TRANSLATION OF THE

# LETTERS

OF A

# HINDOO RAJAH

TRANSLATION OF THE

# LETTERS

OF A

# HINDOO RAJAH

Elizabeth Hamilton

*edited by Pamela Perkins & Shannon Russell*

broadview literary texts

**Canadian Cataloguing in Publication Data**

Hamilton, Elizabeth, 1758-1816
   Translation of the letters of a Hindoo rajah

(Broadview literary texts)
Includes bibliographical references.
ISBN 1-55111-175-6

England – Social life and customs – 18th century – Fiction.  I. Perkins, Pamela Anne. II. Russell, Shannon Lee. III. Title. IV. Series.

PR4739.H164T72 1998      823'6      C98-932523-7

Broadview Press Ltd., is an independent, international publishing house, incorporated in 1985.

North America:
P.O. Box 1243, Peterborough, Ontario, Canada K9J 7H5
3576 California Road, Orchard Park, NY 14127
TEL: (705) 743-8990; FAX: (705) 743-8353;
E-MAIL: 75322.44@compuserve.com

United Kingdom:
Turpin Distribution Services Ltd.,
Blackhorse Rd., Letchworth, Hertfordshire SG6 1HN
TEL: (1462) 672555; FAX (1462) 480947; E-MAIL: turpin@rsc.org

Australia:
St. Clair Press, P.O. Box 287, Rozelle, NSW 2039
TEL: (02) 818-1942; FAX: (02) 418-1923

www.broadviewpress.com

Broadview Press gratefully acknowledges the financial support of the Ministry of Canadian Heritage through the Book Publishing Industry Development Program.

Broadview Press is grateful to Professor Eugene Benson for advice on editorial matters for the Broadview Literary Texts series.

Text design and composition by George Kirkpatrick

PRINTED IN CANADA

# Contents

# Acknowledgements

We would like to thank the British Library, whose copy of the first edition of the *Hindoo Rajah* was used to check the text of this edition. A faculty research grant from the University of Manitoba provided funds for preliminary research, without which this project would not have been started. We would also like to extend our thanks to Patricia Ingham for her advice in preparing the edition and to Patrick Hartnett for his help with the computers.

# Introduction

A FEW pages before the end of the *Hindoo Rajah*, Elizabeth Hamilton finally allows the character Charlotte Percy to make her belated appearance in the novel. The sister of the English officer who sets the story in motion, Charlotte has been mentioned in passing throughout the book, and just before she appears on the scene, Zāārmilla, the eponymous Rajah, has been listening with sympathetic interest to a reading of one of her poems, a reading cut short because everything on the page following the line "Hope lost! Joy gone for ever!" has been made illegible by tears. Readers accustomed to the lachrymose excesses of eighteenth-century sentimental fiction will be prepared for Charlotte's brave but droopingly melancholy introduction to the Rajah; less expected, perhaps, is the following scene in which Charlotte's old friend Mr. Denbeigh tells her sharply to stop feeling sorry for herself and to start publishing her work and using her talents for the public good. Any readers of the *Hindoo Rajah* familiar with the outlines of Elizabeth Hamilton's life would have immediately recognized Charlotte as a self-portrait: when Hamilton published the *Hindoo Rajah*, she was, like the fictional Charlotte Percy, an orphaned, unmarried woman who had lived with and cared for a widowed uncle until he died in 1788, when she was thirty. When Denbeigh rather impatiently asks Charlotte if "the powers of the mind [are] to lie dormant" because a woman does not have "the management of a family," Hamilton is justifying her own foray into print.

Until the publication of the *Hindoo Rajah*, when she was thirty-seven, Hamilton had lived an exemplarily retired and domestic life. She was born in Belfast, Ireland, in July, 1758, the third and youngest child of a Scottish merchant and his Irish wife, but when in 1762 the widowed Katherine Hamilton found herself unable to care for all the children, she sent Elizabeth to be raised by a paternal aunt and uncle near Stirling, Scotland. Aside from this dramatic break with her family, Hamilton's childhood and youth were uneventful. According to her biographer, Elizabeth Benger, she attended school in Stirling for several years, boarding in town during the week; she read voraciously, taking Achilles and Sir William Wallace as her early heroes; and she wrote and destroyed at least one novel, a historical romance about Lady Arabella Stuart (1: 35-7, 34, 52).[1] Hamilton's own childhood experiences seem to lie behind her praise of the beneficial effects of mixed public education in the *Hindoo Rajah*, as even though Benger insists that Hamilton did not attend mixed classes, her favourite childhood playmate was a boy who "stimulated [her] to feats of hardihood and enterprise" (1: 36-7, 32-3). Elsewhere, Hamilton reminisces happily about learning needlework with a group of girls "of very different ranks in society" who were nonetheless "perfectly upon an equality" in the classroom (*Letters on ... Education* 1: 206-7). While much of her study was apparently done without any particular encouragement or guidance – she was, for example, warned by her aunt, Mrs. Marshall, "to avoid any display of superior knowledge" and so took care to hide such reading material as Lord Kames' *Elements of Criticism* (1: 50) – in later life Hamilton nonetheless recalled with considerable fondness the physical and intellectual freedom of her youth. This apparently happy childhood gradually gave way to a directionless young womanhood. By the time Hamilton was twenty-two, in 1780, her mother and aunt were dead, her sister Katherine was married, and her brother Charles was serving in India with the East India Company. Hamilton spent the next half-dozen years in rural isolation, keeping house and caring for her uncle, in what seems to have been a period of almost unrelenting tedium. Benger, determined to present her subject as a model of feminine self-abnegation, insists that she "submitted without murmur to live in solitude and seclusion" (1: 220). Yet letters to Charles from that time make it clear that Hamilton did murmur, at least a little.[2] "You blame me for repining at the solitude in which my lot is cast," she writes in 1780, then, instead excusing herself, admits frankly that she has "sometimes sighed after the pleasure that society affords" (1: 80). Two years later, she writes that the winter "is the most solitary ... I have ever passed" (1: 87); were it not, she adds, for her "good flow of spirits,"

---

1   All quotations from Hamilton's letters and all specific references to details of Hamilton's life are, unless otherwise noted, taken from Benger's biography.

2   Patricia Meyer Spacks discusses the difficulties which eighteenth-century women confronted in writing about boredom in her book on the subject. She argues that not only was admitting boredom presented as a moral weakness in the conduct literature of the era, but, perhaps more seriously, admissions of tedium forestalled options for narrative. See *Boredom* 62-7, 83-92.

I should be apt to feel the effects of continued dulness; and still, in some cross moments, I can't help thinking it a little hard, that with all the good will imaginable towards the pleasures of society, I should be condemned to pass the best days of my youth in such a solitude, that I might, to all intents and purposes, be as well shut up in a monastery; for, though I am not forbid the use of my tongue, unless I were to utter my complaints to the groves and purling streams, I must be silent; and I am not far enough gone either in love or romance, to talk to woods and wilds. (1: 86-7)

Charlotte Percy might have longed passionately for her old life of domestic tranquility, but however devoted to her uncle, Hamilton herself was apparently less able to see unrelieved domesticity as the height of feminine bliss.

The remainder of Hamilton's life divides into two unequal sections: the years with Charles in London, where she finally found the society she craved, and her years as an increasingly famous and popular author, most of which she spent with her widowed sister Katherine. According to Benger, it was Charles who encouraged Hamilton to "explore" the "latent and hitherto unappropriated treasures" (1: 109) of her mind while he worked on his translation of the Hedaya, the Muslim code of laws. His death from tuberculosis in 1792, just before he was due to return to India, was a profound shock to his sister, who memorialized him in her creation of the rather improbably brilliant, saintly, handsome, and charming Captain Percy in the *Hindoo Rajah*. The "fatal event" which Hamilton laments at the end of her "Preliminary Dissertation" is, of course, Charles' death, and it is Charles whom she credits with sparking the interest which led her to write on the "interesting and instructive" subject of "the state of our dominions in India." Like a more famous pair of sister and brother writers who were raised apart, seeing little of one another until they were adults – Dorothy and William Wordsworth – Elizabeth and Charles Hamilton seemed to have drawn inspiration from each other. In the Hamiltons' case, however, it was the sister who drew on the brother for her own much more popular writing. Charles' work received respectful reviews and earned him a place in footnotes in histories of India, but Elizabeth's efforts were rewarded by multiple editions of most of her books, a considerable degree of celebrity during her lifetime, and the friendship and admiration of some of the most important authors of her day. Sir Walter Scott, who paid a polite public tribute to her work at the end of *Waverley*, was also a friend in private life, on sufficiently casual terms for Hamilton to send him notes in playful verse when they were meeting socially in Edinburgh.[1] Maria Edgeworth, whom Hamilton first met in Edinburgh and then visited several years later in Edgeworthstown, wrote a long, affectionate, and admiring obituary of Hamilton for *The Gentleman's Magazine*, praising her contributions both as a novelist and as an educational philosopher.[2]

Indeed, as if to make up for her years of isolation near Stirling as a young woman, Hamilton established herself at the centre of the Edinburgh literary world at a time when it was becoming increasingly vibrant and exciting. She wrote at one point that her shyness about claiming "the character of an author" prevented her "from seeking opportunities of literary conversation" (2: 40), but whether she sought them or not, she undoubtedly found them. The people she knew or met reads like a roll-call of early nineteenth-century Scottish literature: Sir Walter Scott, James Hogg, Mary Brunton, Joanna Baillie, Francis Jeffrey, Dugald Stewart, Hector McNeil, and Anne Grant, among others. Grant, a poet, essayist, and literary hostess, reported to a friend in 1810 that Hamilton "is much sought after in society here" (Grant 1: 228); in 1816, following Hamilton's death, Grant depicted her not as a timidly retiring gentlewoman but rather as something of a Scottish saloniste. Even leaving aside questions of personal affection, Grant lamented,

> her departure makes a blank not easily filled. Others [in the literary world] were more confined to the society of their relations, or those with whom business connected them; but at her house a more selected circle met, where there really was little or no town gossip: the topics were literary or general; and a

---

1  A note of this sort is preserved in the Scott papers of the National Library of Scotland, ms. 3886 f 86.

2  Reprinted in Appendix D. *The Gentleman's Magazine* also printed a shorter obituary in its August 1816 issue.

stranger once introduced there, was immediately received into the accredited company of the place. (2: 129-30)

If Hamilton's career began with Charles, it by no means ended there, and she moved well beyond her pious initial desire to pay a literary tribute to her brother.

The degree of Hamilton's success as an author in those years was matched by her relatively high rate of publication: in the nineteen years of her literary career, she published nine works, despite her frequent travels and active social life in the first years and increasingly poor health towards the end of her life. She wrote on an impressive variety of subjects, including India, contemporary radical thought, educational philosophy (as opposed to straightforward conduct-book advice on female education), classical Rome, and rural Scottish life. Her works also demonstrate considerable range in tone, from the grave didacticism of *Agrippina* to the lively if occasionally cruel burlesque of *Modern Philosophers*, from the class-based comedy of *The Cottagers of Glenburnie* to the wide-ranging and somewhat unstable irony of the *Hindoo Rajah*.

Despite Benger's picture of an impeccably decorous women, Hamilton was touching the boundaries of acceptably feminine subjects and styles in her work. Hamilton herself apparently worried a little that her sense of humour might at some point push her beyond strict decorum. "I have always found myself in more danger of being forsaken by my prudence than my spirits," she confessed to Charles at one point (1: 73). She might have been right about that: Benger comments solemnly that Hamilton "had from nature that quick sense of the ridiculous which often misleads its possessor" (1: 44), and after she established her career, Hamilton apparently shocked one of her admirers, when, in a discussion of the "gross indecency" of Restoration drama, she retorted sharply that "she conceived the sickly sentiment of the modern ones to be more pernicious to the mind."[1]

---

1   Quoted in the unpublished diary of Miss Ewbank of York, National Library of Scotland, ms. 9481 63v. Miss Ewbank, a niece of the Rev. Andrew Ewbank of Londesborough, was, judging by her diary, a rather serious-minded young woman (she earnestly hoped that Maria Edgeworth was "uninfected by her father's infidelity" [25v]) as well as an extravagant admirer of Elizabeth Hamilton, whom she met twice. The conversation about the play is in an entry dated March 27, 1805.

Even when serious, Hamilton's work can display ambition at odds with the feminine self-deprecation for which Benger praises her. For example, in her *Letters on the Elementary Principles of Education*, Hamilton spends so much time discussing the educational theories of John Locke as well as of various Scottish Enlightenment thinkers that some of her male friends warned her that the work would be "above the comprehension" of the average female reader (Hamilton happily refuted them by pointing out the book's popularity with women [2: 32]). The other writing is no less innovative: of the four works on topics other than education, the only one which can easily be called a novel is *The Cottagers of Glenburnie* (1808). *Memoirs of Modern Philosophers* (1800), probably her most popular work after *Cottagers*, is a satire of contemporary radical thought, while *Agrippina, Wife of Germanicus* (1804) is a lightly fictionalized biography which attempts to make Roman history palatable to an audience of young women jaded by the supposedly facile pleasures of novel-reading. This was perhaps the work which worried Hamilton most, sensitive as she was about her lack of a classical education and concerned that "the period of history may be deemed too classical for a female pen" (2: 58). Yet she persevered, and even, perhaps defiantly, imagined following it up with biographies of John Locke and Seneca – subjects who might perhaps be deemed even less suitable to a female pen than an exemplary Roman matron. *Translations of the Letters of a Hindoo Rajah* is the most difficult of her works to classify. Part anti-jacobin satire, like *Modern Philosophers*, part oriental fable, it is an ambitious piece of writing, one in which Hamilton engages directly with a range of the major issues of her day, from colonialism to the "new" philosophy to the present state of literature to female education.

This is an ambitious program for a first book by an almost unpublished author (her only previous publication was an essay which had appeared anonymously in Henry Mackenzie's periodical *The Lounger* in 1785). Yet when *Translations of the Letters of a Hindoo Rajah* first appeared in 1796, it was, in general, warmly received (see Appendix A). What criticism there is is predictable – the *Monthly*, a fairly conservative journal, is condescending about Hamilton's ability to grasp oriental scholarship, while *The Analytical*, by far the most liberal, is offended by the novel's unapologetic support for the British presence in East India and its attacks on the radical philosophers. *The Analyti-*

*cal's* hostility reflects the extent to which the book was immediately recognized as a contribution to the increasingly polemical literary battles of the 1790s and early 1800s, despite Hamilton's insistence on her own moderation.[1] In her views on education and women's issues, Hamilton was a moderate, as critics such as Alison Sulloway and Eleanor Ty have observed. Yet in the battle between the "jacobins" and "anti-jacobins," Hamilton was clearly in the anti-jacobin camp.

Long overlooked, the political novels of the 1790s have, in the last couple of decades, been the subject of a number of excellent studies by critics such as Marilyn Butler, Gary Kelly, and Claudia Johnson.[2] The jacobin novelists have been particularly well-served by this renewed critical interest, perhaps in part because their agenda is more immediately attractive to a twentieth-century audience. Very roughly speaking, the so-called "jacobins" – their ideological opponents inaccurately labelled them with the name of the most radical of the French Revolutionary movements – favoured a broad program of social and political reform. Concerns raised in individual novels include unjust marriage laws (Mary Wollstonecraft's *The Wrongs of Woman*, 1798), the tyrannical powers of the church and landed elite (William Godwin's *Caleb Williams*, 1794, Robert Bage's *Hermsprong*, 1796), the intellectual and emotional stifling of women by social convention (Mary Hays' *Emma Courtney*, 1796, Eliza Fenwick's *Secresy*, 1795), and the meaninglessness of class-based distinctions (Thomas Holcroft's *Anna St. Ives*, 1792). The anti-jacobins, reactionary in every sense of the word, tend to attack the reforms proposed by the jacobins, by showing either villains hypocritically manipulating the

---

1  In a journal entry dated February 21, 1808, Hamilton writes: "Were I to indulge myself in condemning others with asperity for their opinions, I certainly should deserve to be condemned: for in the course of my life, how often have my own opinions varied...." (Benger 2: 237).

2  Kelly's *English Fiction of the Romantic Period 1798-1830* includes a valuable analysis of characteristic stylistic devices differentiating the two forms; Johnson's *Equivocal Beings* features an excellent discussion of the cultural politics of the era and its influence on the fiction. J.M.S. Tompkins provides a very useful survey of both the radicals and the conservatives in her chapter "Philosophers and Christians." Other writers who discuss the political fiction of the late eighteenth century include Ty, Spacks, Scheuermann, Craft-Fairchild, and Schofield. Most of these focus on the radical novels; Kowaleski-Wallace's is one of the relatively rare studies devoted to the conservative fiction, although as the subtitle – "Patriarchal Complicity" – suggests, its treatment of the writing is less than sympathetic.

new philosophy to destroy their victims or misguided but well-meaning converts ruining their own or their associates' lives through their ludicrous enthusiasms. Most of the novels are formulaic, employing a number of stock techniques. Generally speaking, as Gary Kelly has shown, the anti-jacobins tend to prefer third-person narratives to the confessional modes favoured by the jacobins, to employ often heavy-handed satire, and to rely upon a gallery of stock figures: the foolish philosopher who can speak only in nearly unintelligible jargon, the "amazonian" feminist, and the hapless innocent ruined by his or her encounter with new ideas.[1]

*Letters of a Hindoo Rajah* is thus, in a number of ways, a fairly typical anti-jacobin novel, particularly by the end of the second volume, which concludes in something of a rush with the obligatory self-destruction of the radical thinkers. The Amazonian Miss Ardent elopes with Mr. Axiom, an action which fits comfortably with the anti-jacobin assumption that intellectual women are all, at heart, sex maniacs just waiting to be picked up by the first smooth-talking seducer who crosses their drearily spinsterish paths (an idea which it is difficult to imagine Hamilton taking seriously). The nephew of the freethinker Sceptic, dazzled by the ideas of his elder relative, likewise travels down what anti-jacobin novels assure their readers is the almost inevitable road from idealism to radicalism to villainy to suicide. The other radical philosophers merely continue bumbling from one pointlessly Utopian experiment to another, utterly failing to notice the mayhem spreading around them as each monomaniacally preaches the virtues of his own path to a perfect society. The admirable characters, meanwhile, settle into the rather static bliss that is the usual anti-jacobin reward for those wise enough not to try to change the world.

There are, however, a number of points which make the *Hindoo Rajah* stand out from the mass of conservative propaganda then being produced. For one thing, its treatment of women's education and role in society, one of the main issues being argued in the political fiction of the day, is rather more complex than one might think from the simple triumph of the pious matron Lady Grey and the demure

---

1  See, in particular, chapter two of Kelly's *English Fiction of the Romantic Period 1798-1830*.

ingenue Emma Denbeigh over the radical Miss Ardent. Miss Ardent, whom Zāārmilla is initially prepared to dislike, surprises and even charms him on their first meeting, when she proves to be both well-informed, especially about Indian politics and culture, and a good conversationalist. (His main reservation has little to do with her forth-right outspokenness but rather is that despite her otherwise admirable literary taste, she is so blinded by her own cultural values as to suggest that Shakespeare is a better playwright than the Indian author Kalidasa.) Similarly, Miss Ardent's ward Olivia, who possesses all "the candor of a noble mind," is allowed to be more than the merely hoydenish freethinker of conservative convention. In the setpiece scene in which she and her two sisters help an injured man, there is some doubt as to whether Olivia or Caroline, the admirably decorous pupil of Lady Grey, comes off better. Julia, the sister who embodies sensibility, is dismissed as mindless fluff as she first causes the accident by needless panic, then runs off in artlessly feminine disarray, and finally, as soon as she is assured of an audience, "faint[s] for a decent length of time."[1] The two more practical sisters, however, each insist that the other's virtues were more useful. Olivia credits Caroline's feminine skills as a nurse with saving the man's life, while Caroline insists that without the example of Olivia's firm "courage" and "pres-ence of mind" to inspire her, she would have fled with Julia, leaving the man to his fate.

This hint, slight as it is, that the exemplary woman might be better for a dash of "amazonian" firmness is picked up in Hamilton's treat-ment of her alter ego Charlotte Percy. Despite the obvious autobio-graphical elements in the presentation of Charlotte, Hamilton's treatment of her sentimentality has a decidedly ironic edge. Indeed, Hamilton stacks the decks against her fictionalized counterpart, as after several pages dripping with melancholia, the reader is likely to endorse Mr. Denbeigh's exasperated exclamation that Charlotte's

---

1   By the mid-1790s, writers of all political stripes were attacking the woman of feel-ing and accusing the systems of their opponents of producing uselessly and annoy-ingly emotive women; see, for example, Johnson's discussion in *Equivocal Beings* of the way in which Burke and Wollstonecraft both attempted to distance themselves from – and associate their opponents with – the figure of the sentimental woman in their discussion of the French Revolution. Todd's *Sensibility* is probably the best short discussion of the changing fortunes of the concepts of sensibility and senti-mentalism.

complaints that she is left without a purpose in life "are the mere subterfuges of indolence." By putting the attack on indolent women who
neglect their talents in the mouth of the sensible, admirable Mr.
Denbeigh rather than of Charlotte herself or the avowed feminists
Miss Ardent and Olivia, Hamilton downplays the issue to some
degree. Yet at the same time, she implicitly validates Miss Ardent's
assumptions that society damages women: if even talented, intelligent
Charlotte Percy is left hopeless and helpless until she has the good
luck to be pushed into action by an open-minded man who exhorts
her to ignore the "mere mob who receive every opinion on trust"
and hence dislike women authors, then women's education serves
them badly indeed.

Denbeigh's advice to Charlotte is, of course, limited by the implication that it applies only to those who would be called "odd
women" a century later – single women who "have not ... the management of a family" to employ "the powers of the mind." Yet even
so, the book raises insistently and repeatedly the problem of what
women should be educated for and emphasizes the social hypocrisy
of pretending that women need little education because they will be
cared for by men. This issue is initially raised in Sheermaal's second
letter, in which he expresses astonishment at what he can only see as
the cruelty of European men who expect their helpless, ill-educated
widows to raise and support a family. Hamilton's irony here recalls
Mary Wollstonecraft's more familiar account of a sweetly ineffectual
widow in the *Rights of Woman* and her attack on the frivolity of typical female accomplishments. Like Sheermaal, Wollstonecraft insists
that no society which believes women to be rational beings can afford
to educate them in the way that England does. Hamilton – who has
an admirable character praise Wollstonecraft's critique of Rousseau in
*Memoirs of Modern Philosophers* – was not necessarily demonstrating
any marked degree of feminism here; by the late 1790s it would be all
but impossible to find any writer willing to defend a female education consisting only of the "ornamental" accomplishments, no matter
what her political allegiance. Yet throughout Sheermaal's letter on
education, Hamilton is echoing ideas to be found in *The Rights of
Woman*. Both writers, for example, defend mixed day schools, arguing
that they help women achieve what the horrified Sheermaal

describes as "such an odious degree of firmness, as often enabled [women] to sustain, with dignity, the most bitter degrees of adverse fortune."[1] They both criticize the concept of an "ornamental" education which teaches women only to "render[ ] themselves objects of pleasure to the eyes of men." Indeed, in making the Asian Sheermaal see this type of education as one of the few praiseworthy practices he has encountered in England, Hamilton recalls Wollstonecraft's bitter attack on the "eastern" decadence of Rousseau's program of education for his decorative Sophie. More generally, both argue strongly that society is willfully damaging itself by hobbling half of its members. Ultimately, Denbeigh's argument that the "odd women" ought to be able to employ the powers of their minds for the good of society translates into an argument to educate all women for self-sufficiency and usefulness.

The main difference between Hamilton and Wollstonecraft on the question of women's education is that while the radical Wollstonecraft frames the question in terms of future improvement of society, the conservative Hamilton suggests that improved education for women will return society to a happier past and that in providing that education, society will be true to the religious principles it already claims to embrace. Zāārmilla, shocked but intrigued by Captain Percy's firm belief that women have minds and souls, imagines from his reading of the Bible that in England he will find a land of rational, well-educated women; Sheermaal uses what he has seen of women's education to argue that Zāārmilla has, in some fundamental way, misconstrued Christian beliefs. What Hamilton is attempting to do is to create a conservative, explicitly Christian justification for giving women a proper education and recognizing their contributions to society. Whether or not she succeeds, it is important to recognize that positions we might today call "feminist" or "proto-feminist" did not necessarily arise from a unified political radicalism.

Indeed, leaving aside the typically anti-jacobin attacks on the "new" philosophy in volume two and – for the moment – the treatment of India, Hamilton's satire is generally what we might call pro-

---

1   Benger states unequivocally that Hamilton did not attend mixed classes, but Hamilton seems to have had no objection to mixed schools.

gressive in the values it espouses. Yet these attacks on social and political cal abuses and corruption arise mainly from the strongly Christian principles which simultaneously produce the book's social conservatism. For example, Sheermaal's horrified description of the slave ship – which so distresses the idealistic Zāārmilla that he flatly refuses to believe it – places the novel firmly on the abolitionist side of one of the era's hottest debates. Yet Hamilton here aligns herself as closely with Hannah More as with Mary Wollstonecraft; some of the strongest opposition to the slave trade came from evangelical Christian groups. Hamilton likewise blames mistreatment of the poor at home on false or inadequate Christianity, a point which is all the easier for her to make as her poor are, almost invariably, pious and deserving – the cottagers who give Sheermaal shelter on a stormy night are, in effect, the contented peasants of Burns' "Cotter's Saturday Night" moved south. Entirely content with their limited lot, they break even what Hamilton presents as the blatantly unjust game laws (which, under severe penalties, reserved hunting rights for the wealthy) only by spectacular mischance, as Sheermaal's young host manages the quite breathtaking feat of bringing down seven partridges with a single accidental discharge of a borrowed shotgun. As Sheermaal draws the only conclusions he can from the severity with which the magistrates treat the young man's misfortune, that the English revere partridges instead of cows, Hamilton all but bludgeons the reader with the message that the law is, with casually vicious injustice, more interested in protecting game birds than the poor. Even if her satire here lacks subtlety, however, Hamilton's larger point about the basis of such abuses is made with considerable verve. England might see itself as being culturally superior to and thereby justified in ruling people who supposedly worship cows or who confine women to zenanas,[1] but Hamilton satirically presents it as a country sliding into a confused morass of legal and cultural practices which, unlike India's, lack even the virtue of being true to the values preached and at least

---

1   It was an eighteenth-century commonplace that the treatment of women was a measuring stick by which cultures could evaluate their progress towards civilization. This idea is perhaps best encapsulated by William Alexander who, in his *History of Women* (1779), sets out to demonstrate, with Panglossian complacency, that eighteenth-century British women live in the best of all possible female worlds.

nominally accepted by its rulers. The magistrate who is more concerned with the violation of game laws than with a case of violent domestic assault differs from simple religious hypocrites – such as the lady who shocks Zāārmilla by driving a poor woman from her pew, even as she is repeating the prayers for the poor in the Anglican litany – only in being even farther along the continuum of anti-Christian behavior which, Hamilton implies, ultimately produces the huge social evils troubling the Britain of her day.

⁕

The *Hindoo Rajah* is very much part of the jacobin and anti-jacobin quarrels of the 1790s, but it also has another context which is at least as important: European literature about the East. Hamilton was writing at a time when the "oriental" tale was wildly popular, although the orient in the work in question did not necessarily have to have anything to do with any version of the East that existed then or ever. Samuel Johnson's Abyssinia, William Beckford's Arabia, and John Hawksworth's Persia bear little more than coincidental resemblances to the actual places bearing those names. Throughout the eighteenth century and into the Romantic era (and, of course, well beyond), the "orient" connoted romance, and for the purposes of romance readers and writers, it made relatively little difference whether the orient in question was the Levant or China. Indian women in their zenanas were more or less interchangeable with Turkish women in their harems, and an eastern ruler, whether the east in question was near-,

---

Writers such as Hamilton and Wollstonecraft were thus mounting implicit attacks on society as a whole through their complaints about its trivialization of women. The argument (which Hamilton implicitly opposes) that Hindu religious and cultural practices justified colonialism was made with increasing frequency in the early nineteenth century when the missionary movement became established in India. (For an early example of this type of argument see *The British Critic*'s 1817 review of William Ward's *View of the History, Literature, and Religion of the Hindoos* (1817), in which the reviewer attacks earlier presentations of Hinduism as the "amiable" faith of "a decent and harmless people" [570].) In the late eighteenth century, however, one could still find numerous expressions of the idea put most forcefully, perhaps, by Edmund Burke in a 1788 speech: "Whatever fault they [the Hindus] may have, God forbid we should go to pass judgment upon people who framed their Laws and Institutions prior to our insect origins of yesterday" (*Works* 7: 46).

mid-, or far by European reckoning, was almost axiomatically a tyrant. There is no need here to discuss the limitations and inherent racism of these conceptions of the East; Edward Said's *Orientalism* and the numerous works influenced by it have thoroughly done so already. The important point, for the moment, is that Hamilton was working both within and against a flourishing genre.

Most obviously, Hamilton is writing an Oriental version of what Gary Kelly has called the quasi-novel or the footnote novel, a form which gave the author opportunity for commentary on a wide range of subjects, as characters roam through a book which is only loosely anchored by a plot.[1] Hamilton's presentation of the romantic East is complicated by the demands of her genre, in which she uses the commentary of a naïve or inadequate observer to defamiliarize English society. Specifically, the *Hindoo Rajah* belongs with the relatively small but significant body of work focusing on the reactions of imaginary Oriental travellers in Western Europe.[2] Hamilton's most important and obvious predecessor in this rather specialized genre is Montesquieu, whose *Persian Letters* (1721) gives a richly satiric picture of the French ancien régime, while closer to Hamilton's day, Oliver Goldsmith uses a Chinese traveller, Lien Chi Altangi, as the main "author" of the linked essays of his *Citizen of the World* (1762). Montesquieu, Goldsmith, and Hamilton, like other writers who employ this genre, share a number of interests and techniques in their treatment of Eastern travellers to Western Europe.[3] The flowery rhetoric

---

1   Kelly has discussed this genre in a number of places; see, for example, *Women, Writing, and Revolution* 157.

2   Such travel was, of course, not always fictional. One of Hamilton's reviewers praised her for choosing such a realistic basis for her novel, commenting that "[w]e know that about ten or twelve years ago Hindoo Rajahs have been in England" (see Appendix A). Rozina Visram, who has done the fullest study so far of eighteenth- and nineteenth-century Indians in Britain does not mention any eighteenth-century visits by Rajahs, but establishes that such visits were quite frequent in the nineteenth century. According to Jonathan Spence, Arcadio Huang, a young Chinese man living in Paris in the early eighteenth century, was "one of the models for the naive Persian questioners" in Montesquieu's *Lettres Persanes* (18).

3   There were a few other specifically oriental travellers in eighteenth-century literature; some of these were mentioned in the reviews of the *Hindoo Rajah* (see appendix A). One should also include in this genre books which feature American travellers, such as Voltaire's *L'Ingénu* (1767) and Bage's *Hermsprong*, published in the same year as the *Hindoo Rajah* — even though in both of those books the "Ameri-

in which Hamilton's correspondents indulge is, for example, a marker used repeatedly to indicate Eastern sensibilities – and not only in fiction. In 1762, the historian Richard Owen, who was writing about British wars with France in India, reported rather irritably that he had been advised to embellish his style and to include "adventures full of wonder and novelty" if he expected to fulfill readerly expectations of a book with the word "India" in the title (vii-viii). Goldsmith mocks this convention as Lien Chi Altangi disappoints an English gathering by passing the time with "mere chit-chat and common-sense," displaying nothing of the "great, obscure, magnificent, and unintelligible" rhetoric which the entire company knows is the true mark of "oriental" conversational style (110). Yet notwithstanding this mockery, Goldsmith still has his character Fum Hoam open his first letter to Lien Chi Altangi with a salutation whose intricacy rivals that of any of Māāndāāra's or Zāārmilla's. Flowery "orientalisms" are not the only point of similarity; a number of targets also recur in all these works. Māāndāāra's disgust at discovering that in England adultery is merely punished by a fine is, for example, anticipated both by Lien Chi Altangi's dismay that a cuckolded husband might actually still have to support his wife and by the amusement with which Montesquieu's Rica reports that Frenchmen have completely given up any attempt to keep their wives faithful. Indeed, a catalogue of targets mocked by all three works – journalists, the rage for the new in literature, women's passion for gaming, and the contemporary theatre – could almost be used as a checklist of eighteenth-century satiric preoccupations.

Hamilton's satire is thus part of a well-established if minor genre, typical in both its approach and its targets. Like Montesquieu's Persia, her India can be read as an allegorized version of the society she is mocking. Even if the allegory is not as detailed as the careful satire of French society which Lisa Lowe (for example) reads in the growing disorder of the Persia left behind by Montesquieu's travellers, Hamilton's readers might well see a light allusion to the disorders across the channel in the violent disruptions in Māāndāāra's and Zāārmilla's

---

can" is really a displaced European – and books such as Robert Southey's *Letters From England* (1807), which feature "travellers" from other European cultures.

India, as Gary Kelly suggests.[1] Yet Hamilton does more than simply update *The Persian Letters* for an English audience. If her orient does not echo and thereby satirize western society with the sophistication which Lowe traces in Montesquieu's work, part of the reason is that Hamilton is attempting to create an historically specific India, with a degree of cultural particularity which prevents it from reflecting Western failures and absurdities back to the novel's Western readership in quite the same dazzling manner as one finds in *The Persian Letters*. Hamilton's India, unlike Montesquieu's Persia (and very unlike Goldsmith's lightly imagined China), serves a double purpose: it emphasizes the shortcomings of English society both by the techniques of defamiliarization employed in previous oriental satires and by offering a vision of a society which is, unlike England, true to its own values. Zāārmilla's misunderstanding of English society is simultaneously a measure of his comic naïveté and an indication of his superior principles. Unlike the English, he lives the principles he espouses, and in Zāārmilla and his India, Hamilton (however naïve one might argue this makes her understanding of Indian society) shows a character and a society in which the gap between principles and actions which is threatening to destroy contemporary England has been considerably narrowed.

It is in her presentation of that society that Hamilton is perhaps most innovative; the *Hindoo Rajah* is not, after all, a romance, even though it is an orientalist work. Hamilton takes considerable pains to evoke a specific time, place, and culture – Hindu society of Northern India during the mid- to late 1770s – even if this view of India is one which is very clearly shaped by the debates which raged in England in the late 1780s and early 1790s, during the long impeachment trial of Warren Hastings. Throughout the last quarter of the eighteenth century, as the East India Company was in the process of evolving from a mercantile institute to a governing body, the British presence in India was a matter of considerable debate. Robert Clive (1725-74),

---

1   See Lowe, esp. 58-60. Kelly observes that "The novel's principal correspondents are … Indian equivalents of the French *émigrés*" trying "to learn how they and their country could have avoided this fall" (*Women, Writing, and Revolution* 135). Similarly, Leask comments that the *Hindoo Rajah* is built "on an analogy between the Islamic conquest of large parts of Hindu India and the impact of the French Revolution on Europe" (101).

whose victory at Plassey in 1757 was one of the major turning points in establishing British control in India, was the subject of repeated political attacks for his tyranny and rapaciousness, attacks which – depending on one's point of view – either cruelly drove him to suicide or were shown to be justified when, by committing suicide, he demonstrated that he was unable to live with his own actions.[1]

Hamilton places her book right in the middle of the political debates about India before the novel even begins. No reader in 1796, opening the first volume and seeing the dedication to Warren Hastings (1732-1818), could be left in any doubt about Hamilton's political engagement and allegiances, at least not on the vexed Indian question. The previous year, Hastings had been acquitted of criminal misconduct in the House of Lords, following a trial which took place between 1788 and 1795 and which, as several recent commentators have argued, effectively put British imperial policy on trial.[2] Edmund Burke and Richard Brinsley Sheridan, two of the most brilliant orators of the era, were Hastings' main prosecutors, and their vividly memorable descriptions of the cruelties perpetrated either in Hastings' name or at his command irreparably damaged his political career despite the acquittal. (It was noted by many at the time and since that Hastings, unlike the hardly less controversial Clive, never received the peerage which would have been the expected reward for his services in India.) Accused of extortion, of condoning torture, of waging unjust wars against neutral peoples, and of deposing supposedly independent rulers, Hastings remained a controversial figure long after his name had officially been cleared.

One of the reasons that Hastings attracted so much controversy and divided opinions so sharply was that, determined as he clearly was to extend British power by whatever means necessary and to extort money from the unfortunate rulers of various Indian territories, he genuinely admired Indian culture and so supported (and had the support of) the "Orientalists" who helped to introduce Hindu literature, laws, and beliefs to Britain. Hastings was patron of Sir William

---

1   Clive was an opium addict, and there has been some debate about whether his death was suicide or an accident arising from his addiction. His enemies at the time insisted it was suicide, as did some of those who saw him as unjustly attacked by political opponents.

2   See, in particular, Suleri, O'Brien, and Teltscher.

Jones (1746-94), the first great translator from Sanskrit to English, and he was also sufficiently interested in other Asian cultures and languages to propose a chair of Persian at Oxford. (It is a measure of how much British imperialist attitudes towards India changed over the course of half a century that Thomas Babington Macaulay (1800-1859), in his famous attack on Hastings in *The Edinburgh Review*, saw this project as an amusing example of the way in which Hastings "was inclined to overrate" the value of Persian literature [74: 167].[1]) In general, Hastings shared the late-eighteenth-century enthusiasm for Asiatic culture which influenced so much European literature of the era. This interest on the part of the colonial administrators in Indian culture was short lived − it didn't survive even to Macaulay's day − and it didn't prevent the often horrifying excesses of Hastings' rule. Yet it does begin to explain how Hamilton was able to reconcile a deep interest in Indian culture with her admiration for Hastings.

Hamilton, like many of her contemporaries, also understood "Indian" culture to mean "Hindu" culture, an idea which further contributed to her support of Hastings. The Mughal court had had bad press in England at least since Dryden's melodramatic presentation of it as a seat of lust and corruption in *Aureng-Zebe* (1676), and this suspicion of the Mughals was reinforced by the reflexive anti-Islamic prejudices of Western Europe. Like many western Europeans of her day, Hamilton was vehemently anti-Muslim; as Edward Said has pointed out in his discussion of western attacks on − and misrepresentation of − Islam, this is a prejudice as old as Islam itself.[2] Christian Europe, in this construction of history, is not just the opponent but the opposite of the Islamic east, its task that of restoring order destroyed by Islamic imperialism and tyranny. The Indians (or, to be more accurate, the Hindus) themselves accept this version of their history in Hamilton's book; even the vehemently anti-English Māāndāāra admits that until he actually spent time with them he had been "prejudiced in favour of a people whose conduct had been so favourable to our nation." "Nation" here clearly means an ethnic/

---

1  Macaulay's attitudes towards eastern literature are most clearly displayed in his notorious comment that "a single shelf of a good European library is worth the whole native literature of India and Arabia" (quoted Anderson 91).

2  See, in particular, Said 58-63.

religious entity, rather than a geographical one, as nobody ever argued that Māāndāāra's homeland of Rohilkhand, which is going up in flames at the beginning of the novel, was immediately improved by British intervention.

To put the matter very simply, Hamilton reads Indian history as the story of an ancient, fundamentally monotheistic and tolerant culture overrun by tyrannical Islamic invaders. In this version of history, the British arrive not as colonizers but as liberators, freeing the Hindus from their long and miserable subjection to a foreign power and allowing them to return to their old forms of government and landownership, which, in a happy coincidence, happen to share a number of principles with traditional British yeomanry. Whatever one might say about the naïveté of this construction of Indian history, it is a story which makes the presentation of Hastings as a friend of India intelligible.[1] In making war on neutral or even friendly rulers, Hastings is not, according to his supporters, an unprovoked aggressor; he is defending innocent Hindu populations against upstarts and tyrants. Hamilton enthusiastically contributes to this sympathetic reinterpretation of Hastings' actions throughout the *Hindoo Rajah*, even when this narrative of disinterested British support for oppressed Hindus seems strained to the breaking point. One of the main charges against Hastings – in fact, the charge which brought him to trial when Prime Minister William Pitt astonished his own party by voting in favour of pressing it – was that he illegally extorted money from and then deposed the Hindu ruler Chait Singh, Rajah of Benares. Late in the first volume, when Zāārmilla visits the unfortunate Rajah and reports disapprovingly on the young man's ambition and disaffection from what Zāārmilla sees as the benevolent new regime, Hamilton is implicitly attacking Hastings' prosecutors. Zāārmilla reports ominously that rather than gratefully accepting Hastings' benign willingness to let him hold a throne to which he has dubious title, his grandfather having usurped power from the legitimate Rajah, Chait Singh is beginning to overreach himself. An

---

1    Leask discusses this construction of Indian history (100–101). Rajan points out that in Hamilton's version of this tale, the British play "St. George to the Muslim dragon," liberating the "imprisoned femininity" of Hindu India (156).

audience in the mid-1790s, with nearly a decade of Parliamentary debate provoked by Chait Singh just over, would have had no difficulty in recognizing the polemical significance of this passing comment.

More central to the novel is the debate about the Rohilla war. Originally one of the main charges against Hastings, although it was overshadowed by other issues during the impeachment, this campaign remained famous well into the next century, when both James Mill (1773-1836) and Thomas Babington Macaulay focused on it as one of Hastings' main crimes.[1] When Zāārmilla condemns Hafiz Rhamut, or when Māāndāāra expresses cautious approval of "Fyzoola" Khan, Hamilton is again dropping names which would have resonated with her original audience, however unfamiliar they are today. The Rohillas were Muslims of Afghan origin who, early in the eighteenth century, had established power over the mainly Hindu territory of Rohilkhand, a fertile area between the Indus and the Himalayas. Their land was bordered to the east by that of the Nawab of Oudh, also a Muslim and nominally an independent ruler, although his independence was debatable, at the very least, by the 1770s, as his territory was vitally important to the British as a buffer state between Bengal and the hostile Hindu Marathas. In 1774, following some diplomatic and military scuffles between Oudh and the Rohillas, Hastings agreed to send British troops to help the Nawab in his campaign. Aside from a small group which was allowed to retain control of Rampur, under the leadership of Faizullah Khan, the Rohillas were utterly defeated, and their leader, Hafiz Rhamut, was killed in battle.

A basic understanding of the Rohilla war is useful to readers of Hamilton's novel, as the book opens in the final days of the campaign and assumes some knowledge of it, and yet a neutral account of it is difficult, as there were few points on which commentators could agree.[2] In his immensely influential speeches in Parliament, Edmund Burke presented the campaign as an unprovoked assault on a peaceful

---

1 Macaulay 181; Mill 3: 385-407.

2 Perhaps the best brief account of both the Rohilla campaign and the debate about it is in the fifth edition of James Mill's *History of British India*, particularly in the long footnote on 3: 403-404. Mill there elaborates on the evidence of Hastings' duplicity; his hostile editor, who in an earlier footnote complained that "[t]he particulars

and prosperous country, one by which England cynically and dishon-
ourably sacrificed the lives and territory of the Rohillas to further its
interests in Oudh. Even while most agreed that the devastation of the
countryside which followed the battle was the fault of the Nawab's
undisciplined troops, Burke and others insisted that the English were
morally responsible for the destruction of the Rohilla people and for
replacing the good government of Hafiz Rhamut and his predecessor
Ali Mohammad with the rapacious misrule of the Nawab. "The
country," Burke proclaimed in 1783, "was laid waste with fire and
sword, and that land, distinguished above most others by the chearful
face of paternal government and protected labour, the chosen seat of
cultivation and plenty, is now almost throughout a dreary desert"
(*Writings and Speeches* 5: 393). Later, in his Articles of Charge against
Hastings, he described Rohilkhand as "a *Garden*, not having *one Spot*
in it of *uncultivated* Ground," reduced by war "to a State of great
Decay and Depopulation" (*Writings and Speeches* 6: 89). It is this
rhetoric which Hamilton mocks when, in volume two, Zāārmilla
meets the coffee house orator who has obviously been listening to
Burke very carefully indeed, although Hamilton avoids mentioning
his name, even when, in the previous volume she quotes Burke
directly in a footnote.[1] It is also rhetoric which stuck. Macaulay,
whose attack on Hastings is fueled by his matter-of-factly racist
indignation at British support for the dark-skinned Nawab of Oudh
against the "Caucasian" Rohillas, echoes Burke's celebration of their
rule, tying their benevolence to their "gentlemanly" fairness – "fairness" in both senses of the word. As late as 1892, Sir John Strachey,
fighting hard for Hastings, spent considerable effort attempting to
refute Burke's vision of a Rohilla paradise lost, an effort which he

---

of the Rohilla war depend chiefly upon statements intended to prejudice Warren
Hastings" (390), then furiously disputes him, in an argument which draws mainly
upon Charles Hamilton.

[1] It is likely that Hamilton intends the figure as a direct parody of Burke, especially as
the orator freely plagiarizes one of Burke's most famous passages in *Reflections on the
Revolution in France*. Even so, Hamilton is sufficiently discreet in her satire to avoid
naming her targets, and when she quotes Burke on India, she attributes the words
only to "those who ought to have known better." (Moreover, both the quotation
and the discreet attribution are themselves quoted directly – although without
attribution – from Charles Hamilton's *Historical Relation*.)

presents as necessary to England's colonial interests. As Strachey argues, in a rather stunningly self-evident point, if educated Indians hear tales of "the extermination of the Rohillas," such information might have "a serious effect on their feelings towards their English rulers" (vi).[1] By opening her novel with a picture of a Hindu landowner in Rohilkhand enthusiastically welcoming the British victory, Hamilton is both making her own allegiances clear and assuming a readership which has heard another version of the story. Her original readers would immediately recognize Zäärmilla's account of being freed from the alien and tyrannical rule of Hafiz Rhamut by the altruistic intervention of Hastings and the British not merely as scene-setting but as a deliberate rebuttal of Burke.[2]

This happy tale of English-Hindu cooperation undoubtedly reads like a rather sour joke to a post-colonial audience. In fact, it was hopelessly outdated by 1813, when missionaries finally defeated attempts to keep them out of India, and even in 1796, after the ongoing scandal of the Warren Hastings trial, it was rather shopworn.[3] Despite Hastings' acquittal, the memorable rhetoric of Burke and Sheridan in arraigning Hastings and the East India Company had raised questions – to say the very least – about the purity of the motives and the conduct of the Company members.[4] Almost nothing of this intense controversy appears directly in the novel, although

---

1    Strachey is also implying that it is more necessary to convince the Indians than the English of Hastings' innocence. In doing so, he is diametrically opposed to Burke's biographer Conor Cruise O'Brien, who sardonically summarizes the "honest case" that might be made for Hastings: "'He saved India, and to do that he had to raise money. We don't give a damn *how* he raised the money, or what he may have done to the bloody Indians in the process. What matters is that he saved India *for us*'" (300). Hamilton's defense of Hastings is equally far from both of these extremes. She wants to convince the English of his innocence, as otherwise their role in India is unsustainable. In her literary world, saving India is not, by definition, saving it for English exploitation, and by the logic of her argument, if that is what Hastings was doing, he was guilty.

2    In addition, of course, this setting is also a tribute to Charles Hamilton, whose first book was a history of the Rohilla wars which Hamilton drew on heavily in her preliminary dissertation and in the first section of the novel.

3    See Leask for a discussion of the changing ideas of imperialism during this period.

4    Sara Suleri provides a close and subtle reading of the Hastings trial, one which emphasizes the extent to which Hamilton's "innocent" India is a defiantly political intervention in a complex and messily contested debate. O'Brien emphasizes in his treatment of Burke and India that questions about the East India Company's con-

Hamilton does vigorous battle in her footnotes. Criticism of English conduct in India is displaced on to the conduct of the government at home. While Zāārmilla is dimly aware that there is some English dissatisfaction with the governor whom he sees as an exemplar of "the pure and blessed spirit of humanity," he is unable to explain that dissatisfaction until he realizes that England is not the paradise of pure virtue he has imagined and that the English are not all saints. Hamilton reverses what Sara Suleri has argued was Burke's tactic in the Hastings trial – turning Hastings into the focal point of all the guilt of colonialism – and suggests that if there *is* guilt, it lies in the failures of English domestic morality. The faults of English colonialism, in other words, lie not in Warren Hastings but in themselves. The *Hindoo Rajah* is thus rather more than a "surreptitious" defense of English colonialism – to use Felicity Nussbaum's phrasing (171) – but it is a defense of a version of colonialism which will work only if the English practice the Christian tolerance and mercy they preach, something which the novel implies is not by any means certain to happen.

It is easy to accuse Hamilton of blind, even willful, naïveté in her views on British India,[1] but this charge could, of course, be levelled at every British writer on India of Hamilton's generation. Sir William Jones himself is not exempt; Kate Teltscher, for one, uses an impressively detailed close reading of his translations to argue that his work distorts Indian culture, "minimiz[ing] the sense of cultural dissonance" by making "Sanskrit" poetry "reverberate with familiar [literary] echoes" (208).[2] One can grant, readily enough, that

---

duct long predated the impeachment, but that would be the most immediate source of information about imperial conduct in India for Hamilton's audience.

1    Balachandra Rajan, in a sympathetic and compelling reading of the *Hindoo Rajah* – by far the most thorough discussion of it to date in the context of Anglo-Indian fiction – calls Hamilton's understanding of Indian politics naive, but adds that "political naivete may be in the end a reproof to those who did things differently in India and in the theater of gender in nineteenth-century England."

2    Some of Jones' contemporaries noted this point, but thought it grounds for praise. According to one of his early reviewers, "it would be injustice to [Jones], not to remark ... [that] the arrangement, and the conduct of the poems, are generally his own" (*Monthly Review* 509).

no single work can capture "the East" – or even Rohilkhand for that matter – but that doesn't mean that British representations of Indian cultures are by any means monolithic or monodimensional. Hamilton's novel is part of a richly complex body of British literature which, however incapable it might be of grasping the full "otherness" of India, nonetheless offers a compelling range of perspectives on the literatures and cultures of the East.

The Romantics' obsession with the East has attracted considerable attention; studies range from analyses of the Romantic poets' debts to Eastern philosophy to studies of motifs and imagery borrowed from oriental writing to critiques of their colonizing imaginations.[1] De Quincey's kaleidoscopic oriental nightmares, Shelley's philosophical dreams, and Byron's brooding melodramas of Eastern passion and tyranny are sufficient in themselves to establish the range of oriental themes explored or exploited by the generation following Hamilton. Yet Hamilton herself worked in a slightly different era and milieu than her more famous successors. For one thing, her orient is rooted firmly in what was then cutting-edge literary and cultural scholarship. While she might occasionally – in typical eighteenth-century manner – be casual in the documentation of her sources, a reader who was familiar with them (or who was prompted to explore them because of Hamilton's work) would have had no difficulty in tracing individual sections of the novel to the writers who inspired them. All of Zāārmilla's comments on Kalidasa, for example, come directly from Sir William Jones' 1789 preface to *Sakuntala*. The casual reference to collyrium in volume two is taken from a note in Charles Wilkins' 1787 translation of the *Hitopadesa*, a note which Hamilton quotes verbatim (but without acknowledgement). Her India takes its geographical boundaries and some of its religious practices from Thomas Maurice's massive *Indian Antiquities* (1793-94); its topography comes from the travel writer William Hodges (*Travels in India*, 1793) and,

---

1  Raymond Schwab's massive study has informed almost anything written on European literature and the East during the second half of this century. Leask offers a more recent overview of Eastern themes and subjects during the Romantic era; Drew's study is more focused on oriental philosophy in Romantic literature. Barrell's *Infection of Thomas De Quincey*, very different in its approach than these other works, spirals out into a fascinating discussion of the fears of what some British perceived as oriental excess.

presumably, from conversations with Charles Hamilton and his friends; its scripture is drawn from Charles Wilkins' translations of the *Bhagavad Gita* (1785) and the *Hitopadesa*; and its literature – unsurprisingly – is drawn largely from Sir William Jones' translations and prefaces. This is an entirely anglocentric version of India of course; what is rather more interesting than this obvious point is Hamilton's emphasis, in this lavishly footnoted novel, on the extent to which she *was* indebted to other writing on India, much of it recent, and all of it more or less esoteric.

In a very real sense, Hamilton was assembling and popularizing a mass of scholarship and literature which would perhaps not normally have found its way beyond a specialist audience. India might have been very much in the news in the 1780s and 1790s, yet that interest did not automatically translate into a large audience for the masses of specialist studies, histories, and translations being published in the last years of the eighteenth century. This is not to say that Hamilton is simply writing pastiche, cobbling together bits and pieces of other writers' more scholarly work without any of the force or originality of more imaginative writers. *The Monthly Review* might complain that she "added nothing new" to the scholarship she draws from (see Appendix A), but she has given it a new twist by using it in an attempt to create a character living the culture described and analysed in her sources. It is true that Zāārmilla is in some respects – and perhaps inevitably – little more than a mirror image of an educated English gentleman, quoting *The Bhagavad Gita* and the *Hitopadesa* where the Englishman would quote the Bible and quoting Kalidasa where he would Shakespeare. Like Jones, in other words, Hamilton is making Indian culture accessible – "minimiz[ing] ... cultural dissonance" – by ensuring that it has numerous British analogues.

Yet even as Hamilton gives Zāārmilla some reassuringly familiar qualities, she also has to show him as being sufficiently culturally removed from the British to be puzzled and alienated by his experiences in London and at Ardent Hall. Zāārmilla is not, of course, the sort of fully rounded character one might expect in realist fiction; given the exigencies of her shifting satiric targets, Hamilton readily makes him more or less naive as occasion demands. (His increasingly bitter disillusionment through volume two, for example, is occasionally interrupted by ingenuous surprise at the failures of the admirable

characters to accept the self-proclaimed wisdom of the philosophers.)
Even so, Hamilton's satiric technique requires him to be an honourable, honest, and cultured – if naïve – observer of the new world
he visits, and it also requires that these qualities be produced by a culture which is sufficiently unlike Britain's to explain the helpless
befuddlement with which he initially views what he expected to be
the brave new world of England. He must, that is, exhibit his sameness
through difference. Hamilton's point seems to be less that Zāārmilla is
an Englishman *manqué* than that Indians, no less than the English, are
"images of the great Pattern ... whether the white people like it or
not" (quoted O'Brien 255). The phrase just quoted is Edmund
Burke's, not Sir William Jones' or Charles Hamilton's, and it is worth
noting that in some cases, at least, Hamilton shares the views of her
political arch-enemy Edmund Burke.[1] Indeed, Hamilton would be
more closely aligned with Burke than Hastings according to Terry
Eagleton's summary of Burke's stance during the trial: "it is part of
[Burke's] polemic against Warren Hastings that ethical commands are
universal rather than parochial, that moral values do not bend to shifts
of geographical locale, that the same standards of liberty and justice
must prevail among the Indian people as among the British" (40).
Like Burke and unlike Hastings, Hamilton was not a cultural relativist
in the matter of ethics, however fascinated she was by the "otherness"
of Indian culture. No matter how much Hamilton relies on her
friends' scholarship, the novel does more than provide a prettily
fictionalized setting for that work, since by transferring it to her
fiction, she inevitably alters it.

One of the most obvious differences between her work and that of
the orientalist scholars who influenced her is, quite simply, that the

---

1   The divisions between Burke and the "Orientalists" were by no means imperme-
able, in any case, as is evidenced by the Bodleian Library's copy of Hamilton's
*Hedaya*, which is signed both by both Charles Hamilton and Edmund Burke.
Burke, in an inscription to a friend to whom he is giving the book, praises "the
great [power?] of mind and a very subtle jurisprudence shown in this work." While
his praise is probably intended primarily for the original author, not the translator,
it shows nonetheless that Burke was able to appreciate the scholarship of his political enemies. (Burke also sadly explains his reason for the gift: "All my public cares
and theories being now at an end. This unfortunate August 1794" – that is, following the death of his only son.)

author is a woman. Much recent post-colonial criticism has analyzed the place of the feminine in colonialist writing, and it has become a commonplace that the colonized society is simultaneously feminized. This does not, in any way, mean that Western women were therefore somehow not part of the colonial endeavour. As Hamilton's Dr. Severan argues, "the history of literature is intimately connected with the revolutions of Empires," and that statement seems equally true whether the literature in question is written by men or women. Recent critics have begun to explore the roles of European women in the colonial enterprise, challenging any naïve assumption that it was in some way a "masculine" endeavour. After all, excusing women from colonialism merely replicates the discourse which deprives them of any stake or role in public life. Felicity Nussbaum, in a detailed and convincing study which builds on the work of post-colonial theorists such as Gayatri Spivak, has examined the ways in which eighteenth-century Western European feminism bases itself upon the "other" women of empire. Nonetheless, for British women such as Hamilton, justifications for and attitudes towards colonization could be rendered more complex by the metaphors used by their countrymen to justify their actions. Macaulay's casual contempt for the feminized – or effeminate – Hindus, which he used to justify British presence in India, might well, in other words, sit a little awkwardly with a female supporter of imperialism such as Hamilton. Sara Suleri has rightly cautioned against too literal or uninflected a reading of a feminine India versus a masculine west, but in late eighteenth-century representations of Hindu culture, the motif is often too glaring to avoid. The Hindus are presented as a gentle, peaceable people who cultivated the fine arts and were powerless against the martial vigour of the Mughal invaders. Soft, gentle, and helpless, they occupy exactly the same rhetorical space as the female in the literature of the day and evoke an entirely predictable mixture of chivalry and scorn in a number of the writers who discuss them and their culture. Charles Hamilton, for one, states bluntly that they are "soft and effeminate" and complains of their "abasement of mind which is the necessary consequence of a long state of slavish subjection" (13-14).

Elizabeth Hamilton apparently had no trouble at all in accepting the feminized version of Hinduism proposed by her brother and his friends, but her attitude towards it is notably different from his. Her preliminary dissertation, while based heavily on – and at times lifted straight from – his introduction to the Rohilla history, incorporates some small but significant differences. For example, when Hamilton suggests that the supposedly innate patience and fortitude of the Hindus may be attributable to their firm religious faith rather than to "constitutional apathy," "their mode of living," or to "the delicate texture of their bodies," she lists and rejects the explanations given by her brother then chooses a rather more flattering one. While accepting the limiting cultural stereotype imposed by her society, she attempts to rewrite what is clearly construed as a weakness in her brother's work as a strength. A more striking example of this departure from her source material occurs when, early in the book, she has Zāārmilla assist the fleeing Afghan father and son. Charles Hamilton's account of the immediate aftermath of the Rohilla defeat pointedly contrasts what he insists was the cruelly and even cowardly vengeful behaviour of a weak people, as the Hindus took advantage of the British victory to mistreat their fallen enemies, with British magnanimity to the Rohillas (240-41). Elizabeth Hamilton's little vignette, however, quietly links Zāārmilla's gentleness with strength and humanity. Indeed, the episode is so completely unconnected to anything else that occurs in the novel that it is tempting to read it as her riposte to her brother's implicit assumption that only the strong are virtuous and that a subordinated class of people will turn cruel as soon as given the opportunity.

Saying that the colonialist culture feminizes the colonized people is thus only a beginning. Hamilton repeats the tropes her brother and his colleagues use to represent India but gives them a different inflexion. As Balachandra Rajan has argued in his discussion of Hamilton's treatment of India, unlike "[m]ale constructions of India as feminine," which "appropriate gender characteristics to political objectives and thereby ... find India ineligible for self-government" (167), Hamilton's feminized India is the site of a culture which is "just and enduring" *because* it is feminine. Rajan is careful not to insist upon a monolithically "feminine" response to India shared by women writers simply by virtue of their gender; he contrasts Hamilton's version of the country with that of Lady Morgan in her slightly later novel *The Missionary*

(1811). Other recent critical responses to these novels bears out Rajan's point, as they find very different attitudes towards India expressed in the works of Englishwomen around the turn of the nineteenth century. Nigel Leask, for example, argues convincingly that *The Missionary* offers a rich and sophisticated version of Indian culture, one to which he gives considerably more attention than he does Hamilton's.[1] Felicity Nussbaum, on the other hand gives a similarly detailed analysis of an earlier novel, Phebe Gibbes' *Hartley House, Calcutta* (1789), a book which she considers more "lively and polished" than the *Hindoo Rajah*, but which Rajan dismisses as "less sophisticated" than Hamilton's novel.[2]

The point here is not to begin or enter a quarrel about which novel comes closest to getting India "right," but rather to suggest the complexity of late-eighteenth and early-nineteenth century representations of Indian culture. Hamilton's India is indisputably a product of English colonial ideas – it could hardly be otherwise – but that does not mean that it can be dismissed as simplistic propaganda which mindlessly replicates some master discourse. If there is a point at which Hamilton's work on India overlaps with that of her contemporaries, it is that in creating her version of India and of Hindu culture, Hamilton is, like them, participating in a lively and ongoing debate about the East, helping to shape conventions for representing India rather than merely following some established template which, with rigidly imperialist logic, presented it as feminine, hence simple, hence weak, hence exploitable.

<hr />

Dr. Severan's theory that "the history of literature is intimately connected with the revolutions of Empires" is also worth considering in relation to the fiction that follows Hamilton's novel. By the mid-

---

1   See also Rajan's discussion of *The Missionary*, in which he finds much of interest in Morgan's India, but concludes that the novel in some ways "underwrite[s] the evangelical view of India" (167).
2   See Nussbaum 172-82, Rajan 154. There has been some debate about the authorship of *Hartley House, Calcutta*, which was published anonymously; Nussbaum follows Isobel Grundy in crediting the book to Gibbes.

nineteenth century, when the Great Exhibition was erected to proclaim Britain's imperial mastery to the world, one can sense the dramatic shift in the literature that has accompanied this cultural development. While Victorian writers like Dickens, Thackeray, and Charlotte Brontë still find the oriental imaginatively appealing and pepper their stories with references to the *Arabian Nights*, there is a difference in the way the "other" operates in this fiction – a difference which can be attributed to those revolutions in empire. The fiction responds both to an emerging British identity as well as to changes in attitudes to those countries and people Britain was in the process of colonizing.

The self-serving construction of easterners as tyrants, and Britain as liberator and not the oppressor of foreign peoples, still exists in the mid-nineteenth century, but added to these ideas are new "scientific" theories of Britain's racial and cultural superiority. Carefully designed hierarchical models which place the British on top usefully provide justification for imperialist policies. In part, one can read into this rage for calibration a nervousness in the Victorians – an attempt to bolster confidence about their right to expand. But what is eroded in the process is the sense of respect for Eastern cultures, which though limited, is still very much in evidence in Hamilton's novel.

Charles Hamilton and the other orientalists of the 1790s were encouraged to translate Muslim and Hindu religious and legal texts out of the obvious self-interest of their country;[1] behind their enthusiasm for things oriental was a desire to dominate through understanding. As Charles Hamilton writes in his preliminary discourse to his translation of *The Hedaya*:

> The diffusion of useful knowledge, and the eradication of prejudice, though not among the most brilliant consequences

---

1  See both Hamilton's Preliminary Discourse to *The Hedaya* (1791) and Nathaniel Brassey Halhed's introduction to *The Code of Gentoo Laws* (1776) for confirmation of this point. This idea was not confined to the oriental colonies; compare Eagleton's discussion of the eighteenth-century Anglo-Irish ruling class. Quoting Sir Samuel Ferguson's observation that the Anglo-Irish are insecure in their power because they have "not embraced a thorough knowledge of the genius and disposition of their Catholic fellow citizens," Eagleton adds that it is that "knowledge, naturally, which will help to keep those citizens firmly in their place" (37).

of extended empire and commerce, are certainly not the least important. – To open and to clear the road to science; to provide for its reception in whatever form it may appear, in whatever language it may be conveyed: – these are advantages which in part atone for the guilt of conquest, and in many cases compensate for the evils which the acquisition of dominion too often inflicts. (1: iii)

By the mid-nineteenth century, despite frequent travel to all points Eastern and elsewhere, the desire to understand the "other" has been subsumed by a frantic need to understand Britain's own place in the world – a need which frequently results in the denigration of other cultures. On a visit to Egypt, the young Florence Nightingale, for instance, comes to the conclusion that it would be better if the eastern races were extinct.[1] The failure of such British ventures as the Niger Expedition convinced many, including Dickens, that popular trade and civilizing missions were too idealistic in their aims. With the waste, in his words, of "good, white" or "inestimable British lives" which resulted from these projects, came both a desire to refocus attention on home problems as well as a violent backlash in terms of dreams of a more final kind of extermination of the "inferior" races ("The Niger Expedition" 110). This violence is most visceral in Thomas Carlyle's *The Nigger Question* (1849). Carlyle's vicious attack on the Quashee whose "laziness" amounts to a refusal to do the white master's bidding exhibits a wide-spread belief in the innate superiority of the white man to all other races.

This racist attitude permeates the fiction of mid-century. In *Bleak House*, Dickens castigates the Mrs. Jellybys who waste their energy on the inferior "savages" of Africa at the expense of home-grown ones like Joe the crossing sweeper. Like Hamilton, Dickens is calling for home improvement in this novel, but he does so against a background informed by a harder-edged racial and cultural bigotry than she exhibits. (It is a difference in attitude that is conveyed subtly in

---

1 Nightingale writes: "a traveller should consider the question, whether it is not less painful to him to travel in America, where there is no Past, an ugly and prosperous Present, but such a Future! or in the East, where there is such a Past, no Present, and, for a Future, one can only hope for extinction!" (Nightingale 74).

Hamilton's desire to protect and preserve her own "black baby"[1] – the sobriquet she gives her novel – from harmful reception in England.) Carrying the white man's burden, the Victorians often see themselves as bringing British "civilization" to what they deem to be not just uncivilized but unworthy cultures. At no point in Hamilton's novel, however, do we have the feeling that Zāārmilla is representative of a culture that is markedly inferior to Britain's own. Indeed, we have the feeling that she echoes the respectful tones of her brother as, at his most admiring, he writes that Asia is "inhabited not by hordes of bar-barians, but by men far advanced in all the arts of civilized life" (*Hedaya* 1: iii). There is an open-mindedness to difference, and even some sense of equality between cultures as represented in Hamilton's novel, that has all but disappeared from the fiction of the mid-nineteenth century. If Hamilton is guilty of using the east as a means of shaming the British into reform, Victorian writers will exploit this same tired trope with decidedly less tolerance and respect.

That is not to say that Victorians in either themselves or their liter-ature have an uncritical confidence in their own cultural supremacy. In fact, what is missing from Hamilton's novel is an anxious quality which pervades this later fiction. What is in question, by the 1840s and 1850s, are issues of British "worthiness" as much as the worthiness of other peoples. One can sense this anxiety in the culture's fervent commitment to abolition – a movement born out of Britain's own guilty involvement with slavery in its empire.[2] Hamilton, too, is con-

---

1   The image of novels as children is not unusual at this time – the most familiar example is perhaps Jane Austen's comment that she could "no more forget" *Sense and Sensibility* "than a mother can forget her sucking child." Later, Austen refers to *Pride and Prejudice* as her "own darling Child" (*Letters* 182, 201). Interestingly, Hamilton sees herself as the "unnatural parent" of this "black baby" because of her gender, more than her race. And though she uses an image of infanticide when she claims that such children of her brain have previously been remorselessly smoth-ered, she adopts a protective attitude to this "baby," and writes of wanting it to live unmolested in its native environment if exposure to the English climate will bring it harm. See Appendix E for Hamilton's letter.

2   Elizabeth Hamilton, too, was committed to abolition. In a letter written to Dr. S— Ambleside, Kendal, June 12th, 1808, she comments: "I have just finished the perusal of a publication which plainly shows what may be accomplished by the persevering exertions of a righteous zeal. I allude to Clarkson's *History of the Abolition of the Slave Trade*, which I think one of the most interesting books I have ever read. One cannot

cerned with moral worthiness, but her satire does not share the obsessive questioning of Britain's right to rule that can be read into the themes of later fiction. Victorian writing betrays a deeply ambivalent attitude to empire and to the other, and a more acute awareness that empires both rise and fall. This nervousness is muted or missing from earlier texts like Halhed's preface to the *Gentoo Laws*, written at the time when Britain's empire was in its relative infancy. Advising that the stability of empire is conditional upon understanding and tolerating native laws and customs, Halhed looks with confidence, not apprehension, to classical imperials models, and claims that "much of the success of the Romans" can be attributed to this maxim (ix). Years later, when Florence Nightingale observes what she deems to be the demise of Egyptian civilization, she cannot help but draw her own, more fearful, conclusion about Britain's imperial survival:

> It is good for a man to be here, – good for British pride to think, here was a nation more powerful than we are, and almost as civilised, 4000 years ago, – for 2000 years already they have been a nation of slaves, – in 2000 years where shall we be? – shall we be like them? (63-64)

Even when the Victorians seem to bluster with confidence about their own superiority, one can sense the insecurity of their position.

This anxiety is expressed in the very way in which the "other" is demonized or banished to the margins of much of this later fiction. Where Hamilton portrays a Hindoo Rajah who occupies centre stage, narratively speaking – and who visits England and mixes with the people of every class on what appears to be an equal, if not elevated, footing – Dickens, in *Dombey and Son*, gives us the voiceless "dark servant" of Major Bagstock. We know nothing about the beliefs and views of this "expatriated prince" who lives in a perpetual "rainy

---

help envying the feelings of this good man in contemplating the effects of his labours; nor can we reflect on the extensive consequences that may produce, in rescuing millions of our fellow-creatures from a state of misery and degradation, and be at the same time insensible to the operation of an over-ruling providence, which almost in every instance raises up some individual mind as the instrument of most extensive good or evil to his creatures" (Benger 1: 70-71).

season of bootjacks and brushes" abusively hurled at him from his colonial master (775).[1] He is neither worthy of a name nor a home. Dickens writes that Miss Tox "is quite content to classify [him] as a 'native,' without connecting him with any geographical idea whatever." Charlotte Brontë creates the mysterious Creole woman, Bertha Mason, who is famously demonized and banished to the attic in *Jane Eyre*. And Thackeray, too, writes in *Vanity Fair* of the rich though socially unacceptable, because racially mixed, Rhoda Swartz, whom George Osborne describes as both a "Belle Sauvage" and "Hottentot Venus"[2] – terms that are insulting by Victorian standards, even if they hint at the exploitative sexual practises of colonizers. These marginalized characters are representative of a perceived threat from both within British society and throughout the British empire. Where the Hindoo Rajah will happily return to his native India, these products of colonial involvement are here to stay, evidence of the first wave of an empire striking back. Such inter-mingling worries a culture that sees these people as inferior and corrupting influences on the racial and cultural standards of Englishness. Whether silent, faceless, or monstrous, these "ominous" forces exist in these novels to be contained. Not surprisingly, then, these characters are killed off, socially ostracized, or made to occupy a subordinate status from within the cultures of these novels, and in this sense these writers adhere to the racist codes of their society, as they enact a fantasy of control over these "others." In *Dombey and Son*, Dickens portrays the Native comically as if to deflate his potential for rebellion – the dangerous threat of riot and revenge of subordinates that lies at the heart of the race and class relations in almost all of Dickens's novels. Dickens, like most Victorians, had little trouble reconciling support for abolition, for instance, with an abhorrence for "native" rebellion against oppressive rule – an abhorrence that reaches its nadir during the historical event known to the British as the Indian Mutiny. Yet in the ridiculous nature of the relationship between the Major and the Native one can perhaps sense an attempt, however awkward or conflicted, to deflate

---

1  See also Suvendrini Perera's discussion of the role of Colonel Bagstock and "the Native," (*Reaches of Empire* 68), and Mineke Schipper's *Unheard Words* (15).

2  See Perera (98-99) for a description of the Victorian fascination with the "Hottentot Venus."

or to process some of the political guilt Victorians have about their own tyrannical imperial involvement.

This concern about the position of the "other" in Victorian culture is coupled with a deeply anxious feeling about women. The Victorian era is an age in which the woman question continues to dominate contemporary discourse, even if the nature of the debate had changed somewhat since the days of Mary Wollstonecraft. Charlotte Brontë, for one, echoes Elizabeth Hamilton's earlier private complaints when she rails against the stagnation and confinement single woman endure in her society in *Jane Eyre*. Brontë also seems to feel just as awkward about her profession as Hamilton did. While Hamilton claimed that she had "always confined to [her] closet" her "character" as an author and "dread[ed] being thought to move out of [her] proper sphere" (Benger 2: 20), unlike Brontë, she did at least feel able – with some encouragement – to publish her first novel under her own name.[1] And while Hamilton's engagement with the philosophical and intellectual material she uses in her novel is cause of some apology on her part, by the mid-nineteenth century such female forays into male intellectual terrain are rare. Harriet Martineau may come to mind as a unique example of someone who could write about politics and philosophy with some of the same enthusiasm as Hamilton, but she, too, espouses the domestic education which will fit women to be better housewives and to raise the next generation of male empire builders.

The political and narrative alliance between women and racial "others" is simply stronger and more direct in the fiction that follows Hamilton's novel. Dickens's Native in *Dombey and Son* is meant to be parallelled with the oppressed females of the novel, like Edith or the under-appreciated Florence. A similar affinity exists between Bertha Mason and Jane Eyre. Dombey's education may involve his acknowledgement of female power as Victorians defined it, but it is, of course, a circumscribed power which leaves the modern reader uneasy. Dickens portrays a father who in valuing his daughter as "base coin" has failed to see her "use." Dombey's reformation amounts to

---

[1] Characteristically, given her interest in Locke's theories of the mind, Hamilton speculates that she perhaps acquired that dread "from early association."

his recognition of the power and value of self-sacrificing love represented by obedient women. Florence is said to be a servant to her master "love," but she also exists to service both masters of father and husband. In this respect, she, like the more obviously enslaved Edith, is aligned with the Native. By giving birth to a son, Florence becomes a breeder for Britain – fulfilling in fiction, the social destiny of women Dickens promoted in fact through his involvement with philanthropic projects like Urania House.[1] Wedded to Walter Gay – the next generation of imperial adventurer – Florence is that angel in the house who becomes the acceptable face for the emerging construction of Britain's "angelic" empire. However ambivalent Dickens's portrayal of the gender and racial slave systems in this novel may be, women, the poor, and racial others are all linked through the oppression they experience in his society.

Perhaps it is because Hamilton is writing at a time when the British empire had just begun to go on trial, and when the anxieties of empire had yet to flower fully, that the *Hindoo Rajah* reads as such an unworried text by comparison to the novels written at the height of Britain's imperial involvement. Encoded in the gender, class, and race relations of the novels of the 1840s and 1850s are Britain's evolving self-definitions as the dominant world power – a fact that novelists, at least, find both exciting and troubling. What is clear is that in the novels of the mid-nineteenth century, the voice of a Hindu – Rajah or not – could never have the same kind of authority, nor command the same kind of respect, that it does in Elizabeth Hamilton's earlier social satire.

⟨━⟩

1   Dickens was involved with the management of Angela Burdett Coutts's philanthropic enterprise – Urania House – a halfway house for fallen and homeless women. In this institution, young women were trained in domestic skills before being shipped to the colonies where they were to take up a future as housewives to colonists. Such plans for managing the poor and socially unacceptable Englishwoman's maternity for the benefit of colonial expansion is also evident in Eliza Meteyard's emigration propaganda masquerading as novella – *Lucy Dean; The Noble Needlewoman* in Eliza Cook's Journal 2 (1850).

IT would be simplistic to explain the respect which Hamilton accords her "outsider" narrator by reference to her own relative "outsider" status as a woman of Scots-Irish parentage; as has just been argued, her historical moment is clearly an important contributing factor.[1] Yet it is perhaps worth noting that if there is any point at which her optimism about imperial expansion develops cracks, it is in the novel's treatment of Scotland. There has been much recent criticism alert to nuances in the treatment of national identity in writing from the British margins – surely a point of some interest in a Scottish writer's work on India.[2] Rajan, quoting Shelley's observation that "the Celt knew the Indian" looks closely (albeit without finding much) for ways in which Lady Morgan's Irishness might shape her view of India. Yet he doesn't raise the question of Hamilton's Scottish and Irish background at all. Granted, she was no Celt, despite her (Protestant) Irish mother, but even so, an eighteenth-century British writer whose earliest childhood hero was William Wallace – an interest encouraged perhaps by a childhood spent almost literally in the shadow of Stirling Castle – had obviously heard at least two sides of the English colonial enterprise.

Nobody would suggest that an interest in William Wallace translates automatically into scepticism about colonialism. (As Jane Porter's impossibly noble version of William Wallace in *The Scottish Chiefs*, 1810, demonstrates, the English could be just as adulatory about a long-dead anti-English nationalist as the Scots.[3]) What is of rather more significance than this Scottish hero-worship is the inevitable concomitant awareness that Britain is itself a multi-national country, one built on past colonial expansion and battles. Hamilton's relatively

---

1  Rajan writes that "the first wave of Oriental scholarship opened a moment of opportunity for understanding between peoples. The moment passed almost before it had articulated itself. 1785 and 1810 might be said to mark its limits, and even during that brief period the view from the window was clouded" (153). Teltscher vigorously – if only implicitly – attacks the idea that there was any such window.

2  Leask discusses the ways in which Scottish writing about national identity intersects with the British discourse of colonialism; see, in particular 87–90.

3  Wallace was something of a British icon around the turn of the nineteenth century, a point which might have affected Benger's emphasis on Hamilton's childhood admiration of him. If readers didn't find Porter's Wallace sufficiently swooningly heroic, they could turn back to Henry Siddons' 1791 *William Wallace*, which is even more extreme in its hero-worship.

untroubled British identity is thus itself the result of colonialism, something which could have helped to shape her positive view of the British colonial policy in India. As Hamilton retains enough of her Scottish identity to be able to write in Scots – even if only for comic effect – and to achieve major British success in a language which (as the *Edinburgh Review* boasted somewhat inaccurately) the English would be unable to read, it might be argued that she is attempting to demonstrate the possibility that the inhabitants of a small nation can maintain their own culture in harmony with, rather than in hopeless opposition to, the dominant culture of an imperial centre.[1] In effect, one might argue, she attempts to model in her literary practice the union of Scots and English with which Sir Walter Scott ends so many of his novels.

Yet despite her optimism about intercultural exploration and her relative freedom from later imperial anxieties, there are still hints in Hamilton's treatment of Scotland that cultural melding isn't quite that simple. While she laughs at Scottish foibles as readily as she laughs at English foibles, taking as a particular target what she presents as the absurd Scottish pride in ancestry,[2] Hamilton also suggests that there are very real values in Scotland which are gradually being eroded by English influence, such as the female independence encouraged by mixed public education. When Sheermaal reports with satisfaction that "the daughter of a *mountain Rajah*, will soon be as amiably frivolous, as engagingly ignorant; as weak in body, and in mind, as the pupil of the greatest Boarding School in London," the relative heavy-handedness of the irony is an index of Hamilton's dismay at this minor instance of English cultural imperialism. It would be reading against the grain of the novel to suggest that the *Hindoo Rajah* registers any serious uneasiness about colonialism, but Hamilton's

1   The reviewer writes, "After having given this just and attractive description of the book [*The Cottagers of Glenburnie*], we have a sort of malicious pleasure in announcing to our Southern readers, that it is a sealed book to them; and that, until they take the trouble thoroughly to familiarize themselves with our antient and venerable dialect, they will not be able to understand three pages of it." *Edinburgh Review* 12 (July 1808) 402. In fact, the language is not that difficult.

2   This was a target on which she did not spare herself; she writes with amusing ironic detachment on her grandmother's self-destructive assumption of gentility without money in the fragmentary memoir printed by Benger.

irony about the direction in which Scottish culture is headed rever-
berates in ways which might complicate the novel's sunny assurance
that the British presence in India is entirely benign. At the very least,
if the rot which Zāārmilla finally has to recognize has set in at the
frivolous, fashion-obsessed centre of the empire has seeped as far as
Scotland, there is no reason to think India would remain immune.

Nevertheless, for all its scepticism about the direction of British society, the *Hindoo Rajah* remains a work which avoids pessimistic gloom.
Hamilton's satire, if not necessarily good-natured, is far from bitter,
and her attacks on what the book presents as the various failings of
English culture are most sharply differentiated from later writing
about empire in being founded more on an optimistic vision of what
society might rise towards than on bleak fears about how far it might
be doomed to fall. In one sense, Zāārmilla returns to India a sadder
but a wiser man, expecting that his letters will have convinced
Māāndāāra only that "to extend our knowledge of the world, is but to
become acquainted with new modes of pride, vanity, and folly." Yet
Zāārmilla himself, however disillusioned by his encounters with the
philosophers, however thankful to leave England, returns to India
only a little less optimistic than he left, and in leaving her central narrator with his faith and principles intact, if somewhat bruised, Hamilton encourages her readers to retain at least something of the
open-minded excitement about inter-cultural exploration with
which Zāārmilla began his journey.

# Works Cited

Anderson, Benedict. *Imagined Communities*. Rev. ed. London:Verso, 1991.

Barrell, John. *The Infection of Thomas De Quincey: A Psychopathology of Imperialism*. New Haven:Yale UP, 1991.

*The British Critic*. Unsigned rev. of Rev. W. Ward, *A View of the History, Literature, and Religion of the Hindoos*. 1817.Vol 8 n.s. (Dec 1817) 568-89.

Burke, Edmund. *Writings and Speeches*. Ed. Paul Langford. 9 vols. Oxford: Clarindon Press, 1980.

Butler, Marilyn. *Jane Austen and the War of Ideas*. Oxford: Clarendon, 1975.

Carlyle, Thomas. "Occasional Discourse on the Negro Question." *Fraser's Magazine* 40 (1849).

Craft-Fairchild, Catherine. *Masquerade and Gender: Disguise and Female Identity in Eighteenth-Century Fictions by Women*. University Park, Penn: U of Pennsylvania P, 1993.

Dickens, Charles. *Dombey and Son*.The Clarendon Dickens. Ed. Alan Horsman. Oxford: Clarendon P, 1974.

——. "The Niger Expedition." 1848. *The Dent Uniform Edition of Dickens' Journalism:The Amusements of the People and Other Papers: Reports, Essays and Reviews 1834-51*.Vol. 2. Ed. Michael Slater. London: Dent, 1996.

Drew, John. *India and the Romantic Imagination*. Oxford: Oxford UP, 1987.

Eagleton, Terry. *Heathcliff and the Great Hunger: Studies in Irish Culture*. London:Verso, 1995.

[Gibbes, Phebe]. *Hartley House, Calcutta: A Novel of the Days of Warren Hastings*. 1789. Ed. Monica Clough. London: Pluto Press, 1989.

Goldsmith, Oliver. *The Citizen of the World*. 1762. London: Routledge, nd.

Grant, J[ohn] P[eter], ed. *Memoir and Correspondence of Mrs. Grant of Laggan*. 2 vols. London, 1845.

Hamilton, Charles. *An Historical Relation of the Origin, Progress, and Final Dissolution of the Government of the Rohilla Afgans in the Northern Provinces of Hindostan*. London, 1787.

Hamilton, Elizabeth. *Letters on the Elementary Principles of Education*. 3rd ed. 2 vols. London, 1803.

——. *Memoirs of Modern Philosophers*. 3 vols. Bath, 1800.

Johnson, Claudia. *Equivocal Beings: Politics, Gender, and Sentimentality in the 1790s*. Chicago: U of Chicago P, 1995.

——. *Jane Austen: Women, Politics and the Novel*. Chicago: U of Chicago P, 1988.

Kelly, Gary. *English Fiction of the Romantic Period 1789-1830*. London: Longman's, 1989.

——. *The English Jacobin Novel 1780-1805*. Oxford: Clarendon, 1976.

——. *Women, Writing, and Revolution 1790-1827*. Oxford: Clarendon, 1993.

Kowaleski-Wallace, Elizabeth. *Their Father's Daughters: Hannah More, Maria Edgeworth, and Patriarchal Complicity*. Oxford: Oxford UP, 1991.

LeFaye, Deirdre. *Jane Austen's Letters*. Oxford: Oxford UP, 1997.

Leask, Nigel. *British Romantic Writers and the East: Anxieties of Empire*. Cambridge: Cambridge UP, 1992.

Lowe, Lisa. *Critical Terrains: French and British Orientalisms*. Cornell: Cornell UP, 1991.

Macaulay, Thomas Babington. Rev. of G.R. Gleig's *Memoirs of the Life of Warren Hastings*. *Edinburgh Review* 74 (October 1841) 149.

Mill, James. *The History of British India*. 5th ed. 10 vols. Ed. Horace Hayman Wilson. London, 1858.

Montesquieu. *The Persian Letters*. 1721. Trans. C.J. Betts. Harmondsworth: Penguin, 1973.

*The Monthly Review*. Unsigned rev. of Sir William Jones' *Poems*. Vol 46 (May 1772). 508-17.

Nightingale, Florence. *Letters from Egypt: A Journey on the Nile 1849-1850*. Ed. Anthony Satton. London: Barrie and Jenkins, 1987.

Nussbaum, Felicity. *Torrid Zones: Maternity, Sexuality, and Empire in Eighteenth-Century English Narratives*. Baltimore: Johns Hopkins UP, 1995.

O'Brien, Conor Cruise. *The Great Melody*. London: Minerva, 1992.

Owen, Richard. *An Account of the War in India. Between the English and the French on the Coast of Coromandel*. 2nd Ed. London, 1762.

Perera, Suvendrini. *Reaches of Empire: The English Novel from Edgeworth to Dickens*. New York: Columbia UP, 1991.

Rajan, Balachandra. "Feminizing the Feminine: Early Women Writers on India." *Romanticism, Race and Imperial Culture 1780-1834*. Eds. Alan Richardson and Sonia Hofkosh. Bloomington: Indiana UP, 1996. 149-172.

Said, Edward. *Orientalism: Western Conceptions of the Orient*. 1978. Harmondsworth: Penguin, 1991.

Scheuermann, Mona. *Social Protest in the Eighteenth-Century English Novel*. Columbus: U of Ohio P, 1985.

Schipper, Mineke. *Unheard Words: Women and Literature in Africa, the Arab*

*World, Asia, the Caribbean and Latin America.* Trans. Barbara Potter Fasting. London: Allison & Busby, 1985.

Schofield, Mary Ann. *Masking and Unmasking the Female Mind: Disguising Romances in Feminine Fiction 1713-1799.* Newark: U of Delaware P, 1990.

Schwab, Raymond. *The Oriental Renaissance: Europe's Rediscovery of India and the East, 1680-1880.* 1950. Trans. Gene Patterson-Black and Victor Reinking. New York: Columbia UP, 1984.

Spacks, Patricia Meyer. *Boredom: The Literary History of a State of Mind.* Chicago: U of Chicago P, 1995.

———. *Desire and Truth: Functions of Plot in Eighteenth-Century English Novels.* Chicago: U of Chicago P, 1990.

Spence, Jonathan D. "The Paris Years of Arcadio Huang." *Chinese Roundabout: Essays in History and Culture.* New York: Norton, 1992. 11-24.

Strachey, Sir John. *Hastings and the Rohilla War.* Oxford, 1892.

Suleri, Sara. *The Rhetoric of English India.* Chicago: U of Chicago P, 1992.

Sulloway, Alison. *Jane Austen and the Province of Womanhood.* Philadelphia: U of Pennsylvania P, 1989.

Teltscher, Kate. *European and British Writing on India 1600-1800.* Delhi: Oxford UP, 1995.

Tompkins, J.M.S. *The Popular Novel in England 1770-1800.* Lincoln: University of Nebraska P, 1961.

Todd, Janet. *Sensibility: An Introduction.* London: Methuen, 1986.

Ty, Eleanor. *Unsex'd Revolutionaries: Five Women Novelists of the 1790s.* Toronto: U of Toronto P, 1993.

Visram, Rozina. *Ayahs, Lascars, and Princes: Indians in Britain 1700-1947.* London: Pluto Press, 1986.

# Elizabeth Hamilton: A Brief Chronology

1758     Born (July) in Belfast, Ireland, the third child of Charles and Katherine (Mackay) Hamilton.

1759     Death of Elizabeth Hamilton's father.

1762     Hamilton is sent to Stirling, Scotland, to be raised by her father's sister and brother-in-law, Mr. and Mrs. Marshall (she returns to Belfast for a brief visit in 1764); her siblings Charles and Katherine stay in Belfast with their mother.

1766     Elizabeth starts day school near Stirling, which she attends for between four and five years; her mother visits her in Scotland.

1767     Katherine (Mackay) Hamilton dies.

1772     Charles Hamilton leaves for India; Elizabeth Hamilton and the Marshalls move to Ingram's Crook, near Bannockburn, where Elizabeth lives until her uncle's death.

1778     Elizabeth Hamilton spends six months with her sister and maternal relatives in Belfast.

1780     Mrs. Marshall dies.

1785     Hamilton publishes an essay anonymously in Henry Mackenzie's journal *The Lounger*. (No. 46, Saturday, Dec. 17).

1786     Charles visits Scotland (arrives December 20) following his return from India on a five-year leave of absence to translate the *Hedaya*.

1788     Elizabeth accompanies Charles to London, returning to Scotland in the summer. Following Mr. Marshall's death that autumn, she returns to London where she lives with Charles until 1791.

1792     Shortly before his planned return to India, Charles Hamilton dies of tuberculosis. Elizabeth and her sister Katherine, now widowed, settle in Suffolk, then Berkshire; they are together for much of the rest of Elizabeth's life.

1796     Publication of *Translation of the Letters of a Hindoo Rajah*. Hamilton has several years of poor health following the appearance of this novel, and she spends some time in Bath to treat her gout.

1800    Publication of *Memoirs of Modern Philosophers*.

1801    Publication of *Letters on the Elementary Principles of Education*.

1802    From April until September 1803, Hamilton and her sister "live a wandering sort of life, visiting Wales, the lakes of Westmoreland, and Scotland" (Benger 1: 152).

1803    Hamilton meets Maria Edgeworth in Edinburgh.

1804    Publication of *Memoirs of the life of Agrippina, the wife of Germanicus*. Hamilton settles in Edinburgh in the autumn and spends six months in 1804-5 educating the daughters of Lord Lucan; Lady Elizabeth Lucan is the daughter of a nobleman to whom Hamilton's next work is addressed.

1806    Publication of *Letters addressed to the Daughter of a Nobleman on the Formation of the Religious and the Moral Principle*.

1808    Publication of *The Cottagers of Glenburnie*.

1809    Publication of *Exercises in Religious Knowledge*.

1813    Publication of *A Series of Popular Essays Illustrative of Principles Connected with the Improvement of the Understanding, the Imagination and the Heart*. Hamilton spends three months in Ireland, during which time she visits Maria Edgeworth at Edgeworthstown, but is too ill that winter to write; she remains in poor health for most of the rest of her life.

1815    Publication of *Hints addressed to Patrons and Directors of Schools*.

1816    Ill and depressed in the spring, Hamilton travels to Harrowgate for her health on 13 May. She dies there on 23 July.

1818    Elizabeth Benger publishes a biography of Hamilton which incorporates a number of Hamilton's letters and a fragmentary, previously unpublished autobiographical sketch; a revised second edition is published the following year.

# A Note on the Text

*Translation of the Letters of a Hindoo Rajah* went into five editions between 1796 and 1811, and there was a subsequent American printing (Boston, 1819). We have used the first edition as our copy text; significant changes and additions to the second English edition (1801), the only one for which Hamilton made any revisions, have been included in Appendix B. Errata have been incorporated, and we have silently corrected obvious typographical errors, but otherwise we have retained Hamilton's punctuation and spelling. In particular, we have made no attempt to regularize her transliterations of Indian words, except in the case of the accents in the names Māāndāāra and Zāārmilla. In the first edition, Hamilton uses them consistently only in the headings of the letters, but in the second she employs them throughout. This was the only important alteration she made in her transliterations (she made little effort to be consistent in her spelling of other terms), and so we chose to follow her second thoughts on this usage. We have put Hamilton's initials in brackets following her notes; uninitialled notes and all comments following the initials are our own annotations. In a few cases, Hamilton repeatedly annotates a term or name which recurs in several places in the novel (Calli, for example), and we have removed second and subsequent notes which merely repeat a definition provided in an earlier one. We have also followed the spelling and punctuation of the original documents in all of the material cited in the appendices.

# TRANSLATION

OF THE

# LETTERS

OF A

# HINDOO RAJAH;

WRITTEN
PREVIOUS TO, AND DURING THE PERIOD OF HIS
RESIDENCE IN ENGLAND.

TO WHICH IS PREFIXED A
## PRELIMINARY DISSERTATION
ON THE
## HISTORY, RELIGION, AND MANNERS,
OF THE

# HINDOOS.

IN TWO VOLUMES.

———

## BY ELIZA HAMILTON

———

VOL. I.

*LONDON:*
PRINTED FOR G.G. AND J. ROBINSON, NO. 25,
PATERNOSTER ROW
1796.

TO

# WARREN HASTINGS, Esq.

LATE GOVERNOR GENERAL OF BENGAL.
UNDER WHOSE AUSPICES,
AS THE DISTINGUISHED PATRON OF SHANSCRIT,
AND PERSIAN LITERATURE
THE MOST IMPORTANT OF THE ORIENTAL TRANS-
LATIONS, HAVE HITHERTO APPEARED.


# TO HIM,

AS THE HONOURED PATRON, AND FRIEND, OF A
BELOVED, AND MUCH LAMENTED BROTHER,

## IS THIS TRIFLE,

(AS A SINCERE, THOUGH HUMBLE TRIBUTE OF
ESTEEM, AND GRATITUDE)

RESPECTFULLY INSCRIBED,

BY HIS MUCH OBLIGED

AND OBEDIENT SERVANT,

London,
June 6, 1796

## ELIZA HAMILTON.

# PRELIMINARY DISSERTATION

IN the extensive plan which is carried on under the direction of the great Governor of the Universe, an attentive observer will frequently perceive the most unexpected ends, accomplished by means the most improbable, and events branch out into effects which were neither foreseen, nor intended by the agents which produced them. A slight view of the consequences which have hitherto resulted from our intercourse with the East-Indies, will sufficiently evince the truth of this assertion.

The thirst of conquest and the desire of gain, which first drew the attention of the most powerful, and enlightened nations of Europe toward the fruitful regions of Hindoostan, have been the means of opening sources of knowledge and information to the learned, and the curious, and have added to the stock of the literary world, treasures, which if not so substantial, are of a nature more permanent than those which have enriched the commercial.

The many elegant translations from the different Oriental languages with which the world has been favoured within these last few years, have not failed to attract merited attention; and the curiosity awakened by these productions, concerning the people with whom they originated, has been gratified by the labours of men, who have enjoyed the first rank in literary fame.

Still, however, the writers in every branch of Oriental literature, have to contend with disadvantages, too numerous and too powerful to be easily overcome. The names of the Heroes of Greece and Rome, are rendered familiar at a period of life, when the mind receives every impression with facility, and tenaciously retains the impressions it receives. With the name of every Hero, the idea of his character is associated, and the whole becomes afterward so connected in the mind, with the blissful period of life at which it was first received, that the recollected scenes of juvenile felicity may frequently, even in the most accomplished minds, be found to give a zest to the charms of the ancient authors. To those, who have not had the advantages of an early classical education, the same objections which render the translations from the Oriental writers tiresome, and uninteresting, will operate with equal force on the most beautiful passages of Homer, or Virgil, and the names of Glaucus and Sarpedon, of Anchises and Eneas, be found as hard to remember, and as difficult to pronounce, as those of Krishna and Arjoun.[1]

Of these advantages, resulting from early prepossessions, the Persian and Hindoo writers are entirely destitute, and the difficulty of reconciling the sounds of the names of their Heroes to an European ear is so great, that it is not till after a greater degree of attention than the generality of readers will bestow, that any appropriate idea of them can be fixed in the mind. This appears to be at least one cause of that ignorance, and apathetic indifference with regard to the affairs of the East, which is frequently to be remarked in minds, that are in every other respect highly cultivated, and accurately informed. For the sake of readers of this description, particularly those of my own sex, who may have been deterred by reasons above hinted at, from seeking information from a more copious source, I think it necessary toward explaining many passages in the letters of the Rajah, which would otherwise have appeared utterly unintelligible, to give a short and simple sketch of the history of the nation to which they belonged. Should my feeble effort lead to further enquiry; should it in the mind of any person of taste give birth to a laudable curiosity, upon a subject where so much is to be learned, my design will be still more fully answered, and my wishes more completely fulfilled.

That part of Asia, known to Europeans by the name of Hindoostan, extends from the mountains of Thibet on the North, to the sea on the South, and from the river Indus on the West, to the Barampooter on the East,[2] comprehending, within its limits, a variety of provinces, many of which have been famous, from the earliest ages,

---

1 Glaucus and Sarpedon appear in *The Iliad*; Anchises and Eneas (more usually Aeneas) in *The Aeneid*; Krishna and Arjoun in *The Bhagavad-gita*, which was first translated into English in 1785 by Charles Wilkins.

2 Hamilton provides more detail in the second edition (see Appendix B). Her revisions might have been prompted by *The Monthly Review's* criticism of her geography (see Appendix A); the information in the second edition is taken from the first volume of Thomas Maurice's *Indian Antiquities: or, dissertations relative to the ancient geographical divisions, the pure system of primeval theology, the grand code of civil laws, the original form of government, and the various and profound literature, of Hindostan*, 5 vols (London 1793-4), I. 233-4. The territory includes present-day Bangladesh. and parts of Pakistan as well as India.

for the salubrity of their climate, the richness of their productions, and the fertility of their soil. Of this country, the Hindoos[1] are the Aborigines. Over the origin of this celebrated people, Time has cast the impenetrable mantle of oblivion. Their own annals trace it back to a period so remote, so far beyond the date of European Chronology, as to be rejected by European pride. The magnificent proofs of ancient grandeur, however, which are still to be found, and which have been sought for with the most successful assiduity, by many of our countrymen in India, give the most irrefragable testimony of the antiquity of their empire, and seem to confirm the assertion of its Historians, "that its duration is not to be paralleled by the history of any other portion of the human race." To account for this extraordinary degree of permanency, we must direct our attention, not to the barriers formed by nature around their territories, but to those internal causes arising from the *nature of their Government, their Laws, Religion, moral Prejudices*, and established manners.

The ancient government, throughout Hindoostan, appears to have been a federative union of the various states, each governed by its own Rajah, or Chief, but subjected, in a sort of feudal vassalage, to the sovereignty of the supreme Emperor, who was head of the whole.

The manner in which the Rajahs of the Hindoos exercised the rights of dominion over their people, bears so little analogy to that practised by the petty sovereigns of such European states as are placed in circumstances nearly similar; that it would be doing the greatest injustice to the amiable and benevolent character of the Hindoos, to bring them into comparison. *There* the right of sovereignty bore the mild aspect of parental authority. The Prince considered the people in

---

1   The word *Hind* from whence *Hindoo*, and Hindoostan, or country of the Hindoos, is of Persian origin, computed by Colonel Dow to have been derived from Hind, a supposed son of Ham, the son of Noah; and by other Orientalists, to owe its origin to the river Indus. For the sake of such as take pleasure in tracing etymologies, I insert a note written on the margin of the copy of Gentoo Laws, now in my possession, by one whose knowledge of the Persian language has not been excelled by any. He says, "The word *Hind* is often used by the Persian Poets to signify *Black*, or *dark-coloured*, and it is probable that *Hindos* may mean no more than a *black man*, as our negro from *Niger*." [E.H.] Alexander Dow was a translator and playwright as well as a soldier; Hamilton mentions his play *Zingis* (1769) and his translations of the poet "Inatulla" (Inayat Allah of Delhi) in the second volume.

the light of children, whom he was appointed by Heaven to protect and cherish; and the affection of the subject for the Prince, under whose auspices he enjoyed the blessings of freedom, and tranquility, was heightened by esteem for his virtues, into the most inviolable attachment.[1]

The division of the Hindoos into four *Casts*, or tribes, to each of which a particular station was allotted, and peculiar duties were assigned, might doubtless be another cause, which lent its aid toward the preservation of the general harmony. This division must have been made at a period too remote for investigation; and which seems to set conjecture at defiance. It is by the Hindoo writers wrapt in the veil of allegory; they say, that Brahma, the first person in their Triad of Deity, having received the power from the Supreme for the creation of mankind, created the Hindoos in the following manner:

From his mouth he produced the Bramin, and destined his rank to be the most eminent; allotting, for his business, the performance of the rights of Religion, and the instruction of mankind in the path of duty.

The next tribe he created was the Khettrie, or war tribe, and this he produced from his arms, his duty being *to defend the people, to govern*, and to command; of this tribe were the ancient Rajahs.

---

1    The descriptions of the Poet, may sometimes be called in to justify, and illustrate, the assertions of the Historian. In this light, the following passage from the beautiful drama of Sacontala, which was performed at the court of an Indian Monarch, celebrated for his love of the arts, and the encouragement he gave to polite literature in the first century before Christ, may not be unacceptable. "There sits the King of men, who has felicity at command, yet shews equal respect to all: here no subject, even of the lowest class, is received with contempt." – "Thou seekest not thy own pleasure, no, it is for the people thou art harassed from day to day." – "When thou wieldest the rod of justice, thou bringest to order, all those who have deviated from the paths of virtue: thou biddest contention cease: thou wast formed for the preservation of the people; thy kindred possess, indeed, considerable wealth; but so boundless is thy affection, that *all thy subjects, are considered by thee as thy kinsmen*." [E.H.] *Sakuntala*, by the Hindu dramatist Kalidasa (or Calidas) was translated from the original Sanscrit by Sir William Jones in 1789. Jones, in his introduction, follows Indian tradition that Kalidasa was the court poet of the legendary emperor Vicramáditya, who reigned in the first century B.C.; there is no historical evidence of such a king, but Kalidasa might have been a member of the court of a king who reigned in the fourth century A.D. and who was one of several rulers known as Vicramáditya. See also page 145, note 2, and page 193, note 1.

He next produced the Bice, or Banyan, from his thighs and belly, assigning him the occupations of *agriculture*, and commerce. And lastly,

He created from his feet the tribe of Sooder, and to him allotted the duties of *subjection, labour,* and *obedience.*

The respective, and peculiar virtues of these different Casts, are admirably described in the following passage of the Bhagvat Geeta, an episode, from their great epic poem, translated into English by Mr. Wilkins.[1]

"The natural duty of the Bramin is peace, self-restraint, patience, rectitude, wisdom, and learning. The natural duties of the Khettrie, are bravery, glory, not to flee from the field; rectitude, generosity, and princely conduct. The natural duties of the Bice are to cultivate the land, to tend the cattle, and to buy and sell. The natural duties of the Sooder is servitude; a man by following the duties appointed by his birth, cannot do wrong. *A man being contented with his own particular situation obtaineth perfection.*"

Though all Bramins are not Priests, none but such as are of this Cast can perform any offices of the priestly function. The members of every other Cast preserve for theirs the most respectful veneration, and a spirit of partiality toward them seems to breath throughout their laws, as well as religious institutions.

Those who take pleasure in pointing the shafts of sarcasm against the order of the Priesthood (without considering, that invectives against any society of individuals, are only satires upon human nature) will readily assign to the Bramins themselves, the formation of laws which appear so favourable to their interests; and produce it as an additional proof of priestly cunning and ambition; but a moment's reflection on the duties, as well as privileges, of this Cast, will put an end to invidious exultation.

An abhorrence of the shedding of blood, is a principle which pervades the whole of the Hindoo religion, but the Bramins observe it in the strictest degree. They eat nothing that has life in it: their food consisting entirely of fruit and vegetables, and their only luxury being

---

1   Charles Wilkins, *The Bhagvat-geeta, or dialogues of Kreeshna and Arjoon; in eighteen lectures; with notes. Translated from ... the Sanskreet* (London, 1785). The "great epic poem" is the *Mahabharata.*

the milk of the Cow, an animal for whose species they have a particular veneration. Not only every act of hostility, but even every method of defence is, to them, strictly prohibited; submitting to violence with unresisting patience and humility, they leave it to God, and their Rajahs, to avenge whatever injuries they may sustain.

The separation of the different Casts from each other is absolute and irreversible; it forms the fundamental principle of their laws, and the slightest breach of it never fails to incur universal reprobation.

Thus those sources of disquiet, which have held most of the empires of the earth in a state of perpetual agitation, were unknown to the peaceful children of Brahma. The turbulence of ambition, the emulations of envy, and the murmurs of discontent, were equally unknown to a people, where each individual, following the occupation, and walking in the steps of his fathers, considered it as his primary duty to keep in the situation that he firmly believed to have been marked out for him by the hand of Providence.

In the spirit of the religion of the Hindoos, a still more efficient cause, of the durability of their state, presents itself to our view. Original in its nature, and absolute in its decrees, its precepts induce a total seclusion from the rest of mankind. Far, however, from disturbing those who are of a different faith, by endeavours to convert them, it does not even admit of proselytes to its own. Though tenacious of their own doctrines, in a degree that is unexampled in the history of any other religion, the most fervent zeal in the most pious Hindoos, leads them neither to hate, nor despise, nor pity such as are of a different belief, nor does it suffer them to consider others as less favoured by the Almighty than themselves. This spirit of unbounded toleration proceeded in a natural course from the sublime and exalted notions of the Deity, taught by the Bramins, and every where to be met with in their writings, and which are only equalled in that Gospel "which brought life and immortality to light."[1]

That Being whom they distinguish by the different appellations of the Principle of Truth, the Spirit of Wisdom! the Supreme! by whom the Universe was spread abroad, whose perfections none can grasp within the limited circle of human ideas, views, they say, with equal

---

1 Timothy 1:10.

complacency, all who are studious to perform his will throughout the immense family of creation. They deem it derogatory to the character of this Being, to say that he prefers one religion to another, "to suppose such preference, being the height of impiety, as it would be supposing injustice toward those whom he left ignorant of his will": and they therefore conclude that every religion is peculiarly adapted to the country and people where it is practised.[1] The Bramins, who compiled the Code of Gentoo Laws, translated by Mr. Halhed, explain their opinion upon this subject in very explicit terms: "the truly intelligent, [say they] well know that the differences and varieties of created things are a ray of his glorious essence, and that the contrarieties of constitutions are types of his wonderful attributes. He appointed to each Tribe its own faith, and to every Sect its own religion, and views, in each particular place, the mode of worship respectively appointed it. Sometimes he is employed, with the attendants upon the Mosque, in counting the sacred beads; sometimes he is in the Temple at the adoration of Idols, the intimate of the Mussulman, and the friend of the Hindoo, the companion of the Christian, and the confidant of the Jew."

A toleration founded upon such systematic principles, would necessarily exclude those argumentative disputations, those cruel and obstinate animosities, which, alas! under a dispensation whose very essence is benevolence, have so often disturbed the peace of society. There the acrimonious censure, the keen retort, the vehement invective against those who differed in opinion, was totally unknown. Under the banners of their religion, the irascible passions were never ranged. "He, my servant," says Krishna, speaking in the person of the Deity, "He, my servant, is dear to me, who is *free from enmity*, merciful, and exempt from pride and selfishness, and who is the same in pain and in pleasure, patient of wrongs, contented, and whose mind is fixed on me alone."[2]

---

1    See Crawford's Sketches. [E.H.] [Quintin Craufurd], *Sketches chiefly relating to the history, religion, learning, and manners of the Hindoos* (London, 1790), 132.

2    Hamilton is quoting Wilkin's translation of the *Bhagavad-gita*, section twelve, verse thirteen (Wilkins does not retain the verse divisions, but most modern translators do.) She quotes this passage again at the end of volume one, following it there by verse fifteen, and alludes to it in her initial description of Lady Ardent in Volume 2.

I shall conclude this account of the notions of the Deity, entertained by the Hindoos, with the first stanza of that beautiful Hymn to Narryána, or the Spirit of God exerted in Creation, translated by the elegant pen of Sir William Jones.

> Spirit of Spirits! who through every part,
> Of space expanded, and of endless time,
> Beyond the stretch of lab'ring thought sublime,
> Bad'st uproar into beauteous order start,
> Before Heaven was, Thou art:
> Ere spheres beneath us roll'd, or spheres above,
> Ere Earth in firmamental ether hung,
> Thou sat'st alone, till through thy mystic love,
> Things unexisting to existence sprung,
> And grateful descant sung,
> What first impell'd Thee to exert thy might?
> Goodness unlimited. – What glorious light
> Thy powers directed? Wisdom without bound
> What prov'd it first? Oh! guide my fancy right,
> Oh raise from cumb'rous ground
> My soul, in rapture drown'd,
> That fearless it may soar on wings of fire;
> For Thou, who only know'st, Thou only can'st inspire.[1]

A further view of their religious system may be necessary, and will, perhaps, be sufficient to elucidate another characteristic feature of the Hindoos, which has forcibly struck all who have had an opportunity of observing them. The patience evinced by this mild and gentle race under the severest suffering, and the indifference with which they view the approach of death, which has been severally assigned to constitutional apathy, to their mode of living, and to the delicate texture of their bodies, may perhaps be equally accounted for, from their firm and stedfast belief in a future state. This belief, indeed, is darkened by many errors. They believe that the human soul must be purified by

---

1   The hymn is printed in Jones' *Works* (1799; 13 vols) 13: 302-309; Hamilton quotes lines 1-18, slightly altering the punctuation.

suffering, and that it is not till after having undergone this expiatory discipline through a series of different bodies, that it becomes worthy of admission to eternal happiness. The evils inflicted upon the seemingly inoffensive, is attributed by them as a punishment for crimes committed in a pre-existent state. Revolting from the idea of eternal punishment, as incompatible with the justice and goodness of their Creator, they believe that the souls of the wicked, after having been for a time confined in Narekha (the infernal regions) are sent back upon the stage of life, to animate the bodies of the inferior creation, till by various chastisements and transmigrations in these probationary states, every vicious inclination is sufficiently corrected to admit of their reception into the regions of perfection and happiness. "Animated by the desire of obtaining that final boon," says a late Historian,[1] "and fired by all the glorious promises of their religion, the patient Hindoo smiles amid unutterable misery, and exults in every dire variety of voluntary torture."

Notwithstanding the sublime notions of the Hindoo concerning Deity; and, notwithstanding the strenuous assertions of the best informed Bramins, even at the present day, that their worship is only directed to one divine essence, and that the many inferior deities, whose images fill their temples, are but so many emblems of his different attributes, it must be confessed, that the religion of the vulgar has degenerated into the grossest idolatry. This may be accounted for by the jealous care with which the tribe of Brahma prevented the intrusion of the multitude into these avenues to science and so truth, of which they were the peculiar guardians.[2] Ignorance naturally leads to superstition, and the vulgar of all ranks, fixing their attention on the external object that is presented to them, lose sight of the more remote and spiritual allusion, and soon transfer that veneration to the symbol, which was at first meant only to be excited for

---

1   See Maurice's Antiquities. [E.H.] See 56, note 2, for the full reference; the passage quoted is on 2: 283.

2   See Introduction to the Gentoo Laws. [E.H.] *A Code of Gentoo laws, or, ordinations of the pundits, from a Persian translation, made from the original, written in the Shanscrit language*, translated and edited by Nathaniel Brassey Halhed (London, 1776), lxxiii-lxxiv. The term "Gentoo" is derived from the Portuguese word for "gentile" and is used to refer to non-Islamic inhabitants of India, in particular, the Hindus.

the thing signified. Nor is it in the religion of Hindoostan alone, that similar effects are produced by causes of a like nature.

To enter upon the disquisition of a subject, so extensive and so intricate as that of Hindoo Mythology, would be to wander far from the purpose of the present Introduction: such an idea of it, however, as may serve to elucidate some passages in the Letters of the Rajah, which allude to their divinities, may be deemed neither unnecessary, nor impertinent.

The first thing that presents itself to our view is the Triad of Deity, Brimha, Veeshna, and Seeva, under which form is represented the three great attributes of the Almighty – Power to create, Goodness to preserve, and Justice to punish. The long list of the inferior Deities, which follow, exhibit such a striking similitude in their character and offices to the ancient Gods of Greece and Rome, that it has led to a conjecture of their being actually the same, and an attempt has been made by a writer of equal taste and erudition, to prove their identity, and to trace their wanderings through the mazes of Grecian and Egyptian lore.[1] Of the members of this numerous Pantheon, it will be sufficient for our purpose to mention the few following.

The first in rank is Ganesa, the God of Wisdom, who is thought to be the Janus of the Grecian Mythology;[2] Carticeya, the God of War, whose prowess is not inferior to that of the Mars of Rome. Seraswattee, the Goddess of Letters, and Protectress of Arts and Sciences, whose insignia, the Palmyra Leaf, and the Reed or Pen (implements used in writing) are surely more appropriate to her character, than the Shield and Lance which graced the Minerva of the Greeks. Cama, or the God of Love, is said, by Sir William Jones, to be the twin brother of the Grecian Cupid, with richer and more lively appendages. And, indeed, if we form our notions of this fabulous divinity from the beautiful Ode addressed to him, by an ancient Hindoo bard, we must confess his superiority to be very evident.[3] And, lastly, Surraya, or the

---

1   Hamilton is referring to Sir William Jones; see in particular his essay "On the Gods of Greece, Italy and India," *Works* 3: 319-97.

2   Hamilton changed this phrase to "the Janus of the Roman mythology" in her second edition, correcting the error pointed out by one of her reviewers (see Appendix A; she did not, however, correct her later use of the phrase "King of Rivers" for the Ganges, also criticized by the reviewer.)

3   Hymn to Camdeo; translated by Sir William Jones. [E.H.] Hamilton printed the entire poem and excerpts from the preface in her first edition. In the second

God of Day, who, in his chariot, drawn by seven green horses, bears so near a resemblance to Apollo, that it is impossible not to recognise them as the same.

These will serve to give the reader some idea of the numerous divinities, whose images are worshipped in the temples of the Hindoos, and to whose honour festivals are celebrated, and votive offerings of fruits and flowers are presented.

The peculiar construction of the Hindoo government, and the precepts of Hindoo faith, though admirably calculated for the preservation of their empire in happiness and tranquility, were not so favourable to the cultivation of the mind, and to its advancement in the paths of useful knowledge.

To expand the faculties of the human soul the passions must be called into action, nor can any of these be laid under such restraint, as dooms them to lie for ever dormant, without injuring the powers of the mind.

In the struggle of contending interests, though peace is sometimes lost, intellectual energy is roused, and while the strife of emulation, and restlessness of ambition disturb the quiet of society, they produce, in their collision, the genius that adorns it: it is accordingly pronounced, by one who must be allowed competent to the decision, that "Reason and Taste are the grand prerogatives of European minds, while the Asiatics have soared to loftier heights in the sphere of Imagination."[1]

But notwithstanding all the disadvantages under which they laboured, the many monuments that yet remain of their former splendour, the specimens of their literature, and the productions of their manufactures, sufficiently evince their advancement in the sciences which dignify life, as well as in the arts that ornament it.

The Bramins, to whom the cultivation of science was exclusively committed, seem to have made no contemptible use of their high privilege. In astronomy they are allowed to have excelled; many works

---

edition, she added a tribute to Jones but printed only a brief section of the hymn. See Appendix C for the full poem and preface.

1   See Asiatic Researches, vol. I. [E.H.] [Asiatic Society of Bengal], *Researches: or, transactions of the Society instituted in Bengal for inquiring into the history and antiquities, the arts, sciences, and literature of Asia.* Twenty volumes were published in this series, in London and Calcutta, between 1788 and 1839. Volumes 1-4 had been printed in the Calcutta edition (which was sold in London) by 1795.

of their ancient writers on metaphysics, and ethics, have already come to our knowledge; and, surely, no lover of poetry can peruse the specimens of that divine art, which have been presented to the public in an English dress; without feeling a desire to be more intimately acquainted with the productions of the Hindoo bards.

The degree of knowledge we already possess, concerning the antiquities of Hindoostan, has not been attained without efforts of the most indefatigable assiduity. But what obstacles are sufficient to deter the spirit of literary curiosity? When supported by philosophy, and guided by taste, it seldom fails to subdue every difficulty, and to see its persevering labours crowned with success!

How much of this observation has been verified in respect to the Asiatic Society, is well known to all who have perused the volumes of their Researches. It is thus briefly described by Mr. Maurice, in the Introduction to his Indian antiquities. "The buried tablet has been dug from the bowels of the earth; the fallen, and mouldering pillar has been reared; coins, and medals, struck in commemoration of grand, and important events, have been recovered from the sepulchral darkness of two thousand years; and the obsolete characters, engraved on their superficies, have, with immense toil, been decyphered and explained."[1]

In the contemplation of these scientific labours, the Governor General, under whose auspices they were commenced, will have the deserved meed of grateful acknowledgment from every candid and philosophic mind; for although he declined complying with the wishes of the members, who were all solicitous to see him at the head of their society, he was eminently instrumental in promoting its success; and in this, as in every other instance, he stood forth the steady friend, the liberal patron, and zealous promoter of useful knowledge.

How much the world has been indebted to the learned Gentleman who was nominated to the Presidentship of the Society, is too well known to require animadversion. Long and deeply will his loss be deplored by every lover of literature, and friend to virtue.

A few of the original members of the Asiatic Society,[2] still continue to pursue the great object of their undertaking with unremitted

---

1   Maurice, 1: 20 (see 56, note 2 for full reference).
2   The names of the original members of the Asiatic Society were as follows:
    Sir William Jones, Knt. President; Sir Robert Chambers, Knt. David Anderson,

ardour, and undiminished success. Of the rest, some have returned to the bosom of their families, and native country, not enriched by the plunder, and splendid by the beggary and massacre of their fellow-creatures, as has been represented in the malevolent and illiberal harangues of indiscriminating obloquy; but possessed of those virtues which ennoble human nature, and that cultivation of mind and talents, which dignify the enjoyment of retirement. Others of that society, equally honoured, and equally estimable, are, alas, no more! The generous esteem, the cordial friendship, the warm admiration which accompanied them thro' life, has not been extinguished in the silent grave; it lives, and will long live, in the hearts of many, calling for the tear of tender recollection, and of unextinguished, though, alas! unavailing sorrow.

The reader of sensibility, will, it is hoped, pardon a digression, into which the writer has been betrayed, by feelings of which they know the power and influence, and from which she hastily returns, to remark that the happiness enjoyed by the Hindoos under the mild and auspicious government of their native Princes, and preserved, without any material interruption, through such a mighty period of revolving time, as staggers the belief of the ever-fluctuating nations of Europe, was at length doomed to see its overthrow effected, by the resistless fury of Fanatic zeal.

The imposter of Mecca had established, as one of the principles of his doctrine, the merit of extending it, either by persuasion, or the sword, to all parts of the earth. How steadily this injunction was adhered to by his followers, and with what success it was pursued, is well known to all, who are in the least conversant in history.

The same overwhelming torrent, which had inundated the greater part of Africa, burst its way into the very heart of Europe, and covered many kingdoms of Asia with unbounded desolation; directed its baleful course to the flourishing provinces of Hindoostan. Here these fierce and hardy adventurers, whose only improvement had been in

---

James Anderson, Francis Balfour, George Hilaro Barlow, John Bristow, Ralph Broome, Reuben Barrow, Esqrs. General John Carnac; William Chambers, Charles Chapman, Burnots Crisp, Charles Croftes, Jonathan Dunken, Esqrs. Major William Davy; Jonathan Duncan, Francis Fowke, Francis Gladwin, Thomas Graham, Charles Hamilton, Thomas Law, John David Paterson, Jonathan Scot, Henry Vansittart, and Charles Wilkins, Esqrs. [E.H.] The "learned Gentleman" praised in the previous paragraph is Sir William Jones.

the science of destruction, who added the fury of fanaticism to the ravages of war, found the great end of their conquests opposed, by obstacles which neither the ardour of their persevering zeal, nor savage barbarity could surmount. Multitudes were sacrificed by the cruel hand of religious persecution, and whole countries were deluged in blood, in the vain hope, that by the destruction of a part, the remainder might be persuaded, or terrified into the profession of Mahommadenism: but all these sanguinary efforts were ineffectual; and at length being fully convinced, that though they might extirpate, they could never hope to convert, any number of the Hindoos, they relinquished the impracticable idea, with which they had entered upon their career of conquest, and contented themselves with the acquirement of the civil dominion and almost universal empire of Hindoostan.

In these provinces, where the Mussulman jurisdiction was fully established, Mussulman courts of justice were erected. The laws which the Hindoos had for numberless ages been accustomed to revere, as of divine authority, were set aside, and all causes judged and decided by the standard of Mussulman jurisprudence; an evil which appeared to the unhappy Hindoo more formidable than the extortions of avarice, or the devastations of cruelty.[1] Nor was the effect of these latter passions unfelt, the peculiar punishment of forfeiting their Cast, which is attached by their law to the most temporary and seemingly trivial deviation from its precepts, and which involves in it the dreadful consequences of irremediable alienation and irreversible proscription, was converted by their Mahommedan rulers into a lucrative source of oppression. Superstition combined with avarice to invent the means of inflicting this dreadful chastisement, and fines, without mercy, were exacted by those bigotted and venal judges.

By the same merciless conquerors, their commerce was impeded by every clog which avaricious and unfeeling power could invent to obstruct it. Neither the mild and tolerating spirit of the religion of the Hindoos, nor the gentle and inoffensive manners of its votaries,

---

1   See Scrofton's Hindoostan. [E.H.] Luke Scrafton, *Reflections on the government &c. of Indostan: with a short sketch of the history of Bengal, from the year 1739-1756; and an account of the English affairs to 1758* (London, 1763).

were sufficient to protect them from the intolerant zeal and brutal antipathy of their Mahommedan invaders. In the effusions of their barbarous enthusiasm, the temples of the Hindoos ornamented with all the ingenuity and skill for which they were celebrated, were utterly demolished, and the monuments of their ancient splendour every where destroyed.

For the support of the Mogul Nobles, assignments were granted on the lands of the different provinces, which were levied by these military lords in person, who, haughty and voluptuous, came to collect their pay from a timid people, whom they hated and despised with all the fervour of bigotry and ignorance.

To enumerate the multifarious load of oppression under which the unhappy Hindoos were doomed to groan, would be a tedious and ungrateful task. A generous mind cannot take pleasure in contemplating the picture of human misery, and human crime, though drawn by the correct hand of truth: let it then suffice to say, that the whole system of Mogul government toward their conquered Provinces was such, as could never fail to shock an European mind.

Hard, however, as was the fate of the poor Hindoos under their Mogul Sovereigns, even in the most flourishing state of their Empire; when that Empire mouldered to decay, and the power of one despot was overthrown, to make way for the uncontrouled licentiousness of numberless petty tyrants, it became yet more truly deplorable.[1]

The vigorous administration of a long line of able Princes, had, alone, for ages preserved this vast, but heterogeneous, and ill-constructed fabric from dissolution; and when, according to the unavoidable consequences of hereditary despotism, the reins of government were transmitted into weak and feeble hands, it fell rapidly to ruin. To the wretched successor of the Imperial throne, the miserable representative of the house of Timur, little now remains, but an universally acknowledged title to royalty, declared by inefficacious expressions of loyalty and attachment; while those who by bold usurpation, successful rebellion, or insidious fraud,

---

1  See Rohilla History. [E.H.] Charles Hamilton, *An Historical Relation of the Origin, Progress, and Final Dissolution of the Government of the Rohilla Afgans in the Northern Provinces of Hindostan*. London, 1787. The passage to which Hamilton is referring is on pp. 18-21.

possessed themselves of the spoils of the ruined empire, have established in their own families the right of succession to the territories thus acquired.

In those provinces which, by a train of circumstances, totally foreign to our purpose to relate, have fallen under the dominion of Great Britain, it is to be hoped that the long-suffering Hindoos have experienced a happy change. Nor can we doubt of this, when we consider, that in those provinces, the horrid modes of punishment, inflicted by the Mahommedans, have been abolished; the fetters, which restrained their commerce, have been taken off; the taxes are no longer collected by the arbitrary authority of a military chieftain, but are put upon a footing that at once secures the revenue, and protects the subject from oppression. The Banditti of the Hills, which used to molest the inoffensive inhabitants by their predatory incursions, have been brought into peaceable subjection. That unrelenting persecution, which was deemed a duty by the ignorant bigotry of their Mussulman rulers, has, by the milder spirit of Christianity, been converted into the tenderest indulgence. Their ancient laws have been restored to them; a translation of them, into the Persian and English languages, has been made, and is now the guide of the Courts of Justice, which have been established among them. Agriculture has been encouraged by the most certain of all methods – the security of property; and all these advantages have been rendered doubly valuable, by the enjoyment of a blessing equal, if not superior, to every other – the Blessing of Peace, a blessing to which they had for ages been strangers.[1]

These salutary regulations, originating with Mr. Hastings, steadily pursued by Sir John M'Pherson and Lord Cornwallis, and persevered in by the present Governor General, will diffuse the smiles of prosperity and happiness over the best provinces of Hindoostan, long after the discordant voice of Party shall have been humbled in the silence of eternal rest; and the rancorous misrepresentations of envy and malevolence, as much forgotten, as the florid harangues, and turgid declamations, which conveyed them to the short-lived notice of the world.[2]

---

1   Review of the British Government in India. [E.H.]
2   Warren Hastings (1732-1818), to whom Hamilton dedicated this novel, was the

The change which has been effected on the character, and manners of the Hindoos, during so many years of subjection, and so many convulsions in their political state, is not by any means so great, as such powerful causes might have been supposed to have produced.

In wandering through the desolated islands of the Archipelago, or even on the classic shores of Italy, the enlightened traveller would in vain hope to recognise, in the present inhabitants, one remaining lineament of the distinguishing characteristics of their illustrious ancestors. *There* the mouldering edifice, the fallen pillar, and the broken arch, bear, alone, their silent testimony, to the genius and refinement of the states which produced them. But in Hindoostan, the original features that marked the character of their nation, from time immemorial, are still too visible to be mistaken or overlooked. Though they have, no doubt, lost much of their original purity and simplicity of manners, those religious prejudices which kept them in a state of perpetual separation form their conquerors, has tended to the preservation of their originality of character, and all its correspondent virtues.

In the few districts which, secured by their insignificancy, or the inaccessibility of their situation, retained their independence, the original character still remains apparent. Such, till about the middle of the present century, was the fate of those, whose territories were situate along the mountains of Kummaoom.

The inhabitants of this lofty boundary of the rich and fertile province of Kuttaher, continued to enjoy the blessings of independence and security, till that province was brought under the subjection of a bold and successful Rohilla adventurer, who establishing himself, and his followers, in the possession of Kuttaher (which from

first Governor General of India; on his return to England in 1785, he was succeeded by Sir John Macpherson (1745-1821), who was in turn replaced by Charles, first Marquis of Cornwallis (1738-1805) in 1786. Cornwallis, who served in India until 1793, helped turn the East India Company from a trading company into a governing body, a process continued by Sir John Shore (1751-1843), who was Governor General from 1793-98. Hamilton's comments about "the rancorous misrepresentations of envy and malevolence" are an allusion to Hastings' impeachment for misconduct during his administration. The charges brought against him in Parliament received considerable attention, in part because of the impassioned rhetoric of his main enemy, Edmund Burke.

thenceforth bore the name of Rohilcund) directed his arms toward the extirpation of those Rajahs, whose vicinity excited his jealousy and alarmed his pride.[1]

He succeeded but too well in the execution of his unjust design, and did not fail to make the most tyrannical use of the victory he had obtained. Some of these Chiefs he banished for ever from the long enjoyed seats of their ancestors; some he removed to the other side of the Ganges, and from the few he suffered to remain, he stipulated the payment of an annual tribute,[2] and the immediate deposit of an exorbitant fine.

The Rajah Zāārmilla, who will soon be introduced to the acquaintance of the reader, appears to have been descended from one of those petty Sovereigns, who were obliged to put on the galling yoke of their unfeeling conqueror. He, however, must be supposed to have been among the number who were permitted to remain on their ancient territories, while the family of his friend and correspondent Māāndāāra, appears to have been banished from the Province, and to have taken shelter in the neighbourhood of Agra.

This short sketch, imperfect as it is, may serve to give some idea of the state of Hindoostan, not only when the Letters of the Rajah, which are now to be laid before the public, were written, but antecedent to that period. Adequate, however, to the purpose of elucidation, as it may be thought by some readers, it may be censured by others, as a presumptuous effort to wander out of that narrow and contracted path, which they have allotted to the female mind.

To obviate this objection, the writer hopes it will be sufficient to give a succinct account of the motives which led her to the examination of a subject, at one time very universally talked of, but not often very thoroughly understood. From her earliest instructors, she imbibed the idea, that toward a strict performance of the several duties of life, Ignorance was neither a necessary, nor an useful

---

1  The "Rohilla adventurer" is Ali Muhammad, who was succeeded by his sons' guardian, Hafiz Rhamat, the Rohilla leader who was defeated and killed at the Battle of Cutterah. Ali Muhammad's son, Faizullah Khan ("Fyzoola" in Hamilton's transliteration), survived to lead the remnant of the Rohilla forces after that defeat. See also 147, note 1, and the introduction.

2  See Rohilla History. [E.H.]

auxiliary, but on the contrary, that she ought to view every new idea as an acquisition, and to seize, with avidity, every proper opportunity for making the acquirement.

In the retirement of a country life, it was from books alone that any degree of information was to be obtained; but when these sequestered scenes were exchanged for the metropolis, opportunities for instruction, of a nature still more pleasing, were presented.

The affairs connected with the state of our dominions in India, were then the general topic of conversation. It was agreeable, from its novelty, and she had the peculiar advantage of hearing it discussed by those, who, from local knowledge, accurate information, and unbiassed judgment, were eminently qualified to render the discussion both interesting and instructive. The names of the most celebrated Orientalists became familiar to her ear; a taste for the productions of their writers was acquired; and, had it not been for a fatal event, which transformed the cheerful haunt of domestic happiness into the gloomy abode of sorrow, and changed the energy of Hope into the listlessness of despondency, a competent knowledge of the language of the originals would likewise have been acquired. Time, at length, poured its balm into the wounds of affliction, and the mind, by degrees, took pleasure in reverting to subjects which were interwoven with the ideas of past felicity. The letters of the Rajah were sought for, and the employment they afforded was found so salutary, in beguiling the hours of solitude, and soothing the pain of thought, that the study of them was resumed, as an useful relaxation, and, being brought to a conclusion, they are now presented to the world, whose decision upon their merit, is looked forward to with timid hope, and determined resignation.

IT has been justly complained, that the different orthography adopted by the Oriental translators is a source of much perplexity to the English reader; but, from the variety of opinions that prevail upon the subject, it is an evil which cannot easily be remedied. Instead of the double vowels *ee* and *oo*, used by Mr. Wilkins, and frequently by Mr. Halhed, Sir William Jones substitutes *i*, and *u* ; and instead of the *K*, made use of by the former Gentleman, he uses the letter *C*. From the different modes of pronunciation among the natives in the different provinces, another difficulty has arisen. It is from that cause that we frequently find the letter *B* a substitute for *V*, as Beena for Veena, &c.

IN the following Glossary, most of the Oriental words that occur in the Letters of the Rajah will be found.

# GLOSSARY.

ARJOON, or ARUN. The dawn. *See* SURRAYA.

AVATORS. Descents of the Deity in his character of Preserver. Ten of these appearances of the Divinity are mentioned by the Hindoos, nine of which have already taken place; the tenth Avator we are told is yet to come, and is expected to appear mounted (like the crowned conqueror in the Apocalypse) on a white horse, with a cimetar, blazing like a comet, to cut down all incorrigible offenders. ——*Asiatic Researches.*

BRAHMA. The creating Power.

BIBBY. Lady.

CARTICEYA. The God of War.

DEWTAH. The Divinity to whom worship is offered.

DEVAS, or DAIVERS. The Hindoos suppose the Universe to be divided into fourteen regions, or spheres, of which six are below, and seven are above this of the Earth, next beyond the vault of the visible heavens is the first Paradise. The proper inhabitants of this region are called Devas or Daivers, they may be considered as Demi Gods, of whom Endra, or Indra, is the chief.

FAKEER, or FAQUIR. An order of religious recluses.

GANESA. In many parts of Hindoostan every temple has the image of Ganesa (the God of Wisdom) placed over its gate; and the door of every dwelling-house is superscribed with his name.

HIRCARRAH. A messenger. A spy.

KRISHNA. One of the Avators. His adventures are celebrated in the epic poem called the Mahabbaret. He is considered by Sir William Jones as the Apollo of the Hindoos.

KHANSAMAN. Land, or house steward.

LACKSHMI, or LACSHMI. The consort of Veeshnû. She, like the other

Hindoo Goddesses, is distinguished by a variety of names; as Lackshmi, she is the Goddess of Fortune: as Sree, the Goddess of Plenty, or Hindoo Ceres.

MAYA. Explained by some Hindoo scholars to be "*the first inclination of the Godhead to diversify himself by creating worlds.*" "But the word Mayá, or Delusion, has a more subtle and recondite sense in the Védánta Philosophy, where it signifies the system of *perceptions.*" — *See Asiatic Researches.*[1]

MAHABBARET. An epic poem in the Shanscrit language, of great antiquity. The Bhagvat Geeta, an episode from this poem, has been translated into English by Mr. Wilkins.

PUNDIT, or PUNDEET. A learned Bramin.

POOJAH. The performance of worship to the Gods.

RYOTS. Hindoo labourers, or peasants.

RAMOZIN. The Mussulman Lent, or great fast, observed for a period of 30 days.

RIGYAJUHSAMAT'HARVA. A compound word denoting the four immortal Vedas, namely, the Rig-veda, the Yajur-veda, the Sama-veda, and the Atharva-veda.

SERRESWATTEE, or SERESWATI. The Patroness of Science and Genius.

SHASTER. Literally a book. The Scripture of the Hindoos, is, for pre-eminence, called *the Shaster.*

SANC'HA. An ancient Hindoo Poet.

SURRAYA, or SURYA. The God of Light, or the Orb of the Sun personified. The Sect who pay particular adoration to this Divinity are called Sauras. He has a multitude of names, and among them twelve epithets or titles which denote his distinct powers in each of the twelve months. The Indian Poets, and Painters, describe his car as drawn by seven green horses, preceded by Arun, or Arjoon, the dawn, who is denominated his charioteer.

SANASSEE. A Hindoo devotee.

SAIB. Gentlemen. Persons of estimation.

VAIDYA. The tribe who practice physic. Physicians.

VARUNA. The Genius of the sea, and wind.

---

1  Hamilton is quoting Jones' "On the Gods of Greece, Italy, and India" (3: 222).

VEDAS, or BEIDS. The sacred books of the Hindoos.

VEESHNU. The preserving Power.

VEENA, or BEENA, or BEEN. A musical instrument of the Guittar kind.

ZIMEENDAR. A Landholder.

# LETTERS

# OF A

# HINDOO RAJAH

---

## LETTER I.

Zāārmilla, *Rajah of Almora*, to Kisheen Neêay Māāndāāra, *Zimeendar of Cumlore, in Rohilcund.*

PRAISE to Ganesa! May the benign influence of the God of Wisdom,[1] beaming on the breast of Māāndāāra, dispel those clouds of wrath which have been engendered by mistake, and poured forth in the whirlwind of impetuosity.

I might justly expostulate upon the harshness of thy expressions; but I call to mind the goodness of thy heart, and they are effaced from my memory. We shrink from the fury of the King of Rivers, when his terror-striking voice threatens destruction to the surrounding world; but when his silver waves return to the peaceful channel allotted to them by the adored Veeshnû, we forget our terrors, and contemplate with rapture the majestic grandeur of the sacred stream who rolls his blessings to a thousand nations. And who would not prefer the casual fury of the mighty Ganges to the apathetic dulness of the never moving pool?

The Angel of Truth, whose dwelling is with Brahma, be my witness, that I have never been unmindful of the vows of friendship we so solemnly exchanged over the still warm ashes of the venerable Pundit; who was the guide and the instructor of our tender years. Twice, in performance of that vow, have I essayed to send the promised information, and twice have my intentions been frustrated.

---

1 The God of Wisdom, a customary introduction to the writings of Hindoos. From several expressions made use of by the Rajah in the course of his correspondence, he appears to have been an adherent of the sect called in the northern parts of India Veeshnûbukt, or Adorers of Veeshnû, the preserving Power. [E.H.]

No sooner had the auspicious arms of the sons of mercy opened the long-obstructed channels of conveyance, and checked the fury of the Afgan Khans, who have so long oppressed our unhappy country,[1] than I dispatched a messenger to thee, with a full account of public affairs, and of all of the incidents that have occurred to me in my retirement. Two months ago I learned that this messenger was drowned in his attempts to pass the Jumna. Again I wrote the same voluminous detail, and sent it by the hands of a Hircarrah, employed in the English camp, and who was sent by them, with dispatches to Agra, his native city. This messenger, more unfortunate than the other, was seized and cut in pieces, by a band of brutal Afgans. Hoping that this account will fully exculpate me from the charge of neglect, and leaving it to the shrill voice of time to acquaint thee with the public transactions of this eventful period, I shall recapitulate such parts of my two epistles as regarded myself alone, and in conformity to the promises that have passed between us, shall lay open to you not only the actions of my life, but the very thoughts of my heart.

Three days after that in which the blood of the Khans had stained the plains of Cutterah,[2] word was brought me by the Zimeendar of Lolldong, that our late oppressors were flying on the wings of despair to the mountains of Cummow. He conjured me, by all that we had suffered from the cruelty of Allee Mohammed, and the tyranny of his successors, not to give passage to the fugitives; but by arming my Ryots to disappoint their hopes of safety, and turn them back upon the swords of their enemies. I returned for answer, that "I gave praise

---

1  "On the 22d day of April, 1774, was fought between the armies of the visier, assisted by the English, and the troops of Hafiz Rhamut, the Rohilla Chief, the decisive battle of Cutterah; in which the complete victory obtained by the former at once annihilated the power and decided the fate of the Afgan adventurers. Wherever the fate of the Rohillas became known (says the historian of their short lived empire) the Hindoo Zimeendars (each of whom is possessed of a strong hold attaching to the chief village of his district) shut their forts, and refusing to their late masters protection, plundered without distinction all whom they found flying toward the hills." [E.H.]  Hamilton is here quoting from Charles Hamilton's *Historical Relation* (239). The "vizier" is Shuja-ud-daula (Sujah Dowla in Hamilton's transliteration), Nawab of Oudh, the territory which lay between Rohilkhand and Bengal. See also 147, note 1; 72, note 2; and the introduction.

2  History of the Rohilla Afgans, page 241. [E.H.] See also 72, and the introduction.

to Veeshnû, who had avenged the wrongs of the Hindoos, but that I had never learned to lift my hand against a fallen foe." I then issued strict orders to all my Ryots to keep within their dwellings, and having performed the customary Poojah, betook myself to rest. Reflections upon the vicissitudes of fortune, agitated my soul. Sleep forsook my eyelids; and, while the earth was yet clothed in the robes of darkness, I went forth with a few attendants, in hopes that the temperate air, and placid stillness of the night would tranquilise my mind. With astonishment I perceived the eastern horizon already tinged by the flame coloured charioteer of Surrayâ.[1] I hastened to ascend the hill, that I might be ready to pay my devotions at the first appearance of the glorious orb, the sacred emblem of the life-giving spirit of the Eternal! I reached the summit of the hill, but, Powers of Mercy! what a sight then presented itself to my view? The vast jungle extending over the northern side of Cumlore was in a blaze of fire. The reflection of the mighty conflagration illuminated the heavens, while sounds more dreadful than had ever pierced my ears, undulated through the fire-fraught air. The shrieks of the affrighted Afgans, the shouts of the Hindoos, who had contrived this method to obstruct their flight, the growling of the tigers, and yelling of the other beasts of prey, who had been disturbed in their dens, the crackling of the flames, and the bright glare of the still-spreading fire, formed altogether an unspeakable combination of horrors.

Many of the wretched fugitives passed the place where I stood; no longer the proud and haughty lords, at whose frown the Rajahs of the earth were wont to tremble: terror now sat upon their humbled foreheads, and despair seemed the leader of their steps. While I contemplated their present calamity, the remembrance of their former tyranny passed into the bosom of oblivion. A young man appeared, the blood still streaming from his wounds, while on his back he bore his aged father. In vain did the old man entreat this dutiful son to leave him to his fate; he still proceeded, with tottering steps to convey him he knew not whither. "Surely," said I, "the actions of this old man

---

1   Arjoun, or the dawn; who is expressively represented in Hindoo sculpture by the upper part only of a man, the rest of his person being supposed not yet emerged from darkness. [E.H.]

must have been meritorious in the sight of Heaven, that he should have been rewarded with such a son." I looked on the old warrior, and called to mind the grey hairs of my father.

I stopped the fugitives, who seeing my dress, looked on me without hope, and prepared themselves to receive the stroke of death. Whatever are your offences, said I to the son, your filial piety has in my eyes made atonement: turn, therefore, to the shelter of my fortress, where you may remain in safety till times of peace. They expressed their thankfulness, and with them I returned to my house. At the foot of the hill I heard a groan, which I perceived to proceed from under the branches of a tree that had lately fallen. I ordered my servants to search for the person who uttered it, and to my astonishment saw one in the dress of an English officer; he appeared to suffer the anguish of excessive pain, and though borne by the servants with all possible care, before we could reach the house, the invisible spirit seemed about to forsake the noble dwelling that had been allotted to it. On examination we found that his leg and many of his ribs were fractured. While I was in despair about this apparently irremediable misfortune, the old Afgan addressed himself to me, and professing his skill in the art of surgery, told me that he thought he could effect a cure. He accordingly applied such remedies as he deemed proper, and with such success that the stranger soon obtained some degree of relief. He no sooner lifted his eyes upon me, than calling to mind the English that had been taught us, by the Vaidya Beass, I held out to him the hand of friendship, saying "how do?" His eyes glistened with pleasure, and from that moment our hearts were united by the seal of friendship. When the tyrant pain had a little loosened the fetters of her power, he spoke to me in the Persian language; of which, as well as the Arabic, and the different dialects of Hindostan, he was *perfect master*. His conversation was like the soft dew of the morning, when it falls upon the valley of roses; it at once refreshed and purified the soul. His knowledge, in comparison of that of the most learned among the Pundits of the present age, was like the mountains of Cummow compared to the nest of the ant. The powers of his mind were deep and extensive as the wave of the mighty Ganges. His heart was the seat of virtue, and truth reposed in his bosom.

He had set out many months before, from Calcutta, with an intention of travelling through the northern parts of Hindostan, in order to trace the antiquities of the most ancient of nations. He had proceeded into Kuttaher, when a band of Afgans, headed by Daunda Adoola, who had been lately dismissed from the service of Hafiz Rhamut, took him prisoner. They confined him in a strong hold, on the banks of the Gurra; and on the approach of the combined armies of the English and Sujah Dowla, they left him exposed to the miseries of famine; but when obliged to fly to the woods of Cummow they forced him to accompany their flight, in hopes that he might be the means of procuring them terms with the English; whose honour they knew to be equal to their valour.[1]

On their rout to Cummow they were discovered by the Ryots of Raey Bandor, who by the orders of their master set fire to the wood in which they lay concealed; attempting, by this act of cruelty, meanly to avenge on these poor fugitives the death of his kindred, and the loss of his Zimeedary. Captain Percy, for this was the name of my amiable guest, fled with the rest; being overpowered by fatigue, and alarmed by the yells of the tiger, had resolved to climb a tree for safety, and there to remain until he could put himself under the protection of a Hindoo. The tree he attempted had been one left almost cut by my servants, but who had neglected to pull it down; it unfortunately gave way to the pressure, and occasioned the fatal accident I have already mentioned.

Thou knowest, O Māāndāāra, how my mind has ever thirsted after knowledge. Thou knowest with what ardour I have ever performed my *Poojah Seraswatee*,[2] and that, at an age when few young men have read the Beids of the Shaster, I had not only studied the sacred pages, but had perused every famous writing in the Shanscrit language.

The acquisition of the Persic tongue opened to me a door of knowledge which I was not slow to enter. History, for some time, became my favourite study. But what did the history of states and empires present to my view? Alas! what, but the weakness and guilt of mankind? I beheld the few, whom fortune had unhappily placed in view of the giddy eminences of life, putting the reins of ambition into the bloody hand of cruelty, lash through torrents of perfidy and slaughter, till, perhaps, overthrown in their career, they were trampled

---

1   "Sujah Dowla" was the Nawab of Oudh; see 78, note 1, and the introduction.
2   Worship to Seraswatee, the Goddess of Letters. [E.H.]

on by others who were running the same guilty race: or if they survived to reach the goal they aimed at, living but to breathe the air of disappointment, and then drop into the sea of oblivion. Such is the history of the few whose guilty passions, and atrocious deeds have raised them to *renown*, and to whom the stupid multitude, the willing instruments of their ambition, the prey of their avarice, and the sport of their pride, have given the appellation of *heroes*.

To the great body of the people I never could perceive that it made any difference who it was that held the scorpion whip of oppression, as into whatever hand it was by them conveyed, they were equally certain of feeling the severity of its sting. Meditating on these things, the deep sigh of despondency has burst from my heart. Can it be, said I to myself, that the omnipotent and eternal Ruler of the universe should create such multitudes for no other purpose but to swell the triumphs of a fellow mortal, whose glory rises in proportion to the misery he inflicts upon the human race? Surely, by what I learn from the actions of the princes of the earth, virtue is a shadow, and the love of it, which I have heretofore cherished in my breast, is nothing but the illusive phantom of a dream!

By conversing with my English guest I got a different view of human nature. Through the medium of the Persic literature it appeared universally darkened by depravity. In the history of Europe it assumed a milder form. In Europe man has not always, as in Asia, been degraded by slavery, or corrupted by the possession of despotic power. Whole nations have *there* acknowledged the rights of human nature, and while they did so have attained to the summit of true glory. The Romans, whom the Persian[1] writers represent as the lawless invaders, and fearless conquerors of the world; and the Greeks, whom they load with every opprobrium, were in fact nations of heroes. Spurning the chain of slavery, they wisely thought that human nature was too imperfect to be entrusted with unlimited authority; while they performed Poojah to the Goddess of Liberty, their hearts were enlarged by the possession of every virtue. She taught them the art of victory, strengthened their nerves in the day of battle; and, when

---

1   See Richardson's Introduction to the Persian Dictionary. [E.H.] John Richardson, *A Dictionary, Persian, Arabic, and English.... To which is Prefixed a Dissertation on the languages, literature, and manners of the eastern nations,* 2 vols (Oxford 1777-80).

they returned from the field of conquest, she gave sweetness to the banquets of simplicity, and rendered poverty honourable by her smiles. At length, Wealth and Luxury, the enemies of the Goddess, entered their dominions, and enticed the people from the worship of Liberty; who, offended by their infidelity, entirely forsook their country, making Happiness and Virtue the companions of her flight. On a re-examination of the conduct of these illustrious heroes, who, while their nation performed Poojah to Liberty, had gained the summit of fame; Percy pointed out to my view many imperfections, which while my breast was enflamed by the first ardour of admiration, had escaped my notice. The love of Liberty itself, that glorious plant as he called it, which if properly cultivated never fails to produce the fruits of virtue, sprung not (he said) in the Grecian, or the Roman breast, from the pure soil of universal benevolence, but from the rank roots of pride and selfishness. It never therefore extended to embrace the human race. This perfection of virtue was unknown in the world, till taught by the religion of Christ. This last assertion of Percy's, appeared to me as a prejudice unfounded in truth. But such are ever the hasty conclusions of ignorance. I had been taught to believe that the pure doctrine of benevolence, and mercy, was unknown to all but the favoured race of Brahma, that the Christian faith like that of the Mussulmans, was a narrow system of superstitious adherence to the wildest prejudices, engendering hatred, and encouraging merciless persecution against all who differed from them. Nothing can be more erroneous than this idea of Christianity. By the indulgence of my English friend I was favoured with the perusal of the Christian Shaster. The precepts it contains, are simple, pure, and powerful, all addressed to the heart; and calculated for restoring the universal peace and happiness which has been banished from the earth, since the days of the Sottee Jogue.[1]

---

1   The age of purity. The Hindoos reckon the duration of the world by four Jogues, or distinct ages. The Sottee Jogue, or age of purity, is said to have lasted 3,200,000 years, when the life of man is said to have extended to 100,000 years. The Tirtah Jogue, or age in which one third of mankind were reprobate, which consisted of 2,400,000 years. The Dwaper Jogue, in which one half of the human race became depraved, endured 1,600,000 years. And the Collee Jogue, in which all mankind are corrupted, is the present era. See Halhed's Gentoo Laws. [E.H.]

The love of liberty in a people who are taught by the fundamental precepts of their Shaster, "to do to others as they would have others do to them," rises above the narrow spirit of selfishness, and extendeth to embrace the human race! Benevolent people of England! it is their desire, that all should be partakers of the same blessings of liberty, which they themselves enjoy. It was doubtless with this glorious view, that they sent forth colonies, to enlighten and instruct, the vast regions of America.[1] To disseminate the love of virtue and freedom, they cultivated the trans-Atlantic isles: and to rescue *our* nation from the hands of the oppressor, did this brave, and generous people visit the shores of Hindostan!

You may imagine how desirous I was to become acquainted with some particulars concerning the form of government, laws, and manners, of this highly favoured nation. Provided the above particulars are *true*, it is of course to expect, that they must all be formed after the model of perfection; and such, according to my conception of the accounts of Percy, they undoubtedly are.

It having pleased Brahma to create them all of one cast, among them are no distinctions, but such as are the reward of virtue. It is not there as in the profligate court of Delhi, where great riches, a supple adherence to the minister, and a base and venal approbation of the measures of the court can lead to titles and distinction.[2] No. In England, the honours of nobility are invariably bestowed according to intrinsic merit. The titles and privileges of these heroes of the first class, descend to their children. We may well suppose what care is bestowed on the education of these young nobles, whose minds are moulded into wisdom, at Universities instituted for the purpose. Where vice and folly are *alike* unknown: and where the faculties of a young man, might have as *great* a chance, of getting leave to rust in

---

1    Hamilton's irony here depends in part on the reader's remembering the date at which the letter is supposedly written: "toward the beginning of the year 1775" (see 144) the increasingly acrimonious disputes between the crown and the American colonies on the subjects of "virtue and freedom" were on the point of breaking into open warfare.

2    Delhi was the seat of the Mughal empire, which was in complete decay by the last quarter of the eighteenth century. The implicit warning against courtly corruption in England also glances towards the European situation and the destruction of what the English tended to see as the corrupt French aristocracy.

ignorance, as to be lost in dissipation! From these seminaries of virtue, they are called to the Senate of the nation; where they debate with all the gravity, and the interest, that might be expected from their early habits of serious thought, and deep investigation. The sons of the King, at an early age, take their seats in that tribunal, from whose decision there lies no appeal. As their example is supposed to animate the young Nobility, it may well be imagined how wise, learned, grave, and pious, these princely youths must be: their actions are doubtless the mirrors of decorum, and their lips the gate of wisdom!

The equality of human beings in the sight of God, being taught by their religion, it is a fundamental maxim of their policy, that no laws are binding, which do not obtain the consent of the people. All laws are therefore issued by the sanction of their representatives; every separate district, town, and community, choosing from among themselves, the persons most distinguished for *piety, wisdom, learning,* and *integrity*, impart to them the power of acting in the name of the whole.

About four hundred of these eminent men, each of whom to all the requisites of a Hindoo magistrate,[1] unites the knowledge of a Christian philosopher, form what is termed the third estate. Uninfluenced by the favour of party, uncontaminated by the base motives of avarice or ambition, they pursue with steady steps the path of equity, and have nothing so much at heart as the public welfare. No war can be engaged in, and no taxes imposed, but by the consent of these patriot chiefs. Judge then, my friend, how light the burden must be, that is laid on by these representatives, these brothers of the people. Never can such men as these be instrumental in sending war, with all its attendant miseries, into the nations of the earth: all of whom they are taught by their Shaster to consider as brethren. In Asia we behold

---

1  It is ordained that "the magistrate shall keep in subjection to himself his *Lust, Anger, Avarice, Folly, Drunkenness* and *Pride*: he who cannot keep these passions under his own subjection, how shall he able to nourish and instruct the people? Neither shall he be seduced by the pleasures of the chace, nor be addicted to play, nor always employed in dancing, singing, and playing on musical instruments. Nor shall he go to any place without a cause, nor dispraise any person without knowing his faults, nor shall he envy another person's superior merit, nor shall say that such persons as are men of capacity are men of no capacity, &c." See Code of Gentoo Laws, page 52. [E.H.]

the gory monster, ever ready to stalk forth with destructive stride at the voice of ruthless tyranny, but in Europe, Princes are the friends of peace, and the fathers of their people.

Many of our Pundits have contemplated with astonishment, the animosities that have arisen among the followers of the Arabian prophet, on account of the different interpretations given by their[1] Imaums to certain passages of the Koran; forgetting that the Supreme Being delighteth in variety, and that He who hath not formed, any two objects in his vast creation exactly similar, took doubtless no less care upon the formation of the human mind, perceiveth with delight the contrarieties of opinion among men. They have carried their presumption so far, that one sect hath dared to conceive hatred, and ill will against another, for not viewing every dark passage in the writings of their Prophet, exactly in the same light! How different is the case with the Christian? The great Founder of their religion having left every man at liberty, to choose the form of worship which he finds best calculated to excite, and to express sentiments of devotion, they each attach themselves to the form most agreeable to their own minds, allowing the same liberty to others, and convinced that all are equally acceptable to the Deity, who acquiesce in his laws, and obey his commandments. In the dominions of the Mussulmans, though all sects are permitted to live, it is one sect alone (the orthodox)[2] that is invested with power, or entrusted with authority. But among Christians what sect exists, that would accept of the most beneficial distinctions, on terms so contrary to the spirit of their Gospel? No. All sects, equal in the eye of Heaven, must needs, by the wise and virtuous Legislators of this happy country, be admitted into an equal enjoyment of every right, and every privilege. The Priests of their religion are, as their characters are fully set forth in their Shaster, men who despite the adventitious advantages of rank and fortune, who regard no distinctions in their flock, but the distinctions arising from

---

1   See Preliminary Discourse of the Bramins, employed by Mr. Hastings in the Pootee, or compilations of the ordinations of the Pundits. — Gentoo Laws. [E.H.]

2   See the Hedaya or Commentary on the Mussulman Laws. [E.H.] 'Ali Ibn Abi Bakr, *The Hedàya, or guide; a commentary on the Musselman laws: translated by the order of the Governor-General and council of Bengal, by Charles Hamilton*, 4 vols (London, 1791).

internal worth, and intrinsic goodness; not thirsting after worldly honours; nor given to luxury; strangers to avarice and pride. Having no bitterness against those who differ from them in opinion, animosity, strife, or wrath, is never heard of among these holy men, who, in the language of their Shaster, "pass through things temporal, only mindful of those which are eternal."[1] Although my unwearied application to the study of the English language, enables me to read a few passages in that tongue, it is to the Arabic copy of those books of the Shaster, called Gospels, to which I am indebted for the accuracy of my information.

Not presuming to lift the veil of mystery, with which some passages are enveloped (a presumption, which in a stranger would be equally unpardonable and unbecoming) I pass over whatever appears to be mysterious, with the most profound respect. But that Power, which taught me to sweep from my heart the dust of prejudice, taught me also to pay homage to excellence, wherever it might be found. In the precepts of the Christian Shaster, I behold the grandeur of sublimity, and the simplicity of truth. There is one particular so novel; so peculiar; so repugnant to the universally received opinions of mankind that it considerably excited my astonishment. In the revelation bestowed upon the Christians, women are considered in the light of rational beings! free agents! In short, as a moiety of the human species; whose souls are no less precious in the eye of the Omniscient than that of the proud lords of the creation! What can be more extraordinary?

The inferiority of women appears so established by the laws of nature, and has been so invariably inculcated, by all the legislators sent by Brahma to enlighten the eight corners of the world, that it seems altogether incontestible. It is true, that our divine laws (incomparable in wisdom!) do not, like the laws of the Mussulmans, absolutely exclude women from the participation of happiness in a future state, it being written in the Shaster, "*that a woman, who burns herself with her husband, shall live with him in Paradise three crore and fifty lacks of years.*"[2]

---

1   Compare 2 Corinthians 4:18

2   Quoted (with slight variations) from Halhed's *Gentoo Laws*, 286. Hamilton was apparently aware that the old European idea that Islam denied women had souls was inaccurate. In her *Letters on .... Education* she mentions in passing that this belief is "vulgarly attributed to Mahommed" (1: 234).

But even in this case, it is contested by the Pundits, that her admission into Paradise, depends on her husband's title to an entrance into that state of felicity. Uncertain tenor! precarious dependance! on which a poor woman commits herself to the flames! Wisely did our lawgivers ordain, that ignorance and submission should be the ornaments of women; seeing how much the privilege of enquiry, might have disquieted their repose!

Christian women are more fortunate; they may enjoy Heaven without the company of their husbands! Throughout the Christian Shaster, they are exalted to perfect equality with man. They are considered as occupying a station of equal dignity, in the intelligent creation; and as being equally accountable, for the use they make of the gift of reason, and the monitions of conscience. What care! what pains! must we then conclude to be bestowed by Christians, on the formation of the female mind? "As the beams of the moon kindles the flowers of the Oshadi, so," says the philosopher, "doth education expand the blossoms of intelligence."[1] Where women are destined to be under no controul but that of reason, under no restraint, save the abiding consciousness of the searching eye of Omnipotence, of what vast importance must their education appear, in the eyes of the enlightened! Accordingly we find that seminaries of female instruction, called Boarding-schools, are in England universally established; where, by what I can learn, the improvement of the understanding is as successfully attended to, and every solid, and useful accomplishment as fully attained, as are the severe morals of Christianity, by their brothers at the university. When the females of England have completed their education in these seats of science, these nurseries of wisdom, they come forth like the mother of Krishna, the torch of reason enlightening their minds, and the staff of knowledge supporting their virtue! In that enlightened country, a wife is the friend of her husband. Motives of esteem influence the choice of both; for there women are at liberty to choose, or to reject offers of marriage, and educated as they are, we may well suppose how wisely they will always choose! By their religion, men are prohibited from

---

1 Usually, the "philosopher" is the speaker of the *Hitopadesa* (see 156, note 1), but this quotation does not appear there. However, the notes do include a reference to the Lotus – "which spreads its blossom only in the night" (315 [1787], 270 [1885]).

having more than one wife at a time, which at first view will doubt-less appear a hardship in your eyes: but if you consider what an endless source of disquiet, the quarrels, jealousies, and strifes, among our wives frequently produce, you will perhaps acknowledge, that to lessen the number is not so great a misfortune.

What I have said concerning the cultivation of the female under-standing, will perhaps, appear ridiculous in your eyes; but take the fol-lowing proof of the veracity of my assertion. One day that I had been studying the Shaster of my English guest, I perceived, written in fair and legible characters, upon the first leaf, these words; "The parting gift of Charlotte Percy to the most beloved of brothers." I carried the book to my friend, who was still confined to his couch, and asked him if Charlotte was the name of his brother? He answered with a smile, that Charlotte was the name of his dear, and amiable sister. "Your sister!" repeated I, with astonishment, "Can it be, that in your country a woman is permitted to touch the Shaster? or, are women taught to write? It cannot be. Such things are not proper for women." He replied, that my surprise was occasioned, by having always been accustomed, to behold the sex in the degrading state of subjection. A state, which, wherever it prevails, subdues the vigour, and destroys the virtue of the human mind. Man, he observed, received from nature no passion so powerful as the love of tyranny. This, the superiority of bodily strength, had enabled him to exercise over the weaker part of his species, with uncontrouled sway. In proportion as society advanced in civilization, the advantages of reason over bodily strength prevailed, and the passions received from the fetters of restraint a degree of polish, which if it did not change their nature, rendered them less disgustingly ferocious. The wife of a Hindoo, continued he, is from this cause treated with more respect, and enjoys a much greater degree of liberty and happiness, than the wife of an untutored Afgan. But it is not in the nature of man, to relinquish claims so flat-tering to his pride; and the innate love of the exercise of despotic authority, must have for ever kept the female sex in a state of subjec-tion, had not the powerful mandate of religion snapped their chains. This, the religion received by the Christians has fully accomplished: and to shew you how much it is in the power of education to improve the female mind, continued my friend, I shall translate, for your perusal, some of the letters of that sister, whose name is written in the leaf of the book you are now reading. According to this promise, my excellent friend translated for me, several pieces both in prose and verse; presenting me at the same time with copies of the originals, that I might compare them together. By that which I have enclosed for your satisfaction, you will perceive, that the sister of Percy has not only learned to read, and write, but is in considerable degree capable of thinking. Nursed in solitude, she in early youth took delight, to string the pearls of poetry. I send you one of the first of these gems of fancy; which, though it boasts not the radiant brilliancy of the Diamond, is pleasing as the varying Opal, and soft as the lustre of the green emerald. It was written after having refused an invitation to a party of pleasure, on account of her duty to an aged uncle, who had adopted her as his daughter, and of whom she speaks, with the language of filial affection. Let it be read with candour, for it is the offspring of youth; with indulgence, for it is the tribute of gratitude!

BLEST be these rural glens, these flowery glades;
 The lov'd retreats of innocence and joy:
Content's sweet voice is heard beneath these shades;
 Her quiet seat no wild wish dares annoy.

Dear to my heart is this sequester'd scene;
 By liberal nature deck'd in robes so gay:
O'er all my soul she breathes her sweets serene,
 As in her walks I take delight to stray.

'Twas her sweet hand that strew'd this bank with flowers;
 She bends these osiers o'er the chrystal stream;
She twines the woodbine round these leafy bowers:
 And turns that rose-bud to the morning's beam.

From her, sweet Goddess, here in youth, I drew
 Spirits as light as airy fancy's wing:
'Twas here I mark'd each glowing tint she threw
 On the fair bosom of the opening spring.

And shall I leave her? leave her lov'd retreat?
   For scenes where Art her mimic power displays,
For the false pleasures of the gay and great;
   Pride's empty boast, and Splendor's midnight blaze.

Can Pride, can Splendor's most triumphant hour,
   Give any pleasure to the breast so dear,
So exquisite, as is the conscious power
   A venerable parent's days to cheer?

Ah! then, from thee, my guardian, and my friend,
   Let never vagrant wish presume to stray;
But on my steps let filial love attend,
   Gently to sooth thy life's declining day.

Can I forget what to thy love I ow'd?
   Forget thy goodness to my orphan state?
Forget the boons thy tenderness bestow'd?
   Or thy unchang'd affection's early date?

When my lov'd father press'd his early bier,
   (From which, alas! nor youth, nor love, could save)
And when my widow'd mother (doom severe!)
   Victim of sorrow! sunk into the grave.

Thy care a more than father's care supplied,
   Thy breast a more than father's fondness knew.
Led by thy hand, or cherish'd at thy side,
   My infant years in sprightly pleasures flew.

No frown from thee repress'd the harmless joy,
   No harsh reproof repell'd the lively thought.
Pleas'd, thou couldst smile on childhood's simplest toy,
   And say, "no pleasures were so cheaply bought."

Can I forget the partner of thy cares?
   Whose kind attention form'd my early youth;

Or with what care she watch'd my tender years;
  And in life's morning, sow'd the seeds of truth?

'Twas her instructions, pious, prudent, wise,
  Taught me the virtues that adorn our sex;
Its humblest duties bade me not despise;
  But rise superior to its weak defects;

Taught me to scorn mean Pride's malignant sneer,
  The tale calumnious, cautious to receive,
To Misery's voice to turn a willing ear;
  Its woes to pity or its wants relieve;

Taught me on pure Devotion's wings to rise
  To the unseen, supreme, eternal Power;
Whose works an equal theme of praise supplies,
  In heav'n's starr'd concave, or earth's humblest flower.

If e'er my breast with love of virtue glow'd,
  Or ardent sought the Muses' hallow'd shrine,
To thee my dawning taste its culture ow'd;
  Each high-born sentiment, dear shade, was thine.

Oh! if thy sainted spirit hovers near,
  With smiles benign my filial vows approve:
Vows like thy conduct, artless, and sincere,
  Pure as thy faith, and spotless as thy love.

But see! where comes my venerable sire,
  With cheerful air, and looks serenely gay:
He comes to lead me to the social fire,
  To warn me of the dews of parting day.

I come, my more than father! best of friends!
  Dear, good old man; how good, how dear to me?
Beyond thy life, for me no hope extends.
  My comfort, and my peace, expire with thee.

Thus far did Zāārmilla write to his friend Māāndāāra, by the slave who perished in the swellings of the Jumna. Captain Percy had been then five months under the shadow of my roof; the skill of the Afgan had not been sufficient to join the fractured bone; so that great pain was inflicted upon him. I had often attempted to get an account of his situation transmitted to the English camp, but without success. The troops of the Afgans surrounded me, and the danger of discovering to them that an English officer was in their power obliged me act with the utmost circumspection. At length, in the month Assen (October) the treaty was concluded between the Khan of Rampore, and the great powers. I besought and obtained leave from Fyzoola Khan to go myself to the camp of the English, which was yet at the foot of the mountains.[1] Captain Percy, weakened by the langour of disease, and sinking under the pressure of incessant pain, revived at my proposal: the big tear glistened in his eye, and pressing my hand between his, God shall bless thee, my dear Zāārmilla, cried he, the God of Heaven shall bless thee for thy kindness to me. In contemplating the approaching dissolution of my being, unshaken confidence in the mercies of my God and Saviour support my soul. Death has for me no terrors; but methinks it would brighten the dark passage that leads to it, could I again behold any of my former friends, and countrymen; their accounts would soften to my sister the tidings of an event that will pierce her soul. She knows not the goodness of Zāārmilla; and will only imagine to herself the figure of her dying brother, expiring among strangers.

Could she be assured, how often my sufferings have been alleviat-ed by the balm of sympathy, and how much the endearing sensibilities of cordial friendship have refreshed my soul, it would be a solace to her affliction.

He then wrote as much as strength would permit, to a British officer, who was his particular friend, and enclosing it in a few lines to the commander in chief, delivered it into my hands.

I pursued my journey to the foot of the mountains, attended only by a small retinue. When we reached the place of our destination, we

---

1   Fyzoola (or Faizullah) Khan, the son of Ali Muhammad, was granted control of
    Rampur, in north-central India near the present-day Nepalese border, after holding
    out against the Nawab of Oudh for some months. See the introduction.

had the mortification to find that it had been for some time abandoned by the English, who were on their march down the country. I did not hesitate to follow them; though, being unused to travel, I was overtaken by fatigue, and annoyed by the rains, which began at this time to set in with great violence.

After a tedious and disagreeable journey, I at length reached Rhamgaut, where the English army, at the request of the Visier, had for some time halted. I was received by the commander with the eye of kindness, and recommended by him to his officers, with the voice of praise. The chief to whom captain Percy had written, welcomed me in the warmth of friendship, and bestowed upon my conduct unmerited eulogium.

Soon as my limbs had recovered from the weariness of fatigue, this Saib, and another dear, and intimate friend of the unfortunate Percy's, who was deeply skilled in the science of medicine, purposed returning with me, in order to solace, and if possible to restore the amiable youth. The rains continued to descend; but the spirit of true friendship rises superior to every obstacle. We carried with us the good wishes of an host of friends, and, supported by hope, accomplished our journey in safety.

From the accounts I had communicated concerning the situation of our friend, doctor Denbeigh, the friend on whose knowledge in the healing art, his brother officers placed so much reliance, had pronounced great hopes concerning him; hopes which inspired the alacrity of cheerfulness. Alas! as the blood-stained tiger of the forest rushes on the timid fawn, who, unconscious of his presence, sports within the reach of his ferocious grasp, so doth calamity dart upon the cherished hope of mortals.

When we approached my dwelling, the Khansaman, under whose particular care I had left my friend, came out to meet us. His eyes were heavy with the tears of grief, and his whole deportment was marked by the pressure of recent sorrow. I was afraid to question him, lest his answer should bereave me of hope; but at length my tongue articulated Percy's name. Alas! my fears were just. The pure spirit had fled from its corporeal confinement, to the boundless expansion of infinity. Three days had elapsed since the body, deserted by its celestial inhabitant, had been committed to the womb of earth: I visited the dust which covered it, and gave vent to the grief that oppressed my soul. The friends of Percy united their tears with mine: they were the pure offerings of friendship flowing from hearts of sincerity. After we had indulged the first impulses of grief, the Khansaman presented us with the papers which our friend had consigned to his care. These were a sealed packet, directed to his sister, a letter to his English friend, with directions concerning his effects, and an epistle to me, written with the pen of affection. To me he bequeathed, as a token of his love, the little shrill-voiced monitor, whose golden tongue proclaims the lapse of time, called in English a repeating watch, his sister's picture, together with all the manuscripts of her writing, his English Shaster, and, in short, all that was about his person when I had the happiness of receiving him under my roof. I have since perused with care the precious relics of this amiable young man. In the leaves of his pocket-book were written many valuable remarks, some of which had evidently been deposited there but a short time before the Angel of Death arrested the hand which wrote them. Among his loose papers were several pages entitled, "Thoughts on the Prevalence of Infidelity"; in which the names of Hume, Bolingbroke, and Voltaire, frequently occur.[1] It will oblige me if you enquire of the Immaum Yuseph Ib'n Medi for some information concerning these men; who, I make no doubt, are of the sect of Hanbal, against whose opinions the Mussulman doctors so bitterly inveigh.[2] What makes me certain they are not Christians is, that from what Percy has said concerning their opinions, it is evident that these unhappy men are unconscious of the precious spark of immortality which glows within their bosoms. Nay, so much are they inflated by vanity, so infatuated by the spirit of pride, as to utter words of arrogance with the tongue of presumption; saying, that men ought *not* to believe in the supreme Inheritor of eternity.

---

1  David Hume (1711-76) was a Scottish philosopher and historian, notorious for his religious scepticism, as was the great French writer Voltaire (1694-1778). Henry St. John, Lord Bolingbroke (1678-1751) was a politician and philosopher whose writings provided the philosophical basis of Alexander Pope's *Essay on Man* and whose posthumously published reflections on religion greatly offended devout readers such as Samuel Johnson.

2  According to Charles Hamilton's translation of the *Hedàya*, the Hanbalites were the "most traditional of the three traditional [Islamic] sects" (xxii).

Our departed friend concludes his remarks upon these people, in the following words:

"Ye who are so keen to disseminate the baneful principles of infidelity, did ye know what it is to watch the slow, but steady, steps of death; to behold his approach in the silence of solitude, where the whispers of vanity are unheard, and the *small still* voice of conscience alone speaks audibly to the soul, ye would not, surely, be so rashly forward to dash from the lips of a fellow mortal the cordial draught of hope, and to offer in its stead, the bitter cup of doubt, uncertainty, and despair!

"The principles of religion are so congenial to the human mind, that I am convinced they would almost always remain permanent, was it not for the adventitious prejudices, with which the pure and simple doctrines of Christianity are so entangled, by the zealous adherents of every sect, and party.

"Of all my contemporaries, they have ever been the foremost to throw off the restraints of religion, who have been what is termed *most strictly educated*; but who never had any religious sentiments impressed upon their minds, distinct from the particular dogmas of their respective sects. With these dogmas their ideas of the truth of Christianity were inseparably combined; and when they afterward came to mingle with the world, and found their prejudices untenable against the attack of argument, the force of reason, or the sneer of ridicule, the whole fabric of their faith was shaken to the foundation. Blessed be the memory of the parent who instructed me; whose care it was to impress upon my mind the strictest principles, with the most liberal opinions. In her eyes the mode of worship was nothing; the spirit from which it was produced was every thing.

"My feelings tell me that the lamp of life is nearly exhausted. Never more shall I behold the face of a friend. No sister's friendly hand to smooth my pillow, or to sooth my soul with the tender accents of affection. My impatience for the pleasure of seeing my friend Grey, has deprived me of the comfort I have hitherto received from the consoling sympathy, and unremitting kindness, of the amiable Hindoo.

"Remote from country, friends, and all that my heart has been accustomed to hold dear; – but what, in a moment like this, could friends or country do for me? what, but to 'point the parting anguish.'[1] I am *not* alone. No. The ever-present God is with me; and his comforts support my soul. Often in the hour of health, have I repeated with rapture the lines of the poet: and now I am called to be an evidence of their truth.

> "Should fate command me to the farthest verge
> Of the green earth, to distant barbarous climes,
> Rivers unknown to song; where first the sun
> Gilds Indian mountains, or his setting beam
> Flames on th' Atlantic isles; 'tis nought to me:
> Since God is ever present, ever felt,
> In the void waste as in the city full;
> And where His spirit breathes there must be joy.
> When e'en, at last, the solemn hour shall come
> And wing my mystic flight to future worlds
> I cheerful will obey; there, with new powers
> Will rising wonders sing. I cannot go
> Where universal love not smiles around."[2]

Such, O! Māāndāāra, was the conclusion of the life of this European. His two friends abode with me for a few days, and departed, loaded with every mark of my friendship and esteem. I was no sooner left alone, than melancholy took possession of my mind. The conversation of Captain Percy gave light to my soul; it was at an end; and darkness again surrounded me.

The Rajah of Lolldong, and his brother, the Zimeendar, heard of my affliction, and came to comfort me. Alas! they were both too full of their own concerns, to take any part in the grief which filled my heart. In the late calamities of our nation, their lands had been ravaged by the troops of the Visier. The protecting hand of the English, had not been able to save their villages from the ruthless

---

1    James Thomson, *Winter* 348.

2    As Zāārmilla was unable to proceed farther in the translation, we have thought proper to fill up the blank with what we imagine to have been the poetical passage alluded to by Captain Percy. [E.H.] James Thomson, "A Hymn on the Seasons" 100–12. Line 112 should read "smiles not around."

hand of the destroyer; and their Ryots were consequently unable to pay their rents. I listened to the story of their distresses with concern, and said all in my power to comfort them. A second, and a third time, they repeated the particulars of their grievances; and though they both usually spoke at once, still I listened with patience. But when I found them obstinately persist in cherishing the feelings of selfish regret, for their own particular misfortune, while the miseries of thousands, who, on the same occasion, had lost their all, found no entrance into their hearts, I could no longer listen to their complaints with the semblance of attention; and, perceiving that they wearied me, they departed.

In the innocent and playful vivacity of the little Zamarcanda, I have found a better substitute for intellectual enjoyment, than in the tiresome solemnity of sententious dulness. But still the soft dew of contentment sheds not its divine influence on the dwelling of Zäärmilla. My mind is tossed in the whirlwind of doubt, and bewildered in the labyrinth of conjecture: but let not Määndäära mistake the words of his friend; let him not imagine that my veneration for the Gods of my fathers can be lessened by the words of a stranger: or, that I am so far misled, as to conceive that the greatest portion of wisdom bestowed by Brahma upon any nation in the world's circumference can bear any comparison with that which has been given in the sacred Vedas. No. I bow with reverence while I pronounce the name of the sacred volumes; and, confess that in Rigyajuhsámát' Harva the immortal treasures of true knowledge are deposited.

But in what text of the Veda, Upa Veda, Vedanga, Purana, Dherma, or Dhersana,[1] is it forbidden to contemplate the operation of Mâya throughout the sea-girt earth? Why should I remain in doubt as to the truth of the accounts given me by the young Christian? Why should I not satisfy my mind by a farther acquaintance with his countrymen, by which alone I can discover, whether his words have been dictated by the spirit of delusion, or emanated from the heart of integrity?

If his accounts are just; if the book he has given me be *indeed* the

---

1  The six great Shasters, on which all knowledge, divine and human, is supposed to be comprehended. See Asiatic Researches, vol.i, article 18. [E.H.]

Shaster of the Christians, I can, in that case, have no doubt of its being the guide of their practice, as well as the rule of their faith; nor help feeling an ardent desire for knowing more of men, whose conversation must be so full of purity, and whose lives are devoted to good works!

What I have already learned from the worthy European, whose death has caused the arrow of affliction to rankle in my bosom, so far from hurting my mind, has served but to invigorate my virtue. It is by the breath of Ganesa, that the flame of curiosity has been kindled in my bosom. And wherefore should I not indulge myself in following that path to knowledge, which the spirit that enlighteneth my understanding, impelleth me to pursue? If the sun of science, which rose with radiant splendor on our eastern hemisphere, now beams its fervid rays upon the regions of the west, why should I be prevented from following its glorious course?

Thou wilt, perhaps, tell me of what I owe to my Cast, my country, and my people. As to the first, thou knowest, that the acquirement of knowledge, is not a duty confined to the race, which sprung from the mouth of Brahma; and though it is necessary that every Hindoo should keep himself free from contamination, yet many holy men have found it possible to do so, in the strictest sense, even while they made their abode in the dwellings of Mahommadans, and Christians. No opportunity could offer more favourable than the present, for quitting my country, without prejudice to my own interest or that of my people. The peace which has been happily restored to us, is ensured by the faith of our deliverers: and, moreover, the wisdom, generosity, and clemency, which adorn the character of Fyzoola Khan, give the best pledge for the security of our possessions.

I have, therefore, no obstacle to surmount in the accomplishment of my wishes but one. It is the disposal of Zamarcanda. Could I leave her in the possession of my friend, my mind would be at rest. And who, so worthy to be the wife of Māāndāāra as the sister of Zāārmilla? She is yet in the tenderness of youth, but is accomplished in all that our laws permit women to learn. Her mind is pure as the lilly, that bends its silver head over the transparent stream. Modesty is enshrined in her cheeks, and beauty sparkles through the deep fringe which encircles her ground-kissing eyes. The blood of a thousand

Rajahs flows through her veins, and her Ayammi Shadee[1] shall be worthy of the love of her brother. If this proposal seemeth good in thine eyes, I will meet thee at Ferrochabad, in the middle of the month Phogoun,[2] and there thou shalt receive the virtuous maiden from the hands of thy friend.

I expect thy answer with impatience. Farewell.

---

1  Ayammi Shadee is the present made to a young woman by her relations during the period of her betrothment, and which is, ever after, considered her own property. See the Gentoo Laws. [E.H.]
2  Answering to part of our February and March. [E.H.]

# LETTER II.

*The most faithful of Friends,* Kisheen Neêay Māāndāāra; *to the Powerful and enlightened Rajah,* Seeta Juin Zāārmilla.

PRAISE be to Veeshnû! The long wished-for letter from the friend of my youth, hath kindled the fire of conflicting passions in the breast of Māāndāāra. The assurance of thy continued kindness, lights the spark of joy; but the intelligence of the infatuation that hath seized thy mind, envelops my soul in the dark cloud of despair. I perceive that thou art under the influence of enchantment, and that that false stranger hath used some charm to deceive thy understanding. What would the spirit of thy father, what would the learned Pundit, to whose instructions we are equally indebted, what would they pronounce, could they hear that Zāārmilla thought it necessary to sojourn among infidels, and impious eaters of blood, in order to acquire knowledge? Can a race who sprung from the dust that was shaken from the feet of Brahma, and who are on that account beneath the meanest Sooder, who is honoured in being permitted to touch thy sandals, a race who though less savage than that of the Mussulmans with regard to those that bear the human form, exceed them in cruelty to all the other animated inhabitants of the earth. Can any of this race be capable of instructing the descendant of a thousand Rajahs? Impossible. From the ant thou mayest learn industry. From the dog thou mayest be instructed in faithfulness. The horse may teach thee diligence, and the elephant instruct thee in patience, magnanimity, and wisdom; but expect not from Europeans to attain the knowledge of any virtue. How should they be learned that are but of yesterday? Their remotest annals extend but to the trifling period of a few thousand years. While enlightened, and instructed in mystery, we can trace the history of revolving ages through the amazing period of the four Jogues.

I am not, however, surprised that you should be the dupe of their enchantments. I know how far the evil genii have assisted man in that art: of their proficiency in it I had myself a very convincing proof.

When the English Saib, to whom Rursha Bedwan was Mounshi,

abode at Agra,[1] he took pleasure in astonishing those who went to visit him, with a display of his magical skill. Among several other tricks, he made the whole company, consisting of more than twenty persons, lay hold of each other's hands, and form a circle, and then by turning the handle of a little instrument, composed only of metal and glass, but which, I suppose, must have contained the evil spirits obedient to his command; he, all at once, caused such a sensation to pass through the arms of the company, as if a sudden stroke had broken the bone, which was not, however, on examination, found to be in the least injured. As all felt it precisely at the same moment, it was impossible that he could have touched each of us, and therefore it is evident that it could be nothing but magic that could produce so extraordinary an effect. At another time he shut out the piercing light of day, which has always been unfavourable to such practices, and made us behold armies of men, and elephants, and horses, pass before us on the wall. When they disappeared, they were succeeded by a raging sea, vomiting fire, and foaming with all the appearance of a tremendous storm. Ships rolled upon the bosom of the deep; and men who appeared wild with distress, and panting in the agony of terror, were exerting themselves to save their lives, and preserve their ships from the pointed rocks which environed them. This sight of horror drew tears from our eyes; and we burst into exclamations of sorrow. When lo! in a moment, the sun being admitted into the apartment, the scene vanished, and we saw nothing but the hangings which formerly adorned the wall.[2]

Would the son of Coashhind forsake the land of his fathers, and wander to regions which the glorious luminary of heaven scarcely deigns to irradiate with his golden beams, to learn tricks like these? Surely there are jugglers enough in Hindostan who would for a small reward, instruct him in the mysteries of the magic art; and as the devils they employ are of our own country, they must be of a less pernicious nature than those of strangers.

---

1   A Mounshi (also "moonshee" and "munshi") was "a native secretary or language teacher in India" (*OED*).

2   Māāndāāra is describing early demonstrations of the principles of electricity and a magic lantern show, in which a picture on glass is reflected and magnified on a wall.

So far from being guided by wisdom, the laws by which the people are governed, are abominable and absurd: which I shall demonstrate to you, by the following facts, of which I was myself an eye witness during my short abode at their camp. Like you, I had suffered my mind to be prejudiced in favour of a people whose conduct had been so favourable to our nation. The order and regularity which prevailed among them, impressed me at first with the highest idea of their virtue and wisdom. I had as yet seen no appearance of any religious ceremony among them, when, on the third day after my arrival, my attention was attracted by a procession, which I immediately supposed to be in honour of their Dewtah. Curious to behold the nature of their ceremonies upon this occasion, I followed the procession, at which part of the camp assisted. When lo! to my equal surprise and horror, I beheld one poor soldier stripped, tied up, and almost lacerated to death; a thousand lashes being inflicted upon his naked shoulders. That one of their priests should have undergone all this in voluntary penance, would not have surprised me. We every day see instances of greater sufferings than this, inflicted by our Fakeers upon their own bodies. But I could not forbear astonishment, when informed, that this cruel ceremony was performed as a punishment upon a soldier, for the trifling crime of purloining a few rupees from one of his officers. Doubtless, thought I, the morals of the people must be very pure, in whose eyes so small an offence can seem worthy of so great a punishment.

While I yet ruminated upon the scene which I had witnessed, I was called to the tent of an officer, who had, ever since my arrival at the camp, treated me with great kindness. I had not long conversed with him (for he spoke very good Mhors)[1] when several of his brother officers came to visit him. They conversed in their own language, and appeared, from the frequent bursts of laughter which escaped them, to have entered upon a very pleasant topic. I was unwilling to lose the knowledge of a discourse, which seemed to produce so much mirth; and applied to my interpreter for information. He told me the subject of their merriment, was the *dishonour* of one of their own countrymen, a Chief of rank and eminence, whose

---

1   "A name for the Urdu or Hindustani language" (*OED*) – More usually "Moors."

wife had suffered the torch of her virtue to be extinguished, by the vile breath of a seducer. How great, cried I, must be the torture awaiting the wretch who could be guilty of so great a crime? If the poor pilferer of a few rupees was doomed to suffer so severely, what must the man undergo, who could basely contaminate the bed of his friend, rob him of his honour, and destroy his peace? If the weight of the punishment keeps pace with the gradation in atrocity, imagination can hardly paint to itself any thing so dreadful as the sufferings to which this wretch must be condemned. This observation, repeated by my Mounshi, redoubled the mirth of the company; and I heard, with astonishment, that the dishonour of one of these *illustrious Europeans* was to be compensated, not by the punishment of the aggressor, not by the sacrifice of his life, and the degradation of his family, but by a sum of money! Can virtue subsist among a people, who set a greater value upon a few pieces of silver, than upon their honour?

This circumstance did not fail to destroy, the impression I had received in favour of these people. But I should, perhaps, have remained some longer time among them, had I not beheld a deed so horrible, as filled my soul with indignation and disgust. Yes, my misguided friend, I saw these heroes, whom you falsely imagine so pure, so harmless, so full of piety and benevolence, I saw them – my heart shudders, and my hand trembles while I relate it, I saw them devour, with looks that betokened the most savage satisfaction, the sacred offspring of a spotted cow. Yes, Zāārmilla, this unhappy calf, for whom a thousand holy Fakeers would have risked their lives, was slain at the command of these inhuman Europeans, and devoured by them, without one pang of remorse.

Does not nature itself revolt at such an action? And, had any spark of religious knowledge enlightened their minds, would they not have perceived, that the calf they slew was, if not so learned, at least more pious and more uncontaminated by the corruption of impure ideas, than themselves. Tell me no more of the virtue of such men. And no more, I conjure thee, think of incurring the wrath of Mahadeo,[1] by

---

1    In the version of "The Hymn to Camdeo" published in *The Asiatic Miscellany*, Sir William Jones adds a note explaining that Mahadeo is a god who has "dominion over the minds of mortals or such deities as he is permitted to subdue" (19). See Appendix C for the version of the poem printed in Jones' *Collected Works*.

dishonouring thy Cast, and forfeiting its sublime privileges, at the instigation of a curiosity, which has doubtless been kindled in thy mind, by the powerful charms of magical incantations. These spells would probably have failed in their effect, hadst thou not incurred the displeasure of the Dewtah, by neglecting to perform the duty to which every Hindoo is bound; that indispensible duty of marriage. Four years have elapsed, since, in obedience to the command of my father, I married the daughter of the reverend Gopaul. She was ill-favoured, and of a bad temper: so that, being disgusted with her peevishness, and still more, with the plainness of her countenance, (for in a beautiful woman many errors may be forgiven) I parted with her some months since, and presenting her with her *ayammi shadee*, sent her back to the house of her father. I will, therefore, with great pleasure accept of your sister for my wife. With this intention, I some time ago enquired after her disposition, and heard that she was beautiful, and good tempered; which is the utmost perfection in women. To what purpose should they have judgment or under-standing? were they not made subservient to the will of man? If they are docile, and reserved, with enough of judgment to teach them to adorn their persons, and wear their jewels with propriety, and never presuming to have a will of their own, follow implicitly the direction of their husbands, studying his temper, and accommodating them-selves to his humour, it is all that can be wished for. As to all that you say of the cultivation of their understandings, I can only look upon it, as the ravings of a distempered imagination.

Bad as my opinion is of those English Christians, I cannot possibly imagine them to be so absurd as to teach learning to their women. Allowing it possible (which I am very far from allowing) that these creatures, whose sole delight, is finery, who were born to amuse, to please, and to continue the race of man, should be capable of entering the sacred porch which leads to the temple of knowledge, what would be the consequence of their being admitted to it? would their steps, be steady enough to conduct them through the labyrinths of that awful fane? No. Contenting themselves with the first tinsel ornament that caught their eyes, they would come out at the first opening of vanity; and having made a deposit of their gentleness and humility, would clothe themselves with the robes of arrogance, and rest dauntless upon the hollow reed of self-conceit. Such are the consequences that would result, from the foolish attempt, of teaching women more than nature designed them to know.

Let Zāārmilla, therefore, hearken to the voice of reason; and, at the same time that he gives his sister to be the wife of his friend, let him accept for his spouse the sister of Māāndāāra. Without being strictly beautiful, her countenance is pleasing: a mole of extreme beauty is seated on her cheek: and her eyes sparkle like gems of Golconda.[1] She has been taught humility and obedience, and has never conversed with any man, except her father and her brother. I know so well the tenderness and extreme lenity of thy disposition, that it is necessary to caution thee against extreme indulgence, and to put thee in mind of the words of the sacred Shastra,[2] which sayeth, "that a man both day and night must keep his wife so much in subjection, that she by no means be mistress of her own actions. If she have her own free will, notwithstanding her having sprung from a superior Cast, she will nevertheless act amiss."

If thou art inclined to dismiss the spirit of delusion and listen to the voice of thy friend, I will meet thee, not at Ferrockabad, but at Rampore; as, through the interest of certain friends, I have some hopes given me that Fyzoola Khan may look *upon me* with the eye of kindness, and probably restore me to the possession of my fathers. I have just received intelligence of the arrival of Sheermaal from England; whither he was induced to accompany the great man to whose services he had lent the assistance of his abilities; and from him I make no doubt of receiving such information respecting the country he has seen, as will satisfy thy mind, and restore thee to the right use of thy understanding.

What can I say more?

---

1  An area in southern India famed for its jewels.
2  See Halhed's Translation of the Gentoo Laws. [E.H.] 282.

# LETTER III.

*From the* SAME *to the* SAME.

THE powerful influence of the *Goitteríe*,[1] which I have employed some expert, and holy Fakeers to use, in order to dispossess thy mind from the influence of the magic of the Christians, will, I hope, be aided in their operation by the following account of the observations of Sheermaal, during his abode in England.

If, then, Zāārmilla has any value for the peace of Māāndāāra, he will instantly quit the wild and fantastic project of seeking for truth in the regions of darkness; and remaining in the land of his fathers, receive the gifts of happiness into the bosom of content.

Let thine ears now listen to the words of Sheermaal; and from his experience be thou contented to receive the fruits of wisdom.

---

1   A Gentoo incantation. [E.H.]

# LETTER IV.

*The Bramin* Sheermaal, *to* Kisheen Neêay Māāndāāra.

THE letter of the noble and illustrious Rajah, I have read with the more profound respect; and at thy request shall hasten to remove from his eyes the film of prejudice, and to convince him that the opinions he has conceived, concerning the Christians of England, are altogether false and erroneous. I do not wonder, that the enlightened mind of the noble Rajah, would have conceived a prediliction in favour of a people, who seem destined to make so conspicuous a figure in the annals of Asia. As a race of brave and daring mortals, chosen by Veeshnû to curb the fury of destructive tyranny, to blunt the sword of the destroyer, and break the galling fetters of the oppressed, I, and every Hindoo, must unite with him in pronouncing their eulogium: but as to the principles which actuate their conduct, their religion, their laws, and their manners, the mind of the noble Rajah has been immersed in error.

The learned Pundit, whose fame has extended from the walls of Lucknoo to the banks of Barampooter,[1] had sufficiently opened my understanding. It became evident, that whatever was in any degree excellent or admirable throughout the Bobor Logue,[2] was an emanation from the shadow of wisdom, a ray of light obliquely darting from the sacred volume which issued from the chambers of the deep.[3] To ascertain the certainty of this truth, I determined to visit the remotest corner of the habitable world, and in the bosom of experience I have found the expected conviction.[4]

Let not the noble Rajah be deceived. Let him not vainly imagine the Christians to be in possession of such an invaluable treasure as the

---

1   The Translator must acknowledge, that the fame of this learned Pundit has not reached so far as to acquaint her with his name. [E.H.]
2   Habitable world. [E.H.]
3   The Vedas, or Hindoo Scriptures, said in their allegorical mythology to have been recovered from the sea, by the God Veeshnû, in the form of a fish; who, after slaying the giant Hayagriva, tore from his belly the sacred volumes which he had profanely swallowed, returned with them in triumph, and presented them to Brahma. A print of Veeshnû performing this ceremony is given in the second volume of Maurice's Indian Antiquities. [E.H.]
4   The meaning of the Bramin is rather obscure; it is however, sufficiently obvious to establish his character as a *systematic traveller*. [E.H.]

Shaster he describes; a Shaster promulgating the glorious hopes of immortality; calculated to produce the universal reign of peace and justice, the exercise of the purest benevolence, and the most perfect virtue. Let not the Rajah think that the knowledge of such a book as this exists among Christians. If it did, is it possible, that in the ten years in which I have intimately conversed with Christians of all ranks and orders; military commanders, chiefs invested with the powers of civil authority, and men who made the study of literature their employment and delight, is it possible, I say, that I should never once have heard of such book? Let the noble Rajah be the judge.

That a book of ancient origin, vulgarly called *the bible*, was once known to the English, I have had certain information: but far from containing doctrines of such a nature as the Rajah has announced, the first proof of genius which a young man gives to the world, upon his issuing from the schools, is to speak of it, with a becoming degree of contempt. Indeed, to extirpate from society all regard for the pernicious doctrines it contains, has long been the primary object of attention to the enlightened philosophers of Europe. How much the book is detested by these sage philosophers, may easily be inferred, when I declare, that of the many philosophers I have met with, who had most vehemently spoken and written against it, not one had contaminated himself by deigning to examine its contents. One of these great men, a profound writer of history, has given to the world a work more voluminous than the Mahabbarat, more brilliant than the odes of Sancha, undertaken, and accomplished, as I was well assured, with the benevolent purpose of convincing his countrymen of the superiority of the Mahommedan to the Christian faith.[1] Whether these enlightened men will ever really succeed in their intention of establishing the religion of Mahomet in England, is, however, in my opinion, rather doubtful.

---

1　Probably a reference to Edward Gibbon, whose notoriously sceptical treatment of Christianity in his massive *Decline and Fall of the Roman Empire* (1776–88) is balanced by a treatment of Islam which is much less harsh than was usual in the eighteenth century. Even the liberal *Analytical Review* complained, in its review of the final volumes of *The Decline and Fall*, about the "illiberal reflections indiscriminately lavished.... On all who seem to be actuated by any religious principles, except the Mahometan" (Vol II [October 1788], 149). Hamilton knew *The Decline and Fall* well. In her *Letters on ... Education*, she approvingly quotes one of Gibbon's condemnations of luxury, and in *Agrippina* she vigorously attacks his treatment of religion.

However alluring the doctrine of polygamy, and the view of the Mahommedan Paradise may be to men of taste and sentiment, there are some obstacles which, I apprehend, would, in the opinion of the people, be insurmountable. The chief of these I take to be the prohibition of wine, the strict fast of Ramozin, and, above all, the injunctions[1] concerning the treatment of slaves, which are so mild and generous, that the Christians of England, who are concerned in the traffic of their fellow creatures (and who form a large and respectable part of the community) would never be brought to submit to its authority.

From the delusive opinion entertained in the sublime mind of the Rajah, of the religion of the Christians, he will, no doubt, be inclined to imagine, that their philanthropy embraces the wide circle of the human race. How far the rule of "doing to others, as they would be done by, in the like case," actuates the Christians of England, may be learned from the following history of my voyage.

As I attended the family of a great man, I had the advantage of being accommodated on board one of their ships of war, a huge edifice, whose sides were clothed with thunder. This mighty fabric contained near seven hundred people, governed by a few Chiefs, whose commands were obeyed with the quickness of the lightning's glance, and the frown of whose displeasure was followed by the severity of punishment. We had made two thirds of our voyage to the coast of Britain, when a ship appeared at a distance, which our skilful mariners soon perceived to be in distress. I had so often witnessed what I thought to be the exercise of cruelty during my abode in this seaborne fortress, that I did not expect the distresses of people, whom they had never seen, would excite much of their compassion. In this, however, I was mistaken. To my astonishment, every effort was instantly made to afford relief to these strangers; and I beheld the toil-strengthened nerves of these lions of the ocean, strained by the most vigorous exertions, to save the almost sinking vessel. At length, the object of their labours was effected and they, who had been so zealous

---

1   See Sale's Koran, and Hamilton's translation of the Hedeya. [E.H.] George Sale, *The Koran, commonly called the Alcoran of Mohammed, translated into English immediately from the original Arabic; with explanatory notes.... To which is prefixed a preliminary discourse* (London, 1734). A new edition of this translation, in two volumes, was published in 1795.

to save, now appeared perfectly indifferent to the expressions of gratitude and admiration which were poured out by the people, whom they had so gallantly delivered from the jaws of destruction. Our carpenter was employed to repair the breaches in the unfortunate vessel. And, as the weather was now calm, curiosity led the principal people of our company to visit the ship of the strangers. I was among the number. But Oh! that I could obliterate from my mind the memory of a scene, the horrors of which no pen can describe, no tongue can utter, no imagination conceive. It was an English vessel, which had been on a voyage to the coast of Africa, from whence it was now proceeding to the British settlements in the West Indies, with a cargo, not of silver and gold, not of costly spices and rich perfumes, but of some hundreds of the most wretched of the human race; a cargo of slaves. These miserable beings, were here huddled together in the squalid cells of a moving dungeon. Their uncouth screams, their dismal groans, their countenances, on which were alternately depicted the images of fury, terror, and despair, the clanking of their chains, and the savage looks of the white barbarians, who commanded them, exhibited such a scene, as mocks description.

Surely, the magnanimous Rajah will not imagine, that the perpetrators of this cruelty could be the professors of a religion of mercy. No. Had a ray of knowledge enlightened their understandings, through the tawny hue of the unlettered savage, they would have recognised the emanation of the creating Spirit; they would have perceived the kindred mind, which, in its progressive course through the stages of varied being, might one day inhabit the bodies of their own offspring. For my part, when I contemplated the scene before me, I anticipated, in imagination, the few swiftly rolling years, which might change the abode of the souls of these tyrant whites into the frames of woe-destined negroes; while the present victims of their cruelty, would in their turns, become the masters, and, seizing the scorpion whip of oppression, retaliate their present sufferings with all the bitterness of revenge. But, alas! the divine doctrine of retribution is unknown to these Christians. No dread of after punishment restrains the remorseless hand of cruelty. No apprehension of the vengeance of an offended Deity, diverts them from the greedy pursuits of avarice, or deters the enjoyments of luxury. For let it not stagger your faith in my veracity, when I inform you, that all this aggregate of human misery is incurred, in order to procure a luxurious repast to the pampered appetites of these voluptuaries, and that the unhappy negroes are torn from their country, their friends and families, for no other purpose, but to cultivate the sugar-cane; a work of which the lazy Europeans are themselves incapable.

When I mention the slaves of Christians let not your imagination turn to the bondsmen of Asia, as if their situations were parallel. No. By the mild laws of our Shaster, and even by the less benevolent institutions of Mahommed, slaves are considered as people who, having bartered their liberty for protection, are entitled to the strictest justice, lenity, and indulgence. They are always treated with kindness, and are most frequently the friends and confidants of their masters. But with these white savages, these merciless Christians, they are doomed to suffer all that cruelty, instigated by avarice, and intoxicated by power, can inflict. Ah! beloved Hindostan! happy country! paradise of regions! the plant which in the trans-Atlantic islands is fattened with the blood of the wretched, with thee raises its blooming head, a voluntary offering to thy pure and innocent children. That luscious cane, which the inhabitants of Europe purchase by the enormous mass of misery, is on the banks of the Ganga, the exclusive property of the laughing Deity, the heart-piercing Cama; with it the son of Maya forms the bow, from which his flowery shafts are thrown at the sons of men: with it the blameless hermit approaches the altars of the rural Gods; and from it the simple repasts of the favoured of Veeshnû receive their highest relish.

But my observations on the religion of the people of England, stop not here. To obtain complete information upon this subject, was the object I kept perpetually in my view. And I hope it is known to the Rajah, that a Bramin of my character is not easily to be deceived. The custom of dedicating the seventh day to acts of piety and devotion, is mentioned by the Rajah as an institution, admirably calculated for keeping up the spirit of a religion, which was intended for the purification of the heart, and of which the duties of penitence and self-examination formed constituent parts. Alas! how grossly has his simplicity been imposed upon. It is indeed observed as a holiday by the lower Casts, and spent by some of the industrious orders of mechanics in the innocent amusement of walking in the fields, accompanied by their wives and children. By those of less sober manners, it is employed in the indulgence of gluttony, and the most depraved intemperance. By the higher Casts, it is altogether unobserved, except as a day particularly propitious to the purpose of travelling. A select number, from all the different Casts, occasionally amuse themselves by attending, for an hour or two, on the mornings of that day, at certain large buildings, called Churches; a practice which they doubtless continue in conformity to some ancient custom, the origin of which is now forgotten, though the practice continues to be partially observed. Curiosity once led me into one of these churches, where a young man dressed in white began the performance of the ceremony. Had it not been for the carelessness of his manner, I should have been tempted to believe that he was engaged in offering prayers to the Deity; and so far as the extreme rapidity of his utterance would permit me to judge, some things he said so plainly alluded to a future state of existence, that one, less truly informed than I was, might have been led into a belief that some such notions had actually been entertained among them. The ceremonies of this day were concluded by an elderly priest, in a black robe, who read, in a languid and monotonous tone, from a small book, which he held in his hand, a sort of exhortation; the truths contained in which, seemed equally indifferent to himself and to his audience. Nor did the little attention that was paid to his discourse seem to give him any offence, or to impel him to speak in a more energetic manner; though it probably hastened his conclusion; at which he had no sooner arrived, than the countenances of his auditors brightened, and they congratulated one another on their being emancipated from the fatigue of this tiresome ceremony.

Had I never penetrated farther into the character of these Christians, I should have considered them as beings altogether incapable of a serious and profound attention to the performance of any religious duty; but a deeper investigation convinced me of the contrary, and that in the performance of such ceremonies as they deemed *of real importance*, these trifling people could evince a degree of assiduity and perseverance, that would have done honour to a Sanée assee.[1]

---

1   A religious recluse. We are now in possession of so many accurate engravings and minute descriptions of the extraordinary sculpture which decorates the temples of the Hindoos, that there are few readers to whom detail of them would not be superfluous. [E.H.]

The rites to which I allude, may, in my opinion, easily be traced to the sacred institutions of the beloved of Brahma; the nation which is the pure fountain of all human wisdom.

To the intelligent mind of the noble Rajah, it is well known how our great ancestors, incomparable in wisdom, ordained such mystical representations of the superior intelligences; as it is not lawful for any but the most holy and learned of the Bramins to explore. The most pious of the sacred Cast, after purifying themselves from worldly thoughts by years of abstinence, spent in the silence of solemn groves are, by much application, and unwearied study, enabled to perceive the true meaning of those representations hewn in the stupendous rock, or carved in the lofty walls of ancient edifices, which, to the eyes of the vulgar, appear uncouth images of stone. And it is doubtless from this wise example of our ancient Bramins, that the priests of all religions have learned the art of concealing the simplicity of truth, under the dark and impenetrable cloud symbolical mystery, which none but they themselves can fully explain. The knowledge of the vulgar is the death of zeal. But deep is the reverence of ignorance.

It was not then, from the people engaged in the rites I mention, that I could expect information concerning them: but I had a better instructor in the depth of my own sagacity, which soon taught me, that the object of their most serious devotion was strictly analogous to the symbols of our Dewtah, not indeed cut in the solid rock of gloomy caverns; not hewn on the walls of sacred temples; but, correspondent to the trifling genius of these silly people, painted upon small slips of stiff paper. Neither is the manner in which these devotions are performed exactly similar to ours. It is not necessary that those devotees should perform the seven ablutions; neither do they rub their bodies with earth; neither do they cover their heads with cow-dung: and, instead of solemn prostration before these painted objects of their idolatry, they take them familiarly into their hands, and toss them one after another upon a table covered with green cloth; turn them up and down, sometimes gazing upon them with momentary admiration, as they lie prostrate on the middle of the table; then again, seizing them with holy ardour, they turn them hastily upon their faces. And to this Poojah of idols, termed CARDS, do the major part of the people devote their time; sacrificing every enjoyment of life, as well as every domestic duty to the performance of this singular devotion.

It is said, that it is incumbent *only* on a "professed hermit *utterly* to renounce his passions, and worldly pursuits: but that it is sufficient for a domestic character to refrain from their abuse."[1] The zeal for the Poojah of cards inspires a more exalted degree of self-denial: I have known it lead its ardent votaries to exclude the soul-enlivening rays of the golden sun, in the finest evenings of their short-lived summer; and while the nightingale warbled its tale of love to the listening rose, and all the beauties of nature glowed around them, I have beheld them turn from the temptation with heroic firmness, and placing themselves at the altars of their idols, remain immoveably fixed in that devotion, which absorbed the powers of their soul.

Little as I am inclined to coincide with the opinion of the Rajah, relative to the superiority of the females of Europe in any other particular, I must confess, that in their unwearied assiduity to the Poojah of cards, they evince a degree of constancy scarcely exceeded by a pious Yogee[2] in the act of penance.

The languor, so visible in the countenances of the people assembled in the church was never to be observed during the performance of this more important ceremony. Here, even the very Priest lost the apathy which had *there* so strongly marked his countenance. The attention of his fellow worshippers was no longer a matter of indifference to him. His zeal was kindled into fervor, and broke forth into the severity of reproach against a female who sat opposite to him, for exhibiting some transient mark of negligence in the performance of the duty in which she was now engaged.

Universally as the Poojah of cards is established throughout the country, it has not, in the remotest provinces, been able entirely to supercede another species of idolatry, which has clearly, and indisputably, been borrowed from the manners of their eastern

---

1  Untraced.

2  An order of religious Recluses, remarkable for the rigorous performance of the penitential duties, esteemed by the Hindoos so essentially necessary toward the advancement of their happiness in a future state. The voluntary penances undertaken by these pious Yogees, are frequently so severe as to excite an equal degree of astonishment and horror. [E.H.]

progenitors. This is no other than the worship of certain birds, and quadrupeds, which are held so sacred by their worshippers, that the preservation of their lives occupies, I am well assured, many volumes of their laws, and has employed the chief study of their sapient Legislators. I should have wished to obtain much information upon a subject so curious; but all that I could learn, was, that the provincial Rajahs, devoted to the worship of these animals, are mostly sprung from the first Cast. (A certain proof of their Braminical origin.) They despise the vain pursuit of literature; and conscious of their native and inherent superiority, they pique themselves upon their ignorance of the sciences that are in esteem among the lower orders of men.[1]

From such exalted personages much information was not to be looked for: but a circumstance which occurred while I journeyed over the remote parts of the kingdom, threw sufficient light upon the subject.

In one particular, however, the higher Casts in that country must be acknowledged to differ widely from the race of Brahma. – They are deficient in hospitality! Never did I see the doors of a great man open to receive the wearied traveller: the milk of his cows flows not into the stranger's dish. Nay, so very rude and inhospitable are the manners of the people of high Cast, that once upon a time, when, being overtaken by darkness in a rainy evening, I attempted to procure lodgings for myself and my attendant, at the house of one of these provincial Rajahs, which was situated near the road, I was not only denied admittance, but repulsed with the language of contempt, and necessitated to continue my route, in a dark and stormy evening, till the sight of a peasant's hut cheered my heart with the hope of shelter. I was not disappointed; for in this country the spirit of hospitality is only to be found beneath a roof of thatch. The decent matron, who inhabited this lowly hut, received me with looks of cordial welcome. Five blooming children surrounded the blazing fire, whose cheerful light was reflected from the bright utensils that

---

1    The bluff, ill-educated country squire was a popular target in eighteenth-century British satire; Fielding's Squire Western is perhaps the most familiar example of the type. Hamilton is also attacking the game laws, which reserved the rights of hunting and shooting game birds and animals for landowners. Penalties for violating these laws could be severe.

adorned the white washed walls. My first appearance dismayed the little train, but some candied sweetmeats, with which I presented them, quickly reconciled them to my complexion. The genii, who delight to revel in the troubled air, howled around this humble dwelling, and pouring the dashing torrent from the black-bosomed clouds of night, they heard with joy the thunder's roar, while nimbly following the lightning's path, they exulted in the mingled tempest. The pale hue of terror sat upon the matron's cheek: she listened, with anxiety, and impatience, for the voices of her husband and her son, who were not yet returned from the labours of the day: and while her own fears increased with the horrors of the tempest, she employed herself in appeasing those of the infant group, who clung to her, demanding, with accents of clamourous sorrow, the return of their father and their brother.

When the storm a little abated of its violence, the little creatures ran by turns to the door, eagerly peeping into the dark abyss of night, in hopes of discovering their approach. The anxious mother added fuel to the already blazing fire; again she swept the unsoiled hearth; and again adjusted the chairs, which had long been placed for the reception of the supporters of her hope. At length the well known steps were heard; every heart fluttered with joy, and every little hand was stretched out, eager to receive the paternal and fraternal embrace. The old man and his son were for some time occupied in returning the caresses of their family; which they did with the tenderness of affection: and then the venerable master of this humble abode came forward, to welcome me to a share of the comforts it afforded. He had looked at me earnestly for some time, when, to my utter astonishment, he addressed me in my native language. The Mhors he spoke was but indifferent, but it was intelligible, and more charming to my ears than the music of the seven genii.

In order to account for what appeared to me such an extraordinary phenomenon, he told me that, in early life, he had been tempted, by the God of Love, to win the affections of a damsel, whose beauty had touched the heart of the village Lord. The place of wife, in the establishment of this great man, was already occupied by the daughter of a neighbouring Rajah; but he had probably been convinced by the philosophers, of the propriety of the system of

Mahommet; and thought that the damsel, though the daughter of a mechanic, would be no unworthy ornament of his zenana.[1] It is not to be wondered at that he should be filled with indignation at the presumption of the young peasant, who dared to interfere with his pleasures, and disappoint his schemes, by marrying the object of his hopes. It is not proper that inferiors should be permitted to defeat the intentions of their Lords with impunity. This great man was of the same opinion; and, in the height of his resentment against his successful rival, he had him torn from the arms of his bride, and sent in a company of soldiers, who were all collected in the same arbitrary manner (probably as a punishment for the same sort of offence) to the East Indies. Here this unfortunate martyr to love spent eleven years in the service of the Company, in the rank of a petty officer: when having, by his economy, saved a sum sufficient for the purposes of humble competence, he obtained leave to return to his native country. As the gay pennant though forced to obey the pressure of the changeful breeze, still clings to its beloved mast, and, at the return of every short-lived calm, flutters round the object to which it was in youth united; so the heart of this honest peasant, in all the storms of fortune hovered round the cottage that contained his wife and child. At length, her obscure retirement was gladdened by his presence. By the employment of her needle, she had procured during his absence, an honourable and virtuous subsistence for herself and son. The little fortune he had brought from India was lost by the villainy of the agent into whose hands he had entrusted it. But in the endearments of mutual affection, this honest couple had a fund of felicity, which the malice of fortune could not destroy. Both the good man and his son found employment for their industry in cutting down the trees of a neighbouring wood: a work which had been committed to their care, and amply recompenced their diligence. When they returned from their labour, the cheerful appearance of the well-ordered family at home, the smiling welcome of the little innocents, and the affectionate tenderness of the worthy matron, presented to them a reward which went farther than the gifts of fortune have power to penetrate: – it reached the heart.

---

1   The women's quarters in East Indian households.

The recital of these circumstances was made to me during the most cheerful repast that I ever saw Christians partake of. When it was ended, a ceremony ensued, which having never seen practised at any other period, I have reason to think *peculiar to themselves*. Upon a hint from the old soldier, his eldest daughter presented him with a very large book, from which, with a clear and solemn voice, he read some admirable instructions and exhortations. The sublime and command-ing energy with which these precepts were expressed, might lead to a conclusion, that this was a copy of the same Shaster with which the departed Saib Percy presented the learned Rajah: but many obstacles oppose themselves to this supposition. Could we believe that a book of such distinguished authority, unheard of among the learned, and totally unknown among the superior Casts, should yet be found familiar in the cottage of a peasant? It is too absurd for the shadow of probability to rest upon.

But to return to the religious rites of these simple people; which, as I have observed, differ essentially from all that had hitherto come within my observation: for instead of the Poojah of cards, which at that hour would have been performed in the families of the higher Casts, when the old man had shut the book, he knelt down, his wife and blooming infants following his example. The latter clasped their little hands, and held them up to heaven, while he lifted up his voice, calling upon the unseen, omniscient, and immortal Preserver, to bless them, and to accept from hearts of gratitude the offering of praise and thankfulness. I cannot account for it, but there was something in his whole ceremony which greatly affected my mind; and I could not help, while I listened to the simple, but fervent devotion of this virtu-ous labourer, feeling for him a degree of veneration, even superior to what I had experienced for the Priest, whose zeal had been so con-spicuous at the Poojah of cards.

In the morning, the same rites were again repeated; after which, I took leave of this innocent and happy family; the old man insisting that, as I had come some miles out of my way, his son should accom-pany me to the village where I had directed my servant and horse to meet me. The lad willingly obeyed the commands of his father, and we set out together. He was a handsome youth, of about twenty years of age, and of a sensible and intelligent countenance. Taking a path through a corn field, it being now the latter end of harvest, we met a young peasant, who carried a gun, which he frequently fired, to frighten the crows and other birds from the grain. My companion took the weapon of destruction into his hand to examine it: and in that unhappy moment, in which the Goddess of Mischance presided, a group of partridges appeared before him: he involuntarily struck the flint; the report resounded through the air, and oh! unfortunate destiny, seven of these sacred birds were laid rolling in the dust. He had no time to consider of the fatal deed; for, in a moment, two men, whom the bushes had concealed from our view, darted on the guilty youth, wrested the weapon of destruction from his trembling hand, and, with many imprecations of vengeance, insisted upon his immediately attending them before the awful tribunal of assembled Magistrates, who were now exercising the sacred functions of their office in the neighbouring village. It was then I learned the real magnitude of my friend's offence. For I was then informed, that to preserve these sacred birds from being injured by the unhallowed hands of any of the lower Cast, the severest laws were promulgated: and as the Zimeendars in the office of the magistracy, before whom these offences were tried, were all of them worshippers of the rural Dewtah, they never suffered the stern sentence of justice to be softened at the suggestion of mercy.

As it is not good to forsake a friend in his adversity, we entered the temple of justice together. In this awful tribunal, seated in two large chairs, we found the offended Magistrates. The first of these judges seemed fully conscious of his dignity; which was indeed very great; uniting in himself the triple offices of Priest, Zimeendar, and Magistrate of the place. The other was a Pundit, learned in the law; called, in the language of these people, an attorney. No sooner did the witness of my friend's guilty deed, present the unhappy culprit before them, producing at the same time the murdered birds, and the destructive engine of their dissolution, than the murmur of indignation arose; the cause in which they were then hearing evidence was instantly dismissed: it was, indeed, only concerning a man who was said to have beaten his wife almost to death: a trifling crime, in the eyes of these Magistrates, when compared to the murder of seven partridges!

The son of the soldier attempted to speak in his own defence, but was prevented by the first judge, who declared that the proof was sufficient for his condemnation, and that he never would hear any thing in favour of a POACHER: (a name given by this sect to the enemies of their idolatry.) From the tone of wrath with which he pronounced these words, I saw that the young man's fate was determined; and when, after some consultation between themselves, the younger judge arose to pronounce his sentence, I expected, with sorrow, to have heard the irrevocable mandate of immediate death; and knowing how vindictive the priests of all religions usually are toward those who have treated with contempt the objects of their superstitious veneration, I should have been well pleased to have compounded for his simple death, unattended by the tortures which I feared might be inflicted on him; for a crime which, I plainly saw, was thought of by his judges with horror. Judge then with what a mixture of astonishment and delight, I heard the mild and merciful sentence uttered by the Pundit, which pronounced no other sentence of punishment, but that of paying a sum of money!

How universal is the sin of ingratitude? When I expected to behold this young man embracing the feet of his merciful judges with grateful rapture, I heard him, with astonishment, venture to expostulate with his benefactors upon his utter inability to pay so great a fine. He mentioned the situation of his parents; said they depended upon his labour for support; and that, should his judges persevere in inflicting the payment of so large a sum upon him, it must deprive them of his assistance; or, by robbing them of the little savings of their industry, reduce their young ones to penury, and cause them to eat the bread of bitterness in their old age. "Let pity for my aged parents induce you to soften the rigour of my sentence," cried the ungrateful youth, "and, though a thousand partridges were to start up before me, I swear I shall never injure one feather of their wings." Alas! his eloquence was lost. The judges remained inexorable till at length, being touched with the sorrow of the young man, I resolved to address them in the best English I was master of. "Mild, upright, and merciful judges," cried I, "believe not that I speak to excuse the crime of which this young man has been guilty. No. I have ever been taught to pay respect to the Dewtahs of whatever country I was in. With the Persic Magi I have bent in solemn adoration of the solar orb; while, with other equally enlightened nations of the earth, I have demonstrated my respect for the crocodile, the jackal, and the monkey. Since fate has brought me into this renowned kingdom, I have, in the great capital, attended, with due solemnity, the Poojah of cards: and now, that I am made acquainted with the religion of the Rajahs of the provinces, I judge of your feelings, most venerable Magistrates, upon the present occasion, by what my own would have been, had any base-born Sooder dared to lift his impious hands against one of the sacred cows who range the flowery meads of Burrampooter. But since, in the overflowing of your clemency, you have condescended to limit the deserved punishment of this audacious youth to the payment of a fine, I hope you will extend the shadow of your goodness so far, as to accept the money from a stranger." They stared at one another, astonished, no doubt, at the boldness of my speech; but, nevertheless, were so kind as graciously to accept of the gold I offered them, and to suffer my companion to depart with me in peace.

After giving him some good advice against meddling, in future, with the Dewtah of the country, and presenting him with some pieces of gold for his family, I dismissed him, and proceeded on my journey.

In the course of this tour, I had the courage to penetrate into the northern regions of this united kingdom of Britain, where mountains, more stupendous than those of Upper Tartary, heave their bare brown backs to the merciless arrows of the keen-edged wind: where the bright-faced luminary of heaven is wrapt in the eternal veil of clouds and storms; but where, in the uncultivated bosom of heath-covered desarts, resides a people, whose origin is more ancient than the rocks, whose gloomy summits overhang their dwellings.

It was with a view of gaining some information in regard to the chronology of this ancient nation, that I was induced to visit it. I had heard that the original Casts into which these, as well as other nations, had been divided at their creation, were here preserved in their original purity and perfection. For this is another particular, in which the Rajah of Almorah has been grossly deceived, or misinformed. Instead of being all of *one* Cast, as he imagines, the people are divided into *three* Casts, all separate, and distinct from each other; and which are commonly known by the several appellations of PEOPLE OF FAMILY, PEOPLE OF NO FAMILY, and PEOPLE OF STYLE, or fashion. The first two are of much more ancient origin than the other

Cast; which, indeed, appears to have sprung from an unnatural mixture of the others; like the tribes of Buhran Sunker,[1] in Hindostan. But what is extraordinary, and entirely peculiar to the Cast of *people of style*, is, that admission may be obtained by those who were not born to it, nay, who have sprung from the lowest of the tribe, called PEOPLE OF NO FAMILY; and these people, thus admitted, I have ever observed to be most tenacious of the rights and privileges of their new Cast, treating those who still remain in that, which they have left, with the utmost contempt, breaking off all connection with them, and frequently denying (particularly in the presence of other *people of fashion*) that they ever had any acquaintance with them: an asseveration always made with peculiar warmth, when these newly made *people of fashion* are known to be under any particular obligations to the PEOPLE OF NO FAMILY. The mode of initiation into this Cast, I suppose to be made by the ceremonies of ablution: and certain streams, and springs, of mysterious efficacy, are to be found in various parts of the kingdom; where I have reason to think the ceremonies of initiation are usually performed. A resort to these springs, called watering-places, at certain seasons of the year, being prescribed to *people of style*, and all the candidates for that Cast, as an indispensible duty.

Among these candidates, the most certain method of procuring success, is an assiduous devotion to the Poojah of cards: liberal offerings of gold, at these altars of the little painted idols, having frequently procured the honours of initiation to the most low-born, low-bred, and illiterate personages in the community. The flood of wealth, which the golden stream of commerce has diffused over the kingdom of England, has greatly contributed to the exaltation of this upstart tribe: but in the northern kingdom, which is now blended with it (as Bahar is now with Orissa)[2] the barrier between *people of*

---

1   See Gentoo Laws, page 43. [E.H.]: "from the Conjunction of Two different Casts proceeds the Tribe of Burrun Sunker; and that there should be a Burrun Sunker is criminal; it is better therefore to desist from these impious practices."

2   According to Scottish supporters of the Union of the Scottish and English Parliaments (in 1707), and to disgruntled English, Scotland had thrived since the Union, benefitting greatly from English trade and imperial ventures, even while maintaining its distinctive culture. Hamilton is, throughout this section, mocking one stereotypical aspect of that culture: the supposedly excessive Scottish pride in lineage.

*family* and *people of no family*, has been too strong for the tide of wealth to break, too powerful for the teeth of time to destroy. I was extremely anxious to gain an insight into the chronological annals of this most ancient nation, but could obtain none that was anywise satisfactory. By a strange custom, the cultivation of letters is confined to the *people of no family*; who are at no pains to trace the origin of the first Cast, beyond that of their own; but by my own observation, confirmed by the hints I received from all the *people of family* with whom I conversed, it is evident that a period of many thousand years must have elapsed between the creation of the two Casts. Indeed, to believe that the venerable and exalted cast of *people of family* should have sprung from one common parent with the *people of no family*, is equally absurd as to suppose, that in the revolution of the few years that are doomed to terminate a transient and uncertain existence, they should moulder into the same sort of dust! Base slander on the inherent superiority of birth! The minds of the *people of family* are filled with too just an idea of their own dignity to admit so injurious a supposition. Conscious of the blessing of superior origin, the ancient Rajahs, and all who can boast a portion of their blood, never fail to express a proper degree of contempt for the people of inferior Cast: nor can the possession of talents, the attainments of science, or the exercise of the sublimest virtue, serve, in any degree, in their eyes, to lessen the invincible barrier that divides them.

Together with the cultivation of letters the exercise of the Priestly function is usually confined to the second Cast. These men are more distinguished for the regularity of their lives, and sanctity of their deportment, than for their dexterity at the Poojah of cards, which in the southern part of this kingdom is so essential a requisite in the duty of a priest. The ceremonies of their religion are somewhat similar to those of the cottager; they are no strangers to the duties of hospitality, and recommend the enlightening study of literature both by their precept and example. In all other respects, the characteristic virtues, and peculiar customs of this nation, are so evidently of Hindoo origin, that nothing, but the most wilful blindness, could make any one assert the contrary.

As the illustrious Rajahs of Hindostan, when sitting in the midst of their wide-extended possessions, forget not to bend before the

Bramin, who, to procure nourishment for his family, laboureth in his garden, in like manner the people of whom I speak, retain the dignity of their Cast, even when compelled by poverty to exercise any trade in order to procure a livelihood: and, as in India, members of the tribe of Brahma are frequently found exercising the employments of commerce and agriculture, so, in this ancient nation, do *people of family* often condescend to become weavers, shoemakers, and barbers, without forfeiting Cast, or in the least abating of the high idea of their own inherent superiority. It is not so with the people of style, who, by entering into any of these employments, lose all the privileges of their Cast; a circumstance, which occasions numbers of the poorer branches of that tribe to live in a humiliating state of dependence upon the richer, rather submitting to any indignity, than run the risk of *losing Cast*, by submitting to work for their own subsistence.

The mode of living among these people, in which animal food is scarcely known, is another argument in favour of their Hindoo origin. Much might likewise be said of the similarity of sound between Laird and Rajah;[1] a similarity which, in the opinion of learned antiquarians, is more than sufficient to establish an etymology. Nor is this all; like us, they consider themselves a *distinct* and *favoured people*, superior to the rest of the inhabitants of the earth, and do not fail to maintain, that whatever instances of courage, magnanimity, or heroic virtue, are displayed by any inhabitant of the other nations of the world, would, in similar circumstances, have been far exceeded by one of their own countrymen.

These highly favoured people, being too tenacious of their dignity to admit strangers (with whose pedigree they are unacquainted) into the honour of their society; the person, to whom I was chiefly indebted to for information, was the lady, at whose house I lodged. She was of the *people of family* Cast; sprung from an illustrious race; her fifteenth grandfather had been a mountain Rajah; and, in the ramifications of his blood, she could boast a degree of affinity to one-

---

1  The joke here is directed mainly at philological investigations into a common Indo-European language by Sir William Jones and others, although there may also be a more specific mockery of eighteenth century fascination with the origins of the Scottish Celts and their language, which some scholars attempted to link to Hebrew (see Howard Weinbrot, *Britannia's Issue* [Cambridge, 1993], 10, 477ff).

and-twenty Lairds! She was forced, by the dictates of necessity, to make up articles of female attire for her maintenance; but never worked, as she herself assured me, for any but *people of her own Cast*; and I was induced to believe her, from the marked contempt with which I observed her to treat all who had the misfortune to be born *people of no family*. This was particularly felt by a young woman of beautiful person, gentle manners, and good education, whom this high-born female, being equally ignorant of orthography, and arithmetic, was under the necessity of employing as an assistant in her business: and whose conversation, had it not been for the difference of the Casts from which they sprung, I should have greatly preferred to that of her mistress; but the cousin of one-and-twenty mountain Rajahs had too just a claim to my veneration, to be put in competition with the paltry advantages of youth, beauty, talents, and understanding!

It was in this house I observed, with pleasure, the practice of that admirable degree of abstemiousness, the reverse of which had, in the southern part of the island, so frequently excited the feelings of horror, and disgust. The servants of this illustrious Bibby did not sit down together to excite one another to acts of gluttony and intemperance: but after long, and rigorous abstinence, they snatched the scanty morsel of simple viands which their prudent mistress had allotted for them; nor, even at her own table, did I ever see a meal displayed, of which the most holy Fakeer might not have partaken without breaking his vows of self-denial!

Thus hath thy servant clearly refuted, two of the propositions of the misguided Rajah: and proved, in the most satisfactory manner, and from the most undoubted authority, that if such a Shaster as he speaks of, *ever did exist*, it is now become altogether *obsolete*, and entirely unknown; that the only devotion known to the majority of the community, is the Poojah of cards, and partridges; and that the people of Great Britain are, at this day, divided into separate Casts, as distinct from each other as the Bramin from the Kettrie.

There are other errors, into which the noble Rajah has suffered his mind to be led, which I could with equal ease refute, did I not know how easily the mind of a great man is disgusted by prolixity.

What can I say more!

# LETTER V.

*From the* Bramin *to* Māāndāāra.

LET the commands of Māāndāāra be obeyed. In the plenitude of my desire to open the eyes of your misguided friend, I hasten to proceed to a more particular description of the education and manners of the females of England; which the illustrious Rajah has so erroneously conceived to be in some measure influenced by the doctrines of that obsolete Shaster, which seems to exalt the dignity of the female mind, to an equality with that of the lords of the creation.

I shall begin with an account of the usual mode of conducting the education of females in England. How far that is of a nature calculated for "lighting the torch of reason and expanding the germ of intellect," let the wisdom of the Rajah decide!

During the period of infancy these Christian females (whose souls are, in the erring mind of Zāārmilla, deemed so precious) are permitted to receive their first ideas from mercenary attendants, always ignorant, and frequently vicious. When the rising plant puts forth the tendrils of curiosity, which may at pleasure be directed to the tree of knowledge, or suffered to twine round the hollow bamboo of prejudice, and folly: at that period, lest from the conversation of fathers or brothers, these young females might, peradventure, acquire some degree of information, they are removed from the possibility of such deplorable consequences, and placed where science, reason, and common sense, dare not to intrude. In these Seminaries, far from being treated as "beings, whose intellectual faculties are capable of progressive improvement through the ages of eternity," their time is solely employed in learning a few tricks, such as a monkey might very soon acquire, and these are called accomplishments!

Judge how ridiculous it would be to make creatures, believed to be accountable to their Creator, for the employment of their talents, and the improvement of their virtues, spend the most precious years of life, in running their fingers over certain bits of wood, which are so contrived as to make a jingling sort of noise, pleasant enough when one is a little accustomed to it, but which, in the manner executed by them, very seldom equals what is every day to be heard from the itinerant musicians that practice in the streets!

Another ingenious contrivance for filling up that portion of time, which the friend of Māāndāāra supposes to be employed in the acquisition of useful knowledge, is, by the assistance of a master (whose attendance is paid for at vast expence) making wretched imitations of trees and flowers, and this is called *learning to paint*! It appears as if great care was taken, to avoid the possibility of the female pupils ever arriving at any degree of perfection in the art, as I am well-informed, that not one in five hundred is ever capable of copying from nature, or of doing any thing, when left to herself, that is not many degrees inferior to the little pictures which may be purchased for the value of a rupee.

Another indispensible part in the education of females of every Cast, of every rank, and in every situation, is the knowledge of the language spoken in their neighbouring nation. I was for some time at a great loss to know what reason could be assigned for so strange a custom, and after many conjectures, I rested in the belief, that as the French nation was frequently at war with the English, it might either be customary to send the women as Hircarrahs, into the camp of the enemy, or, in case of defeat, to employ them in procuring terms of peace, which from the remarkable complaisance of their adversaries to the female sex, it might be supposed, would be negociated by the Bibbys with peculiar advantage to their country. I was, however, forced to give up this conclusion, on being assured, that after years spent in the study of the language, as it is taught at these excellent Seminaries, few are capable of reading, and still fewer of conversing, with any degree of fluency in this tongue: and that the only real advantage resulting from it was, that by what they knew of it, they were enabled to understand the peculiar terms belonging to the articles of dress imported from that country, which had an acknowledged right of imposing its fashions on the other nations of Europe.

Dress is, indeed, *one* science in which full scope is given to the faculties of these females: and the love of it, is at the great Schools of the Christians, so successfully inculcated, that it remains indelible to the latest period of life. Nor is the mode of education I speak of confined solely to the children of higher Casts, it extends to all, even to the daughters of the tradesmen, and mechanics, who are employed, during the years of improvement, exactly in the manner I have described. All of the difference is, that at the inferior Schools, where inferior masters are employed, the girls do not, perhaps, arrive at the art of running their fingers over the bits of wood, called Keys of a Harpsichord, with an equal degree of velocity; they make rather more execrable copies, of more wretched pictures, and the knowledge they acquire of the French language does not, perhaps, enable them to run over the names of the new fashions, with an equal degree of volubility; but as to making any attempt at instructing the daughters of Christians, in any thing useful to themselves, or society, the idea would be deemed equally ridiculous in Seminaries of every class.

So far all is right. We behold women moving in their proper sphere, learning no other art, save that of adorning their persons; and inspired with no other view, but that of rendering themselves objects of pleasure to the eyes of men. But how shall I astonish you, when I unfold the extreme inconsistency of the foolish Europeans, and inform you, that these uninstructed women are frequently suffered to become intirely their own mistresses; sometimes entrusted with the management of large estates, and left at liberty to act for themselves! Nay, that it is no uncommon thing for a man, who may, in other respects, by no means be considered as a fool, to leave his children to the care of his widow, by which means I have frequently seen a little family cast upon the care, and depending for protection, on a poor, pretty, helpless being, incapable of any idea, save that of dress, or of any duty, except the Poojah of cards! How much wiser is the institution of Brahma, by which creatures, incapable of acting with propriety for themselves, are effectually put out of the way of mischief, by being burned with the bodies of their husbands. – Wise regulations! Laudable practice! by which the number of *old women* is so effectually diminished!

From what I have formerly said, you will observe, that women do actually sometimes carry on certain branches of trade; but to infer from this, that they are generally esteemed capable of business, or receive such an education as to enable them, if left destitute of the gifts of fortune, to enter into it, would be doing them great injustice. No, in that country, as well as in this, all men allow that there is nothing so amiable in a woman as the *helplessness* of *mental imbecility*; and even the women themselves are so well convinced of this, that they would consider it as an insult to be treated like rational creatures. The love of independence is, therefore, a masculine virtue, and though some few females are *unamiable* enough to dare to enter upon some employment for their support, this conduct is very much discouraged, and not only properly discountenanced by the men, but held in abhorrence by all women, who entertain a proper sense of the amiableness of female weakness. The females, who belong to the Cast of *people of style*, are particularly zealous in reprobating the exertions of female industry, and are careful to employ *men* only in all these branches, in which fortuneless women have audaciously endeavoured to procure subsistence; for this reason, when a family, by any of those misfortunes occurring in a commercial country, happens to be reduced to poverty, the daughters of the family are either left a prey to ghaunt-eyed indigence, or doomed to eat the bitter bread of dependance, administered with sparing hand, and grudging heart, by some cold relative! Equally ignorant, and equally helpless, as the females of Hindostan, their situation is far more destitute and pitiable. By the admirable institutions of our laws, it is ordained "that a woman shall by no means be left to herself, but that, in case her nearest relations are incapable of taking care of her, that duty shall devolve upon the Magistrate."[1] But, among the Christians of England, they are as destitute of protection as of instruction.

The misguider of the mind of Zāārmilla, has, it must be confessed, mixed some truth with the abundance of his falsehoods. When he told him, that it was customary in this country to teach women to read and write, he did not advance the thing which was not. It is true, that they are actually taught both, though for what purpose those keys of knowledge are put into their hands, it is not easy to imagine; few bad consequences, however, are found to result from this practice, as it is in general so wisely managed, as to be very little prejudicial to the interests of ignorance; and is seldom employed for any other purpose, than that of reading motely tales of love and murder, of which care is taken to furnish them with an abundant supply, from certain storehouses of trash, called circulating libraries.

The system of female education, such as I have described, is now

---

1 See Gentoo Laws. [E.H.]

almost universally practised over the island of Great Britain; though I have heard that, till lately, a system of a different nature was prevalent in the northern part of the united kingdom. There, instead of the Poojah of cards, it was then customary for the mothers of families to employ themselves in the education of their children, in teaching their daughters the duties of domestic life, and instilling into their tender minds the principles of piety and virtue. Beneath the mother's eye, the young females were then sent to certain places of instruction, called Day-schools, accompanied by their brothers; a practice which would inevitably lay the foundation of a degree of fraternal affection, inconsistent with that sort of reserved and austere demeanour, which it is so proper for men to observe toward their female relatives. Nor was this the only bad consequence resulting from the practice of sending boys and girls to the same School. In the pure hearts of the little innocents, attachments were often formed; which, in the minds of the young females, excited such a wish to excel, in order to render themselves amiable in the eyes of their little friends, as was altogether incompatible with the preservation of ignorance. Nor did the evil stop here; being habituated to consider their young school-fellows in the light of brothers, they had none of that restraint, which, before company, seals the lips of the Boarding-school Bibbys, but behaved with the frankness that is natural to the pure in heart. By early discipline, their minds receive such an odious degree of firmness, as often enabled them to sustain, with dignity, the most bitter decrees of adverse fortune, and their bodies acquired such a repulsive degree of health, as rendered them equal to the discharge of every active duty. All these multifarious evils are now no longer to be apprehended: the system of their southern neighbours, is now, I am well assured, practised with so much success, that the daughter of a *mountain Rajah*, will soon be as amiably frivolous, as engagingly ignorant; as weak in body, and in mind, as the pupil of the greatest Boarding School in London.

There are other instances in which these females of England, whom the infatuated Rajah has represented to himself "as exalted in the scale of being to the rank of rational, as capable of receiving the pure principles of virtue, and of steadily performing the various and complicated duties of life," are treated in a manner, at which the soul of humanity revolts. Thousands, and ten thousands, of these Christian women, being yearly suffered to perish in the streets of their great metropolis, under the accumulated misery of want, disease, and infamy!

We now think with horror, of the blood-stained altars of the ancient groves, where, to appease the wrath of the black Goddess,[1] it was permitted that human victims should be immolated: we paint to ourselves the agonizing feelings of the parent, when the blooming virgin was led forth, presenting a spotless offering to the sacrificial knife; and, sickening at the thought, we give praise to the adored Veeshnû, at whose commands these horrid rites were terminated. But callous, and unfeeling Englishmen! they endure to behold with their own eyes, sacrifices in one year exceeding in number, all that, in the course of revolving years, perished on the altars of Asia! sacrifices, not immolated to appease the wrath of their infernal Dewtahs, but victims of the licentious passions of unprincipled men! and yet many of these men are so absurd as to pretend to sensibility: nay, so much is their conduct at war with their professions, that I have heard them declaim, with apparent horror, against the holy ceremony of the virtuous widow, throwing herself upon the funeral pile of her deceased Lord. Yes, I have seen those, who could witness the scene of misery exhibited in their own streets, without betraying one symptom of compassion, affect to shed tears of pity, at the description of a Hindoo female's voluntary sacrifice, by which she attained glory here, and had the certainty of happiness hereafter! Is it thus, by a pretended feeling for imaginary sorrows, that the Christian Shaster teaches men to exercise their benevolence? Is it in conformity to any part of *its* precepts, that they can so freely grieve at equivocal and distant evils, while those, which are before their eyes, excite neither compassion nor remorse?

However unfeeling others might be to the misery of the wretched females, one would think that the voice of nature in a father's breast

---

1   Callee, or the Black Goddess, is exhibited in the Indian temples with a collar composed of golden skulls, descriptive of the dreadful sacrifices in which she took delight. The timid, and benign, character of the Hindoos, has induced many to doubt in the possibility of these horrid rites having ever been practiced in India; but the proofs that are given in many of the Shanscrit writings, of human sacrifices offered in remote ages, to this truly infernal deity, seem too strong to be refuted. [E.H.]

would cry aloud, to save his offspring from a fate so dreadful; but, deaf to her pleadings, parents themselves do not hesitate to devote the unhappy victims, by means of an education which conducts them step by step from vanity to vice, reconciling themselves to all its direful consequences, by a repetition of the cabalistic word GENTEEL, which has such a magical charm, as to change, in their opinion, the very nature of every species of madness, vice and folly!

Can a mind, pure and intelligent as that of Zāārmilla, delight to dwell with such a people? Is it from such a polluted stream that the descendant of a thousand Rajahs would wish to imbibe knowledge? Foolish project! Perverted ambition! How many choice morsels of Shanscrit literature lie mouldering in the temples of Benares, which he may rescue from the ravages of devouring worms, and be repaid with the words of wisdom. Hath the shallow invention of Europeans conceived any work equal to the Mahabharata? Can the aphorisms of their philosophers be compared with the Heetopades of Veeshnoo Sarma? or the imagination of their poets vie in lofty imagery, or sublime expression, with the beautiful dramas of the immortal Calidas?[1] Doth the wisdom-loving Rajah delight to tread the maze of logic? Let him seek for gratification in the Persian writings of the Mussulmans, which, though scarcely lawful for a Hindoo to peruse, are yet to be preferred to the absurd writings of Christian philosophers.

Which of the lawyers of Europe has shewn himself more expert in involving the simplicity of truth in the deep mazes of perplexity, than the Imaum Aboo Yooseff, and the more illustrious philosopher Ib'n Edress al Shaffie?[2] What king of Europe could ever boast of a Minister equal to that Golden Pillar who supported the throne of the renowned Ackber? Or who, in modern times, can, among them, be compared with the Great Eradut Khan Waseh?[3] The memoirs, written

---

1  The Mahabharata is the great Hindu epic; for the Heetopades and Veeshnu Sarma, see 156, note 1; for Calidas, see 58, note 1.

2  See Preliminary Discourse to the Hedàya. [E.H.] Iman "Aboo Yoosaf" (113-182 A.H), the first supreme civil magistrate of Baghdad, was famous for his legal knowledge; Ib'n Edress al Shaffie (150-204 A.H.) was the founder of the third of the four orthodox Islamic sects. His writing "contains all the principles of Muslim civil and canon law" (Hedàya xxxiii, xxvii).

3  Ackber (or Akbar) (1542-1605) was the first of the Mughal emperors to unite northern India under a single ruler; the "Golden Pillar," Abu'l Fazl (d. 1602), a great

by that Nobleman, is a gem of such transcendent worth and lustre, that its imitation as far exceeds the abilities of the puny Nobles of Europe, as does the unshaken fidelity and magnanimous heroism of the illustrious writer. In truth, there was no point in which I was more disappointed, than in the state of learning in England. By multitudes the people of that country, the name of Abul Fazel has never been heard! I conversed with so many, to whom the renown of Veias was unknown, and can with truth aver, that numbers, who have the character of *learned*, are yet so very ignorant, as not to know whether the great city of Canouge was founded by a Hindoo or a Mussulman![1]

With regard to the political state of Great Britain, its laws, and form of government, I am not qualified to speak with certainty; never having been able to find any two people of the same opinion with respect to any of these points. One circumstance alone appeared to be irrefragably established; and this is a circumstance so extraordinary, that it deserves attention.

Know, then, that the Visier, or first Minister, to the king of Great Britain, is, at all times, the weakest, and most wicked man in the kingdom, and that there is not a man in England, however incapable of managing, with propriety, the simplest concerns of private life, who is not much better qualified, than the Minister, to conduct the complex and extensive business of a great nation? You may, perhaps, be inclined to doubt the truth of this assertion; but when I inform you, that I repeat it not from vague report, but from the reiterated and solemn asseverations of the people I have alluded to, the point will appear incontrovertibly established.

I herewith send, for the gratification of your curiosity, a specimen of the painted idols of the Europeans, the examination of which has lately employed much of my time. A rich field of conjecture is already opened, to the culture of which I shall willingly devote some of the remaining years of my existence. That the origin of the rites of these divinities may be traced to the favoured country of Brahma, will not admit of a doubt. The flower, which one of the Goddesses carries in

---

historian and writer, was his confidential secretary (see also 163, note 2); Eradut Khan Waseh was a memoirist and poet of the eighteenth-century Mughal court.

1 Canouge was a Hindu city; see page 205, note 2.

her hand, bears such a striking resemblance to the Lotos, that, at first sight, any impartial person must recognise the adored figure of the bounteous Ganga. If any one of the figures has any claim to European origin, it is that of *Knave*; but who ever heard of a *King of hearts*, in the history of any nation of Europe? In the course of a few years investigation, I do not despair to prove the real family of every one of these painted idols; and in the prosecution of this laborious work, I shall not disdain to imitate the method pursued by the antiquarians of England, for "wise men will not disdain to learn, even from the counsel of fools."[1] I recommend thee to the protection of Veeshnû, and the favour of all the inferior Gods.

What can I say more?

---

1 Untraced.

# LETTER VI.

*Third Letter of the* Bramin.

BEFORE the delivery of my letter into the hands of the Dauk,[1] I resolved to re-examine the counsellors of memory, lest any circumstance, that would have any influence to enlighten the mind of the noble Rajah, should, unfortunately, have been omitted. It was a happy precaution! By it I am enabled to add to the proofs I have already given of the Braminical origin of the English nation, one other proof, which establishes the opinion of the Pundit, beyond the reach of human controversy.

Let it be known then to the friend of Māāndāāra, that the performance of the ceremony of the Purekah[2] is known to the Christian, and so much is the practice of its mysterious rites encouraged, that the most trifling and insignificant disputes are frequently referred to its decision: as, for example; in speaking of the colour of the eyes of a dancing-girl, one man would say that they were black, and another aver them to be blue, the common method of deciding the dispute (either between *people of style* or such as pant for admission into that honourable Cast) is the performance of Purekah. The method of performing this sublime ceremony, is not, it is true, exactly similar, in all respects, to that which is so piously observed in India. A little consideration on the genius of the people, and their deficiency in religious knowledge, will, however, account for the difference. In England, I never heard that the performers of the Purekah took the precaution of preparing themselves for the award of fate, by the observance of long and rigorous abstinence: or that they were particularly assiduous in their acts of devotion; or that they bound themselves by any oath before the Magistrate to abide by the infallible decision of the Gods. All these preparatory duties are, by these trifling people, altogether omitted; and the ceremony itself, instead of being performed in the presence of the Magistrate, and the assembled people, is usually gone through, under the immediate inspection of only *two witnesses*.[3] In the

---

1   Messenger. [E.H.]
2   Trial by Ordeal, still practiced in Hindostan. [E.H.]
3   For an account of the Indian Ordeal, in which  all these methods are mentioned, see Asiatic Researches, vol. ii. [E.H.]

Purekah of the English, they neither thrust their hands into vessels filled with boiling oil, nor do they say to the Balance, "thou, O Balance, art the mansion of truth, thou wast anciently contrived by Deities. If I am guilty, O, venerable as my own mother, sink me down; but if innocent, raise me aloft in air." Neither do they swallow poison, nor cast an Idol into the water, nor take into their hands the red hot iron; nor make any use of the seven leaves of the trembling Pippel, or the seven blades of Dharba grass, but by means of the diminutive *Agnee Astors*, called Pistols, the two disputants attempt to convey little leaden bullets into one another's bowels, or brains. In the opinion of some philosophers, a worthless fellow will continue to be as much a worthless fellow after the performance of the Purekah as before; but in the opinions of the performers themselves, it has efficacy to change the nature of guilt, and to wash away the foulest spot of dishonour.

What can I say more!

# LETTER VII.

Seeta Juin Zāārmilla, *Rajah of Almora*; *to* Kisheen Neaây Māāndāāra, *Zimeendar of Cumlore.*

I BOW with reverence to Ganesa, and submit the ardent struggles of my soul to the decrees of friendship. The request of Māāndāāra I am unable to resist even when his arguments are too feeble to make any impression on my mind: though my reason is unconvinced, I am sub-dued by my tenderness; and should consider myself unworthy of the name of friend, could I persist in tearing myself from my country at the moment that Māāndāāra is about to be restored to its bosom. Yes, my friend! I have this moment received the delightful intelligence, that the Firman,[1] which restores thee to thy Zimeendary, hath been issued! Thou mayest return in peace to the land of thy fathers! The Gods of Baandaresa shall be raised from their hiding places in the earth, to be placed upon the altars of his son: they shall see him per-form the rites of hospitality: spread his feast for the poor, and afford shelter to the oppressed. The Daivers, who delight in beholding the reward of virtue shall hover round your dwelling. Seraswatee shall bless your hours of study, and the bees of Cama, divested of their stings, shall pay you the tribute of pure and genuine sweetness.

I have prepared Zamarcanda for receiving you as her husband. Her mind is too gentle to require the harsh restraint of authority: let me, therefore, conjure you to treat her with tenderness; and you will be repaid by that willing obedience which is the offspring of affection, in a docile and ingenuous mind. For my share, I declare to you, that while I accept, with pleasure, of your sister for my wife, I, at the same time, must inform you of my intention of acting in direct opposition to your advice. From me she shall receive every indulgence. If she has any understanding, I will take pleasure in improving it: nor shall I dread any consequences that can arise from doing so. The more I meditate, the more am I convinced, that to tread firmly in the path of virtue it is necessary that we should be supported by the staff of knowledge. Ignorance is the mother of many follies.

---

1    "An edict or order issued by an Oriental sovereign." (*OED*)

It is with grief that I behold a mind, great and noble as that of my friend's, darkened by the clouds of prejudice. Had you, with me, paid homage to Seraswatee, the soul-enlightening Goddess would have inspired you of ideas more worthy of yourself: you would not then have attributed a desire to enlarge the sphere of knowledge, and an ardent admiration of excellence, wherever found, to the influence of magical spells, or incantation.

There is a period, beyond which, if the human mind remains bound in the chains of ignorance, it loses the power of expansion; and considers the existence of it in others, as the dream of illusive imagination.

He, who loosed the fetters of my understanding, who convinced me, by the cultivated state of his own, how high the minds of mortals might soar – the enlightened Percy – taught me to observe, that the negative ignorance, in which the mind is immersed, when excluded from commerce with the world, is of a nature far less obdurate, than that which has been rivetted by Pride in the bosom of society. Such is the ignorance of Sheermaal. His mind was too much narrowed, by its own prejudices, to receive a fair impression from new images. The few ideas which had been put into it, by his first teacher, had been received without examination, but retained with the pertinacity of the unyielding pride.

Can *he* be a proper judge of the peculiar customs of remote nations, who measures everything by the narrow standard of his own prejudices? Can *he* who, instead of making observations on the variety of human character, pronounces sentence of condemnation on whatever he does not understand; can *he* be qualified for communicating information to others? No. False, and foolish, will ever be the conclusions of presumptuous ignorance!

Ah! What a pattern might Sheermaal have found in the travellers, and the travel-writers of Europe. How many of these does England alone, every year, pour from her maternal bosom? Happy for Sheermaal, if he had followed the laudable example of these sapient youths; how deep would then have been his observations! how important his discoveries!

I am unwilling to speak with disrespect of a Bramin. I view the ignorance of this man with pity, and should only give to his *prejudice*, the smile of contempt, but I cannot perceive his malice, and his false-hood, without feelings of abhorrence and indignation. Is it for a mind, base and ignoble as his, to accuse the ingenuous and enlightened Percy of falsehood?

O that Māāndāāra could have known that incomparable youth! That he could have listened to his instructions, while every word he uttered, was like the vivid flash of lightening, illuminating the dark expanse of night. He would then have been convinced, that a mind, like his, was incapable of swerving from the rigid dictates of truth; and he would have united with me, in reprobating every attempt to calumniate his memory. Dear shall his memory be to Zāārmilla, while the blood of life flows through his veins, and whoever would shun my resentment, must be careful how they suffer the shadow of disrespect to pass over the name of my departed friend!

<hr/>

I HAVE just received the two concluding letters of that ignorant, and deluded Bramin; who has instilled his base prejudices into the mind of my friend. Surely some malignant Dewtah, must have blinded the eyes, and fettered the understanding, of this unhappy man, who could not, otherwise, have been so grossly deceived. – What! during his ten years abode among Christians, never to have heard of, or seen, the Christian Shaster! That Shaster, the most abstruse, and difficult doctrines of which, are so carefully inculcated into the tender minds of youth that every boy, who is sent to the University, is so perfectly master of the subject to be able to give his solemn assent to the unerring explanations of his Church.[1] That Shaster, of which the precepts of Peace, Charity, Humility, and universal Benevolence, form the basics of every law, and direct the practice of every Christian court! That Shaster I have studied with the strictest attention, and do solemnly assure you, that the virtues I have enumerated, are as strictly enjoined to the Christians, as the performance of Poojah to the Hindoo or the Fast of Ramozin to the Mussulman. The Mussulman fasts, and the Hindoo performs Poojah, according to their respective laws,

---

1  Students attending Oxford and Cambridge were required to declare belief in the thirty-nine articles of the Anglican church.

and can we believe that the Christian alone treats with contempt the authority of his God?

How could the lie-loving Bramin expect to be credited, when he asserts that Christians enter into the traffic of blood! That these men, who walk by the rule of "doing to others, as they would be done by in the like case," invade the countries of the defenceless, and seizing, with tiger-like ferocity, their unoffending children, bind them in the galling chains of slavery, and devote them, as a cruel sacrifice, to the black Goddess of affliction! Surely, such a representation cannot fail to appear in its true light to every one, who knows the jealousy entertained, by the sublime Governors of that enlightened nation, for the purity of their honour! so great, that even those Chiefs, whom we have considered as bulwarks, raised by the immortal Veeshnû, to protect us from the destroyer, have fallen short of the standard of perfection created in the immaculate bosoms of their brethren at home! Can such men be supposed to sanction the traffic of human misery? Ah! how little doth he know of the undeviating rectitude of the British Senate!

Indeed, all that he says upon the religious rites, practiced by the English nation is equally false, and absurd. There is no such thing as any Poojah performed to bits of painted paper: neither are partridges held sacred. From examining their Shaster, with the strictest accuracy, I am prepared to assert, that it contains not one word which could countenance such idolatry. And, whether it is likely, that any practices, not warranted by its authority, would be suffered to become prevalent, I shall leave you to judge; after informing you, that, in England, no man is deemed qualified for holding even the meanest employment in the state, but by the performance of an act of the most solemn devotion.[1] An act which is only safe to the pious, and the pure; and of which, to participate unworthily is declared to be a heinous sin! Ah! how pure must be the morals of such a people!

As to what he says of the frivolous education bestowed upon Christian women, it is sufficient to observe, that it is utterly inconsistent with the belief of the immortality and progressive improvement

---

1   Those who served in any government office were supposed to be communicants in the Church of England, a law designed to bar Catholics and dissenters from civic participation.

of the human soul; it is, indeed, too absurd to stand in need of confutation. When he can convince me, that the men are vain, voluptuous, selfish, and unjust, then shall I believe, that the women are frivolous, and ignorant.

In regard to what he asserts of the different Casts, into which the people are divided, I am not so well prepared to answer him. I only know, that nothing like it appears in the Christian Shaster. The *people of family*, and *the people of no family*, are there put upon a level; and, at the time it was written, it is evident the *people of style* had never been heard of.

Oh! that it had been permitted me to have confuted the misrepresentations of this wicked Bramin, by the unerring answers of *experience*, that I could have followed the impulse of my own desires, in the glorious pursuit of wisdom; and traced the obscure and distant path, by which Knowledge disseminated her treasures over the various regions of the earth! Ah! didst thou know what it has cost me to relinquish this favourite pursuit; what self-denial I have been obliged to exert, ere I could turn mine eyes from the enchanting prospect that opened to my view, thou wouldst esteem this act of friendship more, than if I had poured into thy lap the accumulated treasures of my fathers!

Having once determined, thou needst not fear that aught shall have power to shake my resolution. I swear to thee, by the name of my father, *that while Prymaveda lives, Zāārmilla will never forsake her.*

I shall be at Rampore in the space of a fortnight: there I shall give, to the arms of my friend, the lovely and gentle Zamarcanda; and receive thy sister for the partner of my bosom. After the performance of our nuptials, I shall have the pleasure of conducting you to the ancient seat of your fore-fathers. You will be received with joy, by all the Ryots, and welcomed by every surrounding Zimeendar, with the sincerest satisfaction. You must, after this, return with me to Almora; and there, where every scene recalls to memory the early days of felicity, we shall renew the studies, and retaste the pleasures of our youth. We shall mingle our tears of gratitude, at the tomb of the venerable Pundit, who first poured the balm of instruction into our young, and tender minds.

In the fair bosom of creation, and in the gorgeously enamelled vault of heaven, we shall together read those divine mysteries, over which, the wisdom of our holy Bramins has thrown a veil, that is impenetrable only to ignorance.[1] From these we will rise to the contemplation of that

> Omniscient Spirit, whose all-ruling power
> Bids from each sense bright emanations beam;
> Glows in the rainbow, sparkles in the stream,
> Smiles in the bud, and glistens in the flow'r
> > That crowns each vernal bow'r;
> Sighs in the gale, and warbles in the throat
> Of every bird, that hails the blooming spring,
> Or tells his love in many a liquid note,
> While envious artists touch the rival string
> > Till rocks and forests ring;
> Breathes in rich fragrance from the sandal grove,
> Or where the precious musk-deer playful rove:
> In dulcet juice from clust'ring fruit distils,
> And burns salubrious in the tasteful clove:[2]

May the sovereign Maya,[3] present to the mind of Māāndāāra, an ever varying assemblage of fair ideas! but may that which is dearest to his heart, be the friendship of Zāārmilla!

What can I say more!

---

1   This expression seems favourable to the opinion entertained by some of our own writers, that great part of the Mythology of the Hindoos, is nothing more than enigmatical representations of astronomical facts. [E.H.]

2   See the sixth stanza of the Hymn to Narayena, as translated by Sir William Jones. [E.H.] *Works* 13: 308. The phrase "thy sov'reign MAYA reigns" concludes the stanza.

3   It will be sufficient here to premise, that the inextricable difficulties attending the vulgar notion of *material substances*, induced many of the wisest Hindoos to believe that the whole creation was rather an *energy* than a *work*, by which the Infinite Being, who is present at all times, in all places, exhibits to the minds of his creatures a *set of perceptions* like a wonderful picture or piece of music, always varied, yet always uniform: so that all bodies, and their qualities, exist, indeed, to every wise, and useful purpose: but exist only as far as they are *perceived*. This *Illusive Operation* of the Deity, the Hindoo philosophers, call *Maya*, or *Deception*." See the Argument to the above mentioned Hymn. [E.H.] *Works* 13: 302.

[IN the correspondence of the Rajah, we here find a chasm of several years. Though none of the letters bear any date, we have, from circumstances mentioned in the preceding ones, concluded them to have been written toward the beginning of the year 1775. Those, which follow, we presume, could not have been written before the year 1779, or 1780.]

# LETTER VIII.

*From the Rajah* Zāārmilla, *to* Māāndāāra *(Written from Barellee.)*

MAY the powerful Eendra be ever propitious to the most benignant of friends; and the Goddess Sree preserve his heart from the arrows of affliction![1]

An opportunity offers, of which I am not slow to avail myself, of sending thee information of my health and safety. Had not sorrow spread its raven wing over the beauties of every prospect, my journey might have been delightful. But, alas! to him, whose heart is oppressed by recent calamity, the face of nature is veiled in darkness. My person was soon at a distance from the scene of sorrow, but from it I could not, by distance, disengage my mind. Prymaveda, my affectionate, and faithful Prymaveda, expiring in my arms, was the picture that every where presented itself to my eyes. Her last low, and feeble sighs, were still the only sounds which vibrated upon my ears. Change of scene afforded no alleviation to my grief, and Time, whose tongue of fire devoured all things, appeared to move with too slow a pace to leave me room to hope much from his assistance. One only source of con-solation presented itself to my deeply wounded mind, it was the refl-ection of having contributed to the happiness of her, whose image dwells in my heart. Had I ever reproved with harshness, or indulged my pride in the morose exercise of authority, how insupportable would be the bitterness of my affliction?

Let not Māāndāāra reproach his friend for indulging in these melancholy reflections. The woman, who is attached to her husband, will follow the spirit of her departed Lord, even though condemned to the regions of punishment; and shall my soul forget her, who wait-eth for me in the realms of death? She, from whom sprung my final deliverer![2] She, who was the companion of my days, the friend of my

---

1   According to Charles Wilkins, Eendra is the god of weather, "the personification of the visible heavens, or the power of the Almighty over the elements. He is the sprinkler of the rain, the roller of the thunder, and the director of the winds. He is represented with a thousand eyes grasping the thunderbolts. (*Bhagavad-gita* 143). For Sree, see "Lackshmi" in Hamilton's glossary; she appears to have taken her informa-tion from a note in the *Hitopadesa* (1787), 315.
2   Alluding to the ceremony of the Sradh, which the Hindoos believe it necessary should be performed by a man's own son in order to facilitate his entrance to the

heart, whose gentle manners, and prudent counsels, smoothed the rugged path of life, and gave value to every blessing. But alas! the innocent vivacity, the endearing tenderness, which, but yesterday, were the delight of my life, are now recalled, but to aggravate my sorrow. But why should I, with the dart that rankles in my own bosom, wound the breast of my friend?

Let me try to change the subject. At Bissoolee, I was received, by my kinsman, with every mark of kindness. He endeavoured to divert my mind, from the subject of its own griefs, by turning my attention to those great transactions, of which this country had lately been the scene. The first information that is given us upon any subject, that is in its nature interesting, and which is beyond the reach of our own inspection, is so greedily received, that the judgment we form upon it is equally prompt and decisive. I have frequently observed that such hasty judgment, is upon more full investigation, found erroneous; and here I had ample proof of the justice of the observation.

When the fall of the Afgan Cawns had taken place, we rejoiced to hear that this beautiful, and fertile, province, was to be put under the administration of Bêâss Râye;[1] that pious Hindoo, who had shed so many tears over the misfortunes of his country. We imagined that he, who could paint the extortions, and oppressions of the Afgans, in such true, and lively colours, must necessarily be possessed of a good, and feeling heart. Alas! the art of describing human misery, and the Virtue of feeling for it, are two very different things.

This man, who declaimed so eloquently against the rapacity of the Afgans, had a heart *so steeled* by avarice, as to be impervious to every sentiment of humanity. The country groaned beneath his oppressions, and his removal was considered as a deliverance from the pestilence.

---

regions of felicity; it is, therefore, by them esteemed a great misfortune to die child-less. In the drama of Sacontala, Dushmanta thus laments his fate, "Ah me! the departed souls of my ancestors, who claim a share in the funeral cake, which I have no son to offer, are apprehensive of losing their due honour. – My forefathers must drink, instead of a pure libation, this flood of tears, the only offering which a man, who dies childless, can make." See Sac. Page 125. [E.H.] See 58, note 1.

1    See the Rohilla History. [E.H.] Pages 253-54: "Beass Raye, a Hindoo who had been the Dewan of Hafiz Rhamut, insinuated himself into the favour of the Sujah-al-Dowlah by telling him where to find secret deposits of treasure among the Rohillas. The Suja-al-Dowlah rented the conquered country to Beass Raye, but he was soon after displaced because of complaints about the suffering the Rohilla peo-ple endured under his administration."

After having spent a week at Bissoolee, I took leave of my kind, but too officious, kinsman and proceeded to Barellee. The approach to this city, through lofty rows of bamboos, which form a continued arbour, surrounded on every side by gardens, flourishing in all the pride of beauty, extorted my admiration.

I did not fail to visit the tomb of the renowned Afgan who was so long the terror, and the glory of Kuttaher.[1] I chose to visit it alone. There are moments, when the soul, absorbed in its own reflections, feels an elevation which is incompatible with any society.

The sun had just hid the splendour of his beams behind the hills of Bissoolee, and night begun to spread her dusky curtain over the face of nature, when I approached the silent scene, where the tomb of the warrior was reared. Of that ambition before the impetuous career of which the bars of gratitude, and of justice, had been annihilated; that ambition, insatiable as the ocean, and extensive as the firmament of heaven, what were now the limits? Small was the spot which contained the mouldering remains of him, who had struck the Princes of the earth with terror. I listened – but the thunder of his voice was no longer to be heard. I looked – but the crowds of flatterers, who were wont to pay adulatory homage to his smiles, were no longer to be seen. The world, which had beheld the Afgan greatness arise, like a meteor from the womb of obscurity, which had been dazzled by the brightness of its splendour, and astonished by the celerity of its progress, beheld, without regret, its utter extinction in this narrow tomb. I indulged in these reveries the greater part of the night. The remainder of my time, at Barellee, was spent in making enquiries

---

1   Hafiz Rhamut, a Rohilla chief, celebrated for his warlike talents and unprincipled ambition: by that ambition, betraying the trust of his friend, and usurping the inheritance of his wards, he put himself at the head of the Rohilla government; and was killed at the battle of Cutterah, 22d of April 1774. By those who ought to have known better, Hafiz Rhamut has been confounded with *Hafiz*, the celebrated poet of Shiraz, who flourished above four hundred years ago. On consulting the Parliamentary Register, we find Hafiz Rhamut, who was neither a poet, nor man of letters, introduced as *"famous throughout the East for the elegance of his literature and the spirit of his poetical compositions."* Parliamentary Register, No. 76, Page 205. [E.H.] This note is taken verbatim from the Charles Hamilton's *Historical Relation* 239; as Hamilton would certainly have known, the speaker "who ought to have known better" was Edmund Burke. The phrase quoted is taken from his speech on Fox's East India Bill (*Writings and Speeches* 5:393). Hafiz of Shiraz was a Persian writer who lived in the fourteenth century; see 232, note 1.

concerning the remarkable events which have taken place in its vicinity. The difficulty of obtaining information was greater than I was aware of. Every one, whom I applied to for that purpose, I found to be so brimful of that part of the story which particularly related to himself, that I was obliged to listen to a volume of uninteresting anecdotes, before I could arrive at the truth.

The ravages committed by the troops of his Highness, after the battle of Cutterah, were such as have been constantly practised, by every victorious army; but the contrast, exhibited in the behaviour of the English, was altogether new and uncommon: such as no Mussulman army has ever been known to practice; and such as, I greatly fear, they will never be induced to imitate.

After having, by their courage and superior skill, decided the event of the day, while those for whom they fought, rushed upon the spoil of the defeated enemy, and, in their avidity for plunder, were alike regardless of the remonstrances of justice, and the dictates of humanity, the gallant army of the English, satisfied with the glory of victory, disdained all other spoil.[1] They beheld, with indignation and horror, the behaviour of their allies, and exerted themselves for the protection, and relief, of the unhappy sufferers, whom the successful foe had left destitute of every other resource.

All that I have heard in this place, rekindles in my bosom the desire so long cherished, and so unwillingly suppressed, of becoming more intimately acquainted with a people, who have ever been the objects of my affectionate veneration. My resolution is taken; and, in pursuance of it, as soon as I have performed the act of pious ablution in the sacred spot, where the two wandering blessings of Hindostan unite their waves, I shall proceed to the English camp. In listening to the instructive conversation of these enlightened men, the selfish sorrows, which at present occupy my heart, may, for a time, be soothed into forgetfulness. I shall, perhaps, renew my acquaintance with the

---

1  Hamilton is alluding to the dispatch (often cited in the debate about the Rohilla war) sent by Colonel Champion, the commander of the English forces, after the battle: "whatever effects they [the Rohillas] could not carry off, fell a sacrifice to the ravages of the Nabob's people, whilst the Company's troops, in regular order in their ranks, most justly observed, 'We have the honour of the day, and these banditti the profit....'" (quoted Strachey 141). See also Charles Hamilton's *Historical Relation* 241-42.

friends of Percy. I shall, with them, have the pleasure of recapitulating the virtues of that amiable youth: those virtues, whose fragrance perfumed my soul, and left an impression, strong as the incense from the aromatic plant, which time has not the power to obliterate.

Present Zamarcanda with the affectionate remembrances of her brother. I would recommend my son to her affection, did I not know that her goodness will anticipate my wishes. To you my friend, and to her, I trust the precious deposit – the life of my life! And to Camdhaynû my soul is expanded in prayers, for your happiness!

# LETTER IX.

*The* SAME, *to the* SAME.

FROM the King of worshipped places,[1] the renowned Allahabad to the most faithful of friends, Zāārmilla sends health and prosperity. While the divine influence of the sacred stream, into which I have so lately plunged, continues to refresh my soul, I hasten to impart to thee the sentiments which have inspired my heart. But how shall I describe to you the transport with which I beheld the sacred spot, celebrated through all ages! that spot, consecrated by the threefold junction of the sacred Ganges, the health giving Jumna, and the unseen, but not less benignant Serraswattee! I contemplated, with elevated rapture, the junction of those honoured streams, which here mingling their sacred waves, diffuse the exhaustless treasures of fertility, and verdure, over the most favoured of regions. From these blessed emblems of the mystic union of the divinities, my soul, wrapt in gratitude, ascended to the Almighty Creating Power, the grandeur of whose works is only to be equalled by his beneficence.

In the lessons of the venerable Pundit, who was our first instructor, and in the sublime writings of the great luminaries of the world, we have been taught to lift our hearts to Him, who alone, is infinite in power, and goodness! But, alas! the minds of all the Bramins, I have met with here, are completely engrossed by the multiplied symbols of his attributes. From their company, I have received no pleasure; from their conversation, I have reaped no instruction. I shall, therefore, hasten the period of my departure, and, probably, finish this letter from Benares.

---

1    The English reader will find some light thrown upon the subject of this letter, by consulting Mr. Maurice's Indian Antiquities, who having traced the progress of the Ganges, from the Mountains of Thibet to the plains of Hindostan, thus proceeds: "Then flowing on through delightful plains, and diffusing riches, and verdure, in its progress at Allahabad, receives a rich tribute to its stream in the waters of the Jumna. If we may believe the Bramins, another sacred river, called the Serraswatty, joins these rivers under ground; and, therefore this spot, consecrated by the three-fold junction of their waves, has ever been the resort of devout pilgrims, from every province of Hindostan, and is denominated in the Ayeen Ackbery – *The King of worshipped places.*" Maurice's Indian Antiquities, vol.i, page 155. [E.H.]

FROM the Queen of Science, the favoured seat of learning, the celebrated Benares, Zāārmilla again addresses his friend.

Before I say, anything of a place of which you have already heard so much, I shall proceed to inform you of my visit to the English officers, in the garrison of Chunar.

As I stopt to take some refreshments, at the distance of a few coss[1] from the fort, I was informed, by my people, that some English officers, who had been out, on a hunting party, were, at that very time, in the same village. I sent to inform them of my intention of visiting Chunar; and, in a few minutes, I was no less delighted, than surprised, to see Doctor Denbeigh enter the veranda, where I was then reposing myself. He saluted me with that glow of kindness which is excited in the bosoms of the benevolent, by an unexpected interview with those whom the hand of time seemed to have separated for ever. He introduced me to his companions, the urbanity of whose manners formed a striking contrast to the plainness of their dress.

On my arrival at Chunar, I found myself as if I had been all at once transported into a new world. Surrounded by the English Chiefs, whose dress, whose language, and whose manners, were all so different from what I had ever been accustomed to, I could scarcely persuade myself that I did not wander in the realms of delusion.

At first, all Englishmen appeared to me to wear the same aspect, and to have the same manners. But when wonder had sufficiently subsided to admit of the calm accuracy of observation, I perceived that every countenance had a characteristic distinction; a distinction, which extended to the tones of the voice, and gestures of the body. This variety, like the Ráginís which preside over music,[2] served but to render harmony more pleasing. The senior Officers smiled at the playful vivacity of their youthful friends, who frequently ventured to exert their wit in a manner that could not have failed to excite resentment in less amiable minds. The time of each was spent

---

1   A measurement of distance which Zāārmilla later defines as being approximately two miles.
2   The Ráginís, or female passions, are the Nymphs, which, according to the beautiful Allegory of the Hindoos, preside over musical sounds. A translation of some of the many Dissertations upon this subject, which are to be found in the Shanscrit language, is much to be wished for. [E.H.]

according to his own taste. By some, it was employed in the pursuit of literature; and I am certain it must exalt my new friends in the estimation of Māāndāāra, when he is informed, that to the knowledge of the Persian, many of the English Chiefs add a considerable degree of information in the Shanscrit language. The time of vacation from immediate service wasted by the Mussulman Commanders in voluptuous indolence, is spent by these more enlightened men, in studies which add to their stock of knowledge, and do honour to the genius of their country. It is by these strangers that the annals of Hindostan, which her barbarian conquerors have sought to obliterate in the blood of her children, shall be restored! Already, have Temples, Palaces, and Cities, which Calli[1] had covered with the mantle of oblivion, been, by the indefatigable researches of these favourites of Serraswattee, dragged to light.

The Pagodas, whose lofty summits had sustained the clouds, and palaces, which had once spread their golden fronts to the sun, proud of being the residence of the ancient Rajahs of our nation, now bow their time-worn heads to listen to the voice of strangers, and behold the sacred characters, inscribed upon their bosoms, familiarly perused by a people, whose nation had not sprung into existence at the time these towering monuments of Eastern splendour had commenced the progress of decay!

I found great difficulty in tearing myself from the society of these gentlemen, from whom I experienced every mark of kindness, and attention; the pain of parting was, however, in some degree alleviated by the promise made to me, by two of these Saibs, to rejoin me at Benares.

I embarked, for the first time, on the mighty Ganges, and, turning my eyes to take leave of the seat of hospitality, I was struck with the appearance of the citadel, which seems to have arisen from the bed of Ganga; the piety of our fathers is still legible on the walls of this massy pile; nor has the guardian Dewtah forsaken her sacred charge. The seat of her residence remains entire. And though the refreshing breeze of morn wafts her to the seat of Science, she fails not to return to Chunar, before the sultry heats of noon.[2]

---

1   Calli here signifies Time. [E.H.]
2   The Fort of Chunar is said to be of the highest antiquity. In the citadel is a black marble slab, on which the tutelary Deity of the place is traditionally supposed, at all

We gently floated down the unruffled bosom of the Queen of rivers, which expands itself on approaching Benares; and puts on an additional air of grandeur, in honour, it would seem, of this celebrated city. The city appears to have returned the compliment, and to have selected its choicest ornaments to deck the banks of its beneficent visitor. Numerous and beautiful are the Pagodas, all enriched by the piety, and adorned by the ingenuity of our ancestors; which see themselves reflected in the mighty stream. Some, in mouldering ruins, tell of the injuries they have sustained, not only from the insidious hand of Time, but from the ruthless bigotry of the destroying foe. Innumerable Ghauts,[1] some of which are highly decorated, and embankments, which exhibit all the splendour and elegance of architecture, give additional grace and beauty to this most enchanting scene.

My reception from the Rajah was extremely flattering. You will, no doubt, be anxious for my opinion of this man, who now fills so exalted a station.

There is no trial so dangerous to virtue, as prosperity; had the father of this young man continued to occupy the office of Dewan to the Aumeldar[2] of the province, so long filled by his grandfather, and

---

times, to be seated; except from sunrise until nine o'clock in the morning; when he is supposed to be at Benares: during which time, from the superstition of the Hindoos, attacks may be made upon the fort with a prospect of success. See Hodges' Travels in India page 56. [E.H.] William Hodges, *Travels in India, during the years 1780, 1781, 1782, and 1783* (London, 1793).

1   Flights of steps leading up from the river. [E.H.]

2   Bulwart Sing, the father of Cheyt Sing, was the son of Monserans, a Bramin, who had been appointed *steward* to Rushem Ally, then *governor* of the province of Banares; he supplanted his master, and obtained the province for himself: and this was the origin of a man, called, by some in this country, a sovereign Prince! See Broome's Elucidation of the Articles of Impeachment.[E.H.] Ralph Broome, *An Elucidation of the articles of Impeachment preferred by the last Parliament against Warren Hastings, esq. Late Governor General of Bengal* (London, 1790). One of the main charges against Hastings was his mistreatment of Chait Singh, Rajah of Benares; after first extorting considerable sums of money from the Rajah as tribute, Hastings eventually ousted him from power and then looted his treasury to help finance campaigns in Mysore. Supporters of Hastings tended to argue, as Hamilton does here, that Chait Singh had at best a problematic title in the first place. Both "Dewan" and "Aumeldar" (or Amildar) are terms used to describe collectors of revenues in provinces of the Mughal empire, although the term "Dewan" could also be used of the administrator of a territory (*OED*). Zäärmilla uses it in this sense to describe his shipboard companion at the beginning of volume two.

he himself succeeded to the same advantageous, though subordinate employment, he might, perhaps, have conducted himself with temper and discretion: but the height of his elevation has made him giddy; he wishes to quit the staff which hitherto supported him; and by the assistance of which he climbed to his present greatness. If he succeeds, he will probably be made sensible of his folly, by the precipitancy of his fall.

You may imagine in what manner this young man is imposed upon by his people, when I tell you, that they have actually made him believe that the present Governor General is not without enemies, even in the Supreme Council![1] Was ever any thing more absurd, than to imagine that men, who could possibly have no other motive for visiting these regions, than to promote their country's glory, and the happiness of mankind, should yet become enemies to him who has so eminently contributed to both? Ridiculous idea! What is it but to imagine, that from the base motives of *personal enmity, envy of superiour talents,* or *jealousy of superiour power,* these men would prefer the ruin of a rival, to the glory, and preservation of an empire! How unworthy of the character of Englishmen!

I was much rejoiced at the arrival of my two English friends, whose chief motive for visiting Benares at this time, was to inspect and examine the astronomical apparatus still extant in the Tower of the Stars. Both these gentlemen were deeply learned in this divine science. The stupendous engines, constructed by the ingenuity of our ancestors for measuring the expanse of heaven, and tracing through its trackless arch the path of it illustrious inhabitants, filled their minds with astonishment. Alas! that these evidences of the wisdom of fathers should now serve to mark the degeneracy of their children! That science, which exalts the soul to heaven, which enables it to peruse that book of wisdom, where the Supreme hath written his attributes in the most legible characters; even in the golden orbs, whose distant

---

1  The "present governor general" was Warren Hastings, who had, of course, many enemies. In 1780 – roughly the time that Zāārmilla is supposedly writing this letter – Hastings' relationship with Philip Francis, one of the other members of the governing Council, had deteriorated to the point that the two men fought a duel in which Francis was wounded. The implication here is that Chait Singh was encouraged in his stand against Hastings by English disunion but had no real cause for discontent.

glories delight the eye of ignorance. That science, so familiar to our fathers, is now almost lost to their unenlightened sons. But as the splendid luminary of the sky, when, apparently extinguished in darkness, continues still to pursue his course, illuminating with his brightness the various inhabitants of the earth; so doth the Goddess of Science pursue her radiant journey: and when we vainly imagine she is gone for ever, if we open the eyes of our understanding, we shall see her beaming with redoubled lustre on the children of another hemisphere. These strangers could, at one glance, comprehend the use of those instruments, which the Pundits, who attended us, could not explain; and I soon found that the knowledge imparted to us upon this subject, by our reverend teacher, was but ignorance, compared to their superiour attainments. Need we farther proof that the spirit of Brahma is not confined to any particular region, but extendeth over his great creation?

In the conviction of this truth, I have determined to devote some months to the cultivation of a more intimate acquaintance with those, who are so well qualified to impart the light of knowledge to my mind.

I have now fulfilled the purpose of my journey to Benares, but have no pleasure in the thoughts of returning to Almora. Alas! wherefore should I return? The lamp of love is extinguished in my dwelling, and darkness rests upon my pleasant bowers. To my friend, and to my sister, I can, with confidence, entrust the only treasure that interests my heart. Yes, Zamarcanda, I know that thou wilt watch with a mother's care over the helpless infancy of my child. May the Gods of our nation reward thy tenderness!

What can I say more!

# LETTER X.

*From the* SAME, *to the* SAME.

WHOSE happiness, saith the wise instructor, is equal to that of the man who hath a friend to live with, a friend to converse with, and a friend to embrace; and such happiness it is now my destiny to enjoy.[1] Behold me at Calcutta, under the same roof with the gentle Saib, who was the choice friend of the ever-lamented Percy!

Once more embarking on the bosom of the beneficent Ganga, I was conducted by the gentle Goddess to Patna, where the first person that met my arrival was no other than Captain Grey himself. He instantly recognized me, and received me with the spontaneous glow of cordial affection. The few days that I remained there, were chiefly occupied in viewing that ancient city, which the residence of the English has recalled to the vigour of life. Nothing has more forcibly struck my mind, in the whole course of my journey, than the amazing contrast, in point of fertility and cultivation, between the territories of the Christian, and Mussulman Lords of Hindostan. In the Mussulman districts, we behold ruined villages, where, instead of the cheerful noise of the mechanic, or the mingled hum of light-hearted loquacity, universal silence reigns; nor, in some once populous districts, does any human figure meet the eye, save that of some solitary Bramin, who, absorbed in contemplation, forsakes the haunts of men.

The chief stations of the English, on the contrary, may easily be traced by the flourishing state of the country, which surrounds them: there the peasant throws the grain into the liberal bosom of the earth with cheerfulness; assured, that he shall reap the reward of his toil. Having paid his rent, he knows that the remainder will be his own; nor fears that it will be wrested from him by the open violence of the

---

1   *The heetopades of Veeshnoo-sarma, in a series of connected fables, interspersed with moral, prudential, and political maxims; translated from an ancient manuscript in the Sanskreet language,* translated by Charles Wilkins (Bath, 1787). The 1885 edition has been republished in facsimile, edited by William Bysse Stein, by Scholars' Facsimiles and Reprints (1968). Veeshnoo-sarma is the narrator of the fables and the "wise instructor" to whom Sheermaal refers in his attack on the inferiority of European culture. This quotation appears on page 40 of the 1885 edition.

spoiler, or seized by the hard hand of rapacious avarice. Even when the heavens withheld their fructifying distillations from the thirsty earth, and ghastly famine stalked through the provinces around, the benignant charity of the English Chiefs sustained the lives of thousands: and thousands more would have been saved from perishing, had their religious principles permitted them to accept the proffered bounty.[1]

The day after my arrival at Patna, Captain Grey received the agreeable news of his having been promoted by the Governor General, to a new appointment, which demanded his immediate attendance at Calcutta. It was with pleasure that I accepted his obliging invitation to accompany him thither. Several of his friends agreed to be of the party. We proceeded in Budgerows,[2] furnished with every accommodation that could add pleasure to this delightful voyage.

As the channel of the river enlarged, my heart bounded within me at the expanse of waters which surrounded me. "Yet what is this stream, in all its majesty," exclaimed I, "in comparison of that mighty ocean! that fathomless abyss! which all these Europeans have already passed." Such is the degree of knowledge to be acquired in retirement, compared to the attainments of those, whose bosoms receive the waters of wisdom, flowing through the thousand channels of experience!

The novelty of the picturesque, and beautiful scenery, that frequently presented itself to our eyes, produced astonishment and delight; but the uncommon traits of character, which I observed in some of my companions, exhibited a novelty still more interesting. As an example, I shall only attempt to describe to you a few of those features, in the character of one young officer, from which you may form some idea of the many subjects of wonder with which a

---

1   The English reader may, perhaps, object to the account of the Rajah, as being very different from that tale of horrors, which has been so generously received. Which account comes nearest to the truth, those, who have been eye witnesses of the scene described can best determine. [E.H.] Hamilton is alluding to the lurid accounts of Bengal given by Burke in his attacks on Hastings. Burke — like Hamilton herself – never visited India but relied on eye-witness accounts for his descriptions of English conduct.

2   A type of boat used for river travel in India; they could be quite luxurious.

stranger is surrounded when he enters into the society of Christians.

The first thing that attracted my attention toward this young man was the beauty of his countenance; but the prepossession was soon done away by the familiarity of his manners, and that indecorous want of respect toward his superiors, which gave me inconceivable disgust. When the senior Chiefs opened their lips to speak, instead of listening in mute attention to the words of wisdom which proceeded from their mouths, he interrupted their discourse with some sally of wit, which not unfrequently presented all they had said in so ridiculous a point of view, as to excite the laughter of all present. Judge how this shocked and offended me? Not a day passed, in which he did not perform some wild pranks; in these, however, there was such a mixture of pleasantry, as to force mirth to get the better of anger. On expressing to Captain Grey my surprise at the lenity with which this young man was treated, even by those who suffered from him, he gave me to understand that the follies, of which I complained, were occasioned by a disease, called, in their language, HIGH SPIRITS; a malady peculiar to the climates of Europe. This information quickly changed my aversion for the poor youth into compassion; but, surely, if this disease be very common in those climates, it must be extremely troublesome: how happy is it, that it is not infectious? I was very sorry to learn that he intended being of our party to Calcutta, and avoided, as much as possible, having any communication with him; but my efforts were vain; his disorder made him so restless, that he never remained in one part of the Budgerow for ten minutes at one time.

It would be endless to repeat all the fooleries of this youth, during our voyage: I shall only mention the following, which will be sufficient to give you an idea of the effects of *high spirits*.

It was on an evening of unparalleled beauty. The air, which had just been refreshed by a North-wester,[1] breathed sweet fragrance; delightful as the reconciliation of friends, when clouds of resentment have been dissipated by the Sun of Truth. The clear blue sky saw itself reflected on the unruffled bosom of the Queen of Rivers. On the right hand, the lovely Goddess stretched her majestic waves to such a

---

1 A term used in India for a particular species of hurricane. [E.H.]

distance that the prominent and lofty banks, which formed her western girdle, appeared to our view as a black line touching the horizon. At less than half a coss distance on the left, a richly cultivated country smiled upon us, through the various openings of a Mango grove; which frequently intruded upon the verdant slope, to kiss the tresses of Ganga.

We were tempted by the beauty of the evening to go on shore, somewhat sooner than usual: on our landing, innumerable flocks of peacocks, lorys, and other inhabitants of the grove, were in motion, who, waving their resplendent plumage in the golden rays of the declining sun, gave an additional charm to the graces of this lovely landscape.[1]

---

1    A late writer (Mr. Bellham, in his Reign of George the Third) in portraying the horrid deeds of our countrymen in India, and the calamitous state to which that country was reduced, through their oppressions, thus expresses himself: "Striking, indeed, is the contrast between the situation of the country at this period, and that, which we were told it enjoyed, in the *happy times of the Mogul Government*. The kingdom of Bengal during a long period of peaceful repose is described as (*then*) exhibiting the most charming and picturesque scenery, opening into extensive glades, covered with a fine turf, and interspersed with woods, *filled with a variety of birds of beautiful colours; among others peacocks in abundance*, sitting on the vast horizontal branches, displayed their dazzling plumes to the sun." &c.

The benevolent reader will be happy to learn from the account of the Rajah, confirmed by the views of a late ingenious traveler (Mr. Hodges) that the race of peacocks has not been *utterly exterminated* by the cruel rapacity of the British Governors of Bengal! If the misrepresentations of credulity had been always restrained to external objects, their confutation would have been an easy task. But who can follow the historian, who pretends to expose the secret workings of the human mind and pursues the victim of his prejudice even to the throne of God! Who, speaking of the unfortunate death of a man, whose services had been an acknowledged benefit to his country, could presume to say that though acquitted at the highest human tribunal, he could not acquit himself, *or hope for acquital at that far more awful tribunal at which he dreaded to appear!*" History of the Reign of George the Third, vol. i, page 355.

Instead of the quotation from Persius, we would rather conclude such a sentence with the lines of Pope,

> Let not this weak unknowing hand,
> Presume thy bolts to throw,
> Or deal damnation o'er the land
> On each I judge thy foe. [E.H.]

Hamilton is referring to the comments on Robert Clive in William Belsham's *Memoirs of the Reign of George III to the session of Parliament ending A.D. 1793*, 4 vols (London 1795). Belsham presents Clive as being tormented by secret guilt for his

A walk to the next village was proposed, and agreed to by all the party, excepting one little fat man, who seemed, upon all occasions, to make the study of his own ease the principal object of his concern: and whose extreme selfishness had given frequent disgust to all his fellow voyagers. To him young Cooper attached himself, declaring that he could not think of leaving alone, in a strange country so valuable a gentleman. Pleased at this instance of his benevolence, we commended his good-nature, and proceeded on our walk.

Following the course of the transparent Nullah,[1] on whose banks we had landed, we soon arrived at a small village, most of whose peaceful inhabitants we found busied at their looms, beneath the friendly shade of a far spreading banyan. In one of the hundred arbours formed by the descending branches, sat a musician, who softly touched the chords of a veena: to the sweet sound of which, the women, and children, were listening with mute attention.

Our approach presented a new object to their curiosity. The music had ceased; but was renewed at the request of Captain Grey, who entreated we might give no interruption, either to their labours, or amusement.

Mean time the Chief of the village drew near, to perform the duties of hospitality. A young officer, who saw him advancing, hastily enquired, in English, whether we could be supplied with milk from the village? "Archa Sahib, tamorrow Mulluk,"[2] replied the villager, making a profound reverence. "To-morrow won't do for us, friend," replied the Officer, "we can't stay here all night." And returning to Captain Grey, "we have had a fruitless errand," said he, "for the old man here, says, we can have no milk till to-morrow."

The poor fellow, who had been greatly mortified by the abrupt

---

rapacity, despite being cleared by Parliament, then, in a note, quotes the Roman satirist Persius and Dryden's translation of that satire (iii) — which concludes with a wish that God will punish an avaricious tyrant by "mak[ing] him pale to see / His gains immense outweigh'd by lost felicity" (lines 37-8). Hamilton's retort is from Pope's "Universal Prayer," lines 25-28. The italicized phrase "utterly exterminated" would recall the controversy over the Rohilla War, as Hastings supposedly ordered the troops to "exterminate" the Rohillas, instructions which his defenders argued hotly meant only to send them beyond the boundaries of Rohilkhand.

1   Small streams. [E.H.]
2   Is not this your country – command in it what you please! [E.H.]

manner in which the gentleman had received his offered civilities, now repeated them to Captain Grey in the same terms, who laughed very heartily at his friend, for suffering the casual resemblance between the sound of an English and a Bengal word to lead him into such a mistake.

Having received from the village an ample supply of the articles we wanted, we returned, in search of our friends, followed by a train of villagers loaded with milk, eggs, fruit, &c.

We soon reached the Mango grove, but what was our surprise, on entering it, to see the poor fat gentleman straining his unwieldy limbs to grasp the trunk of a large tree, which he was attempting to climb as fast as his untoward bulk would permit. Panting for breath, he cast a look of despair on young Cooper, who sat perching on a bough of the same tree above; and whose voice we heard from a considerable distance, vehemently urging his corpulent companion to proceed: "but two or three feet farther, my dear sir, and you will be out of all danger," cried he. The poor gentleman made an effort but slipped back into the same situation. "One other attempt, for heaven's sake, my dear sir," resumed Cooper, "or the tyger will lay hold of your poor limbs." "Gracious heaven!" cried the gentleman, in agony. At these words, he cast a glance around which was fully descriptive of the horrors of his situation. On perceiving us, he shouted out, that Cooper had seen a tyger: beseeching us, at the same time to assist him, and to take care of ourselves. Captain Grey, who immediately apprehended some trick of young Cooper, enquired of the villagers, whether any tyger had been lately seen in the neighbourhood? and, being answered in the negative, he prevailed on the poor gentleman to descend. On further investigation, it appeared that the young gentleman had been seized with a paroxysm of his disease in our absence, and that the story of the tyger had been invented by him, in order to throw his poor unsuspecting companion into the awkward situation in which we found him; and of which he produced, next morning, so admirable a drawing, as excited a laughter in all who saw it: from me, I confess, it extorted an unwilling smile. But these Europeans do not seem to think the entertainment that is purchased at the expense of the feelings of another, is too dearly paid for.

We arrived at Calcutta in the night, and went directly to the house of a friend of Captain Grey's, where, according to the rules of hospitality, established in this place, we were both invited to take up our abode.

The Governor General is now in the country, and as it is not proper that I should appear, til' after I have been introduced to him, I shall have nothing of any consequence to write for some days.

⌐≈≈≈≈≈⌐

IT has always been my intention to communicate to you a faithful copy of the first impression made upon my mind, by every new object presented to it; but knowing the aptitude of ignorance to fall into the path of error, I am not without apprehensions, that, while I intend to inform I may possibly mislead. This shall not, however, deter me from pursuing my plan, but only render me more careful in forming my judgment.

Experience has already taught me, that the conclusions, which are formed with precipitance, are almost always retracted with shame: thus, for instance, when I hear these Christians introducing, in familiar conversation, the name of their *Almighty Creator*, upon the most trifling occasions; nay, sometimes, as it would appear, merely to supply the lack of matter, and to fill the chasms of conversation; I can scarcely forbear from accusing them of impiety. But a moment's reflection convinces me of the absurdity of supposing that they, who boast the light and privileges of a divine revelation, can be guilty of irreverence to the Supreme! I therefore conclude, that when these Christians pronounce with so much ease, *that Name*, which is held, by every pious Hindoo, in too great reverence to be uttered, except upon the gravest and most solemn occasions; and which no faithful Mussulman was ever known to pronounce, without a pause, it is from a consciousness of their own superior piety, which they, doubtless, imagine, entitles them to this degree of familiarity with their Maker.

Another instance of the same kind has occurred to me, in an expression much in use, the meaning of which, on applying to the Dictionary, I found to be that of *the eternal punishment of the soul in hell!* I shuddered to think, how often I had heard this dreadful doom pronounced by some of my fellow travelers, not only on their own souls, but on that of many of their brethren! but, on more maturely considering the matter, I found it more agreeable to the precepts of their religion, as well as to the dictates of common sense, to conclude, that in my imperfect knowledge of the language, the negative had escaped me and thus, what sounded in my ears as the most dreadful imprecation, was, in reality, an ejaculation uttered in the spirit of that charity, which teaches them to pray for their enemies even in the moment of wrath. Looking upon it in this *proper* light, I could not but admire the fervor with which I last night heard many petitions of this kind preferred for the soul of a General Officer, who had introduced certain regulations into the service, by which these gentlemen considered themselves aggrieved. And I make no doubt, that had the animadversions of these young men been reported to him, he would have had the charity to pray for them with similar fervency!

⬩⬩⬩

"A GREAT man," saith he whose words are incomparable as wisdom, "should speak kindly, without meanness; he should be valiant, without boasting; he should be generous, shedding his bounty into the dish of the worthy; he should be resolute, but not rash." This is the character of a great man![1] And such a one have I this day seen.

It would be vain to attempt describing to you my feelings, while I stood in the presence of this truly exalted personage. Of him, who, uniting the lofty spirit of the renowned Acbar,[2] with the penetrating, and comprehensive genius of his still more renowned minister, has shewn himself superior to both, in schemes of sound and extensive policy; as well as in that pure, and blessed spirit of humanity, which has distinguished every act of his administration.

The pious Hindoo, no longer forced to submit to laws, that are repugnant to the spirit of his faith; no longer judged by the unhallowed ordinances of strangers, beholds with extatic gratitude, the holy Shaster rising, at the command of his enlightened Governor, to be once more the standard of his obedience.

---

1   See Hetopades. [E.H.] 210–11 (1885 ed). Hamilton misquotes slightly; in Wilkins the final words are "resolute but not harsh."

2   The Emperor Acbar was the contemporary of our Queen Elizabeth, and is one of the few monarchs on whose character posterity can dwell with feelings of respect and admiration. The choice of such a minister as the great Abual Fazel, is a sufficient proof of his penetration. Kindred souls naturally discover each other. [E.H] See 133, note 3.

The same benevolence, which has restored to our nation the invaluable privilege of being tried by our own laws, has projected the extension of the same favour to the Mohamaden inhabitants of Hindostan. A translation of the Hedaya, both into the Persian and English languages, I am well assured, is about to take place, and thus the haughty Mussulman will receive, from Christian magnanimity, a degree of favour and protection, which the laws of his Prophet never taught him to bestow! Surely, one such act is worth a thousand of those deeds of heroes, whose fame is written in letters of blood, upon the fields of desolation! just as it is said, that "truth being weighed against a thousand *Ashmavedajugs*, was found to be of more consequence than the thousand offerings."[1]

At the house of the Governor General, I was introduced, by Captain Grey, to several gentlemen, both in the civil and military departments. They were all extremely kind, and obliging to me, and appeared to be no strangers to those laws of hospitality, of which our nation has long considered itself as the exclusive possessor.

I was invited by the Governor General himself to a notch, or, as they express it, *a ball*, which was to be given in the evening, in a house appropriated to that purpose. On enquiry, I found that the dancers were to be all *English*; a circumstance that delighted me, as I have hitherto had no opportunity of seeing any of their females.

I waited with impatience for the hour which was to take us to the place appointed: but as neither Captain Grey, nor any of his friends, had the same degree of curiosity, the greater part of the company were assembled before we reached the room. When we entered it, amazement, and delight, took possession of my soul. It is impossible to convey to you, by words, any idea of the beautiful objects that surrounded me: but you may judge of the transcendent power of their charms, when I tell you, that they shone forth with invincible lustre, in spite of the deformity of a dress, which appears to have been invented by envy, with an intention of disfiguring the fairest works of nature. These lovely creatures, to the number of about one hundred, were seated on benches in the European fashion, and smiled, and talked to the gentlemen who addressed them, with great spirit, and

---

1  *Hitopadesa* 276 (1885 ed; with slight variations).

vivacity: but this I did not wonder at; as I had been told by Grey, that they all either *were*, or, *had been Dancers*: and you know, women of that profession are seldom at a loss for conversation.

The great man having entered, and received the compliments of the company after the manner of his nation, which consists of very little ceremony, the dancing commenced. But judge of my astonishment, when I beheld the dancing girls led out – not by their masters – but – debasing meanness! each by an English Chief! Sincere as my respect for the Governor General certainly is, I could not restrain my indignation at seeing Chiefs, and military Commanders of high rank and authority, thus publicly degrading themselves by dancing for his amusement. How inconsistent, thought I, is the conduct of mortals! These men, who plume themselves upon their notions of liberty, and independence, submit, without reluctance, to an indignity, to which the Omrahs of the empire, who, in the days of its greatness, surrounded the royal Musmud,[1] and prostrated themselves to salute the dust, which was shaken from the feet of royalty, would sooner have died than have submitted! Though, on the part of the English Chiefs, it appeared entirely voluntary, yet I thought I could perceive that many of them felt sufficient repugnance to this degrading business, which they went through with that sort of heroic apathy and indifference, which you have beheld in, a criminal of our nation when about to be hanged. Indeed, I never saw a dance so very little amusing. The gestures of the women were as little graceful as their dress; and had it not been for the extreme beauty of their countenances, I confess, I should soon have been tired with looking at them.

A gentleman, whom I had seen in the morning, told me, that his wife wished to be introduced to me. The request surprised me; but as I knew the gentleman to be a personage of high rank and character, I prepared to follow him. He conducted me to the opposite side of the room, and led me up to a group of Bibbys, whom I had mistaken for superannuated dancing girls, but whom I now, to my infinite astonishment, discovered to be the wives of men of rank and eminence, whose names, according to the custom of their country, they bore.

---

1 An Omrah is "a lord or grandee of a Mohammedan court, esp. that of the great Mogul" (*OED*); a "musmud" is "a seat made of cushions, esp. one used as a throne by the native princes of India" (*OED*).

I could not find myself in the presence of these ladies without experiencing a considerable degree of embarrassment; this was by no means the case with them; like other females, they all spoke at once, and seemed endowed with much loquacity. They looked at me with steady countenances, totally devoid of that modest timidity, which is the most inestimable gem in female beauty. That glare of colouring, which, at first sight, caught my soul in the net of astonishment, lost, by degrees, its power of enchantment. And as the nightingale,[1] after having viewed, with short-lived rapture, the splendour of the gaudy tulip, returns with fresh delight to the contemplation of his beloved rose; so did my soul, in the midst of this blaze of western beauty, turn to the remembrance of the gentle graces, and endearing charms of my beloved Prymaveda! The loveliness of eyes, sparkling in beauty, may attract our admiration, but the bare recollection of those which beamed with the softness of tender affection, is yet more precious to the soul!

Lost in these reflections, I became insensible to the scene around me; and incommoded by the extreme heat of the room, I took the first opportunity of departing. The green horses of Surraya had seen me perform my morning ablutions in the sacred stream, before my friend Grey returned from this nocturnal festival.

⟅⟆

I KNOW you would deem it an unpardonable neglect, should I say nothing to you of the city itself; which, under the auspices of him who is the liberal patron of every useful and every elegant art, is already become worthy of being the capitol of an empire.

Calcutta presents to the eye of a stranger, a spectacle, delightful from its novelty, and amusing from the variety of its scenes. This city which so short a time since as the Subahship of Cossim Ally Cawn,[2]

---

1    This simile, the Rajah seems to have borrowed from the Persian. Of all the poetical fables of the East, none is so frequently alluded to, in the composition of the Persian writers, as that which supposes the nightingale to be violently enamoured with the rose. [E.H.] Hamilton would have known a poem by Hafiz of Shiraz on that subject.

2    "After the British breach faith with this Nabob [Cossim Ally Cawn], the British commanders defeated and pursued him out of Behar, compelling him to seek refuge in the neighbouring province of Oude." (*An Historical Relation of the Rohilla Afgans* 154). A subahship was the governorship of a province (*OED*).

consisted of nothing more than a mean fort, and a few surrounding huts, now sees rows of magnificent palaces, adorned by all the beauties of architecture, stretching along the banks of this favoured Mouth of the Ganges, to the distance of several miles. The extent, and grandeur, of the fortress, have never failed to impress the Asiatic beholder with sentiments of awe, and admiration; but all the descriptions we have received tended rather to give an idea of its strength, than beauty: it is pre-eminent in both: and when the eye surveys, even but a part of this grand and massy structure, taking in, at the same glance, a view of the elegant buildings of the town, separated from each other by gardens, rich in vegetable beauty, the silver current of the river, as it is partially seen, gliding between the ships of every colour, shape, and nation, which here wave their various streamers on its bosom; it is impossible for imagination to conceive a sight more charming. Add to this, the variety to be seen in the streets, where you behold a concourse of people, whose dress, complexion, religion, and manners, all differ widely from each other: and whose numbers are so nearly equalled, that it is impossible to say who is the stranger. All appear to be at home. Here the holy Fakeer, with no other dress than a piece of muslin wrapped round his lean and shrivelled limbs, walks with folded arms, ruminating on some passage of the holy Shaster, and striving, by penance and mortification, to facilitate the moment of absorption and unchanging bliss. There the turbaned Mussulman, from the top of an adjoining minorat, adjures the followers of Mahomet to attend the hours of devotion in the holy Mosque; while the stately Armenian, the money changing Jew, and the no less money-loving Englishman, mingle on the beach; too intent on their affairs of traffic, to listen to any voice save that which calls to the temple of Lacshmi.

European chariots, various in their form, and elegant in their structure, drawn by horses decked in silver studded harness, glide like meteors along the streets; passing, in their career, the country hackery,[1] the heavy loaded camel, and even the majestic, but unwieldy, elephant, who turning up his great proboscis, wonders at the noise and bustle which surrounds him.

---

1 Small covered carts, drawn by bullocks, which are in general use all over India. [E.H.]

SHALL Ignorance be for ever leading me into error? And shall experience never be able to defend me against the dangers of misconception, and mistake? I this morning accompanied Captain Grey into the country, in an open vehicle, called a Buggy, drawn by one horse, which he himself drove. It was the first opportunity we had for conversation, since the Governor's notch; and he was anxious to know my opinion of it. "What do you think of the ladies," cried he; "did you not think some of them very beautiful?" I answered, "that as to beauty, I must confess, I thought the ladies had but a slender share in every respect, *bloom* only excepted, compared to that which adorned the dancing girls; they, indeed, were beautiful!" "'Tis them I mean," returned he; "you do not think I could expect you to admire the old painted witches; to whom —— introduced you?" "I could never have thought of giving the appellation of ladies to dancing girls," returned I gravely. "Dancing girls!" repeated he, bursting into a fit of laughter, "Why the ladies, whom you saw dance, were many of them, married ladies, of rank and distinction; the lovely Mrs. ★★★, and her still more lovely sister, were of that number." "Is it possible," cried I, "that men of rank can basely contaminate their honour, by suffering their wives and daughters to stoop to the degrading employment of dancers to the G. G—." "Why," returned Grey almost suffocated with laughter, "do you imagine they danced to please him?" "Whom should you all dance to please, but him," rejoined I, peevishly, a little picqued by the excess of his mirth. "Forgive me, dear Zāārmilla," returned my companion; "I confess nothing could be more natural than your mistake: I certainly ought to have informed you, that dancing is a favourite amusement in Europe; it forms part of the education of both sexes, and to dance gracefully, is an accomplishment on which women are taught to set a very high value: nor is it without reason that it is thus esteemed, for nothing sets off the charms of a fine woman to greater advantage. Did you not remark the young lady in the blue and silver?" continued he. "The elegance of her figure, the gracefulness of all her motions, the animation that sparkled in her eye, and the sensibility that glowed in her countenance. Never did —" but here a sudden stop was put to the harangue: in the vehemence of his description, my friend had neglected the management of the reins; the wheels of the carriage were intercepted by the stump of a decayed tree, and the horse, impatient of the interruption, begun to fret, and rear, till the love pierced charioteer, applying his whip to the unfortunate animal, forced him to make a sudden spring, which at once extricated him from confinement, and broke the carriage to pieces. We were both thrown to a considerable distance, and though neither of us received any material injury, we were sufficiently bruised to make us remember *the lady in the blue and silver* for some days to come.

⸙

IT is upon those subjects which particularly excite my curiosity, that I find it most difficult to procure information. Captain Grey, who is always willing to oblige me, when I call upon him for instruction, is naturally of so silent a disposition, that I fear to trouble him by a multiplicity of questions. When, happily, he, of his own accord, engages in conversation, he appears to possess a mind, enriched by the ore of knowledge; adorned by the gem of taste; and enlightened by the steady torch of intellect.

The war, in which his nation is at present engaged, is a subject he seems particularly assiduous to avoid: for, alas! my friend, it must be confessed to thee, that these Christians do not always as I have hitherto supposed, carry arms only to redress the wrongs of the injured, to assert the cause of the oppressed, or to defend themselves from the invaders of their country; – they actually make war *upon one another!*[1]

I have, in vain, sought in their Shaster for some precept that might give a sanction to this custom, for some incident, in the life of their great Teacher, that might afford a precedent for human butchery. But, no. Whether I turn to the life and conversation of the Founder, or to the precepts and example of his first followers, I find but one spirit – the spirit of peace, of love, the meekness of charity, and the magnanimity of forgiveness. How then, comes War? that scourge of mankind! nurse of guilt! and parent of desolation! How comes it to be

---

1    The war in which England "is at present engaged" in 1779 or 1780 was, of course, the American Revolution, which (as Captain Grey's silence implies) was not popular with certain segments of the English public. When the novel was published in 1796, England was also in the third year of a war with France, one which lasted with only brief interruptions until 1815.

practised by the professors of a religion, which proclaimed "peace on earth, and good-will toward the children of men?" I confess that this question has greatly puzzled me; and I can solve it in no other way, than by supposing, that the Christian Shaster, presented me by Percy, is *not complete*: and that an additional revelation hath, in after times, been afforded to these Christians: in which supplement to the Gospels, it is ordained, that when a sufficient number of Christian men are united together, to form an army, a brigade, or any other military division; and are dressed in a particular colour, blue, or scarlet, or a mixture of both, they shall be licensed to commit murder, at the command, and by the authority, of their *religious* superiors (provided they are in the regular receipt of pay for so doing); and that all the slaughter, blood-shed, and devastation, so committed upon their *Christian brethren* (for whose salvation they believe a Saviour to have descended from above and in whose society they hope to live for ever in the Kingdom of Heaven) shall no longer be termed, Murder; but Glory!

<hr />

BY whom was constructed that jewel of a word, that monosyllable, friend?[1] Praise to Veeshnû, for the letter I have just received from thee. It was brought by the Dauk from Benares, and its presence refreshes my soul.

Your apprehensions of the inconveniences to which you think I must be subjected, among these Christians, are without foundation. It is true, I meet with many things that would greatly shock me, did I not consider, that that variety of manners, as well as of sentiments, which is pleasing to the superior divinities, ought not to be displeas-ing to us. I nevertheless cannot be easily reconciled to that custom of devouring the flesh of so many innocent, and unoffending animals, whose lives are daily sacrificed, in order to procure a short-lived, and inelegant enjoyment, to the vitiated palates of these voluptuaries. The injustice done to these animals, is, however, amply revenged, by the quantities of the liquors, which it is the custom to swallow at the conclusion of their cruel feasts; and which, when taken in great quan-tities, seldom fails to pervert the senses, and reduce the reason to a temporary level with the victims of their gluttony.

In regard to the ceremonies of the Christian religion, of

---

1  Hetopades. [E.H.] Page 95 (1885).

which you want to be informed, I am sorry I cannot satisfy your curiosity. Were I unacquainted with the peculiar precepts of their Shaster, I should be surprised at the little appearance of devotion that is to be observed among them; but knowing that it is expressly commanded them to "pray in secret,"[1] and not appear unto men to fast, my wonder is changed into admiration at the strictness and punctuality with which they adhere to the precept! The same secrecy is, indeed enjoined them with regard to their acts of charity, but it must be confessed that, in this particular, they are not quite so scrupulous.

I yesterday accompanied Captain Grey to a hall, called a coffee-house, where it is the custom for gentlemen to meet and converse on business, or politics. We no sooner entered, than I observed the eyes of my companions to fix upon a young man of about seventeen or eighteen years, who sat in a corner of the room, apparently retiring from observation. Melancholy and dejection were painted on a countenance, which the hand of nature had endowed with manly beauty. The meanness of his attire proclaimed him to be no favourite of Lackshmi, but his air seemed suited to a better garb. Captain Grey took up a printed paper, which lay before him, but his eyes were frequently turned toward the youth, and his mind appeared absorbed in reflection. A person, at length, entered, who addressed the young man, by the name of Morton. "Morton!" repeated Grey, springing toward the youth, his eyes glistening with pleasure, and his manly countenance animated by the glow which warmed his bosom, "Morton," repeated he, "was the name of my first friend, my worthy tutor; and every feature tells me, that you, sir, must be his son." "The reverend Mr. Morton, of —— , was my father," returned the young man. "Then you are the son of my old friend," cried Grey, taking the young man by the hand; "and you must look on me as a brother: but this is no place," continued he, "to have all my questions answered; you must come home with me, and let me hear every particular respecting the situation of your family, and especially that of your worthy father, who, I hope, is yet alive?" "Alas! No;" returned Morton: "it pleased heaven to take him from us upward of ten months ago." The tear of filial sensibility, which trembled in the eye of Morton, appeared to be infectious; my friend Grey seemed afraid of

1   Matthew 6:6

it; and taking the young man by the arm, he instantly led him to the house that is now our home.

On our arrival there, he engaged the young man to give him a recital of all that had befallen his family, since the period in which he had been under the tuition of his father. The relation was short, and simple.

His father, who it seems was a priest of the order of *Curates* (for so, at my request, he wrote the word) had, in his old age, been assailed by disease, and afflicted by poverty: death, at length, came to his release, and sent him to obtain the reward of virtue in the region of felicity.

The young man, after this event, proposed to visit India; hoping, that in a region, which since the foundation of the world has been pouring out treasures to enrich the various countries of the earth, he might acquire a competence for the support of his mother and sisters. With the reluctance of a fond parent, struggling between the dictates of prudence, and the yearnings of affection, his mother at length yielded to his entreaty. She was the sooner induced to do so, from the consideration of the many affluent relations she had in the capital; all of whom, she fondly hoped, would strain every nerve to promote the interest of her son. To all these affluent relations, she wrote on his behalf, requesting from them letters of introduction to some of the great Chiefs in India, and having presented him with these harbingers of future fortune, she suffered him to depart, loaded with maternal blessings. On his arrival at the capital, which they call London, he did not fail to visit those relations on whom depended his prospects of future felicity.

Some of them, having been under peculiar obligations to his father, would, he doubted not, rejoice in this opportunity of discharging their debt of gratitude; but it unfortunately happened, that he never could find any of them at home.

After repeated disappointments, he wrote to each of them, enclosing his mother's letters to them; and after many days of anxious solicitude, he received the answers of those on whom his hopes had been principally placed. They all grieved at not having it in their power to serve him: they could not but be sorry, extremely sorry, that he had set out in the most unlucky moment possible: for one had just procured an appointment for the son of his taylor, and could not again trouble his friends in power with a similar application. Another had lately made it a point never to solicit any thing, for any person out of his own family. A third, had given up, some years ago, all correspondence with India; and a fourth, had made a recent vow, never to plague his friends with letters of introduction. Mortified, and dispirited, with these various disappointments, he was on the point of giving up the pursuit; when his landlady, who had formerly lived in his father's parish, informed him that her daughter's husband had a friend, who was intimately acquainted with a butcher, who had a vote in a borough, of which one of the Directors of that company of Merchants, who have become the Sovereigns of so great a part of India,[1] was the representative; by this train of interest she hoped to do something for him. (The good woman's hopes, and honest endeavours, were not frustrated.) Through the friend of her daughter's husband she procured for him an introduction to the slayer of cattle, who prevailed with the Director, to favour the Curate's son with a letter of introduction to one of the English Chiefs at this place; and, at the same time, gave him an order for his passage in one of the Company's ships.

His sufferings on the voyage were many, but his ardour was invincible. Immediately on his arrival at Calcutta, he presented the letter, on which was founded all his future, hopes; but, alas! what was his mortification, on being told, by the great man to whom it was addressed, that it was only one of a hundred applications of the same kind, the twentieth part of which it was utterly impossible for him to attend to!

In a land of strangers, without friends, and without bread, too modest to solicit and too proud to bear the harshness of repulse, without feeling its indignity, is it to be wondered that he was reduced to despondency?

It was at this period, in the moment of dejection and despair that he was discovered by the worthy friend of Percy, in whom he has, indeed, found a brother.

This incident seems to have entirely banished that silence, and reserve, which I have hitherto considered as natural to the temper of my friend. Roused by the ardour of friendship, he exerted, in its

---

1   A reference to the East India Company, which was, at the time of writing, trans-
    forming itself from a mercantile institution to a government.

cause, all his eloquence and activity; and, in two days, procured for the young man an appointment, which will soon enable him to return the obligation he owes to paternal tenderness, with the substantial proofs of filial affection.

⁂

I HAVE for some days laboured under an indisposition, which has kept me from going abroad. The most mortifying circumstance attending my confinement, is the deprivation of the pleasure I promised myself, in accompanying Grey to the houses of some noble Saibs, where numbers of Bibbies were assembled. By the accounts received from him, on his return from these parties, I could easily perceive that the remembrance of the bruises, we received in our fall, had not been able to give him any antipathy to the lady in the *blue and silver*. As often as he was disappointed in his expectations of seeing her at any of those feasts, the disappointment was visible in his countenance, and he cut short all enquiries, by declaring, that the visit had been *very stupid*. But if the evening was spent in her presence, hilarity smiled in every feature, and joyfulness beamed from his eyelids.

I longed to see a female, capable of making so deep an impression, on a mind so solid; and as soon as I was able to go abroad, I accepted, with eagerness, an invitation to the house of a friend, where she, and many other ladies, were expected to spend the evening. Captain Grey had, in his impatience, ordered our Pallenkeens[1] at so early an hour, that we were at his friend's house long before any other guest appeared. The ladies, at length, came; and I recognized the features of several whom I had seen at the notch; but methought they appeared more modest, as well as more beautiful, than when I mistook them for dancing girls, so much is our Opinion under the dominion of our imagination. I was now eager to listen to their discourse, and delighted in the expectation of hearing words of wisdom proceeding from the lips of beauty. Wise might be the words they uttered, and truly edifying their conversation; but unhappily for me, I was too ignorant of the topics they discussed, to receive much benefit.

---

1 A covered chair carried on poles by four bearers (*OED*).

Two ladies, who had just arrived from England, engrossed the greatest share of the discourse: innumerable questions were put to them, which they answered with great quickness and volubility. In the course of their conversation, frequent mention was made of *public places*; by which I understand institutions, similar to those formerly established at Athens, where the renowned Socrates, Plato, Zeno, &c. initiated their disciples in the mysteries of wisdom and philosophy. Whatever are the sciences taught at those modern seminaries of taste and learning, the minds of these ladies seemed to have acquired the most lively relish for them; and the name of Vestris[1] (who I take to be one of the principal of their instructors) was never mentioned without the epithet of delightful! charming! divine!

It is not surprising, that to these females, so well instructed, so learned, and sedate, should be entrusted the most important concerns of the state. Such an one's having *had an affair* with a certain great man, was frequently mentioned: but so great was the modesty of these ladies, that not one of them ever hinted at having *had an affair* with any great man herself.

While I was employed in listening to this conversation, my friend Grey was too much occupied with the young lady, whose charms had captivated his heart, to pay attention to any other object. In conversing with her, he seemed inspired with unusual eloquence; and I was happy to perceive that the fair maiden appeared not insensible to his attention; but smiled upon him with angel-like sweetness, and complacency.

I have already observed to you, that nothing can be more awkward, and ungraceful, than the dress of these females; their robes, instead of falling in easy and graceful folds around their limbs, are extended on huge frames, made of bamboo, or some similar material, and gives to their figure very much the shape of a Moor Punky.[2] The

---

1   A celebrated Opera Dancer. [E.H.] Possibly Gaëtan Vestris (1729? – 1808), or more likely his son Auguste Vestris (1760–1842). Both father and son appeared on the London stage for the first time in the 1780–81 season, and the son, in particular, won considerable admiration. Hamilton is slightly askew in her dating here, as anyone who had witnessed the sensation caused by the younger Vestris during his initial London season could not, of course, have been discussing it in Calcutta in 1779 or 80.

2   A country vessel of a peculiar construction, used for the conveyance of cotton and other bulky articles. [E.H.]

only useful ornament they have, is a Choury,[1] which, instead of being carried in the hands of their attendants, is stuck in the heads of the ladies, where, by the continual motion, it is of great utility in driving off the flies, which are here much more troublesome and offensive than in Kuttaher.

After some time was spent in conversation, many of the company sat down to cards: that which Sheermaal ignorantly pronounced *a species of worship*; being, in reality, no other than an amusement, invented by the Europeans, as chess was by our ancestors, for the pastime of the rich, and idle. Judge, then, what degree of credit is due to the representations of that arrogant Bramin, when he asserts, that many of the females of the West, make this pastime the chief business of their existence, sacrificing to it the duties they owe to society, as wives, as mothers, as rational and intelligent creatures. Base slanderer! how little doth he know of the ladies of England!

⟨⟩

I HAVE omitted no opportunity of procuring from the young friend of Captain Grey, some degree of information respecting the order of the Priesthood, to which his father belonged. These Priests, when spoken of collectively, are called *the Church*; and have the precedence of the Sovereign, as may be inferred from the usual mode of expression, *Church and King*.

From the conversation of Morton and his friend, I am convinced that to preserve the primitive purity of their religion, is the first object of attention to the English Government. To ascertain the virtues of those, who are devoted to the sacred function, they are destined to undergo trials of no common kind. Worldly riches and honours are held out, not as rewards to virtue; but rather as means of proving the degree of pride, venality, hypocrisy, meanness, &c. of the individuals; and as they are carefully withheld from all, who have not given unequivocal proofs of some of these qualifications, men of modest virtue, and rigid integrity, run no risk of being spoiled by the pomps and vanities of this wicked world.

By these humble, and lowly men, are performed all the most sacred and important duties of their function. These instruct the

---

1   A bunch of feathers used to drive away the flies. [E.H.] In the late eighteenth century, fashionable ladies often wore plumes in their hair when in formal dress.

ignorant, comfort the afflicted, visit the sick. It is the prayers of these, which ascend to the throne of the Eternal; and it is these, likewise, who from their slender store, impart relief to the children of indigence.

Such were the duties performed by the father of Mr. Morton, who, according to Grey, added to the virtues of a Christian Priest, the learning of a true philosopher. This excellent man was never molested by the offer of what is called *preferment*, but was permitted to exert his superiour talents and virtues in a state of poverty, equal to that of the first teachers of Christianity.

Thus is the purity of the Priesthood preserved. The least worthy of its members are provided for in this world; and those, whose labours have been truly beneficial to mankind, who have diffused knowledge by their writings; inspired the love of virtue, by their precepts; and taught the practice of it, by their example, are permitted to look for their reward in the world to come!

<hr/>

"IN this world," says the philosopher, "the wealthy are every one, every where, and at all times, powerful. Riches being the foundation of preferment, and an introduction to the favour of the Prince."[1] It is likewise, here, a necessary introduction to the favour of the ladies.

My poor friend Grey returned this morning from the house, which is the residence of his charmer, in a state of indescribable agitation. Vexation, displeasure, and disappointment, were written in such legible characters on his countenance, that they could neither be concealed, nor mistaken. I soon discovered that his uneasiness had arisen from that sex, whose fickleness, and infidelity, have been the theme of the satirists of a thousand generations.

We are told, by the sages, "that women have been at all times inconstant, even among the celestials; and that the security for their virtue, is neither a precise behaviour, nor a modest countenance, but depends solely on the want of suitors."[2] These are words of gall, flow-

<hr/>

1   See Hetopades. [E.H.] Page 69 (1885).
2   See Hetopades. [E.H.] Page 67 (1885). The quotation in the next paragraph presents an idea that appears frequently in the *Hitopadesa*, that people foolishly make riches count more than any other qualities.

ing from the heart of the disappointed! It was not, however, on the fickleness of the sex, that my friend poured forth the invectives of his wrath; it was upon their avarice, and ambition.

Had I given credit to his assertions, I should have considered all the young Bibbies of Calcutta, as votaries of Lackshmi; and that, with them, "no man is handsome, none ugly, none virtuous, valiant, or wise, *but as he is rich.*"

The smiles of the lady in the blue and silver, which gladdened the heart of my friend, were not bestowed upon him, but upon the fortune, which, by the mischeivous folly of young Cooper, she was led to imagine he possessed. Charmed by her affability, and misled by the complacency with which she received his attentions, my friend assured himself of having a place in her heart. His fortune is not large, but he imagined it sufficient to preclude every inconvenience; and indulged himself, in forming the most enchanting picture of domestic felicity. He went out this morning, with an intention of imparting his scheme of happiness to her, on whose approbation it was to depend. He was chagrined, at hearing she was not at home: but was met at the gate, by the master of the house, who is brother-in-law to the lady, and who politely entreated him to return. How great was his surprise, on entering the apartment, to which he was led by the gentleman, to see the fair object of his passion, seated beside a rich civilian, to whom fortune has made amends for the sparing boons of nature; and on whom, the young Bibby smiled with the sweetest complacency. Poor Grey, stunned by this appearance, was yet more embarrassed by the distant coldness with which she returned his salutations. He did not long remain in a situation so cruelly mortifying, but casting a look of contempt on his mistress, hastily withdrew.

He was met, in the anti-chamber, by young Cooper, who, reading in the countenance of the rejected lover all that had passed, burst into a loud laugh. "So, she has discovered the trick," cried he, "I could lay a hundred guineas, by the woeful length of your countenance, that she has found us out." Grey, who was in no humour to be trifled with, quickly put an end to his mirth, and forced from him an explanation of the circumstances to which he alluded. Cooper confessed to him, that the very evening on which the lady was first introduced to his acquaintance, he had mentioned him to her, as the worthy possessor of *many lacks.*

Piqued at being thus made the dupe of the mischievous trick of a boy, and the scorn of an ambitious woman, he rails at the whole sex, without considering, that the disappointment is, most frequently, the "fruit of the tree of our own planting."[1] He knew not the character of this damsel – but she was beautiful; and he assured himself it must be excellent! He knew not from whom her mind had received the light of instruction – but she danced gracefully; and he gave her credit for every accomplishment. She smiled upon him – and was it possible to doubt her discernment? The qualities, which alone constitute the affectionate wife, the faithful friend, the tender mother, were the spontaneous offspring of his own impassioned fancy. Born of error, how could they be expected to live to maturity?

This affair has given me much pain, on account of the wound it has inflicted on the feelings of my friend; and, for my own part, I grieve to find, that these lovely females of England, are not totally free from imperfection!

Having just had notice, of an opportunity of dispatching this packet, I hastily bring it to a conclusion.

May the errors of others teach us wisdom, and while the waters of experience flow through our hearts, may they fructify and enrich the soil! The blessing of thy father rest upon thee.

What can I say more?

---

1   Compare *Hitopadesa*: "Sickness, sorrow, and distress; bonds and punishment to corporeal beings, are the fruit of the tree of their own transgressions" (page 41 [1885]).

# LETTER XI

*From the* SAME, *to the* SAME.

SINCE I last held the reed that is dedicated to friendship, my soul has been tossed in the whirlwind of conflicting passions. My desires have been at variance with each other. Friendship calls me to Almora, while the insatiable thirst of curiosity, the love of knowledge, and of novelty, all unite in prompting me to the hazardous undertaking of an European voyage.

Full of dangers, and of difficulties, as this step may appear to you, no obstacle presents itself to my view, half so formidable as thy disapprobation. But why should a difference of opinion between men of sound principles cause a breach of friendship? "*The stalk of the Lotus may be broken, and the fibres remain connected*": and are not the fibres of affection, that unite our hearts, of a stronger texture?

Let not the length of the voyage, or the consideration of its dangers, give any uneasiness to the breast of my friend; for "what is too great a load for those who have strength? What is distance, to the indefatigable? What is a foreign country, to those who have science? Who is a stranger, to those who have the habit of speaking kindly?"[1]

Every thing I have seen, every thing I have heard, since I have been in this place, has tended to create doubt, and aggravate curiosity. My opinion of the morals and manners of Christians, formed upon the precepts contained in their Shaster, has been frequently staggered by the observation of practices, inconsistent with its simplicity; and the knowledge of actions, irreconcilable to the tenor of its precepts.

It is true, these instances are not universal; and that by far the greater number of those with whom I converse, are men who, though they have not the words of their Shaster often in their mouths, seem to have imbibed a part of its spirit in their hearts. Indeed, the extreme delicacy observed by the Christians of this place, in regard to the expression of religious sentiment, is so universal, that I do not wonder, that to such a superficial observer as Sheermaal, it should

---

1   See Hetopades, page 93. [E.H.] Page 102 (1885). The quotation which ends the previous paragraph is also from the Hetopades (page 59).

have appeared doubtful whether they really had any religion at all.

This amiable modesty, which, no doubt, originates in that respect for the opinions of their Mussulman, and Hindoo friends, which renders them anxious not to hurt their feeling by an opposition of sentiment, is carried to such a length, that they, who generously extol the wisdom of Zoroaster, the morality of the Koran, and the sublimity of the Veda, make no more mention of the energetic eloquence of Paul, or the beautiful simplicity of the Gospels, than if they were actually ignorant of both!

But to return to the more immediate subject of this letter. I have not determined on the important step I am about to take, without weighing well all the arguments which I thought you could adduce against it.

The loss of Cast, which to you appears so formidable, has, I confess, to me lost many of its terrors. I have made it the endeavour of my life, to act in the manner that to me appeared most conformable to the will of the omniscient spirit, the eternal Brahma, and "*he*," saith Krishna, "*he is my servant, he is dear to me, who is free from enmity; merciful; and exempt from pride, and selfishness: who is the same in pain, and in pleasure; patient of wrongs; contented, and whose mind is fixed on me alone.*"[1]

Can this Being, whose animating spirit is spread abroad over the whole universe! can he behold with displeasure, the attempt of any of his creatures, to explore the varied forms of being which partake of his essence? Doth not this All-pervading, life-giving soul of universal nature, reside in the piercing regions of the north, as well as in those which are favoured with the smiles of Surraya? And, doth not the knowledge of his truth exalt the children of Brahma more than the descent of a thousand Avators?

Let then Māāndāāra rest assured, that in quitting, for a season, the favoured land of Hindostan, Zāārmilla doth nothing contrary to the spirit of our religion: and as for the censures of the bigotted, and illiberal, I regard them not. "He," saith the Prince of Goverdhan, "is my beloved, of whom mankind is not afraid, and who is not afraid of

---

1  See Bhagvat Geeta. [E.H.] Pages 99-100. For this and the following note, see 59, note 1.

mankind: who is unsolicitous about events, and to whom praise and blame are as one."[1]

But, in truth, from the Bramins I have little to apprehend. I have given orders, that the gifts I have so liberally bestowed, may be continued; so that the accustomary Poojah may be regularly performed in my absence; and I have sent them such reasons for my departure, as, I make no doubt, will perfectly satisfy them.

It is thou Māāndāāra, it is thou, that art entrusted with the hope of Zāārmilla's heart. My son! the tender pledge of the love of Prymaveda, I confide to thy care: my confidence is in thy virtue, and in the tender affection of my sister. I was a father to her tender years, shall she not be a mother to those of my child?

May the rule of the Devas keep thee from evil! May Vreheshpatee[2] watch over thy dwelling, and the bountiful Lackshmi load thee with her blessings.

What can I say more?

END OF THE FIRST VOLUME

---

1　See Mahhabbarat. [E.H.]
2　See the Argument of the *Hymn to Camdeo* (Appendix B). Jones transliterates the name as Vrihaspati.

# LETTERS

# OF A

# HINDOO RAJAH

---

## VOLUME II

## LETTER XII.

*From the Rajah* ZĀĀRMILLA, *to* MĀĀNDĀĀRA.

PRAISE to Varuna! under the guidance to whose potent arm, behold
thy friend, surrounded by the billows of the mighty ocean.

The most sublime objects alone present themselves to my view.
*Above* is the azure canopy of heaven, in which "the gold-crowned
Sultan of the firmament, advances the standard of his brightness"; and
without rival or competitor, enjoys the solitary grandeur of imperial
state. *Below* is the boundless expanse of waters, the congregated waves
of which all, like the chiefs of some great republic, alternately rise
into the majesty of power, and retire into the peace of obscurity.

From the benevolence and friendship of captain Grey, I received
every assistance in preparing for my voyage, and procured every
necessary that could tend to its comfort. I have also from him Letters
of introduction to his friends, with a sketch of the character of each,
so that I shall have the advantage of a sort of pre-acquaintance in a
land of strangers. From Morton, I have received letters for his mother,
and sisters, accompanied by some valuable presents, which the generous hand of Grey, enabled him to procure for them.

This young man has made a rapid progress in my esteem: his mind
seems formed for the residence of virtue; nor is there any reason to
apprehend that the head-strong passions of youth will ever be able to
drive her from her seat.

I have not forgotten the sister of my friend, the long lamented Percy. For her I have made a selection of whatever I thought could be acceptable: and the idea of presenting it in person, affords great delight to my mind. – Jeo-doss, to whom as well as to my other servants, I gave the liberty of returning to Kuttaher, so earnestly entreated for leave to accompany me, that I consented; and also at their own desire have kept two more of my own people, all of whose services I find very useful to me in this floating castle; where, in spite of every precaution, I confess, many things occur, disgusting to delicacy and abhorrent to the nice feelings of propriety.

I was accompanied to the ship by Grey, Morton, and some other friends, who have distinguished themselves by their particular kindness to me. Even Cooper, wild and eccentric as he is, would not suffer me to depart without some token of his kindness. He brought me a cap lined with the finest fur, which he told me would be of service in the cold climate I was about to encounter.

The pang of regret penetrated my heart, when I bade the last farewell to these amiable friends; but when the ship was put in motion, and I saw those blest shores, "the favoured seats of the Gods of India,"[1] recede from my sight, my heart grew faint within me, and my philosophy was insufficient to reinvigorate my sinking courage.

Sickness in a short time took from me the power of thinking. I have suffered under it so severely, that I have hitherto been unable to enjoy the society of my fellow passengers, the female part of whom are still confined to their apartments, by the cruel effects of this sea nausea, the most intolerable of all diseases! Upon the quarter-deck, I have met the husband of one of these ladies, who was —— of——, in which station he acquired a fortune, which though not the tenth of the sum that a Mussulman Dewan would have acquired, will, I am told, be sufficient to give him distinction in his own country. The Commander of the ship, though among his men he appears like a lion of the forest, is to his passengers gentle as the deer of the mountain. I have already been much indebted to his politeness and civility. I have the same acknowledgment to make to the surgeon, a young man, whose quick, and penetrating eye gives the promise of genius, and discernment.

---

1   The quotations on this and the previous page are untraced.

TIME, that great Physician, having in some degree reconciled our stomachs to the motion of the vessel, I have had the pleasure of being introduced to the fair companions of our voyage; who are three in number.

The first, is the wife of the Dewan; her features are regular, but so insipid, that I should not fail to pronounce her equally void of sense and feeling, was it not for the unlimited affection she evinces towards the animal creation, which she carries to as exalted a height as any Hermit of Cummow. Surrounded by Parrots, Lorys, Maccaws, small Dogs, Persian Cats, and Monkeys of every description, she seems attracted towards them by a mysterious sympathy; while if her languid eyes are cast towards any of the company, it is only to express the language of disdain.

Notwithstanding my admiration of this amiable protectress of the brute creation, I cannot help feeling a superiour degree of pleasure, in contemplating the unaffected charms, and unassuming loveliness of a young widow; the beauty of whose countenance is shaded, though not concealed, by the veil of sorrow. Whilst bestowing on her father-less babes the soft caresses of maternal tenderness, I have observed the tear which glistened on the silken fringe of her fine black eyes, mingled with the smiles of tender complacency.

Betwixt this Lady and her husband, at an early period of life, a mutual attachment had taken place. Prudence could not at that time sanction their union: for in a country where luxury has fixed her residence, it becomes difficult to procure the necessaries of existence, and without these, how would a man answer the calls of an infant family? The affection of these lovers, at length, triumphed over every difficulty: the gentleman went to India, where, in process of time he was promoted to the —— of —— and no sooner found himself in a situation to support a family, than he claimed the promise of his betrothed bride, who, throwing aside the timidity of her sex, and unprotected save by the modest dignity of virtue, nobly braved the inconveniences and hazards of an Indian voyage. She was received with transport by her anxiously expecting lover, whose happiness was completed by their immediate union. Their's was not that transient glow of joy, which, like the crimson-tinted cloud of morning, vanishes while gazed on; it was permanent as pure. Each met in each the enlightened companion, the wise adviser, the faithful friend. But, alas! while fondly looking forward to a long period of felicity, the stroke of death, suddenly destroyed the fair, but fallacious prospect. You will, perhaps, think but indifferently of her, who in such circumstances, would persevere in preserving life: – But it is the custom of her nation! And she perhaps imagines, that she may as effectually evince her regard to the memory of her husband, by devoting herself to the care and education of his children, as if she had mingled her ashes with his.

Three fine boys look up to her for protection, and already begin to benefit by her instructions. Their innocent vivacity, though a source of amusement to most of the party, is a great annoyance to the monkey-loving Bibby, who declares, that "of all the odious torments of a long voyage, that of being teized with the noise of children is the worst." At the sound of her voice, the dissonant screams of her feathered favourites, seem to ratify the declaration of their fair benefactress; while the young and lively neice of the Dewan, casts towards the many-coloured objects of her aunt's affection, such an expressive glance as seems to say, they are *almost* as bad.

Of this young lady I can say little, but that she appears gay, and good humoured. The Surgeon, indeed, from whom I have all my information respecting my fellow voyagers tells me, that she had been brought to India by her uncle, in order to be married to the gentleman, who was to succeed him in his appointment; but, that on the voyage from Europe, a mutual affection had taken place between her, and a young votary of Lackshmee, who must obtain the smiles of the Goddess, before he can procure the hand of his mistress. Her uncle, in the mean while, insists on her return to Europe; and from the hilarity of her countenance, I should not suppose the disappointment to have entered deeply into her heart.

A SAD bustle has just taken place. One of the little boys having been allured into the great cabbin, by the comical tricks of a Marmozet, was attacked by a huge Baboon, one of the fiercest animals in

Mrs. ———'s collection. His cries soon gave the alarm; every one flew to the place from whence they issued. No description can give any idea of the confused scene which followed. The voice of the sufferer, was soon lost in universal uproar. The screams of the ladies, the chattering of the monkeys, the barking of the dogs, to say nothing of the squalling of the parrots and maccaws, made altogether such a noise, that the thunder of the contending elements could scarcely have been heard in it. When peace was at length restored, and the little boy, whose leg was sadly torn, had been committed to the care of the surgeon, the Dewan ventured to remonstrate with his fair partner, on the numbers, and bad behaviour of her favourites. It was a tender point; the very mention of it, though managed with the utmost gentleness, threw her into a paroxysm of anger, which at length terminated in a flood of tears. In truth, there appeared to me in these tears, so much more of passion than of tenderness, that I could not regard them, as any ornament to the cheek of beauty! Perhaps you may blame my insensibility, and bestow more unbounded admiration on this benevolent woman, who generously prefers the welfare and happiness of her tailed, and feathered favourites, to the peace and comfort of her husband; and whose heart expands, with more lively affection, for the meanest quadruped in her possession, than for the orphan child of any friend on earth.

Intelligence is just brought me of our having cast anchor in the road of Madrass. – I will from thence send you this letter. May it find you in the possession of the best blessings of life, health, and tranquillity! What can I say more?

# LETTER XII

THE day after I concluded my epistle from Madrass,[1] we returned on board our ship, and the morning following weighed anchor, and proceeded on our voyage, in company with many floating fortresses of superior size, sent by the king of England, to protect the fleet of the Company. The gentleman who I mentioned to you in my last, proves indeed a valuable acquisition to our society. He, alas! returns to his country, *not* loaded with the riches of India, but possessing in his mind a treasure, more desirable than any wealth can purchase. It is from the sneer of worthless prosperity, from the contumely of successful pride, that Mr. Delmond goes to hide his misfortunes in the oblivious shade of retirement. "When the frowns of fortune are excessive, and human endeavours are exerted in vain, where but in the wilderness can comfort be found for a man of sensibility?"[2] Such an one is Delomond; unable to struggle with the tempestuous gales of adverse fortune, he declines the contest. The pride of talents, and the consciousness of rectitude, may, he thinks, support him in his solitude; though he has found, from his experience, that they are often an obstacle to advancement in the world: the path that leads to fortune, too often passing through the narrow defiles of meanness, which a man of an exalted spirit cannot stoop to tread.

The manly elegance with which Nature has endowed this Saib, together with an air of dignity which marks his whole deportment, commands the admiration of the whole party; even the lady of the Dewan, relaxing from the haughty langour of her usual manner, condescends to address him with the utmost civility: and though her mistake as to him being *a man of fortune* which from his appearance she had naturally concluded him to be was soon rectified, she could not divest herself of the respectful deference which his manifest superiority so justly claims. She sometimes, indeed, when he is not present, wonders what people of *no fortune* mean, by assuming the airs of quality?

---

1   Which letter does not appear and is supposed by the Editor to have been lost. [E.H.] In the original, Hamilton repeats this note after her next mention of Madras, on page 193.

2   *Hitopadesa* 70 (1885)

In the conversation of Delomond and the beautiful widow, I have spent many delightful hours. The first possesses a rich mine of knowledge, from which I expect pure and genuine information. The latter is not less sensible, almost equally well informed, more lively in her ideas, and more quick in her discernments but, at the same time, so modest, and unassuming is this lovely woman, that I am sometimes at a loss which to admire most – the perfection of her understanding, or her unconsciousness of its superiority.

The indisposition of these two intelligent companions, has for some days past deprived me of their society; and I should have been at a great loss how to dispose of myself, had it not been for the goodness of the neice of the Dewan, who from her own library supplied me, with a fund of instruction and amusement.

This young lady I have lately discovered to be a great lover of books; of which she has by far the most numerous collection of any person on board. But it is not surprising, that I should never have suspected her taste for literature. No one could possibly find it out from her conversation, which always turns upon the most trifling subjects. Notwithstanding the knowledge she must doubtless have acquired from the number of books she has read, she is so modest as never to utter a sentiment beyond vulgar observation, nor to attempt making use of her reason upon any occasion whatever; so that a person might easily believe her mind to be still immersed in the depths of ignorance.

In the valuable collection of Biography, which this young lady kindly submitted to my perusal, the first book that attracted my attention, was, "the *History of a Nobleman*";[1] but I soon found, that the word *History* has more meanings in the English language, than that which is given to it in the Dictionary. It is *there* said to be, "a narrative of events and facts, delivered with dignity."[2] But the history of this illustrious nobleman, consisted of nothing more than a few letters

---

1 Perhaps intended merely as a generic title, although there was a two-volume novel called *Colonel Ormsby; or the genuine history of an Irish Nobleman in the French Service* published in 1781. It is an epistolary novel, featuring the eponymous hero's letters about his love for the unhappily married heroine.

2 Like the subsequent definitions of "philosopher" and "critic," this is taken from Samuel Johnson's dictionary.

written in the days of juvenile folly, on the subject of love! – Indeed, I cannot imagine why such immature productions should have been preserved at all; and still less can I conceive for what purpose they are given to the world, to whom the opinion which a young man entertains of the unparalleled beauty of his mistress's complexion, can surely be of very little consequence. Other histories I found written in the manner of memoirs; these are said to contain the lives of illustrious personages, whose names adorn the title page. It appears very strange, that the lives of these great personages should abound in incidents so similar; an account of one will serve to give you an idea of the events that have occurred in fifty families, whose histories I have already read.

It happens, that a noble-born infant is deserted by its fond parents, and exposed to the care of chance, and the humanity of strangers. These fortunate foundlings never fail to be adopted by the first person who takes them up, and as these are always people of fortune, they receive from their bounty an education, every way suitable to their *real* rank. As soon as the young nobleman attains the age of manhood, he falls in love with the daughter of his benefactor, a circumstance which involves the loving pair in the deepest misery. At length, a period is put to their misfortunes, by the discovery of the *real* parents, and the young lord is admitted to all the privileges of his order. You may now perhaps expect that the *history* should become more interesting and important, and be curious to hear how the young nobleman conducts himself in his new station; whether the experience he has had of life, serves to expand his benevolence, to invigorate his intellectual powers, and to render him a more worthy member of that august tribunal, in which is concentrated the illustrious mass of hereditary virtue? As to all these points, you must content yourself to remain in ignorance; with the marriage of the hero, the *history* of his life concludes!

From this circumstance, and, indeed, from the whole tenor of these books, it appears evident, that with these islanders, marriage is a certain passport to never failing, and never fading bliss! A state nearly resembling that divine absorption of the soul described by our Yogees, which entirely excludes the cares and concerns of life, and in which the mind is wrapt in a delirium of perfect and uninterrupted felicity!

– Happy country! where the prudence and fidelity of the women of high rank, so plainly evince the care that is bestowed on their instruction, and where the piety, learning, and morality of the men, is only to be equalled by their humility!

I will not conceal from you, that in these true and faithful pictures of the manners and morals of the people of England, I see much that appears to me extraordinary, and incomprehensible. Here, it is said by our philosophers that, "in this life (compounded of good and evil) sickness, and health, opulence, and calamity; fruition and disappointment, are bound up together; *thus everything is produced with a companion which shall destroy it.*"[1] By this scheme of things, the wounds of affliction are ever within the reach of some cordial balm, which, if it does not heal, may at least serve to alleviate its anguish. While, in the purest cup of felicity is mingled such particles, as may serve to remind the mortal to whom it is presented, of the sublunary source from whence it flowed. – In England, on the contrary (if I am to believe these histories) happiness and misery are known only in extremes; there the tide of adversity sets in with such destructive fury, that the bare recital of the unheard of calamities it occasions, is sufficient to melt the hardest heart! Nor when the flood of fortune comes, is the the torrent of prosperity which it produces, less extraordinary and amazing! In its resistless career, every barrier to happiness is broken down. The undeserving husband, the cruel father, and the malicious aunt, are all carried off by death: while riches, honours, titles, fine clothes, and spotless character, complete the felicity of the beautiful and loving pair, who are designed to be overwhelmed in this sea of bliss.

From the authority of these *authentic memoirs*, it appears, that marriage in Europe is never contracted but from the most pure and disinterested motives. Every young woman who is handsome and accomplished, however humble her birth, or small her fortune, is there certain of attracting the love and admiration of numbers of the highest rank in the community. What a glorious encouragement is held forth to the females of that happy island, who must be blind indeed not to perceive that it is their own *obstinacy* and *folly* that

---

1 Heetopedes. [E.H.]

alone can possibly prevent their advancement to the very summit of felicity!

For such folly and obstinacy, whenever it occurs a very peculiar and extraordinary punishment is reserved. After a few years, spent, as it is generally believed, in vain repentance, and useless regret, they all at once, without any exceptions in favour of virtue, merit, useful or ornamental accomplishments, undergo a certain change, and incomprehensible transformation, and become what is termed OLD MAIDS. From all that I have hitherto been able to learn of these creatures, the Old Maid is a sort of venomous animal, so wicked in its temper, and so mischievous in its disposition, that one is surprised that its very existence should be tolerated in a civilized society.

<hr />

AFTER having spent many days in the study of those authors, so warmly recommended by the young Bibby, I began to apprehend that though to more enlightened minds, they might doubtless prove a source of instruction and delight, they were not sufficiently adapted to my weak capacity, to afford any recompence for the time spent in their perusal. Never before did my heart refuse its sympathy to human misery; but the distresses of the Lady Hariots, and the Lady Charlottes, which called forth the overflowings of compassion, in the breasts of their fair correspondents, were of a nature too refined and delicate to be discernable to any save the Microscopic eye of European sensibility!

The change which according to these sage writers of Novels, has taken place in human nature, must have been as sudden as it appears unaccountable. In the days of their great Dramatic Poet, *the Calidas of Europe*, it was certainly unknown; in his masterly delineations of the passions, it is every where, and at every period the same: and from a perusal of his works, one would be tempted to imagine (notwithstanding the evidence of these *authentic memoirs* to the contrary) that though manners may differ, and local customs fall into oblivion, the traits of kindred likeness, which the Creator has been pleased to impress on the great family of the human race, may, by a discerning eye, be traced through every clime, and in every period of its

existence! How otherwise should the immortal Calidas, who flourished two thousand years ago,[1] and the Bard of England, who was
cotemporary with Ackbar, teach the heart to vibrate with the same
sensations? The Sacontala of the one, and the Desdemona of the
other, speak so nearly the same language, that did I not believe the
soul of the Indian poet to have been long absorbed in the regions of
felicity, I should undoubtedly imagine that it was Calidas himself,
who, under the name of Shakspeare, again vouchsafed to enlighten
and delight the world! – It is at least evident that they have both
copied from the same original – *Unchanging, everlasting Nature!*

A CHASM of many weeks has taken place in my journal. Alas! When I
undertook to write it, I was not aware of the tedious uniformity of a
sea voyage. But though void of incident, the scene has not been destitute of instruction. By time, and increasing intimacy, the characters of
my companions have been more fully developed. The first sketch that
was drawn by the hasty pencil of imagination, I confidently pronounced to be a striking likeness; but very different now appears the
picture, that has been delineated by slow-working observation.

In my letter from Madrass, I informed you of the acquisition I
expected from the society of the young officer, whose sprightly manners, and communicative disposition, gave the promise of an ever-
pleasing companion. But, alas! I soon discovered that sprightliness and
loquacity are by no means united with urbanity and cheerfulness. –
The small stock of personal anecdote, with which the incidents of his
life had furnished him, was no sooner exhausted, than he became
dull, insipid, and morose. Nor was the change which seemed wrought
on his temper, less extraordinary, than that which took place in his
manners. This youth, seemingly so gentle; who took such pleasure in

---

1   Calidas, the celebrated dramatic poet of India, flourished, according to Sir William
    Jones, in the first century before Christ; he was one of the nine men of genius,
    commonly called the *Nine Gems*, who were favoured with the patronage, and
    splendidly supported by the bounty of Vicramaditya, a Monarch eminently distin-
    guished by his taste for literature. (See the preface to Sir William Jones's translation
    of *Sacontala*.) [E.H.] See also 58, note 1.

obliging; who lived but to promote the happiness of others, gives every day such convincing proofs of the malignity of his disposition, in the cruel treatment he bestows upon his younger brother, that it is impossible to behold it without feelings of horror, and indignation.

How different from this, is the change that has taken place in my opinion, concerning the character of the Dewan. Alas! I fear, that in more instances than these my first opinion has been like an unjust judge, who suffers his decisions to be influenced by the eloquence of flattery. Self-love whispers that those who are pleased with us, are pleasing; and it is not till experience has convinced us of our error, that we are willing to listen to the voice of truth. The reserve, and silence which at first seemed to give to the character of the Dewan an appearance of sullenness and stupidity, gradually cleared away, by time and encreasing intimacy, and discovered to us incontestable proofs of a mild and placid temper, a deeply-thinking, well-informed mind, and a humane and benevolent heart.

The conduct of his Lady, has not, I confess, undergone much change; but my opinion of it has been somewhat altered, by an insight into its motives.

That haughty, and arrogant demeanour, which I had conceived to flow from the conscious superiority of birth and merit, was, it seems, assumed by folly, to conceal the real meanness of both. Her history appeared to me so very extraordinary, that had I not had the most convincing proofs of the veracity of my informer, I confess, I should have been led to doubt its truth.

This disdainful Lady, whom I considered as some highly exalted personage was the daughter of a tradesman, "whose foolish fondness, said the Surgeon," (for I give you his very words) bestowed upon her such an education, as, without instructing her in the qualities that are alone suited to adorn an exalted rank, rendered her unfit for becoming wife to a man in her own. At the death of this parent, she laid out the small fortune he bequeathed her, in fine cloaths, and took her passage to Bengal, where she did not doubt that her beauty would procure her an advantageous marriage. The event proved equal to her expectations. On her arrival, she was seen by the Dewan, who admired, courted, and married her! "I thought said I," interrupting my informer, "that Europeans had made companions of their wives.

Surely, this woman was not qualified for being the companion of such a man as the Dewan. It is not possible to imagine, that her intellectual deficiencies, would be unobserved by a man of his sense, and penetration." "The Dewan was too much charmed with her beauty, to observe any deficiency in her merit," replied the Surgeon; "or, if he did, she was so young, that he promised himself much pleasure in filling the office of Preceptor. Alas! he considered not that pride is the usual concomitant of ignorance; that it is not the understanding which has been perverted by vanity, prejudice, and folly, that will listen to the instructions of a husband. Her hopes of happiness were from the enjoyment of his fortune.

"Elated by her exaltation to affluence, she thought that to realize the dreams of bliss, formed by her fond fancy, she had only to indulge in every capricious whim of vanity. Her extravagance was unbounded. But soon she found that it was not in the power of splendid equipage, or fantastic finery, to fill the chasm of an empty mind.

"The delight of unrivaled pre-eminence in every article of expensive ornament, soon gave place to sullen apathy, and fretful discontent. New follies were invented, and pursued with no better success, and it will, perhaps, astonish you, to learn, that her mighty fondness for the brute creation, instead of proceeding from the pure source of true benevolence, was in reality, no other than an effort of the animal spirits, to procure an object of employment to her ever restless mind."

Here ceased my kind informer; who left me very much astonished, at the picture he had drawn of an English woman, and a Christian.

After much reflection, I think l can trace the unenlightened state of this woman's understanding, to her want of instruction. Had she received her education at one of those wise, learned, and pious seminaries, called boarding-schools, her mind would no doubt have been vigilantly defended from the noxious breath of vanity and conceit. She would *there* have learned according to the precepts of her Shaster, to have adorned herself with "shamefacedness and sobriety. Not with broidered hair, or gold, or pearls, or costly array, but (which becometh women possessing godliness) with good works."[1] Such, no

---

1   1 Timothy 2: 9-10.

doubt, is the education of *Christian* women, at *Christian* schools! How does it exalt my opinion of the native genius of the young widow; when I contemplate the extent of her acquired knowledge, her unaffected humility, her undeviating discretion; and at the same time, consider, that by her own account, she never enjoyed the advantages of instruction at one of these enlightened seminaries, but was confined during the early part of her life, to the roof of her parents! Is it not surprising, that, notwithstanding this disadvantage, she should have made such proficiency in every accomplishment?

My first sentiments concerning her remain unaltered. Her exalted sentiments continue to excite my admiration, while her sweet temper, and ever obliging disposition, make daily progress in my esteem.

THE morning after I last laid down my pen, we arrived at a small island, which the benignant hand of Nature seems to have erected in the midst of the mighty ocean, as a convenient Choultrie,[1] for the floating caravanseras that traverse its watery bosom. Here we spent nearly twenty days, and were entertained by the inhabitants, who appeared a gay and lively people, with much kindness and hospitality.

The change of scene was relished by all the party, but by none so much as the neice of the Dewan; to whom the uniform life we led on board ship, was become altogether insupportable. She had indeed for a long time, been at a most pitiable loss for employment. The contents of her library, which I imagined, would have afforded her a fund of amusement and edification, during the course of her voyage, were soon exhausted. Having once found out how all the wished-for marriages, of all the heroes and heroines, were brought about; and been let into the secret of the surprising discoveries, lucky accidents, and miraculous combination of circumstances, which uniformly led to that happy event, she had no further interest nor curiosity concerning them. These books had, nevertheless, by giving constant fuel to the vivid flame of youthful imagination, created such an insatiable craving for novelty, as rendered every other sort of reading, tasteless and

---

1 Choultries, are houses built in India, for the accommodation of travellers. [E.H.]

insipid. Even the ever entertaining conversation of our intelligent companions, had no charms for her. I have frequently known the chain of an interesting argument, to which I have been listening with avidity and delight, all at once interrupted, by her abruptly asking, when we should see land? Whatever gave the promise of variety, seemed to re-animate her flagging spirits. Whether it was the appearance of a flying-fish – or the rumoured approach of an enemy; the drowning of a kitten, or the indications of a coming storm, all were equally acceptable; so that they relieved her, from the tedious task of thought. The approach to St. Helena, made her almost wild with joy. No sooner was it announced, than she flew to her cabin, to take from her trunk, some particular dresses, which she had reserved for the occasion, and hastily displaying them before the amiable widow, asked her fifty questions in a breath, concerning the important point, of which was most becoming.

Besides the novelty of the scenes, and amusements at St. Helena, she there made another acquisition, which, I hope, will afford her sufficient variety of entertainment for many weeks to come. This is no other than a fresh supply of novels! This she happily accomplished, by exchanging the contents of her library, with another *reading fair* one, whom she accidently met at a ball, and with whom, on an acquaintance of three days, she commenced an *extreme* and *ardent* friendship. The great loquacity with which her present flow of spirits has inspired this votary of fancy, is sometimes no less teazing than the effects of her former ennui: to the elegant, but somewhat too fastidious Delomond, it is peculiarly irksome.

In truth, it is not a little to be regretted, that this amiable man frequently indulges a certain soreness of mind, which may not improperly be termed the illegitimate offspring of sensibility. What proves its spurious birth, is, that while genuine sensibility is ever alive to the feelings of others, this bastard branch of the family, is only mindful of its own. By being ever ready to take offence, without considering whether offence was intended to be given, it frequently inflicts a wound in the bosom of friendship; but is unfeelingly insensible to the pain which it has produced. What a pity it is, that this impostor, should ever find a place in the breast of a worthy man! I cannot without pain, behold it cherished by the dignified mind of Delomond, and would not fail to remonstrate with him concerning it, was he not so *easily hurt*, that I fear an estrangement of his friendship might be the consequence. Fatal propensity! which presents a barrier to the wholesome succours of advice, and cuts off retreat from error. In the various sketches which this amiable and accomplished Saib, has given me of his life, and his misfortunes, I can plainly discern, that the disposition I have just now alluded to, has been no less detrimental to his fortune, than injurious to his felicity.

I SUSPECT, that you are now almost as much tired of the voyage, as the niece of the Dewan, and begin to re-echo her interrogatory, of when shall we see land? But courage, keep up your spirits, your patience will not be put to a much longer trial. – Land has been just discovered from the topmast-head. – I cannot avoid envying the happy sailor, who from the giddy height, catches the first view of his dear native country. Ah! what pleasing images play about his heart! in that little speck appearing in the distant horizon, he beholds his little home; his tender wife; his endearing infants; and already, in imagination, feels, and returns their soft caresses. I go to participate in the joy of these honest people, it is a bad heart to which the *happiness of a fellow mortal* can be indifferent.

Ah! Māāndāāra, how astonishingly great has been my disappointment! Instead of the expected appearance of felicity, I beheld in the countenances of the hitherto hearty, and contented sailors, the strongest indications of consternation, terror, and dismay! On enquiring into the cause of this alarm, I was told that it arose from the rumoured approach of a *press-gang*; a press-gang I never before heard of, but from the degree of terror it inspires, I can easily conceive it be some infernal species of monster; some cruel servant to the genii of the deep, to whom the long-absent sailor is an acceptable sacrifice. Accursed spirits! the terror of whose name, can put to flight the tender images of hope, and can induce despair at a moment when the sweetest impulses of nature have kindled the torch of joy!

AT the moment I laid down my pen, a fine boy of about fifteen years of age, who had frequently in the course of the voyage, attracted my notice, burst into my cabin. "For the love of God, assist me dear, dear Sir," cried he, "the press-gang are already here, and I know, I shall not escape! For myself, I should not care; but, my poor, poor mother! she will never survive it. I know she won't. Alas! she has no son, but me. – Her heart is now yearning to embrace me. O it will break, if she is disappointed!" I gave him time to say no more, but having hastily emptied a large trunk, made him leap into it, and there detained him, until I was assured that these children of Nareyka[1] had retired. Alas! they did not retire without prey; above thirty of those brave fellows, whose useful labours have conduced to the enrichment, and prosperity of their country; who, after an absence of twenty months, hoped to reap the reward of their toils, by returning to its bosom, were dragg'd reluctant victims to the infernal demon of power!

Nor are these the only monsters that infest the British coast. Much apprehension is entertained by the seamen, and passengers, for certain savages, called *Custom-house Officers*; who, it seems, are particularly ferocious towards those who come from the East.

⚜

PRAISE to the preserving Spirit! – Our watery pilgrimage begins to draw near its close. At ten this morning we cast our anchor, at the distance of about one coss from one of the principal Naval Ports in England. All on board is now hurry and confusion, every eye sparkles with the eagerness of expectation, and every heart seems warm, with the thoughts of once more beholding their friends, and their native country; it is the tumult of delight; the dread of the custom-house officers, is forgotten; I suppose our fleet was too formidable for these savages to dare to make any attack upon it. And now that we are within sight of an English port, we can have nothing to fear. Seeing every one making preparations for going ashore, I retired to spend an

---

1  A god of punishment; compare Charles Wilkins: "A Hindoo's hope of happiness after death greatly depend upon his having children to perform the ceremonies of the Sradha ... by which he is taught to expect his soul will be released from the torments of Naraka [sic]" (*Hitopadesa* 261 [1885 ed]).

hour at my pen; but the encreasing bustle renders it impossible for me to proceed further at present.

⸻⸻

ON going upon deck, I was surprised to observe a number of strange faces, and anxiously enquired, what kind friends had taken this early opportunity of greeting our arrival? – With astonishment, I learned, that the strangers, were no other than the dreaded custom-house officers. In manners, dress, stature, and complexion, nay even in language, these savages bear so strong a resemblance to the English, that they might at a slight view, be mistaken for the same; but, on a more accurate examination of their countenances, evident traces of their savage origin, may be easily discerned. They are less ferocious than the ⸻⸻,[1] and seldom murder those who fall into their hands, unless in cases of resistance. This they did not meet with from any of us; but, got leave to rifle, rob, and plunder, without any hindrance, or molestation. Their avidity for plunder, though eager beyond description, seems to be acquired by the strangest caprice. On the commodities of Europe, they seemed to set no value; but seized with savage rapacity, on the more elegant productions of the East. In respect to these, the neice of the Dewan and myself, have been the greatest sufferers. A beautiful piece of silver muslin, which the fair reader of Novels, had treasured up, as her choicest ornament, and on which, she set a tenfold value, from its being of a similar description to that which was worn by the Right Hon. Lady Araminta Eleanora Bloomville, on the day of her nuptials; was seized by these relentless barbarians, without remorse. With a copious flood of tears, she besought them to spare her favourite robe; but, alas! the supplications of beauty, touched not the heart of these savage plunderers, who beheld unmoved, the pearly drops, which coursed each other down the fair one's cheek! My cabin afforded a still more ample share of plunder. The shawls, the muslins, which I intended to have presented to the sister of Percy; and the less costly, though in the eye of affec-

---

1 Probably a reference to the "Thugs" or "Thugees," Indian robbers who habitually murdered their victims (and from whom the English word is taken).

tion, no less valuable presents, which the generosity of Grey, had enabled young Morton to send to his family; all, all, were seized, by the unhallowed hands of these ruthless spoilers! Had they taken my whole chest of gold Mhors, it would not have grieved me half so much! But, as it is a misfortune, for which I perceive there is no remedy, I must have recourse to that only physic of the hopeless – Patience.

<hr />

FROM the Queen of the ocean, the favoured Island of Great Britain, does the wandering Zāārmilla, now address the most beloved of friends. – Having taken leave of the Captain and officers, and returned, well-merited, thanks for their kind attention during our voyage; we went into a boat, which had been sent from the harbour, for the conveyance of the passengers, and were quickly landed on one of the ghauts of Portsmouth; it is impossible to convey to your imagination, any notion of the magnificence of the spectacle that presented itself to our view, in this short sail. No idea of the sublimity of a fleet of floating fortresses, can possibly be conceived by those who have not beheld the unequalled scene. The army of the most powerful Monarch of the East, though numerous as the grains of sand upon the shores of the sea, the dust of the feet of whose Elephants obscures the noon-day sun, cannot, in point of grandeur, bear comparison with an assemblage of these glories of the ocean, that ride triumphant in an English port.

We have taken up our present abode at a sort of Choultrie, called an Hotel, and are to spend the remainder of the day together. To-morrow, we shall separate, perhaps, for ever! The lovely widow, in whose countenance I see the emotions of tender recollections struggling with that amiable fortitude, which strives to repress the feelings of unavailing sorrow, purposes going to the house of a friend, at a few miles distance from this place, and there to wait the arrival of her mother. I am to have the happiness of Delomond's company, on my journey to London, which is a very great comfort to me, as I find myself almost as much at a loss here, as if I had never before been in an English settlement. The Dewan has been busily employed in preparations for the conveyance of his family. His Lady's extreme delicacy not permitting her to submit to the ordinary mode of travelling, in hired carriages, he has been obliged to purchase one for her accommodation. Happily, the mortality which prevailed amongst her favourites, in the course of the voyage, has so much diminished their numbers, as to render their conveyance, a matter of little COMPARATIVE difficulty; had they all survived, he must surely have had a carriage built for them on purpose!

<hr />

I AM happy I had not closed this packet, as it gives me an opportunity of recording a scene that has just now passed, while my heart still glows with the emotions it has excited.

The youth, whom I had the good fortune to protect, from the ruthless fangs of the press-gang, presented himself before me, at an early hour this morning. – "You will think me a sad ungrateful fellow, Sir," said he, "that I should not have appeared to thank you, for the very great service you rendered me; but, the moment I obtained the Captain's leave, I made the best of my way out of this place; as I did not think I should be in safety, till I reached home. I set off on foot, and had got rather more than ten miles on my journey last night, when I was overtaken by a fellow midshipman, who informed me of the loss you had sustained from the sharks of the custom house; I have got here, a bit of your India sort of stuff, to take home to my mother; but I know she would wear nothing I brought her with any satisfaction, if she thought so meanly of me, as that I could basely forget a debt of gratitude." So saying, he pulled from his bosom a very handsome shawl, purchased, no doubt, with the scanty earnings of his initiating voyage. " Here, Sir," said he, presenting it to me in a careless manner, as if in order to depreciate its value; "it is nothing to be sure in comparison of the fine things you have lost; but, as it is *real Indian*, it may be more acceptable to your English friends, than something much better bought at home." There was something so open and ingenuous, in the countenance of the youth, while he spoke these words, which he did in the most impressive manner, that he altogether overpowered my feelings. Protecting power! I exclaimed, thou, whose mighty breath, can kindle in the human soul, the flame of virtue; oh! grant, that the son of Zāārmilla, may be capable of inspiring in the breast of a stranger, such sensations as the noble action of this youth causes now to glow in mine! But think not, excellent young man (continued I) that I can deprive thy mother of the gift of such a son. No, long may she wear this, and proudly may she exhibit it to her friends and neighbours, as the sweet pledge of filial affection; more honourable than the gifts of princes! more precious than the jewels of Golconda! I was interrupted by the Dewan, who had hitherto been a silent spectator of all that had passed. Shaking the youth heartily by the hand, "You are a noble fellow," said he, "and I must know more of you; but you may make yourself perfectly easy about this gentleman's losses, as, I believe, I have taken such steps as will effect their restitution; but I must let you know where to find me, and assure you, that wherever I am, there you shall have a friend." So saying, he gave him his address, enjoining him to call upon him as soon as he could find an opportunity. While he yet spoke, two men arrived, with the whole of the goods which had been seized by the pirates. The Dewan, desired each of us to pick out our own; but would give us no satisfaction, as to the manner in which he had effected their release.

I am told, the carriage waits for me, and must therefore conclude this long protracted journal.

May the Almighty Preserver, whose omnipotent arm hath safely guided me across the world of waters, to this remote corner of the habitable globe; He, whose essence, pervades all space! shed the dews of his mercy, on the dwelling of my friend! may his choicest blessings rest on the child of my affections! the blossom of my heart! and may the sweet buds of hope, peace, and contentment, continue to expand in the virtuous bosom of my gentle Zamarcanda! What can I say more?

# LETTER XIII.

At length Māāndāāra, behold me in the metropolis of England, the celebrated city of London. My heart bounds within me, at the idea of the new scenes I am about to behold. The pulse of expectation beats in every vein. – I was all impatience, to deliver my letters of introduction; but, unluckily, we arrived at the very season of a solemn festival, which is very properly celebrated by the Christians, in commemoration of an event which opened to their view the glorious hopes of rising from the bed of death, to the regions of eternal glory! – You may well imagine that a festival originating in such a source, is celebrated throughout the Christian world with appropriate solemnity. With them, the forms and ceremonies of their religion, remain not merely as a testimony of the superior piety which produced them. These institutions have not become a reproach to the degeneracy of succeeding ages! They have not, with them, become a solemn mockery! a satire upon a trifling, and frivolous generation! No; at the time of these holydays, most of the families of distinction retire into the country, that they may there enjoy the heart-purifying benefit of solemn meditation, uninterrupted by the business, or pleasures of the world. Ah! how edifying their devotion! How exemplary their conduct! How happy for the community must it be, if the lower orders are induced to tread in their footsteps! The few people of rank who remain in town, are equally sedulous in preparing their minds for this devout solemnity. They frequent no places that are not private: – private theatricals, private concerts, private pharo-banks,[1] I have already heard of; and I make no doubt, there are numerous other places of private resort, equally honourable to religion, and favourable to virtue!

By the kind care of my friend Delomond, I am provided with a very convenient lodging, in the street which leads to the King's palace. This palace is, in truth, but a mean building very unlike the Durbar of an Eastern Monarch.[2]

---

1   Pharo (also spelled faro and pharoah) is a card game; a "pharo-bank" is the house at which pharo is played.

2   The hall in which Indian rulers gave audiences or held court.

I HAVE spent the greater part of the week, in taking a survey of the town, and examining its temples and other public buildings. – The extent of this metropolis, though it shrinks into insignificance when compared with the Imperial residence of our ancient Rajahs, the celebrated birth place of Rama[1] or the Ganga-washed walls of Canouge;[2] is yet sufficiently great, to strike with astonishment the insignificant mortal, who has beheld only the modern cities of Hindoostan. The foot-paths which are raised at the sides of every street, are filled with a busy throng, where it is curious to behold women, as well as men, apparently intent upon business, entering into the shops, and making purchases, with the undaunted mien of masculine appearance. Far from walking along the streets with that timid air of shrinking modesty, which distinguishes the females of our race,[3] when they venture into the walks of men, their fearless eye undaunted meets the glances of every beholder; and happy is it for the men of the country, that it doth so; for if modesty was super-added to their other charms it would be impossible to guard the heart from their fascinating influence. Having heard that the first day of the week, Audeetye-war,[4] was appointed for attending the worship of the deity in public; I expressed to Delomond, my wish of being present at the solemnity. He declined accompanying me; but sent to a Lady of his acquaintance, to beg she would accommodate me with a seat in her pew. – These pews, are little inclosures into which the greatest part of the temple is sub-divided. We walked up to that which

---

1   Oude, said in the Mahhabaret, to have been the first regular Imperial city of Hindoostan, and extended if we may believe the Bramins, over a line of ten Yogans, or about forty miles; and the present city of Lucknow, was only a lodge for one of its gates. [E.H.]

2   Canouge, a celebrated ancient city of Hindoostan on the banks of the Ganges; whose walls are said in the Mahhbaret, to have been one hundred miles in circumference. [E.H.]

3   See the elegant engravings, illustrative of Mr. Hodges's remark on this subject, in his *Travels in India*. [E.H.]

4   It is very remarkable, that the days of the week are named in the Shanscrit language, from the same planet to which they were assigned by the Greeks and Romans. [E.H.]

belonged to this Bibby, preceded by one of her servants, who opened the door of the pew, and followed by another in the same livery, who carried the books of prayer; with which having presented us, he retired. I have already observed to you, how scrupulously the English Christians adhere to those precepts of their Shaster, which seem to discountenance the outward appearance of a religious sentiment; and so rigorously do they abstain from the display of these delightful emotions, that they who will thankfully acknowledge the most trifling obligation conferred upon them by the meanness of their fellow-creatures, would blush to be suspected of gratitude to the beneficent Governor of the Universe! Instead of behaving in this temple, as if they had assembled together to send up their united tribute of praise, thanksgiving, and humble supplication, to the Most High, so successfully did they affect the concealment of their devotional sentiments, that no one would have suspected they had met together for any other purpose, but that of staring at each other's dress! I must, however, make an exception in regard to a small number of people, very plainly habited, who stood during the service, in a part of the church called the aisle; these appeared *not* to have arrived at such a state of perfection. *They* could not affect *indifference*, as they joined in the petition for averting the punishment of sins; nor conceal the interest they had in the glad tidings of eternal happiness. They listened with peculiar complacency to the accounts of him, who "came to preach the gospel to the poor,"[1] and the hopes of his favour seemed to irradiate with joy the bosom of resignation. A female of advanced life, in whom all these emotions were discernable, particularly arrested my attention. The paleness of her countenance, spoke her want of health, and the lines which sorrow had traced in it, accorded with the sable weeds of widowhood, which she wore. She appeared ready to faint from the fatigue of long standing, and made a modest application to a person, who seemed to act as porter of the pews, for admittance into one of them. To my astonishment, she met with a refusal; nor did any one of the gorgeously apparelled Christians, who sat in them, appear to be any way concerned for her

---

1 Luke 4: 18; the quotations later in the paragraph are from the Litany in the Anglican Book of Common Prayer.

situation; indeed, they all seemed to regard those who worshipped God from the aisle, as if they had been beings of an inferior race. I was, however, well convinced, that Christianity admits of no such distinctions; and supposing the Christian lady who sat by me, though her eyes were roving to all parts of the temple,was, in reality, too much engaged in her devotions, to observe what passed, I took the liberty of acting for her, and opening the door of the pew, invited the poor sick stranger to a seat. At that moment, the priest was preferring a petition, in favour of all "fatherless children, and widows, and *all who are desolate and oppressed*"; to which the great Lady had just uttered the response of, "We beseech thee to hear us, good Lord!" – when observing the poor woman by her side, her face instantly flushed a deep crimson; rage and indignation darted from her eyes, and, telling the fainting stranger, that she was very impudent, for daring to intrude herself into her presence, she turned her out into the aisle. I was weak enough, to be shocked at the behaviour of this well-dressed votary of Christianity. Ah! thought I, can it be, that this woman should be so conscious of her superiority, in everything which constitutes distinction in the eye of the Omnipotent, as to consider *herself* worthy of *sitting in his presence*, while she spurns from her own, the humble child of poverty, and affliction?

<hr />

I HAVE just returned from my first visit to Doctor Severan, the gentleman to whose attentions Grey has most particularly recommended me; nor could he, according to the opinion of Delomond, have done me a more essential service. My accomplished friend, who was, it seems, the companion of his youthful studies, tells me, that at the university, it appeared evident that he was born to be the ornament of Science. Whilst other young men were pursuing the gaudy phantom of pleasure, his time was occupied in investigating the laws of Nature, in tearing the choicest secrets from her reluctant bosom, or, in tracing her foot-steps through the various phænomena of the material world. – Nor, continued Delomond, as we drove to this gentleman's house, is he less estimable as a man, than respectable as a philosopher. But, indeed, the connection between philosophy and virtue, is "so natural, that it is only their separation that can excite surprise; for is not the very basis of science, a sincere and disinterested love of truth? An enlarged view of things cannot fail to destroy the effects of prejudice: and while it awakens in the mind, the most sublime ideas of the great original cause; it promotes, most necessarily, a detestation of every thing that is mean or base." We just then stopped at the door of his friend, and were ushered into an apartment surrounded with shelves of books, arranged in no very good order; every table, and almost every seat, was occupied by numerous odd shaped vessels, some of glass, and others of metal, but for what use I could not possibly comprehend. The philosopher himself at length appeared. A tall thin man, of about forty years of age, his dress put on in a manner particularly careless; but his countenance, so mild, and serious! it was the very personification of benignity. He appeared rejoiced at seeing Delomond, who, if possible, was exalted in my esteem, by seeing the degree of estimation in which he was held by the philosopher. Myself he received in the most gracious manner; and, by his kindness to me, he gave the most convincing proof of his regard for my friend Grey, of whom, indeed, he spoke very handsomely. He informed me, that Lady Grey, widow to the brother of our friend, was then at her country residence, but that her brother, Sir Caprice Ardent, for whom I had likewise a letter of introduction, was in London; and added, that he should do himself the pleasure of accompanying me to the house of this gentleman, the day after to-morrow; and hoped that I would come *to eat my breakfast with him, before we went.* You will smile at the invitation: and, no doubt, be surprised to find this philosopher, whom one would expect to soar above the practices and notions of the vulgar, taking such a method of shewing his hospitality; but it is a difficult thing to get the better of early prejudice; nor does the generality of mankind in any country, enquire into the propriety of customs, to which they have been rendered familiar by use. Though to us it appears highly absurd, as well as grossly indelicate, to see people looking in each others' faces while they chew their food, and calling it sociable to swallow their morsel at the same moment; it is possible, that these Europeans may think our solitary manner of eating equally ridiculous; and if they abstain from censuring it, is it not a proof of their being more enlightened? Often have I observed to you, and often do I see reason to repeat the observation, *that it is they only who have conquered the force of prejudice in themselves, that can make any allowance for the effects of it in others.*

COFFEE-HOUSES, similar to that described in one of my letters from Calcutta, are to be met, with in every quarter of this city. Those I have here seen, are schools of politics, resorted to by all who take an interest in public affairs; – a true and authentic statement of which is daily printed on large sheets of paper, and copies are, I am told, sent to every part of the Island. In the Coffee-houses, these are handed about from politician to politician, and furnish matter for the general discourse. For my part, though possessed of a sufficient share of curiosity, I did not care to be too forward in seeking to pry into the state affairs of the country; but having accompanied Delomond, yesterday, into a neighbouring coffee-house, and hearing a gentleman who sat near me, declare, that the paper he was then perusing, was indubitably published under the immediate direction of the British minister, I could not restrain my impatience, to examine its contents, – and the moment he laid it down, I eagerly flew to its perusal.

It is impossible to describe to you the admiration with which the reading of this paper inspired me, for the talents and virtues of this sapient noble, who presides in the supreme councils of this happy nation. So extensive! so multifarious! so minute are the subjects of his concerns, that one contemplates with astonishment, the mind that is capable of grasping such an infinity of objects. In one paragraph, he reports to the nation, the account of a victory which their armies had obtained, *or nearly obtained* over the forces of their Christian enemies; tells the numbers of the slain – of those who are still suffering the agonies of pain, far from the soothing balm of affection! far from the healing consolations of friendship! – To the families of such as are in a situation to afford the expensive insignia of sorrow, the names of their fallen friends are announced; but, to the poor, who can only afford to wear mourning in their hearts, there is no necessity of giving such a particular account of their friends; it is sufficient for them to know, that few, very few of them can ever again behold their native homes!

In the next paragraph, this puissant statesman informs the world of the safe arrival in town of Sir Dapper Dawdle, in his phaeton and four; which, and many similar pieces of intelligence, are, no doubt, given with the beneficent intention of informing the poor and wretched, where they may find their benefactors; those, who by their liberal and repeated acts of charity, have obtained *the blessing of them, who are ready to perish*. Nor is the nourishment of the mind neglected by this wise minister; the public are informed, in this newspaper, where such books are to be had, as are, doubtless, best calculated for their instruction. I have already told you, that the females of this place go themselves into the shops, in order to purchase what they want; and, methinks, it is highly praiseworthy of this good superintendent of the kingdom, to point out to the fair creatures, where they may lay out their money to the most advantage. They are in one part, strongly assured of the superior excellence of the goods at the Pigeons; in another, they are conjured to buy their stockings at the Fleeces, their shoes, their gloves, nay the very powder, with which they disfigure their beautiful hair, are all objects of this good nobleman's tender anxiety; indeed, the proper decoration of their persons, seems to employ no inconsiderable portion of his attention; there is no deformity of the body, no disorder of the skin, against which they are not here provided with a remedy. Nor doth royal dignity itself disdain to extend its cares to beautifying and adorning the female subjects of these realms. You will, perhaps, smile, to hear of the *royal* firman's being attached to the ladies' garters? But there is not a brush for their nails, nor a soap for their hands, nor a powder for their teeth, nor wash for their pretty faces, that is not as highly honoured. Alas! how much are these females indebted to a prince, who evinces such unequalled solicitude for the preservation of their beauty!

Nor doth the parental care of royalty for the welfare of the people stop here; their health is an object of peculiar concern; innumerable are the lists of medicines of approved efficacy, which are here recommended to the public; I reckoned above sixty that had received the *royal* sanction, sealed by the *royal* arms, and mentioned by *royal* authority; when we reflect, how many nauseous draughts the *royal* counsellors must needs have tasted; how many bitter pills they, doubtless, must have swallowed, before they could advise his

Majesty on a subject so important; we can scarcely refrain from pitying the situation of those, whose high stations impose upon them the performance of such disagreeable duties!! – I could furnish you with further proofs of the tender care of this government for the health and happiness of its subjects, but am obliged to leave off, on account of my visit to Sir Caprice Ardent.

⸎

I FORGET whether I informed you, that a necessary part of my establishment is a carriage. A model of which, I have this morning purchased for you, at what is called a toy-shop, that you may form some idea of the manner in which the great are drawn about the streets of this city. Numbers, however, even of an exalted rank, occasionally walk: nor is it thought any degradation, to make use of their own legs. I this morning met the Heir apparent of the throne, walking on foot in the very street in which I live; far from appearing in my eyes as shorn of his dignity, by thus condescending to mingle with his people, it shed upon it, in my opinion, a beam of additional lustre.[1] Ah! what a transcendent degree of excellence must we suppose these highly favoured Princes to possess, who, together with the dignified sentiments of their exalted rank, enjoy the advantages of that instruction, which is only to be obtained by commerce with the world! The mirror of truth is set before them, and, surely, they will never turn from it to view themselves through the distorting medium of venal flattery, and deceitful adulation!! – But, to return from this digression; I took up Dr. Severan, according to appointment, and proceeded with

---

1   The heir-apparent was the future Prince Regent (from 1811) and George IV (1820-30). At the supposed date of this letter, he was around twenty (he was born in 1762) but had already begun his career of wild expense and dissipation. His "commerce with the world" had, by the early 1780s, included a scandalous liaison with the actress and future novelist, Mary Robinson, and a passionate affair with the Countess von Hardenburg, with whom he briefly contemplated eloping. By the mid-1790s, when Hamilton was writing the novel, the prince's circle was notorious for its expensive dissipation, and it was suspected that the opposition Whigs, headed by the prince's friend Charles James Fox, were using him for their own purposes – "venal flattery" was among the least of the sins of which they were accused by their enemies.

him to the house of the Baronet, which is situated at the upper end of a short street, none of the buildings of which are yet completed; they seem as if they were intended for houses of very different sizes and shapes, and at present have a very strange appearance, but it is impossible to form any idea of what they may be, when finished. The entrance to the house of Sir Caprice, was somewhat obstructed by heaps of rubbish, occasioned, as we soon learned, by the destruction of a row of pillars, of Grecian architecture, with which the hall had been originally graced. These proud ornaments, which during the short period of their exaltation, had heard the lofty roof which they sustained, re-echo the voices of their flatterers, were on a sudden, disgraced, dismissed, and hurled headlong to the ground! Their fall was like that of the favourites of Princes, which shakes the throne they once appeared destined to support. A long train of dependants were involved in the mighty ruin, and it was not without some degree of danger, that, following the servant, we scrambled through this scene of desolation, to the apartment of Sir Caprice, whom we found seated at a large table, on which an innumerable quantity of plans, maps, models of buildings, and other various ornaments, were heaped. After reading the letter I had brought him, congratulating me on my arrival in England, and enquiring after the health of Mr. Grey, he turned to Doctor Severan, and expressed, in strong terms, the particular pleasure he at that moment felt in seeing him. – "I know you are a man of taste," cried he, "and shall be wonderfully happy to have your advice on the plan of a new building, which I intend shall be something very extraordinary. Here it is," continued he, holding up a small model; "here, you see, I have contrived to unite all the orders of architecture in regular gradation; here, you will please to observe that the basis is truly Gothic; above that observe the Tuscan; above that, the Composite, the Corinthian, the Doric, the Ionic – all placed as they never were placed before! Still, however, the top is unfinished; for that I have had many plans; but, that which pleases me best, is, the idea of crowning the whole with a Chinese temple; is it not a good thought, eh? Perhaps this gentleman, could furnish me with a hint. Pray Sir," turning to me, "has the Emperor of China done any thing new in this way, of late?" The philosopher, perceiving my confusion, reminded this noble builder, that I was from Bengal, and had never been in China in my life. "From Bengal? Ay, ay, I had forgot; a Hindoo is he?

Well, well, perhaps, then, he could give me a plan of a Mosque, a Minaret, or some such thing, it would oblige me extremely, as it would be something quite new, and uncommon." Perceiving that he waited my answer, I told him, that I certainly had had many opportunities of seeing Mosques, some of the most stately of which, were built from the ruins of our ancient temples, particularly that at Benares, the Minarets of which were esteemed eminently beautiful; but, that as I had never been in one, I was altogether unqualified to give an accurate description of them. "Did not trouble church much, I suppose, Sir?" rejoined he, with an arch smile. "Good heaven!" cried Severan, "do you not know, that a Mosque is a Mahommaden place of worship, and have I not already told you, that this gentleman is a Hindoo?" – "Ay, ay, I had forgot, he is a *heathen*. So much the better; I shall love him, if he hates all priests; all priest-ridden fools; I never knew any good come of either." So saying, he offered me his hand, and shook mine, in a most cordial manner. He then renewed his solicitations for the opinion of Severan, in regard to the manner in which he should finish his projected building[1] (a building for which, he had not yet fixed upon a situation); the philosopher eluded any further dissertations on the subject, with great dexterity, and finally prevailed upon him to introduce us to the apartment of his Lady.

We found Lady Ardent, and her eldest daughter, in the apartment called the drawing-room. They were prepared to go out, and had their carriage waiting for them at the door; but, on our entrance, politely resumed their seats. The countenance of neither of these ladies, exhibited one single line, that could lead to the developement of their characters; all was placid uniformity, and *unspeaking* regularity of feature. Surely, said I to myself, these women must have arrived at the very zenith of perfection! How effectually must every passion have been subdued under the glorious empire of reason, before they could have attained such inexpressive indifference? It is true, that in their eyes, the sparkling chubdar[2] of intellect, doth not proclaim his

---

1  Explanations of the terms of Architecture, &c. though very necessary to the friends of the Rajah, it was thought, would be rather tiresome to the English reader; they are therefore omitted by the narrator, who has frequently been obliged to take liberties of the same nature. [E.H.]

2  The servant whose business it is to proclaim the titles of any great personage. [E.H.] On the beloved of Krishna, mentioned in the next sentence, see 61, note 2.

master's presence – but the apathy which sits upon their foreheads, speaks in plain language, their contempt of the world and its vanities. With them, as with the beloved of Krishna, pain and pleasure are as one! The modesty of female bashfulness, sealed the lips of the young lady, but her mother enquired after my friend Grey, if not with affection, at least with much politeness. She treated me (as I was told by Doctor Severan) with an uncommon degree of attention. She gave me a slip of stiff paper, on which was marked the 10th day of the next month, which, I was informed by my friend, was an invitation to a rout; that is to say, an entertainment, where a vast number of rational, wise, and well informed votaries of immortality, meet together, not to converse, but to look at each other, and to turn over the bits of painted paper, called cards! After receiving this mark of her Ladyship's attention, we took our leave, and retired.

I was curious to know some further particulars of a family, whose manners appeared to me so peculiar; and Doctor Severan, whom I have the happiness of seeing every day, has had the goodness amply to gratify my curiosity. He began with observing, that "to those who take pleasure in investigating the phenomena that fall under their observation, either mental or material, it is not sufficient to say that things are so, they must develope the causes in which they have originated. As there are few substances found in natural state, whose constituent parts cannot be separated from each other, by the methods used in chemistry, so there are few predominant dispositions of the mind, which may not be analized and traced through their origin and progress by any one who will give himself the trouble to pursue the necessary process.

"This investigation, if accurately followed," continued my friend, "will invariably lead us to the *early education* of the object of it. In *it* we will commonly find an explanation of the manner in which the peculiar combination of ideas that ultimately forms character, has been produced; to it, therefore, we must always recur in our analization of the propensities and conduct of any individual.

"The father of Sir Caprice, was three times married. – His first wife, who was the heiress of a wealthy family, died soon after the birth of a daughter, in whom, the fortunes of her family are at present centered. – His second wife, the mother of Sir Caprice, brought him no other dower besides beauty, and good temper. Her premature death overwhelmed him in affliction; but, happily, just as he was erecting a monument to her memory, in the inscription of which, he gave notice to the world, that his affections were for ever buried in her tomb, a consoling angel appeared to comfort him, in the shape of Lady Caroline Beaumont.

"This Lady, who brought him only one daughter, proved an excellent wife, and would have been one of the best of mothers to his children, but for a certain timidity of temper, which restrained her from exerting authority over the children of another. From her, therefore, they met with unlimited indulgence, that most powerful inflamer of the passions, in whose high temperature, fortitude is lost, and selfishness, arrogance, and pride, are inseparably united.

"Their father having a dislike to public schools, and resolving that his daughter should share the advantages of a classical education with his son, provided them with a tutor at home – the reverend Mr. Ergo. Well do I remember him. He afterwards got the living of our parish, and used to stuff his sermons with Greek and Hebrew, in such a manner, as to make the poor people stare at the depth of his knowledge. In truth, he was a most profound linguist; a complete walking vocabulary; – but of every virtue that dilates the heart, of every science that expands the soul, while it enlarges the understanding, he was completely ignorant. The highest idea he could form of the efforts of human intellect, was confined to an accurate knowledge of nouns, verbs, cases, and tenses; and, to commit these to the memory of his pupils, was the chief object of his solicitude. Unqualified to fix the generous principle in the ductile bosom, he attended not to the developement of mind, but, on the contrary, extoled as marks of genius, the early whims and caprices of his pupil, which were, in reality, the ebullitions of an unregulated imagination.

"It is, perhaps, to this want of judgment in the tutor, that the extraordinary degree of ardour and unsteadiness, which has distinguished the Baronet, may, in some degree, be attributed. A recital of the various and opposite pursuits in which he has been at different times engaged, will be the best illumination I can give you of his character, which is such an one, as, I suppose, your Eastern world has never produced. He is, however, by no means, an unique in this part of the world; where the liberty of committing every folly that suggests itself to the fancy, is considered as the most glorious privilege.

"The ardour of Sir Caprice's mind," continued my friend, "was, for the first two years after his father's death, expended upon running horses; at length, finding himself *taken in* by his compeers of the turf, cheated by his groom, and most frequently, distanced at the post, he sold his racers, and foreswore Newmarket for ever."

Here I was obliged to beg an explanation from the philosopher, and found, that it is customary for the great men in this kingdom, in their exertion of the privilege hinted at above, to expend immense sums of money on a very beautiful, though useless, species of horses. These animals are, however, doomed to experience the effects of the capricious humours of their masters. At any time, they are considered as the dearest friends, and most loved companions of their lords, who are never so happy, as when in the apartments of their four-legged favourites. While this fit of fondness lasts, they are attended by numerous servants, who, taking consequence from the dignity of their employment, are at once the most insolent, and most rapacious of the domestic tribe. Some of these are employed in rubbing the skins of the horses into a beautiful polish, while others serve them with the choicest food. Nay, so far does their care extend, that, as if the clothing of nature were not sufficient, they provide them with woollen garments, which completely cover their whole bodies. Will not Māāndāāra think, that the truth hath forsaken his friend, when I say, that the tormenting of these unfortunate favourites, forms one of the chief amusements of the English nobility? But, so it is; – at certain appointed periods, they are brought out in the midst of a concourse of spectators, stripped of their fine clothing, and forced to gallop round a certain piece of ground full speed, while, for the amusement of their cruel masters, they are whipped, and even goaded by sharp instruments of steel, until the blood flows in streams, from their lacerated bodies, and this is called sport! – But, to return to Sir Caprice Ardent. If I rightly remember, the next pursuit upon which, according to Doctor Severan's account, he employed the vigour of his mind, was Hunting. Here are no Jungles in which to pursue the ferocious tyrants of the forest. Here, courage is not called forth in the attack of the wild Elephant, or the roaring Lion. Nor is activity and watchfulness necessary, to guard against the sudden spring of the carnage-loving Tyger. The pursuit of a small animal, called a Fox, employs the vigour of the English Hunters. The mischief, which the Philosopher informed me, was done by Sir Caprice, and his friends, in pursuit of this little animal, I confess, appeared to me altogether unaccountable. He mentioned their having spoiled fifteen farms, by breaking down the fences, and that a young wood, of great extent, which had been planted by his father, was, by the advice of one of the companions of Sir Caprice, in order to give free scope to the magnanimous pursuers of the red fugitive, burned to the ground. Another consequence of this diversion was, to me, equally incomprehensible. Notwithstanding the coldness of the climate, it seems to be productive of the most astonishing degree of thirst. The sum of money, which, according to the calculation of Doctor Severan, was expended by Sir Caprice, on the wine gulped down by his companions of the chace, would, if it had been employed in improving the uncultivated parts of his estate, have been sufficient to have made the barren wilderness, a garden of delights.

"Next to hunting," said Doctor Severan, "succeeded the love of equipage, and fine clothes. It was now the ambition of the Baronet's heart, to attract the attention of the Ladies. His ambition was, perhaps, in no other pursuit of his life, so fully gratified. Wherever he appeared, his exquisite taste was the object of unbounded admiration.

"To have a wife, whose beauty would justify the opinion enter-tained of his taste, and who would likewise give him a new opportu-nity of displaying it, in the choice of female ornaments, now engrossed his cares. Such a one, he soon met with. You have seen his Lady. She is what is commonly called *one of the best of women*. To an evenness of temper, flowing from insensibility, she adds a strict obser-vance of all the rules of politeness and good breeding, taught by that sort of education given at modern boarding schools; which being directed to unessential forms, and useless accomplishments, renders the character cold and artificial. Though incapable of generous friendship, or heart-warming affection, she is never deficient in the external ceremonials of respect; and though she never did a kind or good-natured thing in her life, the low temperature of her passions, assists her in preserving that semblance of placidity, often, very improperly, called *sweetness*, which at all times appears in her countenance.

"With a better understanding, she might, perhaps, have directed the effervescence of her husband's disposition to some useful purpose, and restrained it within the limits of common sense. As it is, she contents herself, if, by the assistance of a *little* cunning, in which women of this class of intellect are never deficient, she can work out any *little* end, to which her *little* selfish mind inclines her.

"It would be too tedious," continued Severan, "to follow the Baronet through all the various whims and fancies, in which his restless spirits have discharged themselves.

"The only period in which I ever knew reading to occupy much of his time, was soon after his marriage, when he took to studying books of education; and had actually from these composed a Treatise, for the instruction of his expected heir; which, however, was forgot before the child had learned to speak, for then he had turned *improver*.

"It was then, that the fine grove of oaks and chestnuts, the massy richness of whose foliage, served equally to shelter and adorn his stately mansion, was levelled to the ground; and every spot within sight of the windows, metamorphosed into "a dry smooth-shaven green,"[1] awkwardly sprinkled with gnarled sapplings, and ill-formed clumps of shrubbery. How far this spirit of improvement might have led him, it is impossible to conjecture, for it was still at its height, when a piece of silver ore, found by one of the workmen, in digging a canal, intended to meander through the grounds, gave a new object to his ever ardent mind.

"For three sleepless nights, his fancy revelled in all the riches of Peru. Miners were brought from various parts of the kingdom, and the greatest encouragement offered to those who should be successful in discovering the vein, of the existence of which, he could not entertain a doubt. Huge excavations were made in various directions, all begun in hope, and ending in disappointment; the miners strictly followed the usual example of our ministers of state; who, when they have plunged the nation into an unnecessary and unsuccessful war take care, when the account of defeat comes from one quarter, to

---

1   John Milton, "Il Penseroso."

amuse the attention of the public, with the prospect of better success in another; and Sir Caprice, like the honest British people, was too willing to be deceived, to suffer himself to discover the trick. At length, finding miners grow rich, in proportion as he grew poor, his patience became entirely exhausted; and with many execrations on their knavery, and his own folly, he suddenly dismissed them all, and set himself diligently to repair the devastations they had committed on the face of his estate. It was this circumstance, which, perhaps, turned his thoughts to agriculture, which, as he contrived to manage it was as unproductive a folly, as any in which he has ever yet engaged. With such avidity, however, did he enter into it, that I well remember him walking about the fields, with a silver spoon in his hand, to taste the different composts, into the specific qualities of which, he thought it necessary to examine; and ignorant of the chemical process, he trusted to his palate, for a discovery of the acids or alkalis they contained. It would seem, that, in this particular, it had proved a deceitful guide; – for, notwithstanding his delicacy of taste, and although he had laid out his fields in the best method, that the best theoretical writers had pointed out, he had the worst crops that were known in the country; he was, at length, contented to replace the old tenants in their farms; and finding his estate considerably incumbered, by his various schemes of fortune-making (avarice having now become the passion which chiefly predominated in his heart) he resolved for a few years, to try the economical plan of travelling. He accordingly set out for the continent, with his Lady, leaving his eldest daughter at the most fashionable boarding school in London; his second, who had been adopted from the hour of her birth by his sister, Miss Ardent, remained with her; and the youngest, had the happiness of being received under the roof of her excellent Aunt, Lady Grey.

"Sir Caprice Ardent and his Lady remained abroad for six years, in the course of which period, his Lady brought him three sons; only one of whom survives; a poor puny boy, so completely spoiled by indulgence, that there is no bearing his petulance and prate. During the residence of our Baronet in Italy, he gave sufficient proofs to his friends, that the change of atmosphere, had no effect on the temperament of his mind. Antiques, Music, Pictures, Statues, Intaglios, and even Butterflies, were, in their turns, the exclusive objects of his attention. The death of a relation, who bequeathed him a large legacy, brought him at length back to his country, just as the rage for building had begun to occupy his mind. With its effects, you are sufficiently acquainted; and you will, probably, before the conclusion of the summer, see it give place to some other absurdity, which will be entered on with equal ardour, managed with equal skill, and ultimately abandoned with equal facility."

Alas! cried I, I find, that folly is a plant, which flourishes in every clime; it only differs in the colouring. But if it is not intruding too far upon your time and patience, I should be glad to know, what hue it assumed in the young Lady who was educated by the same tutor.

My friend willingly gratified my curiosity, and thus proceeded:

"To the eldest sister of Sir Caprice, who inherited from Nature a stronger intellect and quicker perception than her brother, the tuition of Doctor Ergo was attended with more beneficial consequences. The ancient authors, whose works were by him put into her hands, merely as exercises in the dead languages, attracted her attention. She acquired a taste for their beauties, and soon became so addicted to reading as at an early period of life, rendered her mistress of an extensive degree of information. But alas! it is not merely a knowledge of the facts contained in history, nor a relish for the beauties of poetic imagery, nor a superficial acquaintance with any branch of science, that can effectually expand the powers of the human mind. For that great end, the judgment must be qualified to apply them to useful purposes. It was this deficiency, which led Miss Ardent, to value her accidental attainments at so high a rate, as to make her despise not only the weaknesses, but even the domestic virtues of her own sex. Their occupations and amusements, she treated with the utmost contempt; and thought that in this contempt, she gave the surest proof of the superiority of her own *masculine understanding*.

From her mind, though the particles of vanity were not expelled, they assumed a new form – instead of the attention to external beauty, feminine graces, and elegant manners, the vanity of Miss Ardent appeared in an affectation of originality of sentiment, and intrepid singularity of conduct. In support of this character, she altogether loses sight of her own, which is naturally gentle and benevolent; and enforces her opinions in so dictatorial a manner, as renders her equally the object of dread and dislike to the generality of her acquaintance. And, indeed, it must be acknowledged, that this accomplished woman, in her eagerness to display the strength of her mind, too often lays aside that outer robe of delicacy, which is not only the ornament, but the armour of female virtue; and that she never attempts to shine, without exciting the alternate emotions of admiration and disgust." Good heaven, exclaimed I, and is *this* the consequence of female learning? is the mind of woman, *really* formed of such weak materials, that as soon as it emerges from ignorance, it must necessarily become intoxicated with the fumes of vanity and conceit? "And did your highness never see a *male* pedant?" replied the philosopher. "Did you never behold a man destitute of early education, and confined to the society of ignorant and illiterate people, who had by some chance, acquired knowledge of books; and did he not appear as proud of his superiour information, as ridiculously vain, as arrogant, as ostentatious, and conceited, as any learned Lady that ever lived? or, if a more phlegmatic temper prevented the effervescence of vanity from displaying itself in the same manner, it is ten to one, that he was still more insufferable by his dogmatic pedantry and superciliousness. The reason why such characters are not so frequently to be met with amongst men, is, that (in this country at least) the education of boys is, in some degree, calculated to open, and gradually to prepare the mind for the reception of knowledge; that of girls, on the contrary, is from their very cradles, inimical to the cultivation of any one rational idea.

In the mental as in the material world, similar causes will ever produce similar affects; let the combination of ideas be attended to from the earliest period of life; let the mind be early taught to think; taught, to form a just estimate of the objects, within the reach of its observation; and appreciating every thing by its usefulness, led to see, that *genius is less valuable than virtue*, and that the knowledge of every science, and the attainment of every accomplishment, sinks into insignificance, when compared to the uniform performance of any known duty. Will the mind, whether it belongs to male or female, that is thus prepared, be elated into arrogance, by learning the opinions of the people of different ages, even though taught to read them in the language in which they were originally written? will it become less modest, less amiable, less engaging, for having been enlarged by this extent of information; or will it be less qualified for the performance of social duties, because it has been freed from the prejudices of ignorance, and taught to fill its place in the scale of rational beings? Surely, no; I need only mention the name of Lady Grey, to give the fullest proof of the justness of my assertion. This younger sister of the Ardent's, had, under the care of a mother, eminently qualified for the task, the advantage of just such an education as I have described; but though to all the understanding and accomplishments of her sister, she adds that brilliancy of imagination, of which the value is so apt to be over-estimated by its possessors, she is neither vain, ostentatious, nor assuming. Accustomed to compare her actions, not with the triflers around her, but with the pure standard of Christian excellence, her virtues are all genuine. For instance, the quality of gentleness, which, in woman, is seldom more than a passive tameness of spirit, that yields without struggling to the encroachments of the turbulent and unworthy, is, in her, the spontaneous offspring of true humility; it is the transcript of that wisdom which is from above, pure, and peaceable, and lovely! – Modesty is not in her the affectation of squeamish delicacy – it is the purity of the heart. Maternal fondness (and never was the heart of a mother more tenderly affectionate) is, like every other affection of her soul, put under the controul of reason. That blind indulgence, which would be prejudicial to the real interests of its object, is, by her, considered as a selfish gratification, not to be enjoyed, but at the expence of the future happiness of her child; it is therefore wisely restrained, though sometimes at the expence of present feeling. Such tenderness, directed by such wisdom, is the nearest possible imitation of the most amiable attributes of the divinity! – And who would put such a woman as this, in comparison with the most beautiful piece of insipid ignorance, that ever opened its eyes upon the world? Is there a man, who would prefer the vapid chatter of a pretty ideot, to the conversation of such a woman? So good! so wise! so beautiful! Yes, my noble Rajah, she is still beautiful! though her eyes have lost somewhat of that lustre, which, but a few years ago, was the admiration of all beholders, they still beam with animation and sensibility." Ah! my friend, cried I, you need say little to persuade me of her beauty; the accomplishments and virtues of an ugly woman, can make little impression even on the mind of a philosopher. – My friend coloured, but before be could reply, a loud explosion from the other end of the room, burst upon our ears, and filled us with momentary terror. In discoursing on Lady Grey, my friend had forgotten the necessary management of a retort[1] which for want of his attention, burst in pieces. I know not what were its contents, but they sent forth such suffocating effluvia, as had I not been restrained by politeness, would quickly have driven me from the room.

When the smoke which followed the explosion, was somewhat dissipated, I observed my friend, standing in a melancholy posture, with clasped hands, and fixed eyes, ruminating on the misfortune that had befallen him. A course of experiments, the labour of many weeks, were by this unhappy accident, rendered abortive; it was a subject that could not immediately admit of consolation. I therefore, for some time, preserved the strictest silence. Just as I was about to open my lips with the voice of sympathy, the Philosopher, who had never lifted his eyes, from the remains of the broken vessel, suddenly clapping his hands together, exclaimed, in a transport of ecstacy, "I see it! I see it! – Heavens! what a discovery! – Never was there so fortunate an accident!" I was at first somewhat afraid that my friend's senses had received a shock from this alarming incident; but was happily relieved from my apprehensions, on being informed, that the appearance which the matter, contained in the retort, had assumed on its explosion, gave a hint to the philosopher, for the explanation of some phænomena hitherto unaccounted for. In a moment, that fine countenance (and never did Brama bestow upon a human soul, an index so intelligible) which had been so lately shaded by the cloud of despondency, was brightened by the emanations of joy, and irradiated by the smile of exultation and delight. I was not sufficiently initiated in science, to be able to appreciate the value of the discovery, which gave such ecstatic pleasure the mind of the Philosopher; but contemplated with rapture the wisdom of the immortal spirit, who, when he spread the volume of Nature before his rational offspring, passed this

---

1   A long-necked container, usually of glass, used for distilling liquids.

unalterable decree:"That to the mind, devoted to its perusal, the corrosive passions should be unknown. That it should have power to assuage the tumults of the soul; to foster the emotions of virtue; and to produce a species of enjoyment, peculiarly its own!" – Such, O! Mããndããra! such are the advantages of Science!!

<hr/>

ACCORDING to appointment, I went, few evenings ago, to Lady Ardent's rout. Doctor Severan had the goodness to accompany me; a piece of condescension, which, now that I know what sort of a thing a rout is, I cannot but consider as a very distinguished compliment.

A rout is a species of penance, of which the pious Yogees of Hindoostan never conceived an idea; if these people were not the professors of a religion which prohibits the worship of the inferior deities, I should say, it was sacrifice to the Goddess of Fashion; a sacrifice not of the joint of a finger, or a toe, as we are here told it is the custom to present to that Goddess in some newly discovered countries,[1] but of every faculty of the soul, that distinguishes the rational from the brute creation. These remain during the ceremony of the rout, in an absolute state of suspension. You may imagine, my dear Mããndããra, what a sacrifice this must be – to people possessed of so much wisdom, and who are so eminently qualified for the pleasures of conversation. What a sacrifice! to be deprived of the interchange of ideas, of every communication of sentiment, and every advantage of understanding, and to be doomed to sit stifling in a crowded room, during the length of an evening, with no other employment, than that of turning over little bits of painted paper!

It is not surprising, that in such circumstances the countenances of these votaries of fashion, should so frequently be distinguished by the insipid stare of vacancy, or the lowering frown of discontent. For my part, I could not help pitying them from my very soul; I was particularly concerned for a group of young females, who were placed on a sopha in a corner of the room, and who, instead of cards, held each in their hand a small fan, which they from time to time opened,

<hr/>

1   It is supposed by the Translator, that the Rajah here alludes to a custom said to be practised in Otaheite. See Cook's Voyages. [E.H.]

and again shut in a very melancholy manner. As I contemplated their situation with much compassion, wondering, whether silence had actually been imposed upon them, as one of the duties of the ceremony, my feelings were effectually relieved by the entrance of three effeminate-looking youths, dressed in the military habit, whose pale faces and puny figures, rendered it a matter of doubt, to which sex they actually belonged, till one of them being saluted *Lord*, relieved me from the dilemma. Whether there was anything exhilarating in the perfumes which these Saibs had plentifully bestowed upon their persons, I know not; but their appearance seemed to spread a sudden ray of animation over the dejected Bibbys, who in a moment, began to speak to each other with wonderful loquacity; the fans were opened and shut, with encreasing celerity. The Chouries upon their heads, were with one consent put into motion, waving like the graceful plumage of the Auney,[1] when it carries the messages of Camdeo; and their eyes, which had hitherto rolled with languid vacuity, from one head-dress to another, now turned their glances towards that part of the room, where the lady-like gentlemen stood. Two of these heroes, with a degree of fortitude, to which many more gallant-looking men would have been unequal, turning their backs upon the fair creatures, who so sweetly solicited their attention; sat down at a card-table, each placing himself opposite to a wrinkled Bibby, old enough to be his grandmother. The young Lord, either possessing less resolution than his companions, or, not considering this sort of penance necessary for the good of his soul, joined himself to the fan-playing Party of the young ladies. – Dulness and melancholy, vanished at his approach; every word he uttered, produced a simper on the pretty faces of his female audience; the simper, at length, encreased into a tittering laugh. Observing that they cast their eyes to the opposite side of the apartment, I judged it was some object placed there that excited their risibility; following the direction of their glances, I perceived a Lady with a remarkably pleasant countenance, who had indeed no chourie upon her head, and who was in every particular less disfigured by dress, than any other person in the room. I was pondering in my own mind, how this modest and unassuming personage,

---

1   A fabulous bird, frequently mentioned by the Poets of India, as the ambassador of love. [E.H.]

could excite the risibility of the fair group, when a Lady who had for some time stood near them, apparently engaged in over-looking a card-table, turned round, and addressed them in the following manner: "When you, my Lord and Ladies, have sufficiently amused yourselves in ridiculing the dress of that excellent woman, I hope you will next proceed to her character. You cannot do better, than compare it with your own. I do assure you, her dress is not so widely different from yours, as the furniture of either her head or heart. That very woman, with her flat cap and plain petticoat, has an understanding of the first quality; and a heart replete with every virtue. While she has been cultivating the one, and exercising the other in the noblest manner; be so good as to ask yourselves, how you have been employed? but, perhaps, your observations, like those of a monkey, can go no further than the ornaments of the person? Then, poor things! who can blame you, for exercising the highest of your intellectual powers; and for asserting your claim to rationality, though even by the lowest and most equivocal of its characteristics?" – You have beheld a flock of Paroquets basking themselves in the rays of the sun, all exerting their little throats, and squalling and chattering with all their might: when, lo! a Cormorant, or other bird of prey has made its appearance, and in a moment, the clamorous voices of the little green-robed chatterers, has been hushed in silence – becoming as mute as the vegetable tribe, under whose friendly leaves they sought for shelter.

Such was the effort produced upon the pretty group of Bibbys, by this unexpected harangue; and, I confess, I participated so much in their feelings, that I was not a little alarmed, when the orator turning with a look of ineffable contempt from her dismayed auditors, addressed herself to me. – Nor did it greatly tend to relieve me, when I discovered that it was *Miss Ardent*, who thus did me the honour of introducing herself to my acquaintance. My friend, the Philosopher, had said enough to frighten me, at the idea of holding any communication with *a learned Lady*. I found her, however, not quite so formidable as I had at first apprehended. She, indeed, soon found means not only to reconcile me to her company, but to render it quite charming. She directed the conversation to the delightful subject of my dear native country! at her desire, I described to her the peculiar charms of the blooming landscape, whose exhilarating beauties, gladden the hearts of the happy inhabitants of Almora. I painted to her imagination the immeasurable forest, whose trees have their sky-touching heads overshadowed by the venerable mountains of Cummow: I talked of the thundering torrents which are dashed from the stupendous rocks, and which, delighted at their escape from the frozen North, run to hide themselves in the bosom of Ganga. I told her of the names which they assumed upon their rout, expatiated on the charming banks which adorned the course of the river Gumtry, and of the playful meanderings of the Gurra. I had likewise the honour of explaining to her, the present political state of the country; it is a subject upon which, since I have been in England, I have seldom had any opportunity, and still seldomer any satisfaction in conversing. In all that relates to our country, I have indeed found these western lovers of science, most deplorably ignorant. You may believe it impressed me with a very high idea of the superior powers of Miss Ardent's mind, when I found that she had paid particular attention to every thing connected with the history or literature of India. But even Miss Ardent has her prejudices, and I did not find it a very easy matter to convince her that the Mahhabaret was superior to the Iliad of Homer: or that Calidas was a dramatic Poet equal in excellence to Shakspeare. You will smile at her prejudices; but consider, my dear friend, what you would think of the arrogance of any foreigner, who should have the presumption to put the works of his countrymen in competition with those divine Bards, and you will learn to make allowances for this Lady. She was surprised to hear that I had not yet been to see the representation of an English Natac, here called a play, and invited me to be of her party, to see the performance of one the following evening. I was charmed with the invitation; and I did not fail in my attendance on the letter-loving Bibby, at the time appointed.

The building appropriated to this amusement, belongs to the King, and is called his Theatre; and to it he sends his servants for the diversion of the public. They are not, however, paid by their Master, but, like all the servants of the English nobility, are paid *by the visitors*.[1]

---

1  A reference to the expectation that servants would receive vails, or tips, from any visitors to the household in which they worked.

Nor are they so modest as some that I have seen, at the royal palaces and gardens, who never asked for their wages, until they had gratified my curiosity; but these, stipulated for a certain sum, and demanded it before they permitted me to enter.

My expectations in respect to the magnificence of the building, and the splendor of its decorations, were somewhat disappointed: but upon the whole it is very well contrived, for seeing and hearing the performers. – In front of the stage, is an aisle larger than that in the church, in which, the people are, however, treated with more respect, being all accommodated with seats: and I could perceive, that *here* their marked approbation of any passage excited some degree of attention in the great people, who sat in the little pews above them: and although among these great people, some appeared to regard the Natac, as little as the sermon, talking and whispering, almost as much at the theatre, as they had done in church; yet the performance was here, in general, much better attended to by all who had the enjoyment of their senses. – You will think this a strange exception – but you must know, that a part af the royal theatre, is peculiarly appropriated to the reception of a species of fanatics, called Bucks, who are indeed, very noisy and troublesome; but who are treated with an amazing degree of lenity and forbearance, by the benevolent people, who bestow upon them the pity that is due to their unhappy situation.

Great part of the entertainment seemed, indeed, calculated for their amusement, as it is well known that the eye can be gratified by the display of gaudy colours; even where the mind is destitute of the gift of reason. This respect to folly, was, however, in my opinion, carried too far; and though I should have been well pleased to have seen the grown children amused, by the exhibition of a few showy pictures and other mummery, I could not approve of turning the infirmities of old age into ridicule, for their amusement. I had foolishly thought that all English plays were like the plays of Shakspeare; but, alas! I begin to apprehend, that they are not all quite so good! instead of those portraits of the passions, which Nature spontaneously acknowledges for her own, I only see exaggerated representations of transient and incidental folly. Whether it be owing to the peculiar taste of the exalted Omrah, whose office it is to examine the merits of the Natacs that are performed by his Majesty's servants,[1] or to the limited genius of modern Poets, I know not, but it appears evident, that all dramatic writers in this country, are now confined to one plot: A foolish old man devoted to avarice, has a daughter that is petulant and disobedient, or a son of the same character; perhaps, two or three of these old men, differing from each other in the size and shape of the covering of the head, called Wigs, are brought into the same piece, together with an old unmarried sister, who always believes herself to be young and handsome. After the young people have for some time exercised their ingenuity in deceiving the vigilance of the old ones, and have successfully exposed to public ridicule the bodily infirmities and mental failings of their several parents, they are paired for marriage, and thus the piece concludes. This composition is called a *Sentimental Comedy*, and is succeeded by what is termed a Farce. In the Farce, his Majesty's servants make faces, and perform many droll tricks for the diversion of the audience, who seem particularly pleased with their exertions in this way, which they applaud with repeated peals of laughter. – And, surely, it must be highly gratifying to the imperial mind, to see the people pleased at so cheap a rate.

The first time I went to the theatre, was, as I have already informed you, in company with Miss Ardent, who was much disappointed, that the illness of the royal servants should have prevented the representation of a new piece, written by an English officer in the service of the East India Company, which, in the opinion of this Lady, is a piece of much intrinsic merit. It is taken from the history of Zingis, and adorned with the terror-striking spirit of Zamouca, which blazes throughout the whole of the performance;[2] to me, I must confess, the presentation of such a piece would have been more charming, than either the lesson of morality, given in the sentimental comedy, or the fooleries of the farce; but I was informed by Miss Ardent, that I must be cautious how I give utterance to such an opinion, as nothing is deemed so barbarous as the energy of good sense. – "If your highness would have the people of this country," continued

---

1  For "Omrah" see 165, note 1. The specific reference is to the Lord Chancellor, whose office had to license all plays before they could be performed.
2  *Zingis*, by Alexander Dow. See 57, note 1.

she, "entertain a good idea of your life, you must give all your admiration to hollow, but high sounding sentiment. Sentiment and sing-song, are the fashion of the day. That it is so, we are much indebted to the care and talents of our modern Bards, who by such compositions as the present, spoil and and contaminate the national taste. "Pardon me," cried a gentleman, who stood by, "but in my opinion the stage does not so much form, as *reflect* the national taste. Poetry has always reached her maturity, while her votaries were in a semi-barbarous state: with the progress of civilization, she has gradually declined; and if we take the rapidity of her decay in this country as the criterion of our refinement, we may proudly pronounce ourselves one of the most polished nations of the earth." – Miss Ardent's carriage being announced, put an end to the conversation; but before she stept into it, she invited me to dine with her on the following day. "What!" you will say, "a single, unprotected woman, invite you to her house? – Shameful violation of decorum!" – But consider, my friend – custom, that mighty legislator, who issues the laws of propriety to the different nations of the earth, makes that appear amiable and proper in the eyes of the people of one country, which in those of another, is criminal and absurd: and so easily doth custom reconcile us to her capricious degrees, that I received the invitation, and went to the house of Miss Ardent, with as little perturbation as if she had been a gentleman in petticoats.

She received me in an apartment devoted to literature and contemplation, from which it takes the name of *study*; the walls of the room were lined with books, all shining in coats of glossy leather richly ornamented with leaf of gold. That pains which in Asia is bestowed in decorating the illuminated page, being in England, all given to the outside covering, which, it must be confessed, gives to the study a very splendid appearance.

Two gentleman had arrived before me, and were already engaged in conversation. These, as Miss Ardent informed me in a whisper, were great *Critics*. The word was new to me, and I did not choose to ask for an explanation, but seeing a huge book upon the table, which I knew to be an explainer of hard words, I had immediate recourse to it, and found a Critic to be "*a man skilled in the art of judging of literature.*" What information might I not expected to receive from such infallible judges, who, as the subsequent description informed me, must be qualified "*nicely to discriminate, and ably to judge, the beauties and faults of writings.*" – The name of a great author, whose works I had read with satisfaction and delight, met my ear, and the fire of expectation was instantly kindled in my bosom. Conscious that I could only skim the surface of that ocean of wisdom, contained in the work of this great moralist, I now hoped to see such hidden gems produced to view, as had escaped my feeble search; but, judge of my mortification, at being informed only of the size of his wig! – Both the critics produced a thousand little instances of the oddities of his manner, the peculiarity of his dress, and the irritability of his temper. But as to the excellence of his precepts, the strength of his arguments, or the sublimity of his sentiments – the critics said not a word![1]

The name of this author led to that of another – a poet to whose verses Miss Ardent gave the epithet of *charming*. Her learned guests, though, in general, obsequiously submissive to her opinion, did not, in this instance, seem to coincide with her. – But, instead of pointing out the defects of his composition, they only mentioned the badness of his taste, of which they gave an irrefragable proof, in his preferring *a roasted* potatoe to a chesnut! – Miss Ardent, who did not seem pleased at having the taste of her favourite poet called in question, abruptly turned the conversation, and addressing herself to me, told me, she should soon have the pleasure of introducing me to some gentlemen of distinguished talents and acknowledged merit, whose names I had probably heard. – She then mentioned three of the most celebrated writers of the present day, every one of whose works I had had the advantage of reading with Delomond, in the course of our voyage. While she yet spoke, the Chubdar re-echoed the names of these celebrated men; they entered, and paid the tribute of respect to this patroness of science, who, when she was seated among them, appeared in my eyes, like the Goddess Serreswatti, surrounded by the gems of the court of Vicramaditya.

Think, Māāndāāra! think, what I must have felt, at the sight of four live authors! You may well believe, that I could not find myself in the immediate presence of so many learned personages, without

---

1   Probably a reference to the English moralist Samuel Johnson, whose peculiarities of dress and manner were well-known. The anecdote alluded to in the next paragraph is untraced, but might refer to Johnson's Irish friend, the poet, playwright, and novelist Oliver Goldsmith.

experiencing a considerable degree of agitation. I remained immersed in silent awe and breathless expectation. Surely, said I to myself, the conversation of men who are capable of writing books, must be very different from that of common mortals!

One of them opened his mouth – I listened with avidity – and heard – that, the morning had been remarkably rainy. How beautiful is this condescension, said I again to myself, in one so wise! – The Chubdar again entered; it was to announce that the dinner was upon the table. I followed Miss Ardent and her learned guests into the apartment destined for this repast, where, according to the barbarous custom of the country, they sat down to eat at one table, and confined their conversation while they remained at it, to eulogiums on the good things set before them, of which, in compliment (no doubt) to the mistress of the feast, they devoured a goodly quantity. While they were thus employed, I retired to a sopha at the other end of the room, where I contemplated with astonishment, how much men of genius could eat. At length, the long-protracted feast was finished, the mangled remains of the bipeds and the quadrupeds, the fishes of the sea, the vegetables of the earth, and the golden fruits of the garden, were carried off by the domestics; a variety of wines supplied their places upon the table – the liquid ruby flowed, and these disciples of the poet of Shiraz seemed to unite with him in regard to the sovereign efficacy of the sparkling contents[1] of the goblet.

---

1   The allusion is taken from one of the odes of Hafiz, which, as it does not appear among those selected by Mr. Nott, for his very elegant Translation, we think the following LITERAL one, may not prove unacceptable:

1. The season of spring is arrived, let the sparkling goblet go round!

2. Seize, O ye youths, the fleeting hour, and enjoy the extatic delight of the company of the fawn-eyed daughters of love.

3. Boy! fill out the wine, and let the liquid ruby flow, for it is alone that poureth the oil of gladness into the hearts of the unfortunate, and is the healing balm of the wounds of the afflicted.

4. Leave the corroding thorns of worldly cares, and anxiety of ambition, to immortalize the names of Cyrus and Alexander.

5. Let me indulge in my favourite wine, and see which of us shall soonest obtain the object of his desires.

6. Let mine ear listen to the melody of the lute and the cymbal, and mine eyes be charmed with the fair daughters of Circassia.

7. Go, O my soul, and give thyself to joy, for it is needless to anticipate today the sorrows of tomorrow. [E.H.] John Nott, *Select odes, from the Persian poet Hafez* (sic),

So much has been said and sung on the inspiring powers of wine, that I anxiously watched its effects on these men of learning. – But, unfortunately for wit and me, no sooner were the bottles set upon the table, than the subject of politics was introduced: a subject which to me, is ever dull and barren of delight. To Miss Ardent, is appeared otherwise; she entered with warmth and energy into the discussion, and spoke of ministers and their measures, of the management of wars, and the interests of nations, in such a decisive manner, as proved her qualified to become the Vizir of an Empire.[1]

Not seeing the conversation likely to take a turn to any other subject, and considering that the presence of a stranger might throw some restraint on the discussion of affairs of state, I took my leave; and must confess, that I returned from this banquet of reason, not altogether satisfied with my entertainment.

As after having lost a game at Chess, it is my custom to ponder on the past moves, until I find out the false step that led to my defeat, so do I ruminate on the disappointment of expected felicity, till I make a discovery of the source from which it has flowed. In doing so, I am almost always certain of seeing it traced to the fallacy of ill-grounded expectation. Why, said I, should I have expected more from an author, than from any other man of sense? When a man has given his thoughts a form upon paper, and submitted them in that shape to the perusal of the world, is he from thenceforth to be obliged to speak in laboured sentences, and to utter only the aphorisms of wisdom? Carrying my reasonings upon this subject a little farther, I was almost tempted to conclude, that the manners of even a female author, might not differ much from that of other women! – but this, you will think, was carrying the matter rather too far.

<hr />

translated into English verse; with notes, critical and explanatory (London, 1787). See also 147, note 1.

1  There may be a hint of self-mockery here. In a letter to Charles Hamilton written in December 1781, Hamilton comments that she and her uncle discuss politics "to admiration. Had my uncle been commander-in-chief of the sea or land forces, or I prime minister at home, Cornwallis would have been victorious, and Graves had sent the French home with disgrace" (Benger 1: 86).

THE amiable, the engaging Delomond, has this morning left us. His departure is like a dark cloud, which in early spring deforms the face of nature, and checks the gaiety of the season with the sudden chill of a wintery storm. It has particularly affected me, as it has at once shut the prospect of prosperity, which, as I had flattered myself, was fast opening on my friend, and deprived me of the sunshine of his presence. But, perhaps, my disappointment with regard to the success of Delomond, is more in proportion to the eagerness of my wishes, than to the solidity of my hope. The mind, which, like the delicate leaves of the Mimosa, shrinks from every touch, is ill calculated to solicit the assistance of the powerful, or gain the favour of the great. The very looks of the prosperous, it construes into arrogance; and is equally wounded by the civility which appears to condescend, and by the insolence which wears the form of contempt.

From all these multiplied mortifications, some, perhaps, real, and some only imaginary, has Delomond hastily retired; and relinquishing the pursuit of fortune, and the pleasures of society, devotes his future life to the indolent repose of obscurity. But, alas! how shall he, who was discomfited by the first thorny branch which hung across the path of fortune, struggle through the sharp briers of adversity? – Can a mind, formed for the happiness of domestic life, endowed with such exquisite relish for the refined enjoyment of taste and sentiment, find comfort in a joyless state of solitude; or, what is worse than solitude, the company of the rude and ignorant? Ah! my amiable friend, thou wilt find, when it is too late, that the road to happiness is not to be entered by the gate of fastidious refinement.

THE first care that occupied my mind after my arrival in London, was, to procure a safe conveyance for the presents which I had intended to lay at the feet of the sister of Percy.

I have just received an answer to the letter that accompanied them. – It is such as I should have expected from her who was worthy the esteem of such a brother. But, alas! it is written with the pen of sorrow, and blotted by the tears of affliction. The amiable old man, who supplied to her the place of a father, who loved her with such tenderness, and was beloved by her, with such a degree of filial affection, is gone to the dark mansions of death. She has left the happy abode of her infancy, and her dwelling is now among strangers. – This she particularly deplores, on account of depriving her of the power of shewing the sense she entertains of my friendship to her brother, in any other way than by words alone. Her expressions of gratitude have the energetic eloquence of genuine sensibility; they are greatly beyond what I have merited; but, when I consider the tender reflections that excited them – my heart melts into sympathy.

Alas! it is easy to perceive, that this amiable young woman is not to be numbered with the happy. Perhaps, her present situation is peculiarly unfortunate. Perhaps, she has there been destined to experience the cold reception, the unfeeling neglect, of some little, narrow, selfish mind, to whose attentions she had been particularly recommended by her departed relatives. Perhaps, some friend of her brother. – But, no; the *real* friends of Percy, were like himself, noble, generous, and good. Far from being capable of dishonouring the memory of their friend, by neglecting to perform the rites of hospitality to his sister, they have taken an interest in her feelings, and by acts of kindness and attention, have endeavoured to promote her happiness. And surely, for no act of kindness can the sister of Percy, be ungrateful to the friends of her brother!

The loss of Delomond, and the melancholy letter of Miss Percy, dwelt upon my spirits, and sunk them to a state of unusual depression. I spent the night in sadness, and early in the morning, went in search of my friend, the philosopher, whose conversation is to me, as the rod of Krishna, which no sooner touched the eyes of Arjoon, than he saw the figure of truth, as it appears unto the Gods themselves. This amiable friend, had of late been so much engrossed by his scientific pursuits, that I had enjoyed little of his company. He received me with an air of unusual vivacity. "When I last saw you," said he, "I am afraid I must have appeared strangely inattentive; but, in truth, my mind was at that time very much embarrassed, and almost solely occupied on a subject, which I did not then choose to speak of, but which I shall now fully explain. You must know, that I had lately entered on a course of experiments, more interesting than any in which I have ever yet engaged, and from which, I had no doubt, a most important discovery would result. I found it, however, altogether impossible to go on without the assistance of an additional apparatus, the price of which was far more than I could afford. It was fifty pounds! Little less than a quarter of a year's rent of my whole estate! What was I to do? bespeak it of the artizan, without having the money ready to pay for it? This would be nothing less than an act of wilful dishonesty, for dishonesty either to oneself or others, running in debt always is.

Could I hope to save it by retrenching any of my ordinary expences? I calculated every thing, even to living on bread and water, but found it impossible. I had, then, nothing for it, but to relinquish my plan entirely, and since I could not carry it on myself, to communicate my ideas upon the subject to some more opulent philosopher, by whose means the benefit of the discovery might be still given to the world. "Ah ! my friend," interrupted I, " I now see that you have no regard for me, or you would have given me the enviable pleasure, the delight of being able to say to myself, that I, too, ignorant as I am; I too have contributed my feeble aid to the advancement of Science, and the benefit of Society." "You are very good," returned the Doctor, "and I have no doubt of your generosity. But, as the action of heat evaporates fluids, so does the borrowing of money, in my opinion, destroy the independence of the soul: that independence, which gives life and energy to virtue, without which, it becomes incapable of being exerted to any truly useful purpose. No, what I cannot effect by the means which Divine Providence has put into my power, I think is not intended by Providence that I should effect at all."

"I was therefore quietly employing myself in unfixing that great retort; when this morning, a letter was brought me from my agent in the country, informing me of his having obtained for me, from a neighbouring 'Squire, the sum of fifty pounds; for damages done me, by taking, through mistake, a piece of my ground into one of his inclosures. Which sum, he enclosed to me in a letter. Thus, you see my dilemma is quite at an end. I shall now go on with spirit; and as I need lose no more time, I am just going into the city, to give the necessary directions to the work-people; who, if they are any way diligent, may have the whole apparatus completely finished in a week." As he spoke, I contemplated with delight, the glow of pleasure which animated his finely expressive countenance; a pleasure so different from the sparkling extacy of passion, that merely to have beheld it, would have been sufficient to convince the most devoted sensualist of the superiority of *mind*, over every enjoyment of mere sense.

Having accepted my offer of attending him, we were just about to depart, when, prevented by the entrance of a Lady, whose air and manner had in them somewhat so interesting, that the unseasonableness of the interruption was soon forgotten. Grief and anxiety were painted on her countenance. Every feature was labouring with ill-suppressed emotion, and when she attempted to speak, the tremor of her voice prevented her words from being definitely heard. I, however, soon gathered from her broken sentences, and the sympathetic replies of the philosopher. That she was the wife of an old school fellow, one of his early and esteemed friends. – That she had been born to affluence, but forfeited the favour of her family by her marriage; her husband having virtue and talents, but no fortune. His talents, however, had been turned to good account; he had employed himself in drawing plans of the estates of the affluent, which his taste taught him to embellish in such a manner, as gratified the vanity of his employers, by the admiration it excited. He was contented with the profit, while they enjoyed the praise.

"We were doing charmingly," said the Lady, "and had the prospect of soon getting above the world, and paying of all the little debts, which at our first setting out in life, necessity had compelled us to contract. When, in the beginning of last Summer, my husband was seized with a fever, which lasted seven weeks and left him so weak, that many more elapsed before he was able to go abroad. During that time, he lost some of his most advantageous situations; gentlemen who had employed him, having in the time of his illness, contracted with others. Winter came on, and no funds were provided against its wants; my husband, whose tenderness and affection for his family, seemed to be encreased by the difficulty he found in procuring their support, had a genius fruitful in resources. In those months, when the season necessarily put a stop to his employments, he wrote for the printer of a periodical publication, in which work, he taught me to assist him; and thus by our united endeavours, we contrived still to keep up a decent appearance and to maintain with frugality our four little ones, whose innocent endearments repaid all our trouble and made us when we sat down to our little meal, forget the labour by which it had been earned. Ah! my poor babes! it is your sufferings, that, more than his, own, now wrings your father's heart!"

"But where is now my friend?" interrupted Severan, "Is he well? What can I do to serve him? Where can I see him?"

"Alas! he is in prison!" returned the Lady. "He is in a loathsome, dismal prison! – deprived of light, of liberty, of every comfort, and enjoyment; and his dear children, his pretty darlings, of whom he used to be so fond, they too must go, must be nursed in the abode of misery, and made familiar with every species of wretchedness!" – Here tears came to her relief, and for some time choaked her utterance.

At length, recovering herself, and assuming an air of dejected composure, "I beg your pardon," continued she, (observing the marks of sensibility, that overspread the benignant countenance of our friend) "I did not mean to distress you, but it is so few that can feel for one's affliction! – and the voice of sympathy is so grateful to the wounded heart – that I could not deny myself the consolation of speaking to you. But things may yet go better. – My husband has enough owing to him, to enable him to pay every one. But the misfortune is, that his debtors are all people of fortune, whose favour would be forever lost, by an untimely application for money; and should the news of his having been imprisoned for debt, once get abroad, he is ruined for ever! No person of fashion will ever employ him more!"

"I cannot think so," said the Doctor with his wonted mildness; "we see daily instances of the high favour that is shewn to people of ruined circumstances; many of whom, I have known even when worthless and depraved, to meet with attention and support, from people of elevated rank and fashion?"

"Ah! Sir," replied the Lady, "these were the people who had squandered their fortunes in luxury and dissipation; such, indeed, seldom fail to meet with patrons and benefactors; but, it is far otherwise with the poor man, who has been struggling with adversity, and employing his efforts, for the maintenance of a virtuous wife and family: when *he* fails, he is considered as an object unworthy of notice; *his* situation, creates *no* interest. His wretchedness, excites *no* commiseration." – "But your own family, my dear Madam – they have it in their power to extricate you from every difficulty; will you permit me to apply to them in your behalf?"

"Alas! Sir, I fear it would be in vain, they are too fond of money, to give it to those who have none. You know how I offended them by my marriage; yet, had my husband succeeded in the world, and made a fortune, *mine* would not have been withheld from him. It would have been given, if we had not wanted it; but, now that we are reduced to poverty I have no hopes of assistance, from any of my friends. Yet would I thank you, for making trial of an application to them, if they were in town – but they are not. They are all at York except one Aunt who is, indeed very rich; she is also very religious and very charitable, but makes it a rule, never to give assistance to any, who are not of her own sect."

"Then," cried Severan, with unusual warmth, "whatever are her professions, she is a stranger to the religion of Jesus Christ! But, you have not told me the amount of the debt for which your husband is confined; is it not considerable?"

"Alas! yes," returned the Lady. "It is more than forty pounds, and, what with the bailiff's and the jailor's fees, will, I dare say, arise to little less than fifty!"

"Fifty pounds!" repeated the philosopher. "And fifty pounds would release your husband from a jail. Fifty pounds would restore a father to his infant family, and make the heart of a virtuous woman rejoice. It is the noblest of all experiments! – And detested be the pursuit, that would stand in the way of the happiness of a fellow-creature. My good Madam," continued he, addressing himself to the Lady, who looked astonished at the incoherence of his expressions, "you must know, that I this morning made a mistake; I thought that Providence had sent me fifty pounds, to enable me to pursue a philosophical discovery, on which I had vainly set my heart; but I now find, it was for a nobler purpose; it was to contribute to the happiness of an unfortunate family; here it is; and all I desire, is, that you would consider me only as the agent, and keep your thanks for him who sent it."

The various emotions of astonishment, doubt, gratitude, and joy, which took possession of the poor Lady's bosom, struggled for utterance, and at length found vent in tears.

The effect upon my feelings, was too powerful to be supported. I left the room, and when I returned, found my friend advising with the Lady, on the steps necessary to be taken for her husband's release.

I had from the commencement of our acquaintance, regarded the philosopher as the first of human beings. I now looked up to him as something more. To help a fellow creature in distress, is the instinctive impulse of benevolence; but to sacrifice for the good of others, the darling pursuit of one's life! to give up on that account the favourite; the cherished object of one's mind! this belongs only to the philosophy of Jesus. It was now, that I understood what cutting off the right hand, and plucking out the right eye, truly meant. But ah! my friend, if this is really the religion of Christ, how falsely are people often called Christians!

On the arrival of the man of the law, whom the Doctor had sent for to conduct the business, we all set out with the Lady, for the place of her husband's confinement.

When we arrived at the great, gloomy mansion, Doctor Severan, thinking it indelicate to go immediately into the presence of his friend, sent his lawyer with the lady, to inform her husband of his liberation, and in the mean time, indulged my curiosity with a sight of the prison.

You have seen the dungeons in which the Mussulmans confine their malefactors, and in which their prisoners of war are often doomed to suffer the lingering torture of despair; to inhale the noxious vapours of pestilence, and to pine in all the miseries of disease and famine. But after what I have said of Christian charity, you will no doubt, think it impossible that in a Christian country, similar places should be found. This, indeed, at first sight appears very inexplicable; but it only serves to confirm me in the truth of my former conjecture, respecting *a new revelation*, a supplementary code of Christian laws and Christian precepts, which, in many respects, must very essentially differ from the old one.

In this new gospel, I have every reason to believe, from all that I have observed since my abode in England, that poverty is considered as one of the most heinous of crimes. It is accordingly by the *Christians of the new system* not only stigmatised with a degree of infamy, but by their very laws, and under the immediate inspection of their sage magistrates, it is punished in the most exemplary manner. The abhorrence in which this crime is held by those Christian legislators, is, indeed, evident throughout the tenor of their laws.

Can a person contrive by villainy, to possess himself of the estate of another, provided it can be clearly proved, that *poverty* had no share in instigating him to the offence, the law is satisfied with simple restitution. But, should a poor starving wretch, put forth his audacious hand to satisfy the calls of hunger, or still the clamorous demands of an infant family, he is condemned to death, or doomed to everlasting wretchedness. You who are prejudiced in favour of the mild ordinances of our revered Pundits, will, perhaps, think it unjust, that to the miserable mortal who steals the value of twenty rupees, and to him who boldly ventures on plundering the wealth of a family, adding murder to the crime of robbery, the same punishment should be allotted; but, you will admire the principle upon which the laws of these new Christians in this case proceeds. It throws the crime of poverty into the scale, which instantly settles the balance.

Even when poverty constitutes the sole offence, nothing is more equitable than the punishments, which proceed in regular gradation, and correspond in exact proportion to the degree in which the crime exists. For instance, within the massy walls of this prison, whose iron gates open to receive the reeking murderer, the midnight thief, and all those miserable out casts of society, who, lost to every principle of shame, every feeling of humanity, have sunk into all the brutality of vice; those guilty of the crime of poverty, are likewise immured. But think not that they are all equally wretched. No; those who can afford to defraud their creditors, are suffered by these wise legislators, to live in a degree of luxury. Those who can save enough from the wreck of former times, to pay for their accommodation, may still enjoy some comparative degree of comfort. But, it is those wretches who have lost their *all*, and are alike destitute of friends and fortune – it is they who are doomed to suffer the bitterness of confinement, in all its horrors.

It is true, that some who follow the old system of Christianity, as it was taught by Jesus Christ and his Apostles, by whom poverty is *not* considered as so unpardonable a crime, have exerted their endeavours for relieving the sufferings of their fellow-creatures, who for small sums, are shut up in these dreary abodes of wretchedness. But notwithstanding these endeavours, notwithstanding the zealous efforts, the heart-touching remonstrances of one of these Christians of the old school, who devotes his life to the children of misfortune,[1] still in these prisons, many thousands of the inhabitants of this land of freedom, are left to pine out a miserable existence, alike useless to themselves and to society. Many, at whose birth the voice of congratulation has been raised, and over whose infant forms, the tears of parental tenderness have been fondly shed, are here suffered to languish, unnoticed and unknown.

As for those wretches who have committed such offences against society, as all nations upon earth have deemed criminal, they are here held in such just abhorrence, that it is not thought sufficient to visit their sins with mere *temporal punishment*, but every possible pains is taken to preserve them in such a state of wickedness, as may give them every possible chance of being, according to the faith of the lawgivers, *miserable to all eternity*.

This, you may, perhaps, esteem rather an unjustifiable degree of severity. – But consider, O benevolent Māāndāāra, that by the old Christian Shaster, none are excluded from the hopes of mercy, who seek it by sincere repentance. Now nothing is more probable, than that many of those miserable beings, who have been unwittingly swept into the torrent of vice, might, when they find themselves shipwrecked on its barren shores, gladly listen to the voice that would conduct them to the paths of peace and virtue. If kept in a state of separation from the bad, and favoured with means of instruction from the good, this would, no doubt, often be the case. But then consider what might be the consequence: perhaps, some of these vile felons might come to have a higher seat in Heaven, than some of the proud, and jealous guardians of the laws, which had condemned them upon earth. The idea is not to be endured with patience! and to prevent any possibility of its being realized, the poor trembling wretch, new to vice, and whose mind is not yet hardened in iniquity, no sooner commits (or is said to have committed) the most trifling offence, that stands within the cognisance of the law, than, hurled into the society of those veterans in sin, of whose repentance there is little reason to be afraid, the unfortunate offender is gradually trained to an equal degree of depravity.

---

1 We suppose the Rajah points at the benevolent exertions of Mr. Howard. [E.H.] John Howard (1726?-1790) was a noted prison reformer.

Thus, the door of mercy is for ever shut; the returning path to virtue is barricaded, and so filled up by the briers and the thorns, which these new Christians have thrown in the way, that it becomes quite invisible; and lest reflection should point it out, intoxicating liquors are allowed in all prisons to be distributed in sufficient quantities, to prevent the most distant apprehensions of such an event. Thus do these enlightened people, exert their endeavours to fill the regions of Nareyka!!

As for the philosopher, who, I need not tell you, is a Christian, according to the old Gospel, he deprecates the whole system, and was so much shocked at the sight of the young victims, who are here devoted to vice, in order that they may be afterwards immolated on the altars of justice; that no cordial less powerful than the sight of the happiness he had himself created, would have had efficacy to restore his mind to any degree of composure.

Before I conclude this epistle, I must entreat you, to send for the good and pious Bramin Sheermaal, tell him, that my heart reproaches me, for the injustice I was guilty of towards him; I implore his pardon, for the incredulity with which I regarded his account of the conduct of Christians. – Experience has now taught me, to acknowledge, that his words were dictated by truth, and his observations emanated from wisdom!

All that I have written, thou wilt not, perhaps, think it proper to read to Zamarcanda; many parts of it, she certainly could not understand; but, I request, thou wouldst assure her, that the love of her brother is undiminished. – I embrace my son – and implore upon him, the blessing of all the benignant Dewtahs! – May the fortunes of Määndäära, be established for ever! – What can I say more?

# LETTER XIV.

SINCE I last took up the reed of friendship, my heart has been fretted with vexation, and my soul chilled with astonishment. Will the friend of Zāārmilla believe it possible, that I should have found fraud and falsehood, venality and corruption, even in that court-protected vehicle of public information, that pure source of intelligence, called a Newspaper?

The manner in which I made the disagreeable discovery, was, to me, no less extraordinary, than the discovery itself. I went, as usual, yesterday morning, to spend an hour at the neighbouring coffee-house, and, on entering it, was surprised to find myself the object of universal attention. Every eye was turned towards me; some few seemed to regard me with a look of contempt; but the general expression was that of pity and compassion. I had advanced to a box, and called for a newspaper, but was hesitating whether I should retire, or stay to peruse its contents; when a gentleman, whom I observed to eye me with particular eagerness, approaching me with much formality, begged leave to enquire, whether I was indeed the Rajah of Almora, a native Prince of Rohilcund? On being answered in the affirmative, the gentleman, again bowing to the ground, thus proceeded:"I hope your highness will not attribute it to any want of respect, that I have thus presumed to intrude myself into your presence. I entertain too much respect for whatever is illustrious in birth, or honourable in rank, or dignified in title, or exalted in authority, to do any thing derogatory to its greatness. I am but too conscious of the prejudice which your highness must inevitably, entertain against this nation, to hope that you will look upon any individual belonging to it, without suspicion and abhorrence! But I hope to convince you, in spite of the reasons you have had to the contrary, that we are not a *nation* of monsters. Some virtue still remains among us, confined to me, and my honourable friends, it is true; but we, Sir, are Englishmen. Englishmen, capable of blushing at the nefarious practices of delegated authority. Englishmen, who have not been completely embowelled of our natural entrails; our hearts, and galls, and spleens, and livers, have not been forcibly torn from our bodies, and their places supplied by shawls and lacks, and nabob-ships, and dewannes! We have real hearts of flesh and blood, within our bosoms. Hearts, which bleed at the recital of human misery, and feel for the woes of your unhappy country, with all the warmth of unsophisticated virtue." Perceiving my intention to speak, "I know, Sir, what you would say," cried he, with vehemence: – "You would tell me, that your hatred to the English race, was founded in nature and in justice. – You would tell me, that it is *we* who have desolated your Empire, who have turned the fruitful and delicious garden of Rohilcund, into a waste and howling wilderness. – *We*, who have extirpated the noble race of warriors, who were your kind protectors! your indulgent lords! your beneficent friends! – to whom you paid a proud submission; a dignified obedience; a subordination more desirable than the tumultuous spirit of the most exalted freedom!" Again I attempted to speak. – "Ah!" cried he, in a still louder tone, "you need not describe to me, the ravages you have seen committed! the insults you have sustained! You need not tell me, that your friends have been slaughtered; your country plundered; your houses burned; your land laid waste; your Zenana dishonoured; and the favourite, the lovely, the virtuous wife of your affections, perhaps, torn from your agonizing bosom!" This was a chord not to be touched, even by the rude hand of a stranger, without exciting a visible emotion. "I see the subject is too much for you," cried he, "it is too fraught with horror, to be surveyed with indifference. Nature sickens at the recollection, but you need say no more; depend upon it, I shall make a proper representation of your case. Through me, your wrongs shall find a tongue. I will proclaim to the world, all that I have heard you utter. That mass of horrors, that system of iniquity, which your highness would describe, shall be laid open to the eye of day, and its wicked, nefarious, abominable, and detested author, exposed to the just indignation of the congregated universe!" – At these words, again bowing to the ground, he turned round, and departed. As I had no doubt of the unhappy man's insanity, I exceedingly rejoiced at his departure, and that he had done no mischief to himself or others, during this paroxysm of delirium.[1]

---

1   This passage alludes to and parodies some of Edmund Burke's rhetoric about British misconduct in Rohilkhand in his attacks on Hastings; the identification with Burke is strengthened by the additional parody of one of the most famous passages in Burke's *Reflections on the Revolution in France* (1790): "Never, never more

Among the crowd, which the vociferation of this unhappy maniac had attracted round us, I perceived one of the gentlemen I had met at Miss Ardent's; and was happy to take the opportunity of renewing our acquaintance. From him I learned, that the notice of the noisy orator, had been drawn upon me, by a paragraph inserted in a newspaper of that morning, which, after mentioning my name, and describing my person, falsely and wickedly insinuated, "that I had come there on behalf of the Hindoo inhabitants of Bengal, to complain of the horrid cruelties, and unexampled oppression, under which, through the mal-administration of the British governor of India, we were made to groan."

I was exceedingly shocked at the idea of the consequences, that might arise to the chosen servant of the minister, the writer of the newspaper, from having suffered himself to be thus imposed upon. I did not know what punishment might await the confidential conduc-tor of this vehicle of intelligence, should his master discover that he had suffered a falsehood to pollute that pure fountain of public instruction, in which his care for the morals, the virtue, the fortune, the health, and the beauty of all the subjects of this extensive Empire, is so fully evinced. The gentleman observing my anxiety, told me, that the best method of proceeding, was, to authorise the publisher to contradict the paragraph alluded to in the next paper. And that he would, if I chose it, go then with me to his house.

Eager to extricate the poor man from the dilemma into which his ignorance had thrown him, I gladly accepted the friendly offer, and we proceeded immediately to the office of this prime minister of fame, who received us with all the stateliness which an idea of the consequence of situation never fails to inspire. The gentleman took upon himself to open the business; which he did, by saying, "that he had brought with him a stranger of high rank, who considered him-self aggrieved by a paragraph, which had been that morning inserted in his paper; and then pointing it out, he told him, that I would expect to see a contradiction of that part of it, which related to the

shall we behold that generous loyalty to rank and sex, that proud submission, the dignified obedience, that subordination of the heart, which kept alive, even in servitude itself, the spirit of an exalted freedom" (Oxford, 1993, 76). See the intro-duction.

British governor of India, for whom I entertained sentiments of the most profound respect." The conductor shrugged up his shoulders, and said, "the paragraph had been paid for." – "That is to say, the contradiction of it must be paid for likewise," returned the gentleman. "I dare say the Rajah will have no objection." Observing the astonishment that was painted in my countenance, he told me, that nothing was more commonly practised. "Yes," added the news writer, "the gentleman must certainly allow, that when a falsehood has been paid for, it is not reasonable to expect, that it can be contradicted for nothing! It would be quite *dishonourable!*" "What!" cried I, with an emotion no longer to be suppressed, "and is it then in the power of a piece of gold, to procure circulation to whatever untruths the base malignity of envy or of hatred may choose to dictate? Are these the articles of intelligence, diffused at such vast expence, over this Christian kingdom? Ah! ye simple people! whom distance has happily preserved in ignorance of the ways of news writers, how little do ye know the real value of what ye so liberally pay for!"

So much was I disgusted that if my own character alone had been concerned, I would rather have submitted to the evil, than to the remedy. – As it was, I threw down the guinea and departed, with rather less reverence for the authenticity of newspaper intelligence, than I had entertained at my enterance.

The disagreeable consequences of this affair, have not stopped here; I can no longer stir abroad, without attracting the gaze of observation. – Places of public entertainment are filled by the bare expectation of beholding me; all those of resort, in the outskirts of the town, have advertised me, as part of their bill of fare; and I am this evening disappointed of the pleasure I expected, at a new species of entertainment, called a Masquerade, from seeing in the newspaper, that my intention is known to the public. – In fine, I can no longer find happiness in this metropolis, and would with pleasure at this moment re-embark on the bosom of the ocean, whose distant waves now beat against the happy shores of India. Some weeks must elapse, before such an opportunity can be found. I shall therefore, in the interim avail myself of the polite and friendly invitation of Lady Grey, and the family of the Ardents, to go into the country.

If I can prevail on the philosopher to accompany me, I shall indeed be happy. And let not Māāndāāra, too much exult over the disappointment of his friend, when I confess to him, that experience has now convinced me, that, though the novelty of manners and opinions may produce amusement, and variety of human characters afford some degree of instruction, it is the Society of the friend we esteem, that can solace and satisfy the heart!

WHEN I vainly flattered myself, with obtaining the company of Severan, I had entirely forgot his experiments. He has now engaged in them with renewed ardour; and so deeply is he interested in their success, that no motive, less powerful than the possibility of relieving a fellow creature in distress, would be sufficient to make him quit his laboratory. The morning after that in which we had visited the building allotted to the reception of the unfortunate people, whom these good Christians here so piously devoted to Eemen,[1] I paid a visit to the worthy family who had been rescued from the punishment of poverty, and after having done what was in my power to preserve them from being found guilty of a like crime in future, directed them to return to Severan, the sum he had so generously advanced.

But though I am thus deprived of his company for the present, he promises to join me, as soon as his scientific engagements will admit. And in the mean time, he tells me, I may expect amusement (I wonder he did not rather say instruction) from the characters I shall meet at Sir Caprice Ardent's. This man of many minds, has left his temples and his turrets, his pillars and pillasters, his arcades and his colonades, to be finished by the next lover of architecture, who may chance to spring up in the family; and has retired into the country, to enjoy, without interruption, the calm pleasures of philosophy. The philosophy which at present engrosses the soul of the Baronet, is, however, of a different species from that which engages the capacious mind of Doctor Severan. It is a philosophy which disdains the slow process of experiment, and chiefly glories in contradicting common sense. Its main object is, to shew that the *things which are, are not*, and the *things*

---

1    The Prince of Hell. [E.H.]

*which are not, are*; and this is called Metaphysics.

As I understand the matter, the art of these metaphysical champions lies in puzzling each other, and the best puzzler carries off the prize.

While these Christian-born philosophers pique themselves in turning from light, to walk in the darkness of their own vain imaginations, may the words that are written in the "Ocean of Wisdom" never escape from our remembrance!

"Though, one should be intimately acquainted with the whole circle of Sciences, and master of the principles, on which the most abstruse of them are founded; yet, if this knowledge be unaccomplished by the humble worship of the Omniscient God, it shall prove altogether vain, and unprofitable."[1]

I have heard of a conveyance, which, although not eligible for my personal accommodation, yet will serve to transmit this letter to my friend.

May he who possesses the eight attributes, receive your prayers! May you walk in the shadow of Veeshnû! and when by the favour of Varuna, this letter shall reach the dwelling of Māāndāāra, may he read its contents with the same sentiments of friendship, as now beat in the bosom of Zāārmilla. The brother of Zamarcanda salutes the sister of his heart, and weeps over the tender blossom he entrusted to her bosom. O that by her care, his mind may be nourished by the refreshing dew of early virtue! What can I say more?

---

1   This passage appears to have been taken from the Tervo-Vaulever, a composition which bears the marks of considerable antiquity, and which, though written not by a Bramin, but a Hindoo of the lowest order, is held in high estimation, for the beauties of its poetry, and intrinsic value of its precepts; part of it has been lately translated into English by Mr. Kindersley. [E.H.] Nathaniel Edward Kindersley, *Specimens of Hindoo Literature: consisting of translations, from the Tamoul language, of some Hindoo works of morality and imagination, with explanatory notes* (London, 1794), 54.

# LETTER XV.

PRAISE to Ganesa! How would the God, whose symbol is an Elephant's Head, have been astonished, could he have descended to have been a spectator of the scene I have just now witnessed? Had he beheld, in what a ridiculous light he is represented by the Philosophers of Europe, who pretend to be his worshippers, I am afraid, he would have been more than half ashamed of his votaries. But, let me not anticipate. You must travel the whole journey: and, according to my plan of punctual and minute information, you must be told, that I left London the morning after that in which my last epistle was concluded. And travelling, after the manner of the country, in a carriage drawn by four horses, which were changed every six or eight coss, at Choultries, replete with every convenience, and occupied by the politest, the civilest, and the most hospitable people, I have since my residence in Europe, ever encountered.

Wherever I stopped, smiles of welcome sat on every brow, nor was the benign suavity of their manners, confined to myself alone; it extended even to my domestics; and was particularly evinced in the cordial looks, and kindly greetings bestowed on my English Sircar,[1] who has the uncontrouled disbursement of my money.

I had already travelled upwards of two hundred miles (about one hundred of our coss) without meeting with any adventure worth notice; and had turned a few miles out of the great road, into that which leads to the Baronet's, when on stopping to change horses, at the inn of a paltry village, I met with an unexpected delay. They had no horses at home. I was, therefore, under the necessity of waiting for the return of a pair, which the landlord assured me, would be back in less than half an hour, and should then proceed with me immediately. I was a little surprised, to hear him propose having my carriage drawn by *one* pair, as my English servant had assured me, it was a thing *impossible*. And his judgment had been confirmed, not only by the London horse-hirer, but by the Master of every Inn upon the road. But as the road was now more broken, and more hilly, than I had hitherto travelled, I found that two horses would be sufficient. And for these

---

1  A house steward or a clerk; usually applied by the English to their Indian employees (*OED*).

two, I resolved to wait with all possible patience. – I do not know that I have hitherto mentioned to you, that in this country, there are various ways of measuring time: and that, what is with trades-people, inn-keepers, servants, &c. called five minutes, is seldom less than one hour by the sun-dial. What they call an hour, is a very undeterminate period indeed; being sometimes two hours, and as I have frequently known it, with my English servant, sometimes the length of a whole evening. Making up my mind, therefore, to spend two or three hours, at this sorry village, I was not a little pleased, to hear, that I had the prospect of some company; and that two gentlemen from Sir Caprice Ardent's, were in the same house. They soon introduced themselves to my acquaintance; and it was not long before I discovered, that these were two of the Philosophers, mentioned to me by my friend Severan.

They informed me, that they had been brought to the village on a disagreeable errand. They had, it seems, been stopped and robbed in their way from London to Ardent-Hall. The robber was now in custody, but their evidence was necessary for his commitment to prison. On this account, they were desired to appear before a Magistrate; and as I rejoice in every new scene, from which I can hope to acquire a new idea, I gladly accompanied them thither. Little did I know, what acquisitions were to be made to my stock of knowledge! or, that in the simple business of recognizing the person of a robber, I was to be made acquainted with a complete system of Philosophy. Alas! ignorant that I was! I knew not that to involve the simplest question in perplexity, and to veil the plain dictates of common sense, in the thick mist of obscurity and doubt, is an easy matter with metaphysical Philosophers!

We were shewn into the Hall of Justice, and found the Magistrate seated in his chair. This portly personage, who in figure very much resembled those images of the Mandarines of China, which are often to be seen both in Asia and Europe, with due solemnity of voice, addressing himself to the eldest of the two gentlemen, desired him to examine the features of the culprit, who now stood before him and say, whether he was satisfied as to his *identity*. "Much may be said upon the subject of *identity*," replied Mr. Puzzledorf; "the greatest philosophers have differed in their opinions concerning it, and ill would it become me to decide upon a question of such vast importance." "You have but to look in the man's face, Sir," returned the Magistrate, "to see whether he is the identical person by whom you have been robbed; and I do not see, what any philosopher has to say concerning it." "It would ill become me to instruct your worship upon this point," resumed Mr. Puzzledorf, "but his being *identically* the same is in *my opinion*, altogether impossible. Nor is my opinion singular; happily, it is supported by the most respectable authorities. Locke, indeed, makes identity to consist in consciousness, but consciousness exists in succession; it cannot be the same in any two moments. His Hypothesis, therefore, is not tenable; in fact, Watts, Colins, Clarke, Butler, Berkly, Price, Priestley, all have, in some degree, differed from it."[1] "Pray Sir, were these gentlemen Justices of the King's Bench?" interrupted the Magistrate; "if they were not, I must take the liberty of telling you, Sir, they were very impertinent to interfere in such questions! I am not to be taught the business of a Justice of Peace, by any of them. – And again ask you, whether, that man, who calls himself Tobias, alias Timothy Trundle, be the very identical, person, by whom you were robbed on the 18th instant, on his Majesty's highway?" "I must again repeat it," returned the Philosopher, "the thing is impossible; it is proved beyond a doubt, that there is no such quality as permanent identity, appertaining to any thing whatever: – and that no

---

1   John Locke (1632-1704) – One of the most influential of the English philosophers, his *Essay concerning Human Understanding* (1690) shaped much of the eighteenth-century writing on the development of the mind; Isaac Watts (1674-1748) – A dissenting minister, noted for both his hymns and his philosophical writing, in which he was influenced by Locke; Anthony Collins (1676-1729) – A deist and a friend of Locke, best known for his *Discourse of Free-Thinking* (1713); Samuel Clarke (1675-1729) – A follower of Newton and a critic of deism and materialist philosophy, whose most famous work was on the existence and attributes of God; Joseph Butler (1692-1752) – A philosopher and theologian who defended revealed religion and faith in the scriptures against the rationalist arguments of the deists; George Berkeley (1685-1753) – A philosopher and an Anglican Bishop, best known for his anti-materialist ideas – summed up in his famous catch phrase "esse est percipi" (to be is to be perceived); Richard Price (1723-91) – A unitarian minister and political philosopher who was an early supporter of the French revolution; Joseph Priestley (1733-1804) – One of the English "natural philosophers," he was noted for both his scientific experiments (into the nature of oxygen, among other things) and his political radicalism – his house was vandalized during anti-French riots on the first anniversary of the storming of the Bastille.

one can any more remain one and the same person for two moments together, than that two successive moments can be one, and the same moment. And if you will give me the honour of stating my arguments upon the subject, which I shall do in a manner truly philosophical, I make no doubt of convincing you, of the truth of my system. It is, indeed, a system so clear, so plain, so unanswerable, that nothing but the most willful blindness and obstinacy, can resist its truth." "That I deny," said Mr. Axiom, interrupting his friend. "I agree with you, that consciousness, being frequently interrupted, is not strictly continuous, and, therefore, the continuity of consciousness cannot constitute identity: I also allow, that wherever there is a chemical combination, there is a corresponding change of properties, and that the majority of the particles of which the man is composed, are necessarily in succession changed. – But, I assert, and will undertake to prove, that there exists certain stamina which are never carried off. Where this stamina is situated, will, I know, admit of dispute. In the heart, say some; in the brain, say others: for my part, I think it is most probable, that it is placed in the part of the brain which approaches the nearest possible to the very top of the nose, which situation, is, undoubtedly, the most convenient for receiving the notices sent to it from the organs of sight, hearing, smelling, &c. and which may be more incontestably proved, from the following arguments: first" – "Fire, and fury!" exclaimed the magistrate, "this is more than human patience can bear! But do not think, gentlemen, that I am to be made a fool of in this way; I shall let you know, that it is no such easy matter to make a fool of me! And was it not for the sake of my worthy friend, Sir Caprice Ardent, I should let you know the consequences of insulting one of his Majesty's justices of the peace, in the exercise of his duty. A vile misdemeanor! a high breach of decorum! and not to be suffered to pass with impunity. Once for all, I desire you, Sir (to Axiom) to examine the countenance of the culprit, and, without loss of time, to declare – whether he be actually the person guilty of the *alledged crime?*"

"As for crime," replied Mr. Axiom, "I absolutely deny the existence of crime in any case whatever. What is by the vulgar erroneously called so, is, in the enlightened eye of philosophy, nothing more than an error in judgment. And, indeed, according to my friend

Doctor Sceptic (Tim Trundle's former master) we have no right to predicate this much. – For what is right? what is wrong? what is vice? what is virtue? but terms merely relative, and which are to be applied by the standard of a man's own reason. If, for instance, the reason of Mr. Timothy Trundle, leads him to revolt at the unjust distribution of property, and to think it virtue, to give his feeble aid towards redressing that enormous abuse, who shall dare to call it wrong?" "I can tell you, Sir," cried the Justice, "that the law – will think it *right*, that Mr. Timothy Trundle, should be hanged for so doing. – Nor, would it be any loss to the world, if all the promulgators of such doctrines, the aiders and abettors of such acts of atrocity, shared the same fate!" "That Sir," returned Axiom, with great calmness, "I conceive to be an error of judgment, on the part of your worship." – "You, however, declare that this is the person by whom you were robbed?" said the Justice. "Yes," replied Axiom, "I have no scruples on the subject of his personal identity; identity being, as I said before" – "O say no more upon the subject, but let the clerk read your affidavit, and have done with it," cried the magistrate. The clerk proceeded, and the solemn appeal to the Deity – an appeal which so nearly concerned the life of a fellow-creature, was made – by the extraordinary, and, to me, incomprehensible ceremony of kissing a little dirty-looking book!

The prisoner, who had hitherto maintained a strict silence, now addressed himself to Mr. Axiom, to whom, it seems, he was well known, having long been servant to his particular friend. He began in a sullen tone, as follows:

"I did not think as how it would have been your honour, that would have had the heart to turn so against me at last. Many a time and oft, have I heard you, and my master, Doctor Sceptic, say, that all mankind were equal, and that the poor had as good a right to property as the rich. You said, moreover, that they were all fools, that would not make the most they could of this world, seeing as how there was no other; for that religion was all a hum, and the Parson a rogue, who did not himself believe a word of it. – Nay, the very last day that ever I attended you at dinner, did not you say, again and again, that Kings, Princes, and Prime Ministers, were all worse than pick-pockets? And yet now you would go for to hang me, for having only civilly asked a few guineas, to make up a little matter of loss, I had had in the

Lottery. I wonder you a'nt ashamed to turn so against your own words." "No, Timothy," returned the philosopher; "my opinions are not so easily changed. No man, ever yet convinced me, of being in an error. You have only to regret your having lived in a dark age, when vulgar prejudices so far prevail, as to consider laws as necessary to the well-being of society. But be comforted, Timothy! The age of reason approaches. That glorious æra is fast advancing, in which every man shall do that which is right in his own eyes, and the fear of the gallows shall have as little influence, as the fear of hell."

"Ah! that I had kept to my good grandmother's wholesome doctrine of hell and damnation!" (exclaimed the poor wretch, whom the Justice's men were now dragging back to prison) – "I should not now be at the mercy of a false friend, who laughed me out of the fear of God – and now leaves me to the mercy of the gallows!" – He continued to speak, but we could no longer hear. He was dragged to his prison, and we having made our obedience to the Magistrate, departed. I have been enabled thus circumstantially, to detail the particulars of this curious conversation, from the politeness of the Magistrate's nephew, who was so kind as to furnish me with a copy of his notes, taken down in, what is called, Short Hand.

It is possible, that much of it may appear to you unintelligible; but be not discouraged. How should our unenlightened minds, expect to understand the language of philosophers, since from all I can learn, they seldom thoroughly understand themselves?[1]

On returning to the Inn, I found the horses in waiting, the gentlemen's were also in readiness, and we proceeded in in company to Ardent Hall. My reception from the Baronet, was very cordial. That of

---

1  Hamilton refused to admit that she was targetting individuals in her presentation of the metaphysical philosophers; in response to a complaint from Mary Hays, she replied, rather disingenuously, that it was "a strange sort of compliment" to Godwin to assume that he was the target (quoted by Kelly, *Woman, Writing, and Revolution* 143). Nevertheless, both Doctor Sceptic's ideas (as summarized by Axiom in this scene) and Mr. Vapour's (as presented by Zāārmilla later in this letter) are parodies of positions advanced by William Godwin in *Political Justice* (1793). In this immensely controversial work, Godwin advocated, among other things, the abolition of private property and marriage, and argued that emotions such as gratitude and filial affection went against the strict claims of justice. "The age of reason" is a phrase taken from Thomas Paine's 1794 work by that name.

his Lady, was most frigidly polite. Her daughter, did not seem to remember ever having seen me before; but the elder Miss Ardent, shook me by the hand, with a degree of frankness, as masculine as her understanding.

The conversation of the evening, turned upon the same topics, that had been discussed before the Magistrate, Mr. Axiom and Mr. Puzzledorf doing little more than support the opinions they had formerly advanced. Sir Caprice Ardent, seemed, in general, disposed to agree with the last speaker; and Doctor Sceptic, who made one of the party, made a point of agreeing with none. Miss Ardent retired to write letters, and her Ladyship and her daughter, remained as silent as did the friend of Māāndāāra.

---

O SHEERMAAL! – Wise and learned Bramin! – May thy meek and generous spirit, pardon the presumption of my ignorance, which refusing to confide in thy experience, persisted in cherishing the ill-founded notion, that all the people of England were Christians! – With all humility, I now retract my error: and confess – that of the many religions prevalent in this strange country, Christianity (as it is set forth in the Shaster) has the smallest number of votaries: and, according to the accounts of my new friend, is fast journeying to oblivion.

Much do the Philosophers exult, in exposing the weakness and wickedness of its authors. These artful and designing men, who having entered into a combination to lead the most virtuous lives, having bound themselves to the practice of fortitude and forbearance, meekness and magnanimity, piety towards God, and benevolence to all mankind, weakly and foolishly, refused to take to themselves any merit for their conduct; and renouncing all worldly honours and interests, resigned themselves to persecution, pains, tortures, and death, in support of the truth of their doctrines.

All this appears very foolish in the eyes of the Philosophers; who, judging of others by themselves, pronounce so much self-denial, fortitude, and forbearance, to be utterly impossible. The God of the Christians, appears in their eyes, as very unreasonable, in exacting purity of heart – and humility from his votaries. They therefore, think it is doing much service to mankind, to free them from these uneasy restraints, and to leave them to the worship of Dewtah, that are not quite so unreasonable.

To make the attempt, is all that is necessary, towards obtaining the appellation of Philosopher.

On examining the Cosha,[1] I found, indeed, that the word Philosopher, was said to signify, "a man deep in knowledge either moral or natural" – but, from my own experience, I can pronounce the definition to be nugatory: and that those who usually call themselves such, are men, who, without much knowledge, either moral or natural, entertain a high idea of their own superiority, from having the temerity to reject whatever has the sanction of experience, and common sense.

The poojah of Philosophers is performed to certain Idols, called Systems. The faith of each system has been promulgated by the priest, who either first formed the Idol, or first set it up to receive the poojah of the credulous. This faith, is received by the votary of the system with undoubting confidence, and defended with the fervency of pious zeal. It must be confessed, that this zeal, sometimes carries the Philosophers to a pitch of intolerance, that is repugnant to the feelings of a Hindoo. Never did the most bigoted derveish[2] of the Mussulmans, betray more abhorrence at the sight of the Idols of the Pagoda, than is evinced by the worshipper of system towards a Christian priest! And yet, so far are the latter from returning any portion of this dislike, that the majority of them are very careful not to offend the Philosophers, by too rigid an adherance to the precepts of *that* Shaster, to which they know their adversaries have such an insuperable antipathy.

All the Philosophers now at Ardent-Hall, perform poojah to different systems: and seem to have no opinion in common, except the expectation of the return of the Suttee Jogue, which they distinguish by the name of *The Age of Reason*.

---

1 Dictionary. [E.H.]

2 The antipathy of the Mussulmans to every species of Idolatry, is still the occasion of frequent disturbance to the Hindoos, in the performance of the superstitious ceremonies of their religion. [E.H.]

In this blessed æra of purity and perfection, it is believed by each of the Philosophers, that the worship of his Idol shall be established; and the doctrines of his priest, be the faith of the world.

"Then," says Mr. Puzzledorf, "will be evinced the dignity of man," for this is the Idol to which Mr. Puzzledorf, professes the performance of poojah. You are, perhaps, curious to know in what this dignity consists? Know, then, that it appears, from the researches of the priest of Mr. Puzzledorf – that some difference in point of organization, doth actually exist between him and a Bamboo, or Bramble-bush: no brain having as yet been discovered in any of the vegetable tribes. Should such a discovery crown the labours of some future Philosopher, what a sad stroke will it be to the dignity of Man! He will then be reduced to a level, not only with the beasts of the field, but with the very trees of the forest! The similarity is already too conspicuous. Like them, he is doomed slowly to advance to maturity; shortly to flourish, and quickly to decay. Like them too, according to the faith of Mr. Puzzledorf, he is doomed to moulder into dust from which there is no hopes of resuscitation, no prospect of revival! – Such in the eyes of the adherents of this system, is the vaunted dignity of Man!

The Idol of Mr. Axiom, is the little stamina at the top of the nose. This, he declares to be imperishable, and that it must of necessity exist to all eternity. – To the faith of Mr. Axiom, Mr. Puzzledorf opposes an argument, that is frequently made use of by the bigoted of all sects, against the opinions of their adversaries: – viz. That it is *nonsense*. He says, moreover, that in the age of reason, it will incontestably appear, that every particle is alike liable to the decomposition which these poor bodies of our's must undergo in the laboratory of death, who is too good a chemist to suffer the little favourite Stamina of Mr. Axiom, to escape him. Both Philosophers appeal for the truth of their systems, to the experiments or Doctor Severan. Alas! little does the good Doctor think, that the existence of a future state, depends upon the management of his crucible!

I have not been able to discover the name of the system, to which Doctor Sceptic pays his vows, the only thing I have ever heard him attempt to prove, is, that nothing ever was, will, or can be proved. All religions being, in his opinion, equally false, ridiculous, and absurd. But, though he performs not poojah to the Idols of any of his brother Philosophers, it is the religion of Christianity, against which, the arrows of his sarcasm are chiefly pointed. When an opportunity occurs of venting the overflowings of his zeal, in a sneer at any of the opinions or practices of the Christians, his rigid features relax into a smile of triumph, which, for a moment, dispels from his countenance the gloom of discontent. It seems to have been the endeavour of his life, to eradicate from his bosom, those social feelings and affections, which form so great a part of the felicity of common mortals. – A stranger to the animating glow of friendship, and the tender confidence of esteem; he considers all attachments, as a proof of weakness – into which, if he has ever in any degree relaxed – it is in favour of a nephew, a hopeful youth, whom he piques himself upon having freed from the prejudices he had contracted from a pious father, at whose piety, and whose prejudices, the young man now laughs in a very becoming manner!

The Idol to whose service this young man hath devoted himself, is called Atheism. From all that I have been able to learn, Atheism is an infernal deity, who demands of his votaries, such cruel sacrifices – that every one initiated into the mysteries of this faith, must make a solemn and absolute renunciation of the use of his senses – shut his eyes upon the fair volume of Nature – and deny to his heart, the pleasurable emotions of admiration and gratitude!

Such are the sacrifices required by this Idol, even from its speculative votaries. The zeal of its practical proselytes, carries them still farther. – I am told, that the female converts seldom fail to make an offering to Atheism of their peace, purity, and good fame; and that of its worshippers, among the lower orders of men, numbers every year suffer martyrdom, at a place called Newgate; which I suppose to be a temple dedicated to this superstition.

What are the posthumous honours, which the martyrs of Atheism, receive from their brethren, the philosophers, I have not been able to discover, as it, is a subject on which the philosophers modestly decline to expatiate.

From the conversations that I have overheard, between the nephew of Doctor Sceptic, and Mr. Vapour, who is one of the most renowned teachers of this faith; I find, that its adherents perform poojah to certain inferior Dewtah, called Existing, or External, circumstances, energies, and powers, of whom, I am not yet sufficiently prepared to speak.

Mr. Vapour is particularly tenacious of his faith, which, is, indeed, of a very extraordinary nature. Rejecting all the received opinions, that have hitherto prevailed in the world, and utterly discrediting the circumstances upon which they have been founded; he reserves his whole stock of credulity for futurity. Here his faith is so strong, as to bound over the barriers of probability, to unite all that is discordant in nature, and to believe in things impossible.

The age of reason is thought, by Mr. Vapour, to be very near at hand. Nothing, he says, is so easy, as to bring it about immediately. It is only to persuade the people in power to resign its exercise; the rich to part with their property; and with one consent, to abolish all laws, and put an end to all government: "Then," says this credulous philosopher, "shall we see the perfection of virtue!" Not such virtue, it is true, as has heretofore passed current in the world. Benevolence will not then be heard of; gratitude will be considered as a crime, and punished with the contempt it so justly deserves. Filial affection would, no doubt, be treated as a crime of a still deeper dye, but that, to prevent the possibility of such a breach of virtue, no man, in the age of reason, shall be able to guess who his father is; nor any woman to say to her husband, behold your son. Chastity, shall then be considered as a weakness, and the virtue of a female estimated according as she has had sufficient energy to break its mean restraints. "To what sublime heights," exclaims this sapient philosopher, "may we not expect that virtue will then be seen to soar! — By destroying the domestic affections, what an addition will be made to human happiness! And when man is no longer corrupted by the tender and endearing ties of brother, sister, wife, and child, how greatly will his dispositions be meliorated! The fear of punishment too, that ignoble bondage, which, at present, restrains the energies of so many great men, will no longer damp the noble ardour of the daring robber, or the midnight thief. Nor will any man then be degraded by working for another. The divine energies of the soul will not then be stifled by labouring for support. What is necessary, every individual may, without difficulty, do for himself. — Every man shall then till his own field, and cultivate his own garden."[1] — "And pray how are the Ladies to be clothed in the

---

1  Perhaps an echo of the last sentence of Voltaire's *Candide* as well as an allusion to Godwin's ideas of radical self-sufficiency. Most anti-jacobin writers linked English radical philosophy to the French *philosophes*.

age of reason?" asked Miss Ardent. "Any Lady," replied the philosopher, "who chooses to wear clothes, which, in this cold climate, may by some be considered as a matter of necessity, must herself pluck the wool from the back of the sheep, and spin it on a distaff, of her own making." "But, she cannot weave it," rejoined Miss Ardent, "without a loom; a loom cannot well be made without iron tools, and iron tools can have no existence without the aggregated labours of many individuals." "True," returned Mr. Vapour; "and it is therefore probable, that in the glorious æra I speak of, men will again have recourse to the skin of beasts for covering; and these will be procured according to the strength and capacity of the individual. A summer's dress, may be made of the skins of mice, and such animals; while those of sheep, hares, horses, dogs, &c. may be worn in winter. Such things may, for a time, take place. But as the human mind advances to that of perfection, at which, when deprived of religion, laws, and government, it is destined to arrive, men will, no doubt, possess sufficient *energy*, to resist the effects of cold; and to exist not only without clothing, but without food also. When reason is thus far advanced an effort of the mind will be sufficient to prevent the approach of disease, and stop the progress of decay. People will not then be so foolish as to die." "I can believe, that in the age of reason, women won't be troubled with the vapours,"[1] replied Miss Ardent, "but, that they should be able to live without food and clothing, is another affair." "Women!" repeated Mr. Vapour, with a contemptuous smile; "we shall not then be troubled with – women. In the age of reason, the world shall contain only a race of men!!"

Nothing could be more repugnant to the opinions of Miss Ardent, than this assertion. – This worthy daughter of Serraswatti is firmly persuaded, that, in the age of reason, a very different doctrine will be established. It is her opinion, that the perfection of the female understanding will then be universally acknowledged.

She pants for that blessed period, when the eyes of men shall no longer be attracted by the charms of youth and beauty; when mind, and mind alone, shall be thought worthy the attention of a philosopher.

---

1    An eighteenth-century term for a range of mild emotional or psychological disturbances to which women were presumed to be subject.

In that wished-for aera, the talents of women, she says, shall not be debased by household drudgery, or their noble spirits broken by bare submission, to usurped authority. The reins will then be put into the hands of wisdom; and as women will, in the age of reason, probably be found to have the largest share, it is they who will then drive the chariot of state, and guide the steeds of war!

Mr. Axiom, whose deference to the opinions of Miss Ardent is implicit and unvariable, perfectly coincides in her opinion. – "Who," said he, the other evening, in discoursing upon this subject, "who would look for mind, in the insipid features of a girl? It is when the countenance has acquired a character, which it never can do under the period of forty, that it becomes an object of admiration, to a man of sense. Ah! how different is the sentiment which it then inspires!" The tender sigh, which was heaved by Mr. Axiom, at the conclusion of this sentence, in vibrating on the ears of Miss Ardent, seemed to touch some pleasant unison, that overspread her countenance with a smile. You, my friend, will, I doubt not, smile also, at hearing of these glad tidings for grandmothers; and divert yourself with thinking, when this empire of reason shall be extended to the regions of the east, what curious revolutions it will make in the Zenanas of Hindoostan! – May the Gods of our fathers preserve thee from the spirits of the deep – and the systems of philosophers! – What can I say more?

# LETTER XVI.

MAY He, who at all time claims preference in adoration, preserve thee!!

The day after that in which I last took up the reed of instruction, some strangers arrived at Ardent Hall, who had come into the country on purpose to see a celebrated water-fall – on whose beauties, they poured out such encomiums, as kindled the flame of curiosity in my bosom.

I no sooner expressed my desire of visiting this scene of wonders, than Sir Caprice, with great politeness, ordered the chief officer of his household to attend me thither. – It was natural to expect, that some of the philosophers might have felt an inclination to view a scene, to the description of which, it appeared, they were no strangers. – But, alas! to the worshipper of systems, the fair face of Nature has no charms! In vain, for him, does the appearance of Arjoon tinge the cheeks of the cup-bearers of the sky,[1] with the crimson blush of gladness! In vain, for him, do the robes of the seasons, wove in the changeful looms of Nature, present the ceaseless charm of variety! In vain, for him, smiles the soft beauties of the blooming valley, when the linnet, sitting on his rose-bush, sings forth the praises of the spring! And equally in vain, for him, doth Nature expose to view the terrors of her wonder-working arm, in the scenes of sublimity and grandeur! Midst all the beauties of creation, a philosopher sees nothing beautiful, but the system which he worships!

Happily for me, Mr. Trueman, the steward of Sir Caprice, was a stranger to systems; but had cultivated so much taste for the beauties of the rural landscape, as enabled him to point out to my observation, a thousand charms, which might otherwise have escaped my notice. Nor was this the only benefit I derived from his society. From his plain good sense, I received more real and useful information; in our ride of four hours, than I had gained in nearly as many weeks, in the company of the philosophers.

For the distance of many miles round Ardent-Hall, the country is irregular and undulating. It abounds in trees, which, though they

---

1   An appellation for the Clouds, which frequently occurs in Asiatic poetry. [E.H.]

boast not the height of the Mango, or the vast circumference of the Banyan, are neither destitute of grandeur, nor of beauty. These are not clumped together in solemn groves, or gloomy jungles; but are so planted, as to surround the small fields into which the country is divided; each of which small enclosures, now fraught with the riches of the yellow harvest, appears like a "Topaz in a setting of Emeralds." The chearful aspect of the peasants, busily employed in cutting down the grain, while their fancies seemed to revel in the scene of plenty, excited the most pleasurable emotions in my heart; for who but a philosopher, can "breathe the air of hilarity, and not partake of the intoxication of delight?"[1]

The scene, however, soon changed: an extensive plain opened before us, where no yellow harvest waved its golden head – where no tall trees afforded shelter to the traveller – all was waste and barren. Upon inquiring of my intelligent companion, the reason of this wonderful change, he could only inform me, that this was called *a Common*, and that it could not be cultivated, without a solemn act of the Legislature. I now perceived, that it was from reasons of state, that these great portions of land (for Commons occur very frequently in England) were suffered to remain desolate; but, in vain did I endeavour to discover the motives, which could induce the government to lay this restraint on cultivation.[2]

As geese appeared to have here an exclusive right of pasturage, I was inclined to think, that they might, perhaps, be the objects of superstitious veneration to the English court; but on applying to my guide, I found, that geese were not of the number of protected animals; and that far from being honoured in the manner of those which are called *Game*, the murder of a goose might be performed without ceremony, by the most ignoble hands. Perhaps, thought I, it is from

---

1　In several passages of this Letter, the Rajah seems to have adopted the imagery of the Persian Poet Inatulla, of Delhi – with whose writings, he was, doubtless, well acquainted. [E.H.] Inayat Allah, who died c.1671; an English translation by Alexander Dow was published in 1768. See 57, note 1.

2　Commons – so called because they were the common property of the parish – were public lands on which the poor could let their animals graze. Enclosure acts, which effectively privatized these lands, were immensely controversial, as they often made it impossible for day-labourers who owned no land of their own to survive in their villages. Hamilton's commentary here is thus explicitly political.

the benevolent regard of the minister towards the old women, who keep these noisy flocks; but, alas! a little reflection convinced me, that the age of reason, is not yet sufficiently established, to countenance the supposition. It must, then, be from the pious apprehension of endangering the virtue of the people, by an overflow of plenty. – If this really be the case – it must be confessed, that a more effectual method could not be taken to bring about the desired end.

Having passed the commons, we entered into a deep and narrow valley, overhung with frowning rocks; these seemed frequently to close upon us, and sternly to deny all access to the interior scene. A silver stream, which alternately kissed the feet of the precipices on each side, encouraged us to proceed, and gently conducted us to the furthermost end of the valley. It was here, that the glories of the cataract burst upon our senses. – But how shall my feeble hands, do justice to such a scene? Can I, by description, stun the ears of Mããndããra, with the thunder of the falling waters; or present to his imagination, the grotesque figures of the rocks, surrounding the magnificent bason into which they fell? Can I bring terror to his bosom, by the mention of the over-jutting crags, which, on one side, topped the precipice; or produce in his mind, the sensation of delight, by a minute description of the various trees and shrubs, whose thick foliage ornamented the opposite bank? – Ah no! The task is impossible; or possible only to the magic pen of poetry. By Zããrmilla, it must be passed over in silence!

We returned to Ardent-Hall, as the chariot of Surraya was sinking behind the distant hills. On approaching the house, we beheld a scene of extraordinary commotion. All was hurry and confusion. – Men and boys, household servants and labourers, all seemed engaged in the pursuit of some invisible object. At one part of the lawn, we beheld Doctor Sceptic and Mr. Puzzledorf, cautiously stepping along, and carefully peeping into every bush they passed; at another place, we saw Sir Caprice, attended by the rest of the philosophers, carrying a large net – which, with much care, they softly spread upon a hedge, and then began to beat the roots of the shrubs that composed it, in the most furious manner.

"What is the matter?" cried my companion, to a lad who was running past us. "What is the occasion of all this bustle? What, in the name of goodness, are you all about?" "Catching Sparrows, Sir," returned the lad, in breathless hurry. "Catching Sparrows!" repeated the good Steward. "Philosophers, catching Sparrows! That is doing some good with their learning, indeed! – If they had begun to this work sooner, the early corn in the South field would have been the better for it!"

As my mind has not yet been sufficiently contaminated by the practices of Christians, to take pleasure in beholding misery inflicted upon any part of the animated creation, I hastened from this cruel scene, and took refuge in my own apartment. After some time spent in meditating on the cruel dispositions of Europeans, and in performing poojah to the benignant Dewtah of our fathers – I descended, to pay my respects to Miss Ardent, whose voice I heard in the Hall. "How happy it is, that you have returned to-night!" exclaimed she, on perceiving me. "You have come in time, to assist at the most wonderful of all discoveries! What will your friends in India think, when you tell them, that sparrows may be changed into honey-bees?"

It is a subject, on which none of my friends could possibly entertain a doubt, returned I; the transmigration of soul, from body to body, is evidently necessary for its purification. – It is the doctrine of the Vedas – and its authority is unquestionable. "But the change I speak of, has nothing to do with the doctrine of transmigration," rejoined Miss Ardent. "*Our* sparrows are still to continue *good* and *real* sparrows: it is only their instincts, that are to undergo a change, from the power of *external circumstances*. So young Sceptic declared this morning at breakfast, and my brother, whose imagination takes fire at every new idea, declared instantly, that the experiment should be made. It is true," continued Miss Ardent, "this theory is not confined to sparrows – The reasoning faculties, of which we poor two-legged animals are so proud – and the various instincts, which mark each tribe of the brute creation, all equally originate in a combination of *external circumstances*. And, according to the arguments of the young philosopher, I see no reason, why, by a proper course of education, a monkey may not be a Minister of State, or a goose, Lord Chancellor, of England."

Here a stop was put to our conversation, by the entrance of the gentlemen, each of whom was so full of his deeds of prowess, in the engagement with the sparrows, that he could talk of nothing else. One hundred sparrows, were already taken prisoners: – but as this was only one third of the number declared necessary to form a hive, a reward was offered by the Baronet, for each live sparrow that should be brought to the Hall in the course of the succeeding day: – a measure which was crowned with such success, that, before sun-set on the following evening, the number was declared complete.

Another tedious day elapsed, before the hut destined for their future residence, could be finished; this was made exactly after the model of those of the domestic bees, which, in this country, are built of straw, made into small bundles, and bound together by the fibres of an aquatic plant. This hut, or hive, as it is called, bore the same proportion to its model, as the size of a sparrow does to that of a bee; it was furnished with cross sticks for the support of the combs, and that the sparrows might have no apology for not beginning immediately to work, great care was taken that no convenience usually afforded to the bees, should be wanting. – After undergoing a careful examination by the philosophers, this huge sparrow-hive was placed upon a platform, that had been reared for its reception; and the sparrows having been brought in baskets to the spot, Sir Caprice Ardent, in presence of all the philosophers, with his own hand, pair by pair, deposited them in their new abode. The apparent satisfaction with which they entered their hive, gave such a convincing proof of the power of external circumstances, as already rendered Sir Caprice a complete convert to the system. At the conclusion of the ceremony, he cordially shook hands with the young philosopher, and requesting the rest of the party would excuse him for the evening, he retired to his study, to begin a journal of these important proceedings, with which he intended to illuminate the world.

At the first indication of the dawn of morning, I went, as is my constant practice, to the river side, and after the performance of the accustomary poojah, and having bathed in the refreshing stream, I strolled into that part of the garden, where the honey-making sparrows were placed.

It was at an hour when my meditations have here never been disturbed by the appearance of a fellow mortal. Judge then of my surprise, at beholding the Baronet, who, wrapped in his nightrobes, stood at the side of the new erected hut, listening with eager ears, to catch the first sound that should emanate from its precincts – on perceiving me, he made the signal of silence, and then beckoning me to approach – enquired, in a soft whisper, whether I did not hear the sparrows hum? I told him, that I did indeed hear a humming noise; but believed, that it proceeded from a solitary bee, which was hovering over the adjoining shrubs. Chagrined at my discovery, the Baronet turned from me, in displeasure, and went into the house.

Many were the visits, which, in the course of this day, were made to the new hive. It was soon discovered, that the sparrows had been so far impelled by the pressure of *existing circumstances*, as to go abroad in the morning, in quest of necessary food; and it was hoped by the philosophers, that, as is the custom of bees, they would return before the decline of day, to deposit their yellow spoils. But, alas! fallacious is the hope of mortals! The shades of evening arrived, and night succeeded, spreading her dark mantle over the face of Nature, but not a sparrow appeared!

Miss Ardent, whose knowledge extends to all the particulars of rural economy, on perceiving the vexation of her brother, suggested the idea, that the sparrows had probably swarmed on some tree in the neighbourhood, where they might remain in safety till the following day; "and then," continued she, "if they shew any inclination to fly off, they may easily be fixed, by beating the frying-pans, as they do to a swarm of bees."

This hint from Miss Ardent, re-kindled the expiring flame of hope in the breasts of the philosophers. – Next morning, which proved a very rainy one, word was brought, that a number of the fugitives were seen in a hawthorn-tree, at the bottom of the lawn – thither the philosophers instantly repaired, each armed with some culinary instrument, which, as soon as they reached the place, they began to beat, in such a manner as might have arrested the Sun in the entrance of the jaws of the Crocodile!

Lost was the labour of the philosophers! who, in this instance, exerted their talents in vain. Instead of gathering together in a cluster, as was expected, no sooner did the discordant sounds from the instruments of the philosophers reach the hearing of the sparrows, than away they flew to another tree. Thither they were again pursued, but still the more noise that was made, the less did the sparrows seem inclined to listen. The master of the bees, declared, that he had never seen a swarm so unmanageable!

Wet, and wearied, Sir Caprice and his learned guests, at length returned into the house. Miss Ardent, and Mr. Axiom, thought it a good opportunity to laugh at the system of the young philosopher; who, on his part, defended the infallibility of his Idol, by declaring, that the experiment had not been fully made: – that the habits of old sparrows were not easily conquered; – but that young ones, or young birds of any kind, he was still convinced, if taken before their habits were sufficiently formed, would be found to obey the necessity of existing circumstances, exactly as did the little useful insects, of whose instinctive sagacity, ignorance had said so much.

The hint was not lost upon the Baronet. A reward for nestlings, of every description, was again offered: and again attended with the wished-for success. – Ah! how many loving pairs among the feathered tribes, were, for the sake of this experiment, bereft of their infant families! The groves resounded with the plaints of woe! But little pain did the sorrows of the mourners give to the heart of the young systemist. By his advice, the little birds, after having had their bills rubbed with honey, were shut up in the hive, with a portion of the same sweet food, for their subsistance.

On the evening of the third day, which was the conclusion of their destined term of probation, the entrance to the hive was opened, but not a bird came forth; every method was taken to entice them abroad – but in vain. At length, by the assistance of the servants, their habitation was so far raised, as to enable the philosophers to take a peep within. Sight of horrors! and smell, still worse than the sight! The lifeless corses of the three hundred half-fledged nestlings lay at the bottom of their hive, in a promiscuous heap. – "They have effectually swarmed at last!" said Mr. Axiom. – Neither the Baronet, nor the young philosopher, staid to make any remark – but every one putting his fingers to his nose – impelled by the *necessity* of *existing circumstances*, hurried from the dismal scene.

Such, Māāndāāra, are the illusive phantoms which the all-pervading spirit, the sovereign Maya, presents to the perception of metaphysical Philosophers!

May Ganesa, averting calamity, preserve to thee the use of thy senses! And may the poojah performed for thy friend, by the holy Bramins of Almora, preserve his mind from the contamination of systems! What can I say more?

# LETTER XVII.

My time, for these two past days, has been occupied in a manner, that, I hope, will give pleasure to Māāndāāra.

I have been engaged in translating for your perusal, the greatest part of a very long epistle, with which Doctor Severan has had the goodness to favour his unworthy servant.

According to previous agreement, I transmitted to him, all that I had written to you since my arrival at Ardent-Hall; intreating him to favour me with such strictures upon it, as he thought might be necessary, towards giving me more just ideas upon the subjects of which I had treated.

In his observations, the Doctor does not follow me through the particular systems of the philosophers; but speaks, in general terms, of the effects produced, by what he calls Scepticism; which, according to the great English Cosha, is the art of doubting. But you shall have it, as nearly as the different idioms of the two languages will permit, in his own words. – After opening his letter with the usual exordium, he thus proceeds:

"Knowing the ardour with which you pursue knowledge, and the strong inclination that impels you to investigate the causes of the different phenomena which present themselves to your observation, I cheerfully comply with your request.

"The history of Literature is intimately connected with the revolutions of Empires; and among all the rude storms which have assailed it, in none did it suffer more, than in that which it endured, together with the government, of ancient Rome. Literature was, by this event, effectually driven from those countries where it had formerly flourished; and, during a long period (emphatically distinguished by our historians, by the epithet of *dark*) learning was almost completely obliterated. In this æra of ignorance, superstition established her gloomy reign: and when the attention of men was once more turned to literary pursuits, the objects they had to surmount were new and numerous, and of a nature not very easily to be subdued.

"Instead of that free communication, which had formerly been permitted to men, they were now fettered by the tyrannical edicts of King's and Priests; the investigation of truth being equally hostile to the interests of both. While freedom of discussion was thus restrained, the faculties of the human mind were benumbed, and truth and falsehood were confounded together. Crude speculations were ushered into the world, with the authority of truths; and not only was scepticism propagated by means of the promulgation of opinions, nurtured in ignorance, but encreased from the propensity which the mind has, when newly freed from restrictions, to rush from one extreme to another.

"From the nature of our constitution (whose spirit is toleration) and from the freedom of our religion from superstition, scepticism has made little progress here, in comparison of what it has done upon the Continent. There, its triumph has been in proportion to the blind obedience exacted to the national superstition, to which men of sense and observation could not, contrary to the dictates of their reason, subscribe; and from that propensity of the human mind, which I have just mentioned, these formed systems for themselves, as distant from the truth, as the doctrines of the high priests of the country were from the pure precepts of Christianity.

"The only species of sceptics that abound in this kingdom, are not thinking, but may be called *talking* sceptics. These are men of shallow understandings, and cold hearts; who, feeling their incapacity to attract attention, by going on in the ordinary path, endeavour to gain it by stating opinions which may astonish their hearers, and acquire them some degree of applause, for their ingenuity and boldness. It may, indeed, be observed of this class, that they take special care never to utter their oracles before those who are capable of entering into argument with them, though they deliver themselves with dogmatical assurance before the ignorant and illiterate.

"But let not my noble friend imagine from this account of scepticism, or from his own penetrating observation on the conduct of the gentlemen at Ardent-Hall, that metaphysical enquiry is without its use. Such enquiry expands the powers of the human mind, enlarges the understanding, and, by placing the science of morals on a true foundation, tends to encrease the happiness of society.

"Would its professors pursue the same plan of investigation that has been so successfully adopted by natural philosophers, that of first making themselves well acquainted with facts, and thoroughly investigating them, before they draw conclusions, they would perceive the necessity of allowing first principles, which are so self-evident as not to admit of any direct proof. Indeed, I do not hesitate to assert, that almost all the errors of metaphysicians have arisen from their neglect of natural philosophy. – The extreme accuracy, and exact precision, that is requisite in the investigation of the phenomena of the material world, would induce like habits of reasoning in regard to that of the mental: while the Colossus of Scepticism, I mean Atheism, would, by an acquaintance with the works of Nature, be utterly annihilated.

"I have endeavoured to explain myself to my noble friend as clearly as possible on the subject of his letter; and shall only add, that true philosophy is never the companion of arrogance and vanity. While it investigates with assiduity, and pronounces with diffidence; they assert with boldness and give the crude conjectures of fancy, for the sound deductions of truth.

"The natural turn of my mind, and still more the objects which have for the greatest part of my life occupied my attention, have effectually precluded me from sceptical opinions, and rendered me callous to sophistry of their promoters – but it has always appeared to me, that where freedom of discussion is permitted, there scepticism and infidelity will be but little known."

Such, Māāndāāra, are the opinions of the *natural Philosopher*. The Philosophers at Ardent-Hall declare, that it is a pity so good a man should have so many odd prejudices. I confess, that, to me, who have been accustomed to behold with reverence, the self-inflicted torture of holy men – the noble enthusiasm of the worshippers of System is object of more veneration. It is true, these philosophers hold it not necessary to mortify the body, or to bring the irregular passions under subjection. But what is the severest penance of the most pious Yoggee, compared to the utter dereliction of eternal happiness? By hope, a man is supported through many sorrows, but on the shrine of his Idol, the philosophic Sannassee, makes a voluntary sacrifice of even Hope itself. – On the system that he worships, his thoughts for ever dwell; on it, his tongue for ever runs: and while it exclusively occupies every avenue to his soul, he, with a superlative degree of modesty, bestows the epithet of *prejudiced enthusiast*, on the votary of Christianity. How amiable is this condescension!

Shall I confess to my friend – that to my weak mind, the enlightening conversation of the philosophers had become so tiresome, as to render the arrival of Lady Grey, and her blooming party, a considerable relief to my wearied spirits? Till then, I was destitute of all resource: Miss Ardent, being too fond of disputing with the philosophers, and too much engaged by them to attend to me; and her Ladyship so entirely engrossed by her darling boy, as to be incapable of attending to any other object. This boy, is suffered to become so troublesome, that it entirely eradicates that benevolent complacency which one is accustomed to feel at the sight of infant innocence. His parents behold the capriciousness of his desires increase with gratification, and the irascibility of his temper receive fuel from satiety; yet do they continue to pamper the over-pampered appetite, and to indulge each caprice of the wayward fancy, in full expectation, that, in the *age of reason*, he will be able to exercise the virtue of self-control! – Yes, Māāndāāra, when, from the *pressure* of *existing circumstances*, sparrows are taught to make honey, then shall the passions, which have been fanned into a flame by the breath of indulgence, listen to the voice of Moderation!

You may, perhaps, imagine, that the society of a young and lovely female, such as is Miss Julia Ardent, would be a dangerous trial to a man of my sensibility. But, alas! My friend, you know not how effectually the mixture of insipidity and haughtiness can blunt the arrows of Cama! It is, perhaps, for this reason, and to preserve the hearts of young men from the influence of female charms, that these qualities are so carefully instilled at the seminaries of female education, which were described in such true colours by the good Bramin Sheermaal. I was, at that time, too much blinded by the mists of ignorance, to give credit to his report. – I had read the Christian Shaster, and was it not natural for me to suppose, that all who called themselves Christians, were guided by its precepts? From it I learned, that Christian women were not prohibited from the cultivation of their understandings; and how could I conceive, that fashion should lead them to relinquish so glorious a privilege? How could I imagine, that Christian parents should be so much afraid of the improvement of their female offspring, as to give encouragement to seminaries formed on purpose for the exclusion of knowledge? It is true, the information of Sheermaal, might have instructed me in these things, but to the heart that is filled with prejudice, Wisdom lifteth up her voice in vain.

Nothing but experience could have convinced me, that the cultivation of the rational faculties, should, among the Christian women of England, be so rare, that no sooner can one of them emerge from the depths of ignorance, than she is suspected of assuming the airs of self-importance and conceit. If she has the knowledge of a school-boy, she is thought vain of her learning. Nor are there many men of sense among the Christians, who would not prefer to the conversation of such a woman, the impertinent tattle of the frivolous, the capricious, and the ignorant. Nor is this much to be wondered at, when we consider, that, by the pains taken, from the earliest infancy, to sap the foundation of every solid improvement, the imagination becomes so much stronger than the judgement, that of the small number of females who, under all the disadvantages of custom and prejudice, dare to distinguish themselves by the cultivation of their talents, few should do more than exchange one folly for another: – substitute the love of theory, for the love of dress – or an admiration of the mental gewgaws of flimsy sentiment, and high sounding declamation, for that of trifles of another kind.

But though I confess my error, and acknowledge, that I deceived myself in extending my notions of Christianity to every Christian, and of excellence to every female, of England, I still see some who amply justify the expectations that were formed by my sanguine mind. In Lady Grey and her daughters, I find all that I had expected from the females of their country; all that my friend Severan had described.

With them, arrived the two youngest daughters of Sir Caprice Ardent, one of whom has received her education under the care of Lady Grey, while the other had to her Aunt, Miss Ardent, been indebted for her instruction. At first sight, one is struck with the similarity of their features. They are both beauteous as the opening rosebud, when the dew of morning trembles on its leaf. The eyes of each, sparkling with vivacity, are dazzling as a bright dagger suddenly unsheathed. They are both shaped by the hand of elegance, and both move with the same degree of grace. Yet, notwithstanding this similarity, the opposite characters impressed by education is visible in each. –

While over the graces of Miss Caroline, is thrown the bewitching veil of timidity, and her every action is bound in the silken fetters of decorum; the adopted daughter of Miss Ardent speaks her sentiments with an energy that has never known restraint. Though open to conviction, and ready to confess error with candor of a noble mind, she yields less to the authority of persons, than to that of reason; and it is easy to perceive, has been early taught, that to be weak, and to be amiable, are two very different things.

An incident which occurred to the three sisters, in the course of their morning's walk, will serve to illustrate these observations upon their characters.

It appears, that having strayed into a narrow lane, they were frightened at the appearance of a horse and cart, coming towards them so quickly, as to leave them no other method of escaping, than to climb a steep bank, and get over the paling into their father's park. Miss Olivia, with the activity of an Antelope, led the way, and, with some difficulty, assisted her sisters to follow her example. Just as she had prevailed upon the terrified Miss Julia, who long insisted upon the impossibility of her making the attempt, they beheld near them an old man, who excited by the screams and promised rewards of Miss Julia, attempted to lay hold of the horses. To stop them, his feeble efforts were ineffectual; the animals were too strong, and too spirited, to be managed by his aged arm. After a short struggle, the horses sprung over him, and in a moment the mangled and bleeding body was discovered lying, to all appearance, lifeless, in the track which the cart had passed.

Miss Julia redoubled her efforts to escape; she succeeded, and flew to the house, which she no sooner reached, than, as is customary with young ladies upon such occasions, she fainted away. When she had fainted for a decent length of time, she screamed, laughed, and cried alternately, and continued long enough in the second stage of fright, called *An Hysteric Fit*, to draw round her the greatest part of the family. Indeed, there was full employment for them all. One held to her nose a bunch of burnt feathers; another chafed her temples with a drug, called Hartshorn;[1] a third held to her lips drops and cordials,

---

[1] "The aqueous solution of ammonia (whether obtained from harts' horns or otherwise)" (*OED*) – used to help bring people round from fainting-fits.

while the rest ran about the room, opening the windows, ringing the bells, and giving directions to the servants.

While we were thus engaged, in flew Miss Olivia. But what a figure! The few tattered remnants of muslin robe, besmeared with blood, streamed in the air; eagerness sparkled in her eyes, and unspeakable glow of ardour animated her countenance. Totally unconcerned for her sister, on whom, indeed, she seemed to dart a look of contempt, she hastily snatched the hartshorn, and the cordials, and desiring, with a tone of authority, all the men to follow her, she again flew off, with the swiftness of a bird of Paradise, who has been frightened by the voice of the hunter.

Miss Julia was left to recover as she could. Every soul deserted her. Men and maids, philosophers and footmen, all hurried after the fair Olivia; who, like the meteor which floats on the dark-bosomed cloud of evening, was seen gliding before us. At length we reached the lane, and there, seated on the ground, we beheld the twin-sister of Olivia. Her fair arms supported the unfortunate old man, whose wounded head, reclined upon her lap. His wounds were, however, bound up. The robe of Olivia, having been torn in pieces for the purpose. And now, with a tenderness which equalled her activity, she knelt at the old man's side, and carried to his pale lips the cordials she had, with so little ceremony, snatched from her sister. The old man at length so far revived, as to pronounce, with feeble but impressive accents, the blessings of his God on the angel-forms who had saved his life. He was with all possible care, by the direction of the two Ladies, carried up to the house. A surgeon was immediately sent for, who, on examining his wounds, declared them to be of such a nature, that if he had not received the assistance bestowed upon him by the two Ladies, he must inevitably have perished. "Then," cried the lovely Caroline, "it is to my sister Olivia, that he owes his life! – But for her, I should have followed my sister Julia into the house, to call for help; it was Olivia alone, who had the courage to return to him and the presence of mind to afford him relief." "No, Caroline;" replied Olivia, "without you, I could have done nothing. When I looked back, and saw how the poor man bled, I knew he could not live, without assistance; but it was you, by whom the assistance was principally bestowed." "Don't speak any more about it, for Heaven's sake!" cried Miss Julia; "the very thought of it makes me sick. I would not have looked at him, for a thousand worlds! I wonder how you could have so little sensibility!"

"Sensibility, my dear niece," said Lady Grey, "is but too often another word for selfishness. Believe me, that sensibility which turns with disgust from the sight of misery it has the power to relieve, is not of the right kind. To weep at the imaginary tale of sorrow exhibited in a Novel or a Tragedy, is to indulge a feeling, in which there is neither vice nor virtue: but when the compassion which touches the heart, leads the hands to afford relief, and benevolence becomes a principle of action; it is then, and then only, that it is truly commendable." "I perceive that your Ladyship has studied Mr. Hume's Principles of General Utility," said Mr. Axiom. "No," said Mr. Puzzledorf; "it is evident, her Ladyship has taken her opinions from *my Essay on the Eternal and Necessary Fitness and Congruity of Things.*"[1] "I have taken them," said her Ladyship, "from the doctrines and examples of Jesus Christ and his Apostles."

In this life, "composed of good and evil,"[2] this younger sister of the Baronet had had her share of calamity. Her marriage with Sir Philip Grey, was an union of mutual affection, founded on mutual esteem, and productive of mutual felicity.

Though a Baronet, his estate was not extensive; and from it, a numerous family of brothers and sisters were to be provided with fortunes, suited to their birth. Sir Philip and his Lady, having the same views and opinions, easily settled the plan of their future life. They took the management of their estate into their own hands: taste and elegance became a substitute for splendor: and the propriety of domestic arrangement, amply compensated for the absence of a few articles of superfluous luxury. But though they retrenched in ostentation, they decreased not in hospitality; their house was the refuge of the distressed, the home of merit, and the central point of all the genius and the talent which the surrounding country could boast. In addition to the care of their fortune, they took upon themselves the sole care of the education of their children. – But, notwithstanding all

---

1  This title is, of course, imaginary. Hume explores the principles of morality in his *Treatise of Human Nature* (1739-40).

2  See 191, note 1.

these avocations, they still found time for the pursuit of literature, for which their taste remained undiminished. Lady Grey was not only (as is universally the custom in this country)[1] the companion of her husband's table – but the partner of his studies; and by him, her opinions were as much respected as her person was beloved.

Years rolled on, and each returning season saw an increase of the happiness of this well-matched pair. But who can give stability to the felicity of mortals? While yet in the prime of life, this amiable and happy husband was seized by the ruthless hand of disease, in whose rude grasp, the vigour of life was blasted, and the gay hopes of future enjoyment dashed on the rocks of disappointment. His senses, of which he suffered a temporary deprivation, were gradually restored; but the wheels of life were clogged; the vital fluid stagnated in the veins, or moved with such lingering and unequal pace, as was unequal to the re-animation of the palsied limbs: nor did he ever recover a sufficient degree of strength, to enable him to quit his apartment. In such a situation, in vain would a man have looked for consolation to the pretty face of a fool. In vain would he have expected it from the trifling accomplishments, to the acquirement of which, the most precious years of life are commonly devoted. Alas! though Lady Grey could have spoken French, with the fluency of a Parisian; though she could have danced with the grace of an angel; though she could have painted a flower, or a butterfly, even without the assistance of drawing-master, and run over the keys of harpsichord with the most astonishing rapidity – little comfort would it have given to the heart of her sick husband.

In an understanding enriched by the accumulations of Wisdom, a temper regulated by the precepts of Christianity, and a heart replete with tenderness, Sir Philip found a more solid resource. By these endowments, was his Lady enabled to manage the affairs of her family, and the concerns of his estate; to watch over the education of her children; and, by the unremitting attentions of endearing affection, to cheer the spirits that were broken by confinement, and soothe the

---

1   It is by some of the Hindoo authors, mentioned as one of the indispensible qualities of a good wife – "that she never presumes to eat, until her husband has finished." [E.H.] Compare *Gentoo Laws*: "A woman ... who eats before her husband eats ... shall be turned out of the house" (284).

sufferings of a bed of pain. Nor was the performance of these multifarious duties the sudden effect of a short-lived energy. During the six years in which her husband lingered under the partial dominion of death, the fortitude of his Lady remained unshaken, her perseverance unabated, and when at length his soul was suffered to depart from the decayed mansion of mortality, though her heart was possessed with too much sensibility, not to feel with sorrow the stroke of separation, the assured hope of re-union with the object of her affections, in the regions of immortality, afforded consolation to her wounded mind. – Yes, Māāndāāra, notwithstanding all I have said in favour of this excellent woman, truth obliges me to confess, that the powers of her mind are not sufficiently enlarged to embrace the doctrines of Atheism! She is blind enough, not to perceive the evident superiority of any of the systems of the philosophers to the Christian faith; and weakly asserts, that if all that was taught by Jesus Christ and his Apostles, was generally practised, it would be no great injury to the happiness of society. – She takes great pleasure in the contemplation of a future state, and carries her *prejudices* so far, as to declare, that she considers the account of it, as given in Scripture, as little less easy of belief, than the system of Mr. Puzzledorf; and that she finds it more satisfactory to rest her hopes on the promises of her Saviour, than on the permanent existence of the little imperishable stamina at the top of the nose!!

Not contented with making the precepts and doctrines of Christianity the guide of her own conduct, she has endeavoured to instill them into the minds of her children; and so well has she succeeded, that her eldest son, at the age of nineteen, though possessed of an uncommon degree of learning, sense, and spirit – is not ashamed to confess that he is a Christian!

<hr/>

ALAS! my friend, how shall I inform you of the events of this morning? – The number of philosophers is diminished! The promising sprout of Infidelity, whose early genius gave such hopes of future greatness – he, by the prowess of whose pen, it was expected that religion should be routed from the world – the nephew of Doctor Sceptic – this morning, took the privilege of a philosopher, and shot himself through the head!

As I find upon enquiry, that this is a privilege which is often claimed, and a practice, that is very common with the philosophers of England, I suppose it is found to be conducive to general utility, and agreeable to the eternal and necessary congruity and fitness of things.

The *existing circumstances* which impelled this young man to make so philosophical an exit, have been, to all appearance, fully explained; and as you may have some curiosity concerning them, I shall briefly state them for your perusal.

It appears that his father, a man of rigid morals and austere devotion, who lived in the exercise of much piety towards God, and much charity to his fellow-creatures, some years ago, received into his family the orphan niece of his wife. She was educated with his own children, and shared with them the benefit of his instructions and the tenderness of his paternal love. Her beauty made an early impression upon the heart of her cousin, and such was her merit in the eyes of the old man, that, preferring the happiness of his son, to the aggrandizement of his family, he consented that their union should take place, as soon as the young man should have attained his one and twentieth year. It was agreed, that he should employ the interval in what is called an Attendance upon the Temple;[1] and, according to a previous invitation from his uncle, Doctor Sceptic, should during that period take up his residence at his house, in the capital. – There the young man had not long resided, till a new light burst upon his eyes; he saw things as he had never seen them before: saw that religion was a bug-bear, made to keep the vulgar in awe: – saw that his father was a fool; and, as I have before mentioned, learnt to laugh at his prejudices and his piety, in a very edifying manner.

In the summer, he returned into the country; found his cousin lovely and affectionate as ever, and had no great difficulty in initiating her into all the mysteries of Scepticism. They both found it a charming thing to be so much wiser than their instructors; and wondered they could so long have been blinded by prejudices, whose absurdities were so obvious. The young man went again to town, became every day more enlightened, and soon discovered that marriage was a piece of priest-craft – an ignoble bondage – a chain, which no *man of honour* should submit to wear.

---

1   That is, he was studying law.

He hastened to return to the country, to communicate to his cousin this important discovery. Finding some difficulty in convincing her understanding of the truth of this new doctrine, he applied to the softness of her heart; he pretended to doubt her affection, appealed to her generosity, and – completed her ruin.

Still the poor girl was not sufficiently convinced of the propriety of her conduct, not to entertain some doubts and apprehensions, which the young philosopher soon grew tired of hearing. Finding that their connection could not be much longer concealed, she grew more importunate, and he listened to her importunity with increased indifference. At length, to avoid her remonstrances, he came to Ardent Hall, where he had been introduced by his Uncle, who made the offer of his services to assist Sir Caprice in writing his Book upon the *Supremacy of Reason*, with which the Baronet is soon to enlighten the world. – The young man willingly engaged in the task. But fatal are the effects of early prejudices to the peace of a philosopher! His thoughts became gloomy; his speech has often of late been incoherent; and every action betrayed the restlessness of a mind at war with itself. Even his zeal against the advocates of Christianity, had in it a degree of bitterness which shewed that they still retained an authority over his mind, at which, though his pride revolted, his understanding could not conquer.

For the last few days, he appeared to exert more than usual spirits. He laughed, when he had no occasion; talked, when he had nothing to say; and sedulously sought the company of the Ladies, whom he had before neglected with the frigidity of indifference. Yesterday evening, his spirits were raised to a pitch which gave reason to suspect intoxication. When he retired to his chamber, it appears that he did not go to bed, but employed himself in writing letters to his father, all of which he had again torn, and scattered about the room. At four o'clock in the morning, the report of a pistol was heard: the family were instantly alarmed; the door of his chamber was broken open; and, on entering it, the first object that presented itself to view, was the lifeless corse of the young philosopher, extended on the floor.

On the table at which he had been writing, lay two letters. The first was from his father, and feelingly descriptive of the agony of parent's heart, on the first discovery of a son's unworthiness. The other was from his cousin. It portrayed the picture of a virtuous mind, struggling with the dread of infamy, bitterly regretting the loss of peace and self-respect, and gently reproaching the author of its calamities, for depriving her of that hope which is the resource of the wretched, the comfort of the penitent, and the sovereign balm for the evils of life! "To her," she said, "hope was a shadow, which had passed away. Once, there was a time, when she could have smiled at calamity, endured the severity of pain with unshrinking resignation, and, supported by faith, have cheerfully resigned her soul into the bosom of her Creator. Now, doubt and darkness sat upon the realm of death; she feared to die, but she had not courage to live. – "Death," she said, "was the only refuge of despair; to it she fled, to save her from the reproaches of the world, and the torments of her own perturbed mind" – and with an affecting apostrophe to the days of unspotted innocence, this unhappy creature concludes her melancholy epistle; which, it seems, she had no sooner written, that she put an end to her existence, by plunging into the sea!

Such has been the effects of performing poojah to System, in the family of the Sceptics!

Ah! how little do the Christians of this country consider the nature and extent of the obligations they are under to those enlightened men, whose indefatigable endeavour it is, to free them from the narrow prejudices of their religion! O, ye incomparable moralists, who so freely blow out your own brains, from a sense of *general utility*, little doth the world consider how much it is indebted to your labours!

***

### Reverence to Ganesa!

THE previous arguments of the philosophers in praise of suicide, had not sufficiently enlightened the minds of the family of Ardent-Hall, to prevent their regarding the death of young Sceptic as a melancholy catastrophe! Though the difference of character gave a variety to the expression of their feelings, all appeared to feel. The shock was universal.

The worshippers of System, and the votaries of Christianity, appeared indeed, to be affected in a very opposite manner. The former, who had, till this event, been so clamorous in support of the pretensions of their Idols, were all at once struck dumb. Not one appeal was now made to *existing circumstances*. Not one ray of hope darted from *the age of reason*. Nor did either *general utility*, or the *fitness of things*, appear in this juncture, to afford any comfort to their votaries. But while the lips of the philosophers were sealed in silence, those of the Christian religionists were opened. Their prejudices, indeed, appeared to have gained fresh strength: these *prejudices*, which are calculated to foster the sensibility of the tender heart, and to encrease the feelings of sympathy, seemed likewise endowed with power to support their votaries in the hour of affliction, to soften the rigour of anguish, and to preserve from the tyranny of despair.

It must be confessed, that Lady Grey, amiable as she is, had not sufficient greatness of mind to applaud the heroism of the young philosopher, or to speak of his last action – but with a mixture of pity, horror, and regret. With much feeling, did she deplore his having ever imbibed the *liberal opinions* that led to the destruction of his wife; the murder of his child; his own death, and the misery of his family.

The consolation of that unhappy family was the first object of her concern. Having seen Lady Ardent and the young Ladies set off for the house of a friend, to which they had been invited on the first accounts of the melancholy event; she hastened to the house of affliction; there to mingle the tears of sympathy; to speak comfort to the wounded heart; and, by sharing in its sorrows, to lessen their severity. – Such, Māāndāāra, are the offices pointed out by the prejudices of Christianity!

Deeming it improper at such a juncture, to incommode the family by the presence of a stranger, I took my leave of Sir Caprice Ardent, and left the Hall, impressed with a deep sense of the kindness and hospitality I had experienced beneath its roof.

Full of melancholy, I proceeded, without having fully determined on the route I was to pursue. To London, I was averse to return, and yet knew not how otherwise to dispose of myself. As I was debating this point with myself, while the horses were putting to my carriage, at the third stage of my journey, a chaise drove up to the Inn. From it alighted a gentleman – but, O ye Gods of my fathers! What was my surprise, on beholding, in this gentleman, my former guest Mr. Denbeigh, the friend of Percy! He, who had at Chunar, loaded me with so many marks of kindness and affection! Soon as the flutter of spirits which always accompanies an unexpected meeting, was a little subsided, he took from his port-folio a packet, on which I soon recognized the hand-writing of Maāndaāra. How did my heart beat at the sight! I tear open the seals – I read. I hear of the welfare of my friend, of the health of my child. Ah! my son! my son! What tender emotions does the mention of thy name raise in my bosom! When shall the soft cheek of my child, be patted by his father's hand? When shall my ears be gratified by the delicious music of my darling's gentle voice? Detested spirit of curiosity! too long have I sacrificed to thee the truest, sweetest joys, that gem the period of existence!

My heart is too full to proceed. May He, who is Lord of the Keepers of the eight corners of the World, preserve thee! May the adored wife of Veeshnu be the friend of my child!!

<hr />

DENBEIGH, at the time I met him, was on his way to the place of his nativity. He requested me to accompany him to his father's house; and found in me no disposition to reject a proposal so agreeable to my inclination. We proceeded together in the same carriage. Conversed of India – of our friends at Calcutta: talked of all the little incidents that had occurred during my residence in that city: the most trivial of which, appeared interesting to the memory, on account of the pleasing ideas with which it was associated. Swiftly flew the wheels of our chariot, but more swiftly flew the rolling hours, which were occupied by this sort of conversation.

About noon, on the second day of our journey, we, by the direction of Denbeigh, struck into a narrow bye-road, which following the course of a clear stream, winded through the midst of a narrow valley. As we entered upon this road, the agitation of my companion became apparent. Every object that we passed, caused his heart to heave with tender emotion. In every shrub he recognized an old acquaintance, and in every tree he seemed to discover a long lost friend. "Let us stop here," said he, at a turn of the road: "the bridge for carriages is half a mile off, but I can take you a nearer way." So saying, he leaped out of the carriage, and I followed his example. My friend surveyed the scene around, and the soft tear of delight glistened in his eyes. "There," said he, "stands the old thorn, which, at the close of evening, I used to pass with such hasty steps, not daring to look behind, from terror of the fairies, who were said to hold their nightly revels beneath its boughs. Ah! there is the wood, whose filberts were so tempting. There the pool, where I first ventured to beat the wave with my feeble arm. On the outstretched branch of yonder beech, was suspended the swing, in which I have often tossed my little sisters, who, half pleased and half afraid, squalled and laughed by turns, as they were made to fly through the yielding air."

We had now reached a little rustic gate leading into an orchard, in one of the broad walks of which, we beheld an aged pair, enjoying the smiles of the meridian Sun. A little boy and girl sported beside them, joyously picking up the apples, that lay hidden in the grass.

Our approach was at length perceived. The old gentleman paused, and leaning on his staff, endeavoured to recognize us. The emotion of Denbeigh encreased. – He bounded forward – and taking a hand of each – while the bursting sensations of his heart choaked his utterance – gazed for a moment on the revered faces of his parents, and in the next, was in their arms. His poor mother could not, for a few minutes, reconcile herself to the darkness of his complexion, which fourteen years spent beneath the lustre of an Indian sky had changed from the fair red and white, such as now adorns the face of his little nephew, to the deep brown shade, that marks the European Asiatic. The good Lady gently pushed him from her, to examine more minutely the features whose more delicate lines were engraven on her memory. He smiled. – In that smile, she recognized the peculiar expression of her darling's face, and fondly pressed him to her maternal bosom.

During this scene, I stood a silent and unobserved spectator; nor was it till after a considerable length of time, that Denbeigh sufficiently recollected himself to introduce me to his parents. To be called the friend of their son, ensured my welcome; but, that I might not be any restraint on their conversation, I attached myself to the little folks, to whom Uncle Henry was no more than any other stranger.

As we approached the house, I observed, at an open window which fronts the orchard, a lovely girl, who seemed to view the party with a greater degree of interest, than curiosity alone could possibly inspire. Twice she came to the door, and twice returned irresolute. At length, she was observed by one of my little companions, who running towards her, called out, Uncle Henry is come! Uncle Henry is come! the words gave wings to her willing feet, she flew down the walk, and in a minute her beauteous face was hid in the bosom of her brother.

The shrill voice of my little friend, had reached farther than the parlour. By the time we entered the Hall, the servants were assembled. – The old nurse was the first who pressed forward to salute the stranger – by whom she was received with the kindness due to her affection and fidelity. Two other domestic companions of his youth still remained in the family: tears spoke the sincerity of the many welcomes they bestowed on the traveller; while the hearty good-will with which he received their salutations, gave a convincing proof, that neither time nor distance had changed the dispositions of his heart.

Mr. Denbeigh, with the delicacy of attention which is peculiar to a few chosen minds, provided for me an apartment in a detached house, where my Hindoo servants were furnished with every requisite for preparing our simple meals according to the religion and customs of our country. To this apartment I retired during the dining hour of the family; and by the time I returned, I found that an acquisition had been made to the happy party of united friends, by the arrival of the two married daughters of Mr. Denbeigh, accompanied by the husband of the eldest. The countenance of this gentleman justified the character given him by Denbeigh, of worth and good-nature. He was bred to business, and has by industry and application, obtained an ample share of the gifts of fortune, which he enjoys with cheerfulness, and bestows with the frankness of a generous heart. His wife seems happy in his affection, and in the enjoyment of a degree of good temper equal to his own.

The countenance of the second sister bears a stronger resemblance to that of my friend; it speaks a soul endowed with superior powers; a more refined sensibility, a more lively perception, a more cultivated taste. When the arrival of her husband (who had been detained by the business of his profession, which is that of a Physician) was announced, I marked the emotion of her spirits. She presented him to her brother, with an air that seemed to demand his approbation of her choice; nor was she disappointed: the appearance of the young man was too prepossessing to fail of making an immediate interest in the favour of my friend, whose sentiments were no sooner perceived by his sister, who eagerly watched them in the expression of his countenance, than her eyes sparkled with delight. – In a few minutes more, my friend had the pleasure of embracing his two brothers: the eldest, who is a year his senior, is now priest of the neighbouring village. A man of mild aspect, and gentle manners. At an early age, he made a sacrifice of ambition to love, and married a young woman, whose dower was made up of beauty and good temper.

Of the numerous offspring with which she has presented him, the two eldest reside with their grandfather – the youngest has but two days seen the light; and all the other their uncles have promised to provide for. So that the good man looks with a smiling aspect upon futurity.

The youngest brother of my friend, is a Professor of the Art of Surgery. A dapper little gentleman, with a smart wit, and perfumed handkerchief. His brother Henry says, he is a little affected by a disorder called *Puppyism,* but that he has sufficient stamina in his constitution to conquer the disease, which, it seems, is a very common one at his time of life.

Never did Calli, in the progress of his eventful journey, behold a happier circle than that which now surrounded the heart of Mr. Denbeigh. When I saw them sit down at the supper-table, I began to think the custom of social meals not altogether so ridiculous as I had hitherto considered it. At the conclusion of the repast, the cordial wish of health was mutually exchanged; and a glass filled with generous wine, was pressed to the lips of each, in token of sincerity. The cheerful song went round: every voice was in unison to strains of joy, and every countenance was irradiated with the smile of satisfaction. Before they parted for the night, the old gentleman, according to a very strange custom of his own, knelt down in the middle of his family, and while the tear of joy strayed down his venerable cheeks, offered up the sacrifice of thanksgiving to the throne of the Eternal!

Alas! this poor gentleman is not sufficiently enlightened to perform poojah to System. He has never been convinced, that vice and virtue are only qualities of imagination; and is deplorably ignorant of all theories, save that of a good conscience. – Nor has his wife advanced one step farther than himself, towards throwing off the prejudices of Christianity. – And what is still worse – the manner in which they have rivetted these prejudices in the minds of their children, scarcely admits a hope, that any of them will ever become converts to Atheism, or have sufficient spirit to exchange the morality of their Shaster, for the doctrine of external circumstances. On making enquiry of my friend concerning the cause of this phenomena, he informed me, that his father and mother, who were of different sects of Christians, agreed, that the religion taught their children should not be indebted for its support to the peculiar dogmas of either; but should chiefly rest on the authority of that Shaster, which has so deeply incurred the displeasure of the philosophers. – His mother was the daughter of a priest of the sect of Dissenters, who had bestowed such particular pains on the cultivation of her understanding, as actually qualified her for conducting the education of her own children.

It is, perhaps, to this uncommon and extraordinary circumstance, that the children of Mr. Denbeigh are indebted for many of those peculiarities which at present distinguish their characters. It is from this cause, that the daughters have become learned, without losing their humility: that they are gay, without being frivolous: that in conversation, their sprightliness is free from the lightness of vanity, and their seriousness from the arrogance of self-conceit. Mrs. Denbeigh, not considering the preservation of ignorance absolutely necessary towards the perfection of the female character, never sent her daughters to the seminaries that are established for that purpose, but suffered them from infancy to partake with their brothers in every advantage of solid instruction. – Being early taught to make a just estimate of things, they learned how to value the performance of every duty; nor was their attention towards those annexed by custom to their situation, lessened from a consideration of their simplicity. In their minds the torch of knowledge was too fully lit, to lead to the dangerous path of singularity, into which unwary females have by its feeble glimmering, been so oft betrayed. I can almost venture to assert, that the blooming Emma, at this moment manages the domestic economy of her father's house, with as much prudence and activity as could be expected from the most ignorant and accomplished female that ever issued from a *genteel boarding-school*. That she is as dutiful, as affectionate, as obedient to her parents, as if she had never looked into any book but a Novel; and will regard their memory with as much filial veneration, as if they had never furnished her mind with an idea, or taught her any other duty, save how to dress and play at cards!!

THE week that has elapsed since my arrival at Violet-Dale, has been spent in alternate visits to the sons, and sons-in-law of Mr. Denbeigh. As the most beautiful symmetry of feature eludes the skill of the painter, so do the quiet satisfactions of life, though sources of the truest pleasure, bid defiance to the powers of description: I shall therefore of this week only mention one little incident, which pleased, in spite of its simplicity.

On the second day after our arrival, while Mr. and Mrs. Denbeigh, and the lovely Emma, were listening, with looks of complacency and delight, to the recital made by my friend of some of his adventures in India, Mr. Denbeigh was informed, that a person wanted to speak with him. – It was a country-man, who being by universal consent, admitted into the parlour, declared his business. It was, to pay to the old gentleman a small sum of money, which, it appeared, had been lent, with little prospect of return. He received for his punctuality, the encouragement of praise; and Emma, unbidden, arose from her embroidery, to present him some wine for himself, and sweet-cake to take home to his children. The poor man was, by this kindness, emboldened to loquacity. "Yes," said he to Mr. Denbeigh, "I defy the whole world to say, that Gilbert Grub ever remained one hour in any man's debt, after he was able to get out of it. And as your honour was so good to me in my necessity, and lent to me when no one else would, it was good reason to pay your honour first. But, perhaps, you have not heard of the strange behaviour of Mr. Darnley?"

"Mr. Darnley!" repeated Emma, suspending her work to listen.

"What of Mr. Darnley?" said Mr. Denbeigh.

"Why, Sir, you must know," said the peasant, "that Old Benjamin Grub, who lived in one of Mr. Darnley's free cottages, to whom, I am sure, both your honour and these two good ladies have given many and many a shilling, died on Friday was eight days; and on opening his will, who do you think he should have left his sole heir, but Mr. Darnley?"

"What could the poor creature have to leave?" said Mrs. Denbeigh. "He was the very picture of wretchedness."

"Aye, so he was," returned the garrulous old man; "and that was the very way he took to scrape together such a mine of wealth. Would you believe it, Madam? In the very rags that covered him, fifty golden guineas were concealed, and a hundred more were found in his house; but no matter for that, if it had been ten times as much, it all went to Mr. Darnley. – And though to be sure, we could not blame him for taking it – yet some of us thought it main hard, that while so many of his own flesh and blood were in a starving condition, all this store of wealth should go to one who had enough of his own."

"But, whilst his own relations left him to starve, had he not been supported by Mr. Darnley's bounty?" said Mr. Denbeigh.

"Aye, that is true," said the peasant: "but, as old Sam Grub of the Mill, says, if any one of us had a-known of his wealth, we would all have been as kind to him as the 'Squire."

"Mr. Darnley ought certainly to have made some present to the old man's relations," said Mr. Denbeigh. "Aye, Sir, I thought he might ha' given some small thing among us," said the peasant; "but never could have imagined, that he would have behaved in the way he did."

"Go on," said Mr. Douglas, knitting his brows.

The cheek of Emma grew pale: she took up her needle, but remained in the attitude of attention, while the peasant proceeded.

"You must know, Sir, that after having had a long confabulation with the Sexton, who is himself a Grub, the first thing the 'Squire did, was to send for all the Grubs in the parish, man and woman, to come to the funeral. Some of us were so much stomached, that we did not much like to go. But, says I, though Benjamin has been unnatural to us, that is no reason that we should be unnatural to him. So we all went yesterday morning, at the hour appointed, and found all things prepared for the funeral – and a gallant funeral it was; it would have done good to the heart of any of his friends to have seen it. When we returned from the church-yard, Mr. Darnley, who was himself chief mourner, desired us all to go back with him to Ben's Cottage, where wine was poured out for us by Mr. Darnley's butler, who is himself a very grand gentleman. – When we had drank a glass, Mr. Darnley got up, and said – 'My friends,' says he, 'I hope none of you will have any cause to repent the choice made by your kinsman of a trustee, for the distribution of his property, for I cannot look upon his Will in any other light. – Here are twenty of you present. Ten grand-children of his brothers, and as many descendants from his Uncles. To the first I have allotted ten guineas each to the latter five, which disposes of the whole hundred and fifty found in his possession – and I hope it is a division with which you will all be satisfied.' We all cried out with one voice, that his honour was too good! too generous! that he should, at least, keep one half to himself. 'God forbid!' said he, 'that I should take a farthing, that my conscience told me, was the property of another!' – And he looked so pleased, and so good humoured! And we were all so astounded with delight! For your honour must know, that ten guineas to a poor man, is a mighty sum! Ah! your honour can have no notion what it is, when a man has been working from hand to mouth, now scrambling to get out of debt, and then falling back into poverty - what it is to be at once, as I may say, set above the world!"

The eyes of Emma glistened with delight, and the sweet tint of the opening rose-bud again mantled over her lovely cheek. – The peasant continued —

"Well, Sir, we were scarcely come to our sense, as I may say, when Farmer Stubble's cart came to the door, with old Martha Grub, who kept the penny-school on the Green Common, and who broke her leg last year on going up to the hen-roost. We had every one of us forgotten old Martha, but were all willing to club her share. 'No, no,' said the Squire; 'you must all keep what you have got, it was my fault, for not being better informed; but Martha shall be no loser, said he; I will give her five guineas out of my own pocket!' – Who would have thought he would have behaved in such a manner?"

"It was indeed acting very handsomely," said Mr. Denbeigh.

"Noble, generous Darnley!" said Emma. "It is just what I would have expected from him!"

The old man took his leave. – "And pray," says my friend, as soon as he was gone, "who is Mr. Darnley? Is it he whom I well remember breaking down your fences, in following his fox hounds?" "No, no," returned Denbeigh, "that was the elder brother of this Darnley, who was then, in obedience to the will of his father, preparing for the Bar. He was, as you have just heard, too fond of Justice, to be very partial to the practice of the Law; and on the death of that elder brother, who broke his neck one morning in hunting, he came down to Darnley-Lodge, where he has ever since resided.

"He was soon discovered to be a very strange, whimsical sort of a creature, by the neighbouring 'Squires. – The sufferings of a poor timorous animal, harassed by fatigue, and tortured by the agonizing sensations of excessive fear, were not necessary for his amusement.[1] He could enjoy much pleasure in walking over a fine country, without being the butcher of either hare or partridge: and take delight in rambling by the side of our river, though his heart never felt the triumph of beholding the dying struggles of a poor trout, or exulted in its writhing agony while tearing the barbed dart from its lacerated entrails. His mind sought for other objects of gratification. The study of Mineralogy and Botany, and exquisite relish for the beauties of nature, refined by an acquaintance with the sister arts of Poetry and Painting, gave sufficient interest to the rural scenery, without any aid from the misery of inoffensive animals. To the amusements of elegant Literature, he has added those of Agricultural improvement. He comes here to take my advice about the latter; and on the former, I believe, he comes to consult Emma, who will give you the best account of his taste."

Emma at the moment very suddenly recollected something she had left in her own room, for which she went in great haste, and the old Gentleman proceeded. "At the time that our acquaintance with

---

1   Foxhunts were controversial; compare the account of them in Severan's description of Sir Caprice Ardent (Letter XIII). Late eighteenth-century theories of sensibility led to increasing concern about mistreatment of animals – see G.B. Barker-Benfield's discussion of the subject in *The Culture of Sensibility* (Chicago: U of Chicago P, 1992).

Mr. Darnley commenced, Emma was in her seventeenth year. He found her mind more cultivated than is common with girls of that age, and took delight in improving her already formed taste. His conversation was far superior, in point of elegance and information, to that of any person she had ever met with: besides, it must be confessed, that there is a charm in the manners of a man who has seen something of the world, and been accustomed to move in the upper circles of life, which is very captivating to a delicate mind. I saw the impression that was made on my poor Emma's, and trembled for the peace of my sweet child. I feared, that by acquiring a taste for that sort of refinement of sentiment and manners, which is so rarely to be met with in the country, she might injure her future happiness. I know not if Darnley perceived my uneasiness, but he soon took an opportunity of speaking to me on the subject. He told me, that his affection for my daughter should long ago have led him to make proposals to me on her account, but that the disparity of their ages had rendered him anxious to make such an interest in her esteem, as might supply the place of that romantic passion, which, during the reign of fancy, is deemed essential to nuptial happiness. I approved of his conduct, and told him, that in regard to my daughters, I had laid down a rule to which I had invariably adhered, and that was, never to give my consent to their entering into any engagement, before they had entered their twentieth year."

"Then you did not intend they should marry Nabobs," said my friend. "Why, we Indians, never think of any thing beyond sixteen."

"Then you do not think of the blessing of mutual happiness," said his father. "Why not?" returned my friend. "*We* think of happiness in the possession of youth and beauty; and our young wives think of it in the enjoyment of our fortunes. – Is not this being mutually happy?" "Short-lived happiness!" rejoined his father, "which is certainly extinguished by satiety, and probably succeeded by disgust. – The first sight sympathy of souls," continued Mr. Denbeigh, "is laughed at by any well educated girl; but such an union of minds as includes a similarity of taste and sentiment; – such a degree of esteem as is essential to mutual confidence, is, in my opinion, absolutely necessary between two people, who are to be bound in partnership for life. And is a girl of sixteen a proper judge of the qualities necessary for such an union?" – "But, if I mistake not," returned my friend, "the age of Mr. Darnley very nearly doubles that of my sister." "True," replied the old Gentleman; "but Mr. Darnley does not marry Emma merely on account of her pretty face. Neither does she bestow her affections on his fortune. The tender friendship that already subsists between them, is cemented by esteem for real virtues. – If it had been otherwise, it is not Mr. Darnley's fortune (though far beyond what a child of mine is by any means entitled to) that should have tempted me to witness the sacrifice of her future peace."

Here the good Gentleman was interrupted by the entrance of this very Mr. Darnley, who had come to pay his compliments to the family, on the arrival of my friend. His noble aspect and graceful manner, apparently justified all that had been said in his favour; and the sweet blushes that spread themselves over the countenance of the fair maiden, on unexpectedly beholding him – told, that the old Gentleman had not been wrong in his conjectures, concerning the state of her heart.

But what does Māāndāāra think of the doctrine of Mr. Denbeigh? Not suffer a daughter to enter into an engagement of marriage before she is twenty! – Twenty! – why twenty is old enough for a grandmother! – I fear the reasonings of Mr. Denbeigh would make as few converts in Hindoostan, as in the English seminaries, where young Ladies are *genteelly educated*.

<hr />

WE have just returned from spending the day with the eldest daughter of Mr. Denbeigh.

The company assembled were numerous and gay, and the entertainment given them by the Merchant, was at once substantial and splendid. – I should not, however, have thought of mentioning it, but for the sake of one of the guests, whose behaviour will give you some idea of the manners and conversation of such *people of style* as are suffered to go abroad after the loss of their senses. – When such people visit, they make use of the company as their *Chubdars*; and always keep them waiting for their appearance such a length of time, as may give them sufficient opportunity for discussing their birth, titles, and situation. This Lady was accordingly announced, before her appearance, to be the wife of a recruiting officer, and fifteenth cousin to an Irish Lord – a circumstance, of which we might have remained in ignorance, had she arrived at the same time with the rest of the company.

When she entered, the height of the chowry that adorned her head; the length of the train of silk which followed her into the room, and which did not disdain to wipe the feet of the gentlemen; the scanty size of the veil of modesty, which covered, or rather which did not cover, her bosom; the quickness of her step, the undaunted assurance of her mien – all spoke the consciousness of her own superiority. I listened to her conversation with the most respectful attention, till she mentioned a circumstance, that at once struck me with astonishment and horror. "London," she said, "was now become quite a desert, not a single being remained in town." "London!" repeated I. "London! that populous city, which was late the residence of so many hundred thousand people; is it possible, that it can so suddenly have been rendered desolate?" "Lard bless me," returned the Lady, "every body knows that there is not at this time a single creature in London: and so I told the Captain before we went, but he would go, and staid whole ten days; you never knew any thing so horrid! Not one creature was to be seen."

"Horrid, indeed," repeated I. "Alas! poor Doctor Severan, what, in the general calamity, is become of him?" A smile which sat upon the faces of the company, and a look of compassion with which the benevolent Mr. Denbeigh at that moment seemed to regard my informer, made me suspect her of insanity, and she, indeed, said enough afterwards fully to confirm my suspicion.

Poor thing! she was so incapable of concealing her misfortune – that she seemed to pique herself on having fainted at the sight of a red gown in the month of July, a convincing proof that she was not then in the possession of her understanding. – The derangement of her faculties, may, perhaps, be accounted for from the many *frights* and *shocks* she has met with in a country town, where her husband is unfortunately quartered.

"The *frights*," she said, "came to visit her, and some of their heads were so *hideous*, that she thought she would have died at the sight."

No wonder that such a circumstance should have produced fatal effects upon a feeble mind. Like most people who labour under this sort of delirium, she was altogether unconscious of her unhappy situation, and really seemed to enjoy a fancied pre-eminence over the daughters of Mr. Denbeigh, and many other females of sound mind, who were assembled upon this occasion. "Alas! poor lady," said I to myself, "how pitiable is thy situation! How much more would it have been to thy advantage, to have possessed one grain of the good sense of these amiable females, whom thy folly holds in such derision, than to have been cousin to all the Lords in Christendom! Had not thy malady brought blindness to thine eyes, thou mightest, doubtless, have beheld in the streets of London, thousands, and ten thousands of thy superiors in the scale of human excellence!" – But thus it is, that the dust of folly which is shaken into the eyes by the hand of affectation, produces the false perception of objects.

May we have our eyes enlightened by the Collyrium[1] of judgment – so shall we be able to observe ourselves in the Mirror of Truth!

<hr />

I HAVE had the unexpected satisfaction of beholding the sister of my first English friend. Yes, Māāndāāra, Charlotte Percy is now the guest of Mr. Denbeigh, and you may judge how much such a circumstance has augmented the pleasure of Zāārmilla.

I did not till lately discover, that Morley-farm was in the neighbourhood of Violet-dale, and not many hours elapsed after the discovery, till, in company with Denbeigh and his sister Emma, I went to visit the late residence of the benevolent old man, whose character is still spoken of in this neighbourhood in terms of respect, gratitude, and affection. The weather was serene and temperate, such as, at Almora, we frequently enjoy in the depth of winter; it was what is here called a fine autumnal morning. The trees, which were so lately clothed in the livery of the Mussulman Prophet, have now assumed a

---

1 Collyrium. Crude Antimony, and sometimes Lead ore, ground to an impalpable powder, which the people of India put into their eyes, by means of a polished wire. They fancy it clears the sight, and encreases the lustre of the eye. [E.H.] Hamilton quotes this passage from Wilkins, 101 (1885).

greater variety of colouring – while some have had their green coats changed into the sober tint of the cinnamon: and others have taken the tawny hue of the orange. The leaves of many, which like ungracious children, had forsaken their parent stem, rustled in our path. Of all the vocal inhabitants of the woods, one little bird alone, like the faithful friend, who reserves his services for the hour of adversity, sitting on the half-stripped boughs, raised the soft note of consolation to the deserted grove.

Emma, who was our conductress, said she would take us by the private road, which had been a few years ago made my Mr. Morley and her father, to facilitate the intercourse of their families. We soon arrived where the wooden bridge had stood; but, alas! it was now no longer passable. A few of its planks half floated on the stream – the rest had been carried away by the farmer, to make up a breach in the fence. "Ah!" said Emma, "could poor Mr. Morley now see that bridge! – but do not mention it to my father. I know how it would vex him to hear of it." We proceeded on another road, and at the distance of a few paces from the house, we met with a second disappointment. Attempting to open a small gate that led to the front door of the house, a little boy came out to tell us that it had been nailed up, and that we must go through the yard where the cattle were feeding.

Emma begged we might proceed no father, and we were about to comply with her request, when the wife of the person who now rents the farm came to us. "Ah! how glad Miss Percy will be to see you Miss!" cried she. "I did not think that my son could have been back from the Dale so soon."

"Miss Percy!" said Emma. "What of Miss Percy? When did you hear of her?"

"Did you not know that she came here yesterday?" returned the woman. "She sent a letter to let you know that she intended going over to the Dale tonight."

"Sent a letter!" returned Emma. "Charlotte used not to be so ceremonious."

"Indeed she is not what she used to be," returned the farmer's wife. "She is so melancholy, that I never saw the like. Soon after she came yesterday evening, she went out to the garden, and, would you believe it? The sight of the potatoes my husband planted in the place my old master used to call his Velvet Walk, and which he used to have mown every week (though the grass was good for nothing, to be sure, but to be swept away as if it had been rubbish) and where he used to sit of an evening in the queer-looking chair, that now, when it is turned upside down, does so well for a hay-rack for the young calves; would you believe it? Her eyes filled with tears at the very sight of it. Now what could make any one cry at the sight of a good crop of potatoes, is more than I can imagine. But, says my husband, don't you see that it is being very lonely that makes Miss so melancholy? So I went to her, and thought she said she liked to be lonely, I would not leave her to herself the whole evening."

"Your company would be a great relief to her spirits, to be sure," said Denbeigh.

"Yes, for certain," returned the good woman; "though she took on a little still. And when she went into the paddock, where the little poney that Mr. Morley used to ride about the farm now runs, La! See Miss, says I, if there is not your uncle's poney, I dare to say it knows you. She held out her hand, and called it by its name, and, would you believe it? It no sooner heard her voice, that it came scampering up. – Poor Mopsy, said she, as she stroked its ears, and again the tears came into her eyes. She turned away, but the beast still followed her, neighing, till we came to the gate. She then so begged me to leave her for a few minutes, that I went on the other side of the hedge, and saw her go back to poor Mopsy, and laying her hand upon its head, as it held it out for her to stroke – she burst into tears. Dear heart, says I, Miss, don't take on so; my husband will buy you a surer-footed beast than Mopsy, at any market in the country, for five pounds."

"Poor Charlotte!" said Emma: "but why did she expose herself to this torture?" The good woman stared at Emma, who declined listening to any more of her conversation; but demanding which way her cousin had walked, she hastily requested us to follow.

"How nicely this gravel walk used to be kept!" said Emma (as we walked along) "and see how it is now destroyed. These shrubs too, so broken down by the cattle, how the good old Mr. Morley used to delight himself in taking care of them! He is gone! and, alas! how quickly are the favourite objects of his attention likely to perish! – But the remembrance of his virtues shall not thus fall into oblivion. – No!" continued the lovely Moralist: "the trees he has planted may be cut down by sordid avarice; and the hand of brutish stupidity may root out the flowers of his garden; but his deeds of benevolence and charity shall be held in everlasting remembrance!"

We were now arrived at the gate of a meadow, which was almost encircled by the stream. A narrow path winded through the plantation of young trees that ornamented its banks. – At the root of one of these trees, I perceived a small bright object glittering in the rays of the sun. I approached it, and found some leaves of ivory, fastened by a silver clasp, which on touching it, flew open, and discovered the hand writing of Miss Percy. "It is Charlotte's tablets," cried Emma. "It was in these she used to sketch the effusions of her fancy, on any subject that occurred. – It is still so," continued she, turning over the leaves. "Here is some poetry – she cannot think it any breach of faith to read it." "Read it then," said her brother.

She complied, and read as follows —

> Why, shades of Morley! Will you not impart
>     Some consolation to my grief-worn mind?
> 'Mid your delightful scenes, my sinking heart
>     Had hoped the sweets of wonted peace to find.
>
> Dear scenes of sweet content, and careless ease,
>     Where in unchanging bliss the seasons roll'd,
> Where Winter's storm, or Summer's genial breeze,
>     Could some peculiar beauty still unfold.
>
> The charmer Hope then perch'd on every bough,
>     And sung of Friendship true, and Love sincere;
> While Fancy twin'd her wreath round youth's fair brow,
>     And Mem'ry's annals mark'd no transient tear.
>
> But now – the charmer Hope is heard no more!
>     Gone are my youth's lov'd friends; – for ever gone!
> The dear delusive dreams of bliss are o'er,
>     And all fair Fancy's airy train is flown!
>
> Sad Mem'ry now must these lov'd haunts invade
>     With the dark storms of many a heart-felt grief,

With bosom'd sorrows, silent as this shade,
    Sorrows from lenient Time that scorn relief.

As to each well known object Mem'ry clings,
    She bids the tear of deep regret to flow;
To every former scene of bliss she brings
    The throb of Anguish, and the sigh of Woe.

As she retraces every blissful hour,
    Here spent with cheerful Hope, and youthful joy,
Hope lost! Joy gone for ever; ————————

✳ ✳ ✳ ✳ ✳ ✳ ✳ ✳ ✳ ✳ ✳ ✳ ✳ ✳

The tears which had fallen on the remaining lines had rendered them totally illegible. Those which suffused the blue eyes of the gentle Emma, stopt her utterance, she hastily put the tablets in her pocket – and we proceeded in silence.

In a spot that was peculiarly sheltered by a row of beeches, whose leaves have now assumed the colour of the dried cinnamon, stood the remains of an arbour, which had once been covered with the most beautiful creepers this ungenial climate can produce, but which unsupported now fell upon the ground; no bad emblem of the mind of their former mistress, who sat at the entrance of the arbour, on the trunk of the fallen tree. Her countenance wore the traces of melancholy, but the manner in which she received the salutations of my friends, shewed that her heart was still capable of the most animated affection. Me too she received with kindness; though the ideas associated with my appearance gave a perceptible emotion to her already agitated spirits. She made an effort to banish the melancholy ideas which had of late been so familiar to her mind; and having satisfied Emma as to the reasons that induced her to stop at Morley-farm, she cheerfully acquiesced in her proposal of returning with us to Violet-dale, where she was received with the cordial welcome of sincere affection; and where, in the happiness of her friends, her own sorrows appear to be forgotten.

IN this Temple of domestic bliss, the flight of time has been so imperceptible, that a whole week, which has elapsed since I laid down my pen, appears but as a day.

We know that one of the fourteen precious things which were produced in the churning of the ocean, was a learned physician: but which of the sages of the tribe of Vaidya ever contrived a remedy of such approved efficacy, as the conversation of a faithful and judicious friend?

Such a one has Miss Percy experienced in the father of Denbeigh. He has already convinced her that the indulgence of melancholy, instead of being an amiable weakness, rather deserving of admiration than censure, is, in reality, equally selfish and sinful. – It is, he says, the height of ingratitude to the Giver of all good, peevishly to refuse the enjoyment of the many blessings that are left us, because we are deprived of a few, which were in their very natures perishable. – "But, alas!" replied Miss Percy, "what is left to those whose earliest and dearest friends have been snatched from them by the hand of death?"

"Much is left to all," replied Mr. Denbeigh. "No one, who enjoys the blessings of health, and a peaceful conscience, can, without ingratitude, repine. The proper discharge of the duties of life is a source of happiness to every well regulated mind."

"But how circumscribed are the limits of those duties to a female, who has no longer any parent to attend on: no family to manage: no fortune to bestow in deeds of charity: and who has it little in her power to be useful, even to a friend?"

"And is the gift of reason then nothing?" retorted Mr. Denbeigh. "And are the powers of the mind to lie dormant, because, forsooth, you have not now the management of a family: or the exercise of the benevolent affections to be given up, because you have not a fortune to build alms-houses? These are the meer subterfuges of indolence. Believe me, my dear Charlotte, that whoever seriously resolves not to suffer any opportunity of benefiting a fellow-creature to pass unemployed, will find, that the power of doing good is not circumscribed within very narrow limits.

"Why, (let me ask you farther) should your mind, cultivated as it has been by education, and improved by listening to the conversation of the enlightened and judicious; why should it not exert its powers, not only for your own entertainment, but for the instruction, or innocent amusement of others?"

"Ah! Sir," returned Charlotte, "you know how female writers are looked down upon. The women fear, and hate; the men ridicule, and dislike them."

"This may be the case with the mere mob, who receive every prejudice upon trust," rejoined Mr. Denbeigh; "but if the simplicity of your character remains unchanged – if the virtues of your heart receive no alloy from the vanity of authorship; trust me, my dear Charlotte, you will not be the less dear to any friend that is deserving of your love, for having employed your leisure hours in a way that is both innocent and rational."

Thus did this venerable old man persuade Miss Percy to reconcile her mind to the evils of her destiny, and, by the exertion of activity, to seek the road to contentment. Nor has his attention been confined to her. Me also, he has honoured with much of his instructive conversation. He has been particularly solicitous to know my opinions concerning all that I have seen in England; and expecting to reap advantage from his observations, I have put into his hands a copy of all my letters to you. These it was easy for me to give in English; it having been my custom to write down such conversations as I intended to recite to you, in that language, and after having given it to some English friend to translate, have from the corrected copy made the translations intended for your use.

Mr. Denbeigh was much entertained with my account of the philosophers, but said, "if it was known in England, people would think that I intended to turn philosophy itself into ridicule." Thus it is that the designs of authors are mistaken! Perhaps this is not the only passage in my letters that might, to an English reader, appear to be absurd. – Happily they will never be exposed to any eye, save that of my friend. – It is therefore sufficient, if to him they convey a picture of the truth, such as it appears to the mind of Zāārmilla.

I have already hinted my astonishment at the number of new books that are every year produced in England; but now that I know what these books have to encounter, before they fight their way into the world, my astonishment is increased tenfold! Many and various are the evils which these poor adventurers have to encounter. Besides the smarting, though superficial wounds, which they may expect to receive from the small-shot of the ladies and gentlemen *genteelly educated*, who call every thing *stupid* that is beyond the limits of their slender comprehensions, they have to sustain the *heavy* blows of those who cut down every thing as *nonsense*, that swerves from the beaten track over which they have been accustomed to trot. Should they be endowed with sufficient strength to survive the attack of both these adversaries, they have still to pass before the formidable phalanx of Reviewers, each of whom, like the mighty Carticeya,[1] brandishes in his hundred arms a hundred instruments of destruction. These terrible Genii are said to judge of books by the smell, and when that has happened to be offensive to their nostrils, have been known, by one well-aimed dart, to transfix an unfortunate book to the shelves of the booksellers' shops for ever. But with the powerful is found mercy. Instead of the dread weapons of war, these imitators of the sons of the Mountain-born Goddess, sometimes condescend gently to tickle the trembling adventurer with a feather plucked from the plumage of the Peacock.

Ah! if ever friend of Zāārmilla's venture to send forth a book into the world, may it find these terrible Reviewers in this favourable mood! May its perfume be pleasing to their nostrils, and its form find favour in the sight!!

---

I HAVE just received a letter from my friend Severan, it contains the desirable information, that a ship will in a few weeks sail for India – the commander of which, is his particular friend. In it I shall take my passage – and if the powerful Varuna is favourable to my prayers, shall, in the progress of a few returning moons, again behold the blessed shores of Hindoostan. O thought replete with extacy! How does the bosom of Zāārmilla pant, for the period of thy realization! – Yet shall I not purchase that felicity, without having paid the debt of anguish,

---

1   The Hindoo God of War. He is represented with six faces, and a number of hands, in each of which he brandishes a weapon. He rides upon a peacock, and is usually found in company with his Mother Parvati, or the Mountain Goddess, one of the characters of the consort of Seeva. See Asiatic Researches, vol. ii. [E.H.]

in many a tear; before my eyes can be solaced by beholding the companions of my youth, they must have been moistened with the sorrow of an eternal separation from every English friend.

From this amiable family, from the worthy Denbeigh, and the excellent Severan, I shall have been parted for ever. – But the remembrance of their virtues shall be the companions of my life; and the idea of their happiness shall solace every hour of my existence.

Nothing can equal the delight of my friend Severan, at the success of his experiment; which has opened a new field for discovery, of which he will not be slow to take possession. It is a peculiar advantage attendant upon science, that the gratification it affords is not more delightful to the individual, than beneficial to society; and it is this consideration that enhances every enjoyment of the scientific philosopher.

I cannot help thinking, that this sort of philosophy is more favourable to the happiness of its votaries, than that sort professed at Ardent-Hall; but this may be owing to the advantages enjoyed by the former, of a happier method of conducting their experiments. It certainly does not arise in the latter from any want of zeal, or from a backwardness to repeat experiments, that have already been found unsuccessful. As a proof of this, my friend Severan informs me, that Mr. Axiom, has persuaded Miss Ardent to accompany him to the Continent, on an experiment of *abstract principle*, which, he says – "should put a learned female above the censure of the world." My friend seems to doubt whether the result of this experiment, will bring peace to the poor Lady's bosom; and adds, "that it would be no less surprising, to see the flame of the taper brighten, on being plunged into mephitic air,[1] than that a female, who bids defiance to modesty and decorum, should preserve her honour, and her peace."

Miss Ardent has resigned her charge of the younger daughter of Sir Caprice, to Lady Grey. The eldest daughter of the Baronet, the Novel-reading Julia, has, it seems, suffered much from the unexpected metamorphosis of a charming swain; who, soon after he had introduced himself to her acquaintance, as a hero of exalted sentiment and tender sensibility, was unfortunately recognized by certain sagacious

---

1   Carbonic acid (*OED*).

men, from a place called Bow-street,[1] to be one of the tribe of Swindlers – the discovery gave such a shock to the nerves of the young Lady, that she has been ordered to a place called Bath, for the recovery of health. Thither her father and mother have accompanied her; and there the former, at the instigation of a teacher of a sect called Methodists,[2] has renounced the poojah of System; and, instead of building a house for sparrows to make honey, he now intends to erect a church, for the edification of the saints. Thus doth one folly succeed to another, in the breast of him who is void of all permanent principle! – May the mind of Māāndāāra be furnished by Ganesa with the protecting shield of judgment, and preserved from the evils of instability!

<hr>

As this letter will be sent by a small vessel called a Packet, which carries dispatches from this government to the council of Calcutta, it will probably reach the happy region of Almora some weeks before thy friend.

I anticipate the comments which thou wilt make upon its contents. Thou wilt observe, that to extend our knowledge of the world, is but to become acquainted with new modes of pride, vanity, and folly. Thou wilt perceive that in Europe, as in Asia, an affected singularity often passes for superior wisdom; bold assertion for truth; and sickly fastidiousness for true delicacy of sentiment. Thou wilt see that the passions of men are every where the same; and that the variety made by the Idol of Doctor Sceptic (existing circumstances) is not in the passions themselves, but in the complexion of the objects which excite them. Thou wilt remark, that though vice and folly have the appearance of being every where predominant, that it is only the superficial observer, who will from thence infer the non-existence of Wisdom and Virtue. These have been traced by Māāndāāra to the bosom of retirement, where he will have observed them employed in scattering the sweet blossoms of domestic peace: and though the

---

1 A London street; the site of Britain's first organized police force.
2 Methodism was, at this time, often associated with religious hypocrisy or extremism.

torch of vanity glares not on their dwelling, and the trump of fame sounds not at their approach, he will nevertheless have remarked with pleasure the extent of their silent reign, and, with Zāārmilla, will pity the man who can form a doubt of their existence.

Of the various religions of the English, I have given you a full and distinct account. You will perceive by it, that notwithstanding the progress of philosophy, and the report of Sheermaal, that that of Christianity is not *yet entirely extinct*; but that, like Virtue and Wisdom, it has still some adherents, in the retired scenes of life. – You will, perhaps, not have been able to discover how the practices enjoined by its precepts can be injurious to society; and inclined to think, that the love of a Being of infinite wisdom and goodness, and such a government of the passions, as enables a man to love his neighbour as himself, can do no great harm to the world. – Obnoxious as the precepts which command purity of heart, unfeigned humility, sanctity of morals, and simplicity of manners, may be to the philosopher; you will conclude, that they have, in reality, been found as little detrimental to the repose of the individual, as the expectation of everlasting felicity has been to his happiness. I am sorry, that the want of success attending the experiments of the worshippers of System, presents me with nothing to oppose to your conclusions better than assertion: but if you have half the complaisance of the people of England, you will think that ought to be sufficient to overturn the dictates of common sense, though confirmed by the experience of ages! – Such faith do these good people put in the assertions of philosophers!

I am called from my pen to witness a ceremony called Signing the Settlements,[1] which is preliminary to the marriage of Mr. Darnley and the blooming Emma. The day after to-morrow is fixed for their nuptials, and on the day following, the amiable bride departs with her husband, loaded with paternal blessings. Though every thing is to be conducted in common form, and exactly in conformity to Christian prejudices, I do not know but this gentle and unassuming girl may have as great a chance for happiness, as if she had gone off with her lover on an experiment of *abstract principle*.

"May the conduct of those who act well, afford pleasure to the

---

1    The legal documents arranging the financial affairs of an affianced woman and her future children.

mind! – May you, ye good, find friends in this world! May virtue be for ever to be found!"

In reading the letters of a friend, may the goodness of his intention be put in the balance with his errors; and where the former is found predominant, may the latter be consigned to oblivion! What can I say more?

F I N I S .

# Appendix A: Select Contemporary Reviews

## 1. *The Critical Review*, vol. 17 (July 1796): 241-49.

There is no better vehicle for local satire than that of presenting remarks on the manners, laws, and customs of a nation, through the supposed medium of a foreigner, whose different views of things, as tinctured by the particular ideas and associations to which his mind has been habituated, often afford an excellent scope for raillery; and the mistakes into which such an observer is naturally betrayed, enliven the picture, and furnish the happiest opportunity for the display of humour and fancy.

The justly admired Montesquieu employed this vehicle for the conveyance of instruction of a graver complexion; under a despotic monarchy, and writing for a light and fantastical people, he found means, beneath this pleasing garb, to attract the public attention to some of the most important topics of politics and morals, while by this contrivance he escaped the censure of a jealous administration, who would have been less tolerant of a work, which professedly treated of these subjects with equal freedom. Lord Littleton, in his Letters written in imitation, or rather in continuation of those of Montesquieu, has nearly followed the same track. The Letters before us are in a different style, and are more upon the model of Addison's humourous Epistle from the Ambassador of Bantam, than of the Persian Letters. In the course of the work we find a regular narrative, enlivened with many interesting and well drawn characters. The whole is founded on the supposed fact of a young Indian of rank forming an intimacy with an accomplished Englishman, whose representation of the state of his own country produces in the Rajah an insatiable curiosity to visit a country which his romantic imagination had pictured as the wonder of the universe. From this design he is dissuaded by one of his countrymen, a man of letters, who had been in England; but the scheme is afterwards revived by a domestic misfortune, which induces him to endeavour to forget his sorrow by visiting a foreign country. Through the whole, miss Hamilton displays a considerable knowledge of modern life, with very strong powers of ridicule and irony, and no inconsiderable acquaintance with the manners and literature of the East.

We have thought we discovered in different parts of the work some well-known characters in real life: but as no key is offered to explain these, it would be improper to intrude on our readers our own conjectures; and it will be a more candid mode of proceeding, both to the writer and the public, to extract a few specimens, where the satire is general.

The following observations our readers will probably think not unseasonable, as the subject was in some degree agitated in the last session of Parliament –

[Quotes Sheermaal's letter on the game laws from "Universally as the poojah of cards is established...." to "... suffer my companion to depart with me in peace," omitting the description of the peasant household.]

The following strictures on the system of female education in England are entertaining: – we wish we could say they are not just.

[Quotes Sheermaal's letter on female education from "During the period of infancy...." to "Wise regulations! Laudable Practice!]

We shall conclude our review by one more extract, which is from the second volume –

[Quotes Zaarmilla's description of newspapers from "Coffee-houses, similar to that described in one of my letters...." to "... my visit to sir Caprice Ardent."]

There are some very pretty and pathetic pieces of poetry introduced in these volumes; and we can very cordially recommend the whole as abounding in good sense, lively description, well-pointed (though not ill natured) satire, and general entertainment. Miss Hamilton is, we understand, the sister of the late Mr. Charles Hamilton, the learned translator of the Arabic code of Mussulman laws.

### 2. *The British Critic*, vol. 8 (September 1796): 237-241.

Matters of fact, as well as of opinion, too trite and common to command attention, and excite emotion by a bare recital, may derive an interest from the new lights in which they are capable of being contemplated. In all ages, even the rudest, the ingenuity of men has attempted, with more or less success, to enliven and impress moral and political truth on the mind, by fable and other machinery, whether in verse or prose. In the less cultivated ages, when the imaginations of men, but little restrained by the precision of philosophy, are more open to the art of the fabulist and poet, there is a boldness of fable, allegory, and poetical fiction, that would not be indulged in times of more reasoning and refinement. The machinery which so much enlivened the satire of Lucian, has very little effect in the hands of modern writers of the dialogues of the dead. The English nation of the present day scarcely endures every bold fiction of her best poets. The German nation, whatever may be the particular circumstances which occasion that difference, can bear a bolder degree of invention than Britons, and easily admit all the extravagance of a Dante or an Ariosto. As a proof of which, we have found in the German language, a kind of philosophical romance, entitled Mammuth,[1] or human Nature displayed on a grand Scale, in a Tour with the Tinkers into the central Parts of Africa; where the travellers meet with the remains of tribes, animals, &c. on a gigantic scale of stature and duration; and the remains of arts and sciences known to certain ancients, wiser than us, but now lost in the gulf of time. It appeared, on reading a critical preface, that this production was a translation from the English language: though in England the book is difficult to be found, and scarcely to be heard of. The machinery and humour which, it would seem, appeared too extravagant to Englishmen, was acceptable to the Germans.

From these observations, we may perceive the sound judgement of those writers, who confine the machinery by which they endeavour to excite attention and awaken imagination, as nearly as possible, within the bounds of probability. Such a writer is Eliza Hamilton. We know that about ten or twelve years ago Hindoo Rajahs have been in England. From the connection between India and Britain, it is extremely natural that a friend of a Rajah should write to him from England: that the prince, whose curiosity is strongly excited by the

---

1   The name given to the unknown animal, whose enormous bones have been found in America and Siberia. [Reviewer's note] The book refered to is [William Thomson], *Mammuth....* London, 1789.

correspondence, should himself pay a visit to this imperial country, and, in his turn, send an account of what appears most remarkable in this, to his friends he had left behind him, in his own country. Such is the ingenious and natural plan (the more ingenious for being so natural) of this writer; who, as appears not only from the letters, but from her preliminary dissertation, has acquired a very intimate acquaintance with the history, religion, and manners of the Hindoos, and is also a sensible and very extensive observer of the opinions, manners, and customs of our island. The following extracts will serve as specimens of this ingenious and amusing work of imagination.

[Quotes Zāārmilla's account of Mr. Vapour's ideas of the Age of Reason and the conversation between Grey and Zaarmilla about the Governor's ball.]

Miss Hamilton has illustrated her work not only by a glossary of Oriental words, but, for the convenience of the reader, by notes explanatory of them, when they occur, at the foot of the page. It is but justice to say that, for sound observation, rich imagination, and delicacy of taste and humour, this work is not inferior to the Persian Letters, or any thing that we have had of the same kind for many years.

### 3. *Monthly Review*, vol. 21, second series (October 1796): 176–81.

Impressed, from the moment at which we begin to think, with many gratuitous notions; bred up with local prejudices; accustomed to respect certain institutions, and to confound acquired habits with natural instincts; we view at a maturer age, without surprise, the complex structure of refined society. It becomes difficult to disentangle the perplexity of its combination; to separate that which is essential to its existence, from what is added by caprice; and that which is conducive to our happiness, from what is illusive or pernicious. An ingenious device practised, for this purpose, by the learned, has been the introduction of individuals of a distant nation, unacquainted with our opinions, and untainted with our prejudices of a contrary tendency; the opposition of which furnishes us at once with an agreeable entertainment, and an instructive moral lesson. By the illusion of fine writing, we can place ourselves in the situation of this stranger; admire and wonder at objects which we have before viewed without either wonder or admiration; and possibly withdraw our reverence from others which we have hitherto considered with respect. A Persian, a Turk, a Chinese, and a Jew, have each taken the trouble of publishing their remarks for our edification; and we are now introduced to a Hindoo Rajah, who is come to laugh at our follies, to condemn our vices, and to contrast the capricious fluctuation of our modes and sentiments with the perennial simplicity of eastern manners. It is, indeed, scarcely necessary to inform our readers that this is a work of fiction and fancy, designed to place before the view of the English reader a picture of the prevalent manners and customs of his country, in the novel colours of a supposed Hindoo painter. It may be more acceptable, because the circumstance is less apparent, to acquaint them that the actual delineator of this sketch is sister of the late Capt. Charles Hamilton, translator of the "History of the Rohillas," and of the "Hedaya"; of which works the reader will find accounts in our 77th vol. p. 395 and vol. vii. N.S. p. 417. The chief point to which we shall direct our attention will naturally be the *keeping* preserved by the fair artist, in handling her oriental pencil.

The prefixed dissertation is designed for an epitome of the religious and political opinions of the Hindoos, in order to familiarize the reader with the allusions and images introduced in the work. From the perusal of it, we derive no addition to our stock of information collected from the same recent publications which have supplied this lady with her materials: but such works are not yet sufficiently numerous, nor are the antiquities of which they treat sufficiently explored, to permit us to rely, with much confidence, on many curious conjectures which they seem to authorize, relative to the antient state of the nation which now inhabits the fertile region washed and enriched by the Ganges. Our knowledge is confined to a few isolated facts; while all around is buried in "darkness visible." In proportion, however, to the accumulation of these facts, and the degree of critical acumen and philosophic research with which they may be investigated and appreciated, we shall gradually be enabled to tread with a firmer step, among the antiquities of this singular people: to whom, perhaps, much of the mythology, much of the science, and many of the arts, cultivated by the western nations, may ultimately be traced: – but, with the scanty materials which could be drawn from English authors, it will not appear surprising if our fair writer herself should sometimes fall, and sometimes lead her Rajah, into mistakes, which a moderate degree of local knowledge would have enabled her to avoid. In assigning the Barampooter as the eastern limit of Hindostan, she cuts off some of its richest provinces; in bestowing on its antient government a federative form, she has embraced too readily a most questionable hypothesis; and in exempting the Hindoos from all hatred or contempt of other nations, she has totally mistaken the genius and character of the sons of Bramha, in whom a contempt of foreigners is inculcated and excused by the precepts of their religion. A less venial error occurs in the passage where Ganesa is said to be the "Janus of the Grecian mythology," in which this Italian deity had no place.

The dissertation is in general well written, though we must except the following ungrammatical sentence: "those religious prejudices which kept them in a state of perpetual separation from their conquerors *has* tended," &c. "A pathetic indifference," too, is an expression to which we cannot reconcile ourselves.

We now come to the fable of the work. When the arms of the late vizier, assisted by his European auxiliaries, wrested the province of Rohilcund from that tribe of Afghans to which it owed its name, a party of the fugitives sought refuge in the mountains of Almora, and carried with them a young captive, an English officer named Percy. Zāārmilla, Rajah of Almora, received them with that hospitality which is the characteristic of a liberal mind and a feeling heart. This prince had already attained a degree of general knowledge which was very uncommon in Hindostan; and during a long confinement, in consequence of an accidental fracture, young Percy found leisure to instruct him in the English language, as well as in many particulars of our manners and political institutions. The pure precepts of the gospel, which, he did not doubt, were literally practised, impressed him with the highest ideas of our morals; and a letter to Percy from his sister inspired him with an equal respect for the talents and sensibility of the fair; when the death of his guest deprived him of this intellectual entertainment. It was then that he conceived the design of visiting England: but the dissuasion of his friend Maandaara, corroborated by the narrative of Sheermaal, who had lately returned from this country, and who gave a representation of our manners which was very different from the ideal perfection figured by the Rajah, succeeded in deterring him from executing his design. The friendship between our hero and Maandaara is now farther cemented by the interchange of sisters: but the Rajah losing his wife soon afterward by a premature death, he quits a scene in which every object reminds him of his loss, intrusting the education of his son to the superintendence of his friend, to whom the letters are addressed. He visits Allahabad and Benares, and presents us with an account of his voyage down the Ganges, enlivened by occasional description of the rich and romantic scenery; as well as by the portraits of his companions, the friends of Percy, who accompanied him to Calcutta. During his residence in that city, he discovers that the conduct of his new associates was not so uniformly modelled on the examples furnished by the sacred writings, as might be wished: yet he sees more to applaud than to condemn; and he determines to prosecute his design of visiting England. The novelty of many scenes and characters which occur in Calcutta, and the surprise which they afford to our traveller, – particularly, the astonishment excited by seeing our ladies so far forget the modesty of their sex, as even – to dance at a ball, – are amusing and well described.

The second volume commences with the Rajah's embarkation: but, for the portraits of his ship-mates, the incidents of the voyage, and the characters of those with whom he becomes acquainted in England, we must refer to the work itself. Suffice it to say that he too soon learned to appreciate the difference between the *practice* of Christians, and their *professions*.

Although this publication is well supported throughout, and affords much entertainment, and many just and pointed remarks respecting the present state of our own country, we must acknowledge our opinion that the portion of the work which is evidently most laboured is the least deserving of commendation; and that Miss H. is less happy in her descriptions of Hindoo manners, than in her delineations of scenes at home, where she is better acquainted. It might seem fastidious to object to the impossibility of a Hindoo partaking of our tables, since that is a difficulty inherent to the subject:

but we perceive other incongruities, which a more perfect knowledge of that people would have taught her to avoid. A party at cards is mistaken by the Rajah for a poojah, or act of adoration: but cards are well known though not frequently used in Hindostan; and they are mentioned by Abul Fazil as one of the amusements at the court of Akbar. The names of the hero and his sister, (Zaarmilla and Zamarcanda,) are such as a Hindoo could not pronounce without difficulty. The letter Z is not to be found in the Shanscrit alphabet, nor in any of the dialects derived from that source; and in the pronunciation of those Persic words in which that letter occurs, it is converted by the Hindoos into J; as Jemindar for Zemindar. The Ganges we find in one passage styled the "king of rivers"; elsewhere, indeed, the goddess is restored to her real sex. Angels and genii are both improperly mentioned in this work, being equally foreign from the Hindoo mythology. The term Faquir cannot be applied, with propriety, to any but Mohammedan mendicants. A correct taste should have led this ingenious lady to reject the frequent recurrence of Persic or Moorish words, where both the sound and the sense would gain by a translation. "The sparkling chubdar of intellect," applied to the eye, is an expression too remote from common sense to be agreeable.

We feel no pleasure, however, in pointing out defects, particularly where there is much to approve; and we will now proceed to offer a specimen of the performance to our readers, which shall be the beginning of the fourteenth Letter. A paragraph inserted in a newspaper at Calcutta, after having mentioned the Rajah's name, and described his person, falsely and wickedly insinuated that he had come there on behalf of the Hindoo inhabitants of Bengal, to complain of the horrid cruelties and unexampled oppression, under which, through the maladministration of the British governor of India, the natives were made to groan.

[Quotes from the beginning of Letter XIV to "... bowing to the ground, he turned round, and departed."]

A number of mistakes occur in the orthography, which we imagine to be typographical; comparitive, frivilous, infallable, phenomona, prodominant, imposter, &c.

The original hymns addressed to the Hindoo deities by Sir William Jones are here termed *translations*: an error which we think it necessary to notice, because sublimity of invention, and an ingenious display of appropriate imagery, constitute a principal beauty of those poems.

## 4. *The Analytical Review*, vol. 24 (October 1796): 429-31.

The author of these letters seems to have taken the hint of conveying her sentiments to the public in the present form, from Montesquieu's and lord Lyttelton's Persian Letters, Goldsmith's Citizen of the World, the Turkish Spy, &c. It might be invidious to draw comparisons, but we confess, with pleasure, we have received entertainment from the perusal of this lively and amusing little work.

The writer displays, both in the letters and preliminary dissertation on hindoo mythology, history, and literature, considerable knowledge of india affairs: but it is doubtful, whether the generality of readers will perfectly accord with her in opinion, respecting the happy change which the long-suffering hindoos have experienced under the dominion of Great Britain. Many, it may be, will be rather inclined to believe, that, however mitigated in some respects by the more tolerant principles of the british legislature, on the subjects of law and religion; these injured people have merely *changed masters*, and one species of oppression for another. The interference of foreign states in the internal government of nations is generally equivocal in it's motives, and always mischievous in it's tendency. A simple, commercial intercourse would perhaps have been attended with more beneficial consequences to both countries. The compliments which are paid by our author to governor Hastings, to whom her production is dedicated, will be adjudged by the reader, either as just, or the grateful language of private obligation or friendship, according to his own preconceived opinions on the subject. We expected from the title of this work, to find the follies and vices of our contemporaries satirised by the fictitious indian prince, nor were we disappointed: a vein of ingenious pleasantry runs through it, mingled with a number of judicious, and sensible observations, on various subjects, especially on the female mind and manners, from which we select the following as particularly just and important.

[Quotes Sheermaal's letter on women's education from "you will observe, that women do actually, sometimes, carry on certain branches of trade...." to "... as destitute of protection as of instruction," and Zaarmilla's comments on novels from "the whole tenor of these books ..." to "... tolerated in a civilized society."]

Had the design of these volumes been less evidently *systematic*, they would have been more generally interesting. In the writer's laudable, because *apparently sincere*, zeal for christianity, she sometimes betrays a spirit not perfectly consistent with the mildness and simplicity of the religion of Jesus: railing is substituted for reasoning, and a frightful picture held up of the adversaries of revelation, in which truth and soberness are sacrificed, as is not unusual with controversialists, to *undue alarm*. A *sceptic* is described as a monster, for whom, "the fair face of nature has no charms" – who must necessarily have "a shallow understanding and a cold heart," – who confounds all distinction between vice and virtue, and preaches *profligacy* and *suicide* as conducive to *general utility*. Candid and calm discussion, not *abuse*, is the proper method of making *rational* converts: if conscious of the justness of our cause, we surely injure it by having recourse to calumny. Our author is still less successful, and equally illiberal in her attack upon moral philosophy and metaphysical inquiry, in which little knowledge and great assumption are manifested. Pursuing these subjects, which can interest or be understood but by a few readers, a wide field of fashionable follies, which might have yielded an abundant harvest, remains untouched, or is but slightly passed over. The style of these letters is agreeable and appropriate, though less glowing and metaphorical than the admired oriental compositions of Drs. Johnson and Hawkesworth; some incorrectnesses, and occasional harsh and illconstructed sentences, have escaped the writer's pen: but upon the whole, her production manifests a cultivated understanding and benevolent affections; and is one of those publications, which are calculated to undermine and destroy the barbarous, sensual prejudices, which have hitherto been indulged respecting the female mind and manners, and to confute the pertinacious sophisms of witlings.

## 5. *Scots Magazine*, vol. 59 (January 1797): 47-8.

These letters are filled with sound sense and observation; they illustrate in a very lively manner the remark, that many of our practices, habits, and sentiments, depend entirely on custom, prejudice, and education.

As a specimen we shall transcribe his shrewd remarks on the public worship of the capital.

[Quotes Zaarmilla on his visit to a church in London; the following month, the magazine reprinted Sheermaal's letter on female education.]

# Appendix B: Major Revisions in the Second Edition

**Page 56:**

"That part of Asia ... many of which have been famous...." is omitted.
*Replaced by*:
"That part of Asia, known to Europeans by the name of Hindoostan, extends from the mountains of Thibet in the north, to the countries of the Deecan in the south. It is separated from Persia and Uzbec Tartary by deserts on the west; and on the east, is bounded by the kingdoms of Tysra, Assam, and Arracan; comprehending within its limits a variety of provinces, many of which have been famous...."

**Page 233:**

The sentence following "... that of other women!" [" – but this, you will think, was carrying the matter rather too far"] is omitted in the second edition, and the following reflections on friendship are added:

Every day presents me with some new subject of meditation and perplexity. Nothing however has appeared to me so very extraordinary, so altogether incomprehensible, as the notions which the enlightened people of London entertain of the duties of Friendship. These are capacious as the firmament of Heaven – extensive as the bounds of space! To have a few real, affectionate, and disinterested friends, we esteem as a blessing reserved by the God for their peculiar favourites. One such friend appears to our narrow minds as a cordial drop in the cup of life, of sufficient efficacy to sweeten its bitterest contents. Judge then of the portion of happiness enjoyed by a nation, where every man and every woman of fashion boasts of hundreds of thousands of *friends*, all equally dear and equally deserving! In this point of view the Ladies of London betray an expansion of soul, which I had vainly thought reserved for beings of a higher sphere. The greater part of these fair creatures devote their lives to the duties of friendship – duties, which are in many respect incompatible with the duties of domestic life. – You will, perhaps, imagine from this, that the powers of the soul are expended in the necessary interchange of sentiment, with such a numerous host of friends. You will conceive, that these amiable women neglect their families in order to attend the sick beds of the friends who are afflicted with disease – to console the sorrowful, and to sympathise in the felicity of the fortunate – No such thing. The Ladies of London know no more of the joys or the sorrows of their *friends*, than they know of what is now doing in the house of Maandaara. Reciprocal good offices, which to our little minds appear to be the cement of friendship, have not the smallest influence in uniting the souls of people of fashion in the bonds of amity. The only essential duty of friendship, in this metropolis, is to be regular and punctual in leaving one's name (written, or printed, upon a bit of stiff paper) at the door of the friend's house, as frequently as the friend leaves a similar talisman at your's! You can have no idea of the zeal with which females, in the superior ranks, endeavour thus to keep alive the divine spark of friendship in the breasts of their sister beauties. With equal astonishment and veneration have I beheld them hurrying in their splendid equipages, from street to street, dropping these talismanic tickets at the dwelling of every fair friend. To notify the approach of these votaries of friendship, a certain great hammer is suspended at every door, with which the servant, who may be called the high priest of friendship, beats such an alarming peal, as is sufficient to strike terror to the stoutest heart. This, it would appear, is a very necessary part of the ceremony – as wherever the offering is not made in this manner, it fails to produce any of the feelings of friendship in the breasts of the visited. "Do these friends then, you will ask, for ever remain strangers to each other's persons? Do they never meet? Methinks such a species of friendship can be very little beneficial to either party."

Be not so hasty, my friend, in your conclusions. The ceremony I have described is, it is true, the only means by which the breath of friendship, between these enlightened people, can possibly be kept alive. An omission of this ceremony would inevitably convert the warmest friendship into the most bitter enmity. But think not that this is all that is demanded of friendship. No, this is a trifling sacrifice in comparison of that which follows. Every Lady, who can boast some hundred of friends, makes it a point to be *at home* on certain evenings, a circumstance which from want of habit is extremely irksome; and no sooner is it known to her friends that she is under the necessity of performing this penance, than they croud to her house, in order to amuse and comfort her. The person, who upon these occasions sees only as many friends as her house will conveniently hold, considers herself quite deserted. To have not only the apartments, but the passages and stairs filled with friends who pant for admission, is a felicity reserved for the peculiar favourites of fortune! At the time I visited Lady Ardent, I did not know that her Ladyship was then performing penance *at home*. I did not know the cause of that air of dissatisfaction which was visible on her brow. Her apartments were, in my opinion, sufficiently filled; as I am sure the heat was sufficiently offensive; but I have since learned, that, of three hundred friends to whom she had notified her intention of being at home, *only* one hundred and fifty made their appearance! This was surely sufficient mortification to a woman of sensibility. But, added to this, was her kind participation in the feelings of her servants. In the countenances of her domestics she read the language of disappointment, and the good lady's soul sympathized in their distress. For be it known to my friends, that at every cardtable a present is made to the servants, so considerable, as to enable them to imitate their masters in every species of folly and dissipation. The money thus given is indeed, as I am well informed, considered as a fund sacred to profligacy and extravagance. As without this extra pay, the servants of the great could neither afford to game, nor to get drunk with generous wines, not to keep expensive mistresses, they would, but for this happy contrivance, be deprived of many enjoyments, which are considered by their superiors as the prime privileges of existence!

In addition to the methods of making and preserving friendship, which I have already described, there is another now fast coming into use, which bids fair, as I am informed, soon to become universal. With many people of sentiment, those are already considered as the *best friends* who give the best dinners and suppers. It is in this manner that people of low birth and mean education contrive to make friends among the great. Could Maandaara listen to the praises sometimes bestowed upon these entertainments, he would surely conclude that the souls of people of fashion were destined, in their future state of existence, to animate the bodies of the most detested quadrupeds! – What can I say more!

[Elizabeth Hamilton's own feelings about the hypocrisy of the social convention of calling on one's "friends" is exemplified in a letter To Dr. S——, Leyton, Essex, Aug. 23d, 1804, in which she writes: "Nothing can be more hostile to thought than the society of Bath. The very air is inimical to every thing serious; and the old game of 'Neighbour, I'm come to torment you,' occupies one half of its inhabitants from morning till night." (Benger 2: 65).]

## Pages 272:

"Crude speculations.... the ignorant and illiterate" is omitted.
*Replaced by*:
.... confounded together.

The errors that are mixed with truth, and promulgated by authority, enlist for a time the prejudices of mankind in their favour: but when from the detection of error these prejudices are taught to mutiny, they desert not only the error, but the truth to which it was united. There is a propensity in the human mind to rush from one extreme to another, and thus implicit belief is succeeded by universal scepticism.

Wherever the mind had been bound by the fetters of authority; wherever inquiry has been deemed a crime, and the free use of reason has been condemned as impious, there shall we find the throne of superstition usurped by enthusiasm or *overturned by infidelity*.

Such is the natural progress of events. We, vain and presumptuous mortals, who in the short span of our limited duration, can behold but one of the oscillations of the balance, are too apt to conclude, that whichever scale we see descend must there for ever rest! Could we extend the sphere of our observation, we would I make no doubt, perceive these vibrations of public opinion at length fixed by the immutable law of TRUTH!

In this kingdom, which has long held freedom of investigation as one of its most glorious privileges, conscientious sceptics (if I may so call them) are but rare. Our wisest legislators, our greatest philosophers, whose names are the boast and honour of our country, were all firm believers in the truth of that revelation, whose doctrines accord with all that sound philosophy has ever taught. The only species of sceptics in which we abound, are men of shallow understandings, and cold hearts; who, feeling their incapacity to attract attention by going on in the ordinary path, endeavour to gain it by stating opinions, which may astonish their hearers, and acquire them some degree of applause, for their ingenuity and boldness. It may, indeed, be observed of this class, that they take special care never to utter their oracles before those who are capable of entering into argument with them, although they deliver themselves with dogmatical assurance before the ignorant and illiterate.

**Page 273:**

The line "How amiable is this condescension!" is omitted in the second edition.

**Page 283:**

"Ah! how little do the Christians.... labours" is omitted.
*Replaced by*:
Blessed they, who can extract from the passing events of life, the divine essence of Wisdom! To me it is now made evident that the Eternal Being, who fills all space, hath immutably decreed – that belief in existence, and hope of his protection, shall be necessary to the soul in every region and in every clime. This is the divine breath, or spirit, of which it is said by a royal poet of the Jewish nation – "Thou sendest forth thy spirit, they are created; and thou renewest the face of the earth. Thou hidest thy face – they are troubled – *thou takest away thy breath* – they die, and return to their dust."[1]

May this life-giving spirit continue to animate the soul of Maandaara, with confidence in the mercies of the eternal!

What can I say more!

---

1  Psalm 104:29-30

**Page 284:**

"It must be confessed ... his family" is omitted.

*Replaced by*:

Lady Grey was the person who evinced at the same time the greatest degree of sensibility, and the most perfect presence of mind; she deplored the untimely death of this rash young man, with the most lively pity, mixed with feelings of horror and regret: But for his family, she expressed a compassion that rendered her in my eyes the first of human beings.

# Appendix C: Sir William Jones, Hymn to Camdeo (from Works XIII, 236-9).

[In the first edition, Hamilton prints the poem in its entirety – with a few minor differences in punctuation – in the notes of her Preliminary Dissertation, although she includes only the first sentence and the sentence beginning "His bow of sugarcane..." from the Argument. In the second edition, she omits the poem entirely, simply referring readers to "the beautiful Hymn to Camdeo, by Sir William Jones."]

### THE ARGUMENT

The *Hindú* God, to whom the following poem is addressed, appears evidently the same with the *Grecian* EROS and the *Roman* CUPIDÓ; but the *Indian* description of his person and arms, his family, attendants, and attributes, has new and peculiar beauties.

According to the mythology of *Hindustán*, he was the son of MAYA, or the general *attracting* power, and married to RETTY or *Affection*; and his bosom friend is BESSENT or *Spring*: he is represented as a beautiful youth, sometimes conversing with his mother and consort in the midst of his gardens and temples; sometimes riding by moonlight on a parent or lory, and attended by dancing girls or nymphs, the foremost of whom bears his colours, which are a *fish* on a red ground. His favourite place of resort is a large tract of country round AGRA, and principally the plains of *Matra*, where KRISHNAN also and the nine GOPIA, who are clearly the *Apollo*, and *Muses* of the *Greeks*, usually spend the night with music and dance. His bow of sugar-cane or flowers, with a string of bees, and his *five* arrows, each pointed with an *Indian* blossom of a heating quality, are allegories equally new and beautiful. He has at least twenty-three names, most of which are introduced in the hymn: that of *Cám* or *Cáma*, signifies *desire*, a sense which it also bears in ancient and modern *Persian*; and it is possible, that the words *Dipuc* and *Cupid*, which have the same signification, may have the same origin; since we know, that the old *Hetruscans*, from whom great part of the *Roman* language and religion was derived, and whose system had a near affinity with that of the *Persians* and *Indians*, who used to write their lines alternately forwards and backwards, as furrows are made by the plough; and, though the two last letters of *Cupido* may be only the grammatical termination, as in *libido* and *capedo*, yet the primary root of *cupio* is contained in the three first letters. The seventh stanza alludes to the bold attempt of this deity to wound the great God *Mahadeo*, for which he was punished by a flame consuming his corporeal nature and reducing him to a mental essence; and hence his chief dominion is over the *minds* of mortals, or such deities as he is permitted to subdue.

### THE HYMN

WHAT potent God from *Agra*'s orient bow'r
Floats thro' the lucid air, whilst living flow'rs
With sunny twine the vocal arbours wreathe,
And gales enamour'd heav'nly fragrance breathe?
    Hail, pow'r unknown! for at thy beck
    Vales and groves their bosoms deck,
    And ev'ry laughing blossom dresses
    With gems of dew his musky tresses.
I feel, I feel thy genial flame divine,
And hallow thee and kiss thy shrine.

"Knowst thou not me?" Celestial sounds I hear!
"Knowst thou not me?" Ah, spare a mortal ear!
"Behold" – My swimming eyes entranc'd I raise,
But oh! they shrink before th' excessive blaze.
    Yes, son of *Maya*, yes, I know
    Thy bloomy shafts and cany bow,
    Cheeks with youthful glory beaming,
    Locks in braids ethereal streaming,
Thy scaly standard, thy mysterious arms,
And all thy pains and all thy charms.

God of each lovely sight, each lovely sound,
Soul-kindling, world-inflaming, star-ycrown'd,
Eternal *Camá*! Or doth *Smara* bright,
Or proud *Ananga* give thee more delight?
 Whate'er thy seat, whate'er thy name,
 Seas, earth, and air, thy reign proclaim;
 Wreathy smiles and roseate pleasures
 Are thy richest, sweetest treasures.
All animals to thee their tribute bring,
And hail thee universal king.

Thy consort mild, *Affection* ever true,
Graces thy side, her vest of glowing hue,
And in her train twelve blooming girls advance,
Touch golden strings and knit the mirthful dance.
 Thy dreaded implements they bear,
 And wave them in the scented air,
 Each with pearls her neck adorning,
 Brighter than the tears of morning.
Thy crimson ensign, which before them flies,
Decks with new stars the sapphire skies.

God of the flow'ry shafts and flow'ry bow,
Delight of all above and all below!
Thy lov'd companion, constant from his birth,
In heav'n clep'd *Bessent*, and gay *Spring* on earth,
 Weaves thy green robe and flaunting bow'rs,
 And from thy clouds draws balmy show'rs,
 He with fresh arrows fills thy quiver,
 (Sweet the gift and sweet the giver!)
And bids the many-plumed warbling throng
Burst the pent blossoms with their song.

He bends the luscious cane, and twists the string
With bees, how sweet! but ah, how keen their sting!
He with five flow'rets tips thy ruthless darts,
Which thro' five senses pierce enraptur'd hearts:

Strong *Chumpa*, rich in od'rous gold,
Warm *Amer*, nurs'd in heav'nly mould,
Dry *Nagkeser* in silver smiling,
Hot *Kiticum* our sense beguiling,
And last, to kindle fierce the scorching flame,
*Loveshaft*, which Gods bright *Bela* name.

Can men resist thy pow'r, when *Krishnan* yields,
*Krishnan*, who still in *Matra*'s holy fields
Tunes harps immortal, and to strains divine
Dances by moonlight with the *Gopia* nine?
   But, when thy daring arm untam'd
   At *Mahadeo* a loveshaft aim'd,
   Heav'n shook, and, smit with stony wonder,
   Told his deep dread in bursts of thunder,
Whilst on thy beauteous limbs an azure fire
Blaz'd forth, which never must expire.

O thou for ages born, yet ever young,
For ages may thy *Bramin*'s lay be sung!
And, when thy lory spreads his emerald wings,
To waft thee high above the tow'rs of kings,
   Whilst o'er thy throne the moon's pale light
   Pours her soft radiance thro' the night,
   And to each floating cloud discovers
   The haunts of blest or joyless lovers,
Thy mildest influence to thy bard impart,
To warm, but not consume, his heart.

# Appendix D: Obituary attributed to Maria Edgeworth

(*The Gentleman's Magazine*, **supplement, 1816: 623-643**).

CHARACTER and writings of Mrs. ELIZABETH HAMILTON

The following account of the late Mrs. *Elizabeth Hamilton*, is understood to have been written by Miss Edgeworth. – She was born at
Belfast, in Ireland, and the affection for her country which she constantly expressed proved that she had a true Irish heart. The lady is
well known to the publick as the author of "The Cottagers of Glenburnie," "The Modern Philosophers," "Letters on Female Education,"
and various other works. She has obtained in different departments of
literature just celebrity, and has established a reputation that will
strengthen and consolidate from the operation of time, that destroyer
of all that is false or superficial. – The most popular of her lesser works
is "The Cottagers of Glenburnie," a lively, humourous picture of the
slovenly habits, the indolent *winna-be-fashed* temper, the baneful content which prevails among some of the lower class of the people in
part of Scotland. It is a proof of the great merit of this book, that it
has, in spite of the Scottish dialect with which it abounds, been universally read in England and Ireland, as well as in Scotland. It is a
faithful representation of human nature in general, as well as of local
manners and customs: the maxims of economy and industry, the principles of truth, justice, and family affection and religion, which it
inculcates by striking examples, and by exquisite strokes of pathos,
mixed with humour, are independent of all local peculiarity of manner or language, and operate upon the feelings of every class of readers in all countries. In Ireland, in particular, the history of the
Cottagers of Glenburnie has been read with peculiar avidity, and it
has probably done as much good to the Irish as to the Scotch. While
the Irish have seized and enjoyed the opportunity it afforded of a
good-humoured laugh at their Scotch neighbours, they have secretly
seen, through shades of difference, a resemblance to themselves; and
are conscious that, changing the names, the tale might be told of

them. In this tale, the difference and the resemblance between Scottish and Hibernian faults or foibles are both advantageous to its popularity in Ireland. The difference is sufficient to give an air of novelty that wakens curiosity, while the resemblance fixes attention, and creates a new species of interest. Besides this, the self-love of the Hibernian reader being happily relieved from all apprehension that the lesson was intended for him, his good sense takes and profits by the advice that is offered to another. The humour in this book is peculiarly suited to the Irish, because it is, in every sense of the word, *good humour.* The satire, if satire it can be called, is benevolent – its object is to mend, not wound the heart. Even the Scotch themselves, however national they are supposed to be, can bear the Cottagers of Glenburnie. Nations, like individuals, can with decent patience bear to be told of their faults, if those faults, instead of being represented as forming their established unchangeable character, are considered as arising, as in fact they usually do arise, from those passing circumstances which characterize rather a certain period of civilization, than any particular people. If our national faults are pointed out as foul indelible stains, inherent in the texture of the character, from which it cannot by art or time be bleached or purified, we are justly provoked and offended; but if a friend warns us of some little accidental spots which we had perhaps overlooked, and which we can at a moment's notice efface, we smile, and are grateful. – In "The Modern Philosophers," where the spirit of system and party interfered with the design of the work, it was difficult to preserve throughout the tone of good-humoured raillery and candour: this could scarcely have been accomplished by any talents or prudence, had not the habitual temper and real disposition of the writer been candid and benevolent. In this work, though it is a professed satire upon a system, yet it avoids all satire of individuals, and it shews none of that cynical contempt of the human race which some satirists seem to feel or affect, in order to give poignancy to their wit. Our author has none of that misanthropy which derides the infirmities of human nature, and which laughs while it cauterizes. There appears always some adequate object for any pain that she inflicts; it is done with a steady view to future good, and with a humane and tender, as well as with a skilful and courageous hand. The object of "The Modern Philosophers" was to expose those whose theory and practice differ; to point out the difficulty of applying high flown principles to the ordinary but necessary concerns of human life; and to show the danger of bringing every man to become his own moralist and logician. When the novel first appeared, it was perhaps more read and admired than any of Mrs. Hamilton's works; the name, the character of Bridgetina Botherim passed into every company, and became a standing jest, a proverbial point in conversation. The ridicule answered its purpose; it reduced to measure and reason those who, in the novelty and zeal of system, had overleaped the bounds of common sense. – "The Modern Philosophers," "The Cottagers of Glenburnie," and the letters of the "Hindoo Rajah," the first book we believe that our author published, have all been highly and steadily approved by the publick. These works, alike in principle and in benevolence of design, yet with each a different grace of style and invention, have established Mrs. Hamilton's character as an original, agreeable, and successful writer of fiction. But her claims to literary reputation as a philosophic, moral, and religious author, are of a higher sort, and rest upon works of a more solid and durable nature – upon her works on education, especially her "Letters on Female Education." In these, she not only shews that she has studied the history of the human mind, and that she has made herself acquainted with all that has been written on this subject by the best moral and metaphysical writers, but she adds new value to their knowledge by rendering it practically useful. She has thrown open to all classes of readers those metaphysical discoveries or observations which had been confined chiefly to the learned. To a sort of knowledge which had been considered rather as a matter of curiosity than of use, she has given real value and actual currency. She has shewn how the knowledge of metaphysicks can be made serviceable to the art of education. She has shewn, for instance, how the doctrine of the association of ideas may be applied in early education to the formation of the habits, of temper, and of the principles of taste and of morals – she has considered how all that metaphysicians know of sensation, abstraction, &c. can be applied to the cultivation of the attention, the judgment, and the imaginations of children. No matter how little is actually ascertained on these subjects, she has done much in wakening the attention of parents, of mothers especially, to future inquiry – she has done much, by directing their inquiries rightly – much by exciting them to reflect upon their own minds, and to observe what passes in the minds of their children. She has opened a new field of investigation to women – a field fitted to their domestic habits, to their duties as mothers, and to their business as preceptors of youth, to whom it belongs to give the minds of children those first impressions and ideas which remain the longest, and which influence them often the most powerfully through the whole course of life. In recommending to her own sex the study of metaphysicks, as far as it relates to education, Mrs. Hamilton has been judiciously careful to avoid all that can lead to that species of "vain debate" of which there is no end. She, knowing the limits of the human understanding, does not attempt to go beyond them, into that which can be at best but a dispute about terms; she does not aim at making women expert in the "wordy war," nor does she teach them to astonish the unlearned by their acquaintance with the various vocabulary of metaphysical system makers – such jugglers' tricks she despised: but she has not, on the other hand, been deceived or overawed by those who would represent the study of the human mind as one that bends to no practical purpose, and that is unfit and unsafe for her sex. Had Mrs. Hamilton set ladies on metaphysic ground merely to shew their paces, she would have made herself and them ridiculous and troublesome; but she has shewn how they may, by slow and certain steps, advance to an useful object. The dark, intricate, and dangerous labyrinth she has converted into a clear, straight, practicable road – a road not only practicable, but pleasant; and not only pleasant, but what is of far more consequence to women, safe. – Mrs. Elizabeth Hamilton is well known to be not only a moral, but a pious writer; and in all her writings, as in her conversation, religion appears in the most engaging point of view: her religion was sincere, cheerful, and tolerant, joining in the happiest manner faith, hope, and charity. All who had the happiness to know this amiable woman will, with one accord bear testimony to the truth of that feeling of affection which her benevolence, kindness, and cheerfulness of temper inspired. She thought so little of herself, so much of others, that it was impossible she could, superior as she was, excite envy – she put every body at ease in her company, in good humour and good spirits with themselves. So far from being a restraint on the young and lively, she encouraged, by her sympathy, their openness and gaiety; she never flattered, but she always formed the most favourable opinion that truth and good sense would permit, of every individual who came near her; therefore, all, instead of fearing and shunning her penetration, loved and courted her society. Her loss will be long regretted by her private friends – her memory will long live in public estimation. Much as Mrs. Elizabeth Hamilton has served and honoured the cause of female literature by her writings, she has done still higher and more essential benefit to that cause by her life, as by setting the example, through the whole, of that uniform propriety of conduct, and of all those domestic virtues; which ought to characterize her sex, which form the charm and happiness of domestic life, and in which in her united gracefully with that superiority of talents and knowledge that commanded the admiration of the publick.

# Appendix E: Selections from Letters.

All quotations are from Elizabeth Benger, *Memoirs of the late Mrs. Elizabeth Hamilton* (London: Longman, Hurst, Rees, Orme, and Brown, 1818).

[*An Indian acquaintance of Charles Hamilton's comes to visit Elizabeth during her 1778 trip to Ireland. After her return to Scotland she writes:*]

I believe I have not yet told you who my fellow-travellers were: the one was Mr.———— , and the other an Indian acquaintance of yours, Mr. A. In the month of May he came to see my sister and me; and you may be sure his visit was very acceptable, as he had seen you in India. As he brought nobody to introduce him, we were all at first a little at a loss, when he addressed me as Miss Hamilton: he thought you had but one sister, and from my resemblance to you, he said he should have known me as such any where. Indeed, many people at Belfast complimented me with the name of little Charles. I was always very well pleased to be told of this likeness, though my Aunt Marshall does not take it so well; for she says, that at weel I'm muckle better faurd. Have you still Scotch enough to make out that sentence?

I have some hopes that while you are at Calcutta, you will have an opportunity of sending me, what I have so long wished for, your picture. You may be sure you shall have mine, when in my power to get it: but, in the mean time, you may take your looking-glass, and the face you will see there may serve to bring your Bess to your mind. Mr. A used all his rhetoric to persuade us to take a trip to India, to pay you a visit. Indeed, from his representation, it were well worth one's while to traverse the globe to arrive at such a blessed country; and we both said, that, but for the strong ties of duty to those who have been more than parents to us, we should willingly follow his advice. But, for my own part, I would much rather have our happy meeting in Scotland. (1:70-71)

*[Fragment from a letter to Charles dated 1781.]*

Many thanks also for the muslin which you mention for a wedding suit. If it is to be laid up for that occasion, I don't think it need be in any hurry; but if it arrive in safety, I shall perhaps use the freedom of wearing it before hand. (1: 82–83)

*[Fragment from letter to Charles, dated 1783, about his proposal that she come to India.]*

I must now, my dear Charles, thank you for the pains you have taken on the subject of the trip to India; a subject, on which I never once entertained a serious thought at the first view: the objections to it were so many and so insuperable, that nothing but my having been left in a most helpless situation could have induced me to admit of such an idea; and even in that case, unless some very happy change had taken place in your affairs, I never could have been tempted to throw such a burden on your generosity. In the pleasure of enjoying your company, and living under your protection, I should indeed have had a temptation, such a temptation, as, had no other obstacles stood in the way than danger and fatigue, would soon have overcome them: but the thousand delicacies that form a barrier to every woman possessed of true female feelings, I never could have attempted to overleap; nor would even the certainty of getting a husband weigh so very deeply with me, as you gentlemen may perhaps imagine; nor am I sure I should be quite so saleable as you might partially suppose: I believe the pert adventuress would have the advantage of me: some antiquated notions of refinement might stand in my way, such as that there were some other requisites besides fortune essential to happiness, – a similarity of disposition, an union of heart and sentiment, and all those little delicacies, which one, whose only ambition is to possess wealth, and whose most ardent wish is the parade of grandeur, may overlook, but which one of a different education, and another manner of thinking, could not dispense with. Seriously and deeply, however, do I think myself indebted for the tender solicitude you express for my happiness.

All girls build castles: for my own share, I confess, I have raised structures of all dimensions.

A few years ago I beheld you placed in a lordly seat, with all the grandeur I have ever seen displayed by any of our eastern nabobs: I then descended so far as to give you four or five hundred a-year, with a house and equipage to correspond. But now that time has taught me the fallacy of all these fantastic hopes, my wish is to see you even in the humble sphere of Ingram's Crook, where with a competence sufficient to procure the necessaries and comforts of life, I sincerely believe you might possess more real happiness, than most of those who enjoy all its superfluities. (1: 92-94)

<hr>

[*Charles Hamilton returns to England only to plan a departure again in 1791, but he dies before he can accomplish it. The following letter to his sister after he has parted from her mirrors the style and tone of the Hindoo Rajah.*]

September 16th, 1791

Joy be to Shiraz, and its charming bowers! O Heaven preserve thee from decay! Thus sang the immortal Hafiz on first quitting the place of his nativity; and thus sang I, as I quitted the mansion of soft tranquillity and domestic peace, to engage once more in the turmoils of a world for which I begin to fear I am but indifferently qualified. Alas! what are those wild, delusive passions, which so eternally lead mankind out of the road of rational felicity, and, urging them to grasp at the shadows of avarice, vanity, or ambition, cause them to forget or overlook the humbler but more substantial blessing, which they may command. But soft, is not happiness equally the portion of every state of life? and may not that very tranquillity which, on a transient view, we so much admire and sigh after, carry in its train the daemons of soul-rusting torpor and stagnant apathy? Bow, then, my soul, with humble resignation to the decree of Providence, in whatever sphere it is thy lot to move. Such, my dearest Bess, was the train of reflections, which occupied me on the day of my departure from your sweet mansion! (1: 115-16)

[*Elizabeth Hamilton's poetry conveys her dejection at parting from her brother and replicates the poetic effusions of Charlotte Percy.*]

Written on 31st December, 1791:
Year of vicissitude, when thou wast born,
Thou sawst my heart in sweet contentment blest;
Responsive greetings haild thy primal morn,
And kindred friends the hand of friendship pressd.

[*Speaking of the social pleasure with which she was then encircled, she adds:*]

In one alone I saw, Oh, pleasing sight!
The minds first gifts the hearts best virtues blend
In a lovd brother saw them all unite,
And mine the pride to call that brother friend!

Such were thy early scenes, deceitful year!
From these they closing hour beheld me torn;
Condemnd to leave whateer my soul holds dear,
Reluctant, sorrowing, hopeless, and forlorn. (1: 117)

[*Depressed at the death of her brother, Hamilton begins to pursue the literary career he had encouraged; she writes the Hindoo Rajah and sends it on to her friend Mrs. Gregory with the following comments:*]

I am afraid to enquire what you will say to my black baby: I had no sooner given it out of my hands, than I passed sentence of condemnation on it myself, and was almost ashamed at having exposed it even to your eye; but there is one thing of which I must beg leave to assure you, and that is, I have so little of authorship about me, that there is no occasion for the smallest degree of delicacy in pointing out its defects, or, indeed, in condemning in toto, any child of my brain, towards whom I am so unnatural a parent, that I have hitherto seen them smothered without remorse. That which has been done by my own diffidence, will be still more easily accomplished, when aided by the judgment of a friend; on you, then, my dear madam, it will depend, whether my poor Rajah shall sleep in peace on his native mountains, or expose himself to the dangers of criticism, by a trip to England; if you think him too weak to stand the dangers of the voyage, he shall never move a step further. (1: 126-27)